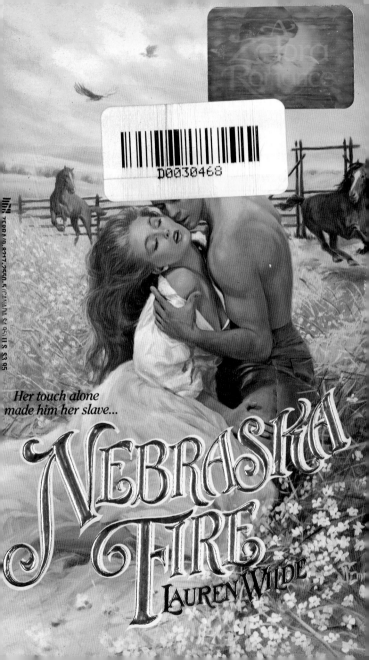

A Zebra Romance

D0030468

Her touch alone
made him her slave...

NEBRASKA FIRE

Lauren Wilde

0-8217-2550-5

UNCONTROLLABLE DESIRE

"What are you doing here?" Alex demanded as he slammed the door to the corral shut behind him.

Liza didn't answer—couldn't answer—her voice caught in her throat.

Alex stared at her. Her face was flushed, her eyes glazed. She had tempted and teased him for days, and now, his control snapped. He grabbed her shoulders roughly, throwing her to the straw-covered floor, holding her down as he covered her mouth with his in a long, punishing kiss.

Liza lay stunned, still in a state of shock from what she had witnessed. She was barely aware of Alex's demanding kisses, but when she felt his hand on her thigh, she struggled, pushing his hand away, trying to squirm from under him.

Alex threw one powerful leg over hers, holding her thrashing ones. He raised his head and looked into her wide, frightened eyes. "You're just like that little mare out there, aren't you, Liza?" Then, nuzzling her neck, he muttered, "Teasing, taunting, pretending you don't want it, when all the time you really do. Well, I'm tired of playing games with you, Liza. No more games!"

NEBRASKA FIRE

Lauren Wilde

ZEBRA BOOKS
KENSINGTON PUBLISHING CORP.

ZEBRA BOOKS

are published by

Kensington Publishing Corp.
475 Park Avenue South
New York, NY 10016

First printing: January, 1989

Printed in the United States of America

For all the girls in Labor and Delivery and all of my old friends at St. Lukes, especially those who supported and encouraged my writing over the years. . . .

Chapter 1

Liza Wentworth stood on the wooden platform of the train station, her beautiful violet gaze locked on the rusty rails beside her. Despite her exhaustion from the emotional trauma she had suffered in the past few days, she knew that she had a decision to make, an important decision, one that might change the course of her life.

Her eyes drifted to the east. She could leave the train station and go back to New York City and start all over trying to find a job. She shrugged her small shoulders wearily. She knew what a chore that would be. She had already been down that road. The crowded, teeming city was overflowing with new European immigrants, all seeking employment. The memory of standing in long lines in the hot sun, being rudely shoved, pushed and sometimes cursed by the other women, brought tears of frustration to her eyes.

She turned and faced westward, her extraordinary eyes following the metal rails that glimmered like two silver streamers in the light of the late afternoon sun. She could also continue westward, as Anne had desperately urged her to do.

Anne's words came back to Liza with startling clarity. *Go to him. Go to Alex Cameron.*

Liza frowned. She knew nothing of this man, this Alex Cameron. What was he like? Young or old? Handsome or ugly? Refined or crude? Kind or cruel? She shivered. The thought of traveling into the wild, untamed frontier and putting her life in the hands of a total stranger terrified her. Why, she hadn't even heard of Alex Cameron until a month ago. Her mind drifted back, remembering that day—and the fateful day that followed.

"Liza," Anne had said, "look at this advertisement in the newspaper here."

Liza had looked up from her book and had smiled at her roommate, Anne Garrett. The older woman sat at a small desk, her brow creased thoughtfully as she absently pushed a greying strand of hair from her face, her soft eyes still locked on the newspaper before her. Thank God, Liza thought, their landlady had suggested she and Anne room together to save on expenses. Not only had the arrangement helped both women's dire finances, but if Liza had never agreed to sharing a room, she would have missed the opportunity to meet the best friend she had ever had.

Liza rose and walked across the small room, peering over Anne's shoulder to look at the newspaper advertisement. It read:

8

Wanted: Matronly, experienced, loving woman to care for small boy. Must have a good command of the English language and be capable of basic tutoring. Must be willing to relocate to a ranch in the Nebraska Territory. Send applications to Alex Cameron, c/o General Post Office, Fort Laramie, Nebraska Territory.

"Are you thinking of yourself?" Liza asked.

"Yes," Anne answered. "What do you think?"

Liza frowned. Having just arrived from England, she was not familiar with the geography of this new, still-growing country. "Where is the Nebraska Territory?"

"Out west," Anne answered. "Not as far west as Oregon or California, though. Somewhere between the Rocky Mountains and the Mississippi River."

"Out west?" Liza asked in a shocked voice. "You mean . . . the frontier?"

"Yes," Anne replied calmly.

"Why, that land is still wild and untamed. Swarming with Indians! Wouldn't that be terribly dangerous?"

"I'm not afraid. Besides, it must not be too dangerous. He said to send the letter in care of Fort Laramie, so there must be soldiers nearby."

Fear raced through Liza. Not fear for her friend's safety, but fear for herself. She had just recently lost both her parents in an influenza epidemic and her brother, Dan, in a shipboard accident when they sailed from England to America, and Anne was Liza's only friend in this strange, new country. The thought of being left alone in this big, bustling, noisy city terrified her. "But that must be over a thousand miles away!" she cried.

"Yes, it is," Anne answered. Then, in an agonized voice, she said, "But what else can I do, Liza. I've been looking for work for over three months with no success. My age and my frail appearance work against me. There are too many strong-looking, young immigrant women competing with me, women with years of experirence as domestic servants. And, like you, I can't get a position as a governess or companion here in New York City without references. Didn't you notice? This Mr. Cameron didn't ask for references. Just experience. And I've certainly had enough experience, having nearly raised two sons myself."

Liza heard the pain in Anne's voice when she mentioned her sons. Her heart filled with compassion for her friend. Anne, too, had suffered the loss of loved ones recently. Her husband and sons were all killed in a sudden nighttime fire. It had been their mutual loss of family that had bonded the two women in the first place. In time, as they had gotten to know one another, their friendship had grown, strengthened by mutual respect and admiration as they discovered each other's unique qualities.

Suddenly, Liza's fear of being left alone was replaced with shame. She realized that she was being selfish by trying to hold her friend back. Anne's meager savings were even more depleted than her own. And Liza certainly couldn't support them both on her pitiful wages.

Pushing aside her feelings, Liza said with a

determined voice, "Yes, you're right, Anne. You should apply for the position. There's no telling when you might get another opportunity like this one."

Anne looked up, her own doubts and dread at leaving Liza filling her. "I don't know," she said in a soft, hesitant voice. "I hate to leave you."

"Nonsense," Liza answered with a bravado she didn't feel. "I'll be fine, now that I've finally found a job."

Anne frowned. To her, it was an outrage that the beautiful young woman standing before her had been reduced to a scullery maid. Better educated than most of her gently-reared contemporaries, Liza would have made an excellent governess. But because she had never worked in such a capacity and had no work references, she had been unable to attain such a position.

Anne studied her friend silently, noting her slim, yet shapely body, her magnificent golden-red hair framing her lovely face, her striking, beautiful violet eyes. No, she didn't believe that the lack of references was the real reason Liza had been refused by the well-to-do women who had interviewed her. The young Englishwoman was just too beautiful. Liza would be too much of a threat, living day after day under these women's roofs, often thrown into the company of their husbands. Unless she was supremely confident of her husband's love and fidelity, no woman would be foolish enough to take that risk.

Anne gazed at Liza's mouth, a sensuous, generous mouth with soft, full lips. She remembered her late husband once telling her that a man could judge a

11

woman's capacity for passion by the shape of her mouth. If this theory was true, then Liza was a passionate young woman. So why had she never married? Anne wondered for the hundredth time. Were the men in England blind? Or had the young woman never met that special man, the one man who could awaken her passion and love?

While Anne had been thinking these thoughts, Liza had been busy bustling around the room, gathering pen, ink and stationery. She set them firmly before Anne. "Now, write your letter. And, Anne, when you take it to the post office, ask if they have some kind of special delivery service. That way, your letter will get there first."

Now as Liza stood on the platform, she thought back to that fateful day less than a month after Anne had posted her letter, when Liza had rushed back to the boarding house, her violet eyes brimming with tears of humiliation and rage. Stumbling up the stairs and into their small room, she had thrown herself into Anne's comforting arms, her composure finally shattering and her tears spilling over as she sobbed out her story.

"Oh, Anne, something terrible has happened. I've been fired."

"Fired?" Anne asked in astonishment. "But why, for heaven's sake?"

Liza shuddered violently in remembrance. "Oh, it was horrible," she cried. "That revolting, repulsive man!"

Fear clutched at Anne's heart. What in the world

had happened? She had never seen Liza so distraught. "Man? What man? What are you talking about?"

Liza struggled to control herself, chewing on her lip. Anne led her to the bed and sat beside the young, trembling woman, wrapping her arms around Liza again and saying in a soothing voice, "Sssh, sssh, child. Tell me all about it."

"I was scrubbing the hall in the foyer," Liza sobbed. "I knew I was running late . . . that it was past four-thirty . . . but I wanted to finish it before I left . . . so I wouldn't have to do it over tomorrow. . . ."

Anne frowned. She had always thought it strange that Mrs. Banks, Liza's employer, had insisted that Liza be finished with her work and gone by four-thirty every afternoon. All of the scullery maid jobs she had applied for were live-ins, offering room and board in compensation for the low wages. Now, she sensed that leaving by that specified time had something to do with Liza's distress. "Go on," she urged.

She swallowed hard before continuing. "Mrs. Banks had gone shopping, and her husband came home. I'd never seen him before, but suddenly he was standing over me." Liza's nose wrinkled in disgust. "Oh, Anne, he was the most repulsive man I've ever seen. Fat, red-faced, gross-looking. Like a big, ugly pig!"

"What happened?" Anne asked weakly, fear and dread rising in her.

Liza looked up, a wild look in her eyes. "He attacked me!"

"Oh, my God, no," Anne muttered, her face draining of all color. "He raped you?"

Liza was shocked by the ugly word, a word never mentioned in the presence of well-bred women, not even between those women themselves. The word had the same effect on her hysteria that a slap in the face would have. For the first time, she was aware of Anne's pale face and the look of raw fear in her friend's eyes. Suddenly, she was filled with guilt for having alarmed Anne unduly. Now, it was Liza trying to soothe Anne as she said in a rush of words, "No, he didn't do *that*. I mean, he may have meant to, but he didn't succeed. He had me backed into a corner, slobbering all over me, his big, fat hands pawing me all over. Then his wife came in."

A wave of relief washed over Anne, relief so intense it left her feeling giddy. "Thank God!" she muttered.

"But, Anne, he blamed *me!*" Liza cried, her outrage overriding her fear and humiliation. "He told her *I* was trying to seduce *him!*"

Now that Anne realized that Liza had been badly frightened but not harmed, she was her usual calm self again. "That doesn't surprise me. You know, I always thought there was something strange about that no room and board business. I suspect Mrs. Banks has had trouble with her husband bothering her maids before. That's why she was so insistent that you be out of the house before he got home."

"But she acted like she believed him!" Liza cried, even more outraged at the injustice of it all.

"Of course. What else could she do?" Anne replied patiently. "Stop and think, Liza. She's completely dependent on him. They probably have an under-

14

standing. She pretends to believe his innocence, if he continues to support her."

"You mean, he might throw her out if she didn't pretend to believe him?"

"No, he probably wouldn't go that far. If nothing else, they have a social image to maintain. But there are many other ways he could make her life miserable. He has her over a barrel, and she knows it."

"And now, I've got to find another job because of him," Liza said with disgust. "Men!" she spat contemptuously. "I hate them!"

Anne laughed. "All men aren't like that, Liza. What about your father and brother?"

"That was different. I mean other men." She blinked back fresh tears. "Oh, Anne, I couldn't stand his hands on me, his slobbering all over me. It was so humiliating. I'll never get married if that's what you have to put up with. It's disgusting!"

Anne frowned. "Don't you think you're over-reacting? Just because one repulsive man paws you, is no reason for you to swear off marriage."

Liza remembered the young men back in England who had tried to court her. Their simpering compliments, their wet, messy kisses and awkward fumbling at her body had disgusted and repelled her just as much. "No, I mean it," she said with determination. "I just can't stand for a man to touch me that way. Any man!"

Anne smiled. "That's because you haven't met the right man yet." She turned Liza to her, forcing the girl to look into her face. Her eyes were knowing, her smile reassuring. "Someday, Liza, the right man will

15

come along. That special man. The man you'll love. And then you will ache for his kiss and his touch."

"No! Never!" Liza denied vehemently.

Anne studied her young friend. "How old are you, Liza?"

"I'm twenty-two. Why?"

Anne's brown eyes twinkled. "Do you know, I was thirty before I met the right man. And I was just like you. I couldn't stand the thought of a man touching my body. I had sworn to remain a spinster for the rest of my life." Her eyes warmed with remembrance. "Then Sam walked into my life, and all that changed. I took one look at him and fell in love."

Liza frowned. "But how will I know it's love?"

"Oh, you'll know, Liza," Anne answered gently. "Your heart will tell you. Just listen to your heart."

Liza gazed at Anne for a brief moment. "You loved your husband very much, didn't you?"

"I still love him. I always will. His death didn't change that. That's why I know I'll never remarry." She took Liza's small hands into her own frail ones. "There are some women who love only once, and then it's forever. I'm one of those women." She scrutinized Liza carefully before saying, "And I think you're one of those women, too. Yes, you'll love once—deeply—and then forever."

"I don't think so," Liza muttered doubtfully.

Anne smiled knowingly. "We'll see."

Anne turned and walked to the battered desk in a corner of the room, saying, "I have a surprise for you. I could hardly wait for you to get home so I could tell you, but now I feel almost guilty about my good fortune after what happened to you today."

"What is it?" Liza asked.

"A letter from that rancher, Mr. Cameron. He wants me to come right away. Look, he sent me my entire itinerary: train schedules, suggested hotels. I go by train to Saint Joseph, Missouri, and then by stage to Fort Laramie, where he'll meet me. And he even sent me a bank draft so I would have money for traveling expenses and new clothes. I cashed it today."

"New clothes?" Liza asked in disbelief. "He's paying for a new wardrobe?"

"Yes," Anne replied excitedly. "He says the winters are very cold, and he wants me to be sure and have plenty of warm clothes. But he suggested that I wait until St. Joe to buy them. That way, I won't have to drag them all that distance. He even allowed me a few extra days in St. Joe just for shopping and sent a list of what I would need."

Anne handed the list to Liza. As the young woman studied it, she remarked, "Well, he certainly seems to have thought of everything."

"Yes, I can't believe my good fortune. Why, he's even going to pay me fifty dollars a month plus room and board."

Liza gasped. "He must be rich!"

Anne laughed. "Well, apparently he's comfortably situated. And that's reassuring." She hesitated and then said, "He wants me to leave Friday."

"Friday?" Liza asked in a shocked voice. "Why, that's less than a week away."

Anne frowned, hating to leave the young woman behind. Their separation was the only thing marring her happiness. "I don't know. Maybe I shouldn't go.

17

I hate to leave you. Particularly now."

"Don't be silly. Of course you'll go," Liza insisted. Then, with a confidence she didn't feel, she added, "Besides, I'll find another job."

Anne was still doubtful. If it took as long as it had for her to find the first job, Liza would be in dire straights. But then, how could she help her young friend when she herself was jobless? At least, if she took the job being offered her, she could send Liza money. And she wouldn't be needing her savings, either. No, she would insist that Liza take it before she left, as a loan if nothing else.

Having settled that in her mind, Anne said, "All right, I'll go. But let's go out and celebrate tonight. Let's dine at a nice restaurant and then go see a play."

Liza started to object, thinking of how low her funds were. She gazed at her friend. She had never seen Anne so excited, looking so alive. She couldn't spoil her friend's happiness. She smiled. "That sounds like a marvelous idea."

Thirty minutes later, the two women skipped down the stairs in front of the boardinghouse, both excited at the prospect of an enjoyable evening.

"Hurry now," Anne said, "we don't want to be late for the play. We only have an hour to eat."

Liza winced and limped a few steps. "Just a minute, Anne. I've got a rock inside my shoe."

In her excitement, Anne didn't hear Liza and kept walking, stepping off the curb into the street. Then, realizing that Liza wasn't with her, she turned and looked back for her. At that moment, a carriage turned the corner behind Anne. It was traveling at a fast clip, and the driver, temporarily blinded by the

18

setting sun, didn't see the frail woman until it was too late.

"Look out!" the driver yelled as he viciously sawed on the horses' reins, trying desperately to avoid hitting the figure standing in the street.

Liza looked up when she heard the man yell and froze in terror as the carriage bore down on her friend. She saw Anne's tiny body thrown to the ground with a sickening thud as one of the wild-eyed horses hit her. Liza watched helplessly, horrified, as one carriage wheel rolled over her friend.

"Anne!" Liza screamed, running to the limp form lying so deathly still in the street, then pushing frantically at the crowd already gathering around the injured woman. She crouched over her. "Anne, Anne! It's me, Liza."

"It was an accident," the distraught driver mumbled in a shocked voice. "I didn't see her. The sun was in my eyes. It was an accident."

Liza looked down at Anne's pale face. She was unconscious, but there were no signs of blood. "Someone help me," Liza pleaded. "Please, help me get her into the house."

A big, burly man stepped forward and lifted Anne's body in his arms. "Which way, lady?"

"This way!" Liza cried, running ahead of him. Seeing their landlady standing on the doorstep, she called out, "Send for a doctor. Anne's been run over by a carriage."

The woman hurried away as Liza led the big man into the house and up the stairs to their room. Silently, the stranger placed Anne on a bed and then faded away.

Liza knelt beside Anne's body, tears streaming down her cheeks. "Oh, Anne, wake up," she sobbed. "Please, talk to me."

Anne's eyelids fluttered, then slowly opened. Liza gasped at the vacant look in her eyes. "Liza?" Anne whispered weakly.

"I'm here, Anne," Liza assured her. "Everything is going to be fine. The doctor is on the way."

"No," Anne breathed, her voice so weak Liza had to strain to hear it. "I know I'm dying. I can hear Sam calling me. I don't have much time left."

"No!" Liza cried in an anguished voice.

"Hush, child. Listen to me," Anne whispered. "That letter from Mr. Cameron wasn't meant for me. It was for you. Don't ask me how I know. I haven't got time to explain, but I know." The dying woman drew a shuddering breath and then continued, her voice surprisingly stronger, "Go to him, Liza. Go to Alex Cameron. Promise you will." She squeezed Liza's hand with urgency. "Promise me."

"Yes, yes, I promise," Liza sobbed, hardly aware of what she was saying, thinking only to comfort the dying woman.

Anne smiled, a soft happy smile, her gaze fixed on a point over Liza's shoulder. "I'm coming now, Sam," she whispered. "I'm coming, my love."

Liza sensed a strange presence in the room. The hair on her nape rose, and she whirled, fully expecting to see Anne's husband standing behind her. The room was empty, but for several seconds, she felt the eerie presence. And then, suddenly, it was gone.

She turned back to Anne. Her friend's eyes were

closed again, the same soft, happy smile frozen on her face.

Anne was dead.

The low, mournful sound of a train whistle brought Liza back again to the present. She peered down the railroad tracks. The train was still a mere black speck in the distance.

Should she go west? Liza wondered. Had Anne really known something she didn't? Had the older woman had some mystical insight into the future? Or were her words just the ramblings of a confused woman on the threshold of death?

Liza absently fingered her reticule, feeling the roll of bills through the thin material. But that wasn't her money, she remembered. It belonged to Alex Cameron. It had taken almost all of hers and Anne's meager savings to ship her friend's body to a small upstate town to be buried beside her beloved husband. Now, Liza was almost destitute.

A small, bitter smile played at her lips. *Do I really have any choice?* she wondered ruefully.

She turned and walked to the ticket window behind her, then said to the man standing behind the window, "I want to buy a ticket, please."

"East or west?" the man asked impatiently.

Liza hesitated. And then she heard it again— Anne's voice whispering urgently, *Go to him. Promise me.*

For better or worse Liza's decision was made. She took a deep, ragged breath, lifted her chin, and said in a firm voice, "West."

21

Chapter 2

Liza lurched as the stage suddenly hit a deep chughole and slammed her shoulder into the wooden frame of the stage window. Grimacing, she massaged the painful injury, knowing it would be yet another bruise. Every muscle in her body screamed in protest from the jolting and swaying of the stage. Her jaws ached from clenching her teeth to keep them from rattling, and she seriously feared her internal organs were permanently misplaced. Besides being exhausted and bruised, her face was windburnt from the hot, arid wind, and her body and clothing were sweaty and grimy.

She sighed deeply, reminiscing over her journey. The train trip from New York State to St. Joseph, Missouri, had not been too bad. She had actually enjoyed her stay in St. Joe, particularly shopping for her new clothes, following Mr. Cameron's instructions to the letter. The only thing she had bought that was not on the rancher's list was a beautiful violet silk gown with delicate lace over the low bodice and tiny puffed sleeves. Liza knew that it was extravagant and frivolous, but she had never seen such a beautiful gown and had been unable to resist it. Now she knew she would never have an occasion to wear such a dress in this raw, desolate, backward country.

And that is exactly what this country is, she thought despairingly, her eyes drifting across the landscape. Had she known what she was getting into before she left St. Joe, she certainly would have turned around and taken her chances in New York City instead. As she had traveled farther and farther west, the land had become more and more barren and forbidding, and the inhabitants more uncivilized and crude.

Since leaving Fort Kearny, she had seen only one woman. Otherwise, her traveling companions had been an assortment of dirty, smelly, barely civilized men. And whether young or old, they had all seemed to have only one thought in mind. She had learned to ignore their lustful, raking leers, but had been at a loss as to how to handle their obvious attempts to fondle her body. She knew some had argued, and some had openly fought, over who would sit next to her, and it hadn't mattered who had won the argument. Inevitably, she had been pawed, if not openly, then under the excuse of the lurching stage coach.

In England, had she been treated in such a coarse manner, she would have indignantly told the men to keep their eyes and hands to themselves, but Liza had been terrified of the awesome arsenal of weapons these men carried. First, there was the large handgun strapped low on the hip; then the large hunting knife at the waist or tucked into a boot. And as if that weren't enough protection for any one man, they also carried rifles that they carelessly tossed into a corner of the stage or balanced precariously between their knees. At times, Liza had wondered if she were in more danger of rape or of being killed by a gun going off accidently.

Other than her traveling companions' unwanted attentions, the trip had been surprisingly without incident, considering the violence that occurred every day in this wild, lawless land. They had seen only one band of Indians, and they were at such a distance, Liza could barely distinguish man from horse. The event had touched off a series of tales by her fellow travelers of the savages' brutality, each tale more bloodthirsty and grizzly than the one before. For days, Liza had been terrified, expecting to see a band of Indians trailing the coach any minute.

While Liza had feared an Indian attack, the incident that had disturbed her the most had been the day they had come across a buffalo herd. She shuddered involuntarily as she remembered. The stage had had to stop for the large herd of buffalo as it lumbered across their path. Huge, shaggy, almost ugly, they had had a certain majestic aura about them that had left her breathless. But the magic of the spell had been broken as the men began shooting the beasts, bragging about who was the best shot and who could kill the most. Liza had stood dumbly, watching as the buffalo had dropped one by one, and then was terrified when the animals stampeded. After the dust had cleared, almost two score of the animals

24

had lain dead, either shot or trampled to death. Liza had been sickened by the needless carnage. It had been the first time she had seen animals killed for mere sport by men mad with blood-lust. The sight had been etched into her memory, never to be forgotten or forgiven.

My God, Liza thought, *what have I gotten myself into?* What if Alex Cameron were no better than the rest of these crude, uncivilized men she had been exposed to? What if he was as disgusting and savage as they were? She fought down her rising panic, telling herself firmly, *No, you read his letter.* It was a letter from an intelligent, refined man. After all, he was the respectable owner of a ranch and not some lawless drifter like these other men.

Liza chewed her lip nervously as she tried to create a mental picture of Alex Cameron. He would be middle-aged, she decided, kind and definitely a gentleman. Oh, yes, he might be a little displaced at her audacity to come in Anne's place, but surely after she had explained everything, he would be understanding, perhaps even grateful. Reassured by this picture of her future employer, Liza relaxed.

"Almost there," a gruff voice shocked Liza from her thoughts.

She glanced at the wiry, old man sitting across from her. "Have you been to Fort Laramie before?" she asked.

"Yep."

Liza waited anxiously, naturally curious about her destination and hoping for more information, but the old man was grimly silent.

Leaning forward, she peered out the window to get

25

a look at the town, but as usual, all she could see was the thick cloud of dust kicked up by the horses. Several minutes later, she felt the familiar lurching of the stage and heard the driver cursing the horses as they were pulled to a rough, jerking halt. Then the only sounds were the labored breathing and pawing of the horses, their harnesses jingling.

The coach door opened abruptly, and the driver announced, "Fort Laramie! All out!"

Liza slowly descended from the stage and stood in the dusty, rutted street, looking curiously about her. *Well, it's certainly not much of a town*, she thought with keen disappointment. There were only several small, roughly planked buildings, a blacksmith's shop, a saloon, and two larger buildings down the street. She gazed in the opposite direction and saw the tall log walls of the fort's stockade as a column of blue-coated soldiers rode out from the gate.

Apprehensive, she glanced around her, looking for Mr. Cameron, but no one seemed to be paying any attention to her. The stage driver and his assistant were busy unhitching the exhausted, sweaty horses from the stage. Two men, dressed in buckskins and fur caps, argued loudly in the doorway of a building across from her. Then she had the uncomfortable feeling of being watched and turned to face a veritable bear of a man, scrutinizing her from across the street.

My God, Liza thought, was that Alex Cameron? He was huge and barrel-chested. A wild bush of black curly hair covered his head; another bush formed a short beard on his face. His shirt sleeves were rolled up past his elbows, and his massive arms were covered with black hairs. *My goodness, he's all hair and muscle,* she thought as she glanced quickly into a pair of black eyes staring at her curiously.

As the man walked toward her, Liza had the ridiculous urge to turn and run. But when he spoke, his voice, although gruff, was not threatening. "Excuse me, ma'am, but would you by any chance be Anne Garrett?"

"Are you Alex Cameron?" Liza asked, her voice trembling slightly as she looked up at the huge man.

"No, ma'am." He chuckled. "No wonder you looked so shocked. I'm Jake Webster, and I own that trading post down the street there." He motioned vaguely to one of the larger buildings. "I'm a friend of Alex Cameron's. Something important came up at the ranch today, and he couldn't get away. He asked me to meet you for him and see that you were taken care of." The whole time he had been talking, Jake had studied her, obviously baffled.

"I see," Liza answered, both disappointed and irritated that Mr. Cameron hadn't met her himself. She was anxious to get their first meeting over with, so she would know where she stood. She glanced up to see Jake Webster's dark eyes openly scrutinizing her. His look made her uneasy. "Is something wrong, Mr. Webster?"

Jake shuffled his feet awkwardly, embarrassed at being caught staring at her. She was undoubtedly the most beautiful woman he had ever seen, but that was not what baffled him.

"No, only . . ." Jake began. "Well, I sort of got the idea you would be a much older woman. Kinda young to be a widow woman, aren't you?"

27

he asked bluntly, looking her directly in the eye.

Liza swallowed nervously. Now she wished she hadn't insisted that Anne give Mr. Cameron so much of her personal history. How much had the rancher told this man? she wondered. She felt absurdly guilty. Tears of frustration and fear stung her eyes.

Seeing her tears, Jake mistook them for tears of bereavement and cursed himself for being so thoughtless. He apologized quickly. "I'm sorry, ma'am. I didn't mean to bring back unpleasant memories. I just wasn't expecting a young, pretty woman like you, that's all."

Liza sighed in relief and quickly changed the subject. "Is that Fort Laramie?" She pointed to the tall stockade in the distance.

Jake nodded, his piercing gaze still on her.

"It's not very big, is it?" she asked, thinking, *Goodness, he's like a dog with a bone. He just won't leave it alone.*

"No," Jake answered, finally looking away from her and gazing thoughtfully at the fort. "But those soldiers do a mighty big job."

"Just what is their job?" Liza asked, hoping to distract him.

"They protect the wagon trains going to California and Oregon from Indians." Seeing the fear that had come into Liza's eyes, he added, "Now, ma'am, I'm sure you've heard all kinds of wild tales about Indians, but you can't believe half of what you've heard. Besides, you'll certainly be safe with Alex, particularly since he's a good friend of Standing Bull."

"Who is Standing Bull?" Liza asked, puzzled.

"Why, he's one of the most powerful Sioux chiefs around here."

"Indian?" Liza asked in a shocked voice. "Mr. Cameron is a personal friend of an Indian?"

Jake frowned, his look resentful. "Now, just a minute, ma'am. I got Indian friends, myself, and if you're an Indian-hater, you might just as well turn around and go back East. Alex don't like Indian-haters."

Liza was ashamed, realizing that there had been a strong hint of disgust and disapproval in her voice. Truthfully, she didn't really know anything about Indians, only what she'd heard on her trip west. "I really don't hate Indians. As a matter of fact, I've never seen any up close. But from the stories I've heard, I was led to believe that all white men and Indians were enemies."

Jake's stance relaxed, and he smiled sheepishly. "Not all Indians, ma'am. Just like white men, some Indians are enemies and some aren't."

"I see," Liza muttered, his answer confusing her even more. She turned about, again trying to change the subject. "Is that your trading post?" she asked, pointing to one of the larger buildings.

"Yes, ma'am," Jake answered proudly.

Liza glanced about the small settlement, wondering how he managed to keep any kind of a business going.

As if guessing her thoughts, Jake said, "I don't make my living just off this town or that fort. Nope, most of my business comes from the fur trappers, miners, and wagon trains passing through. But there won't be any more trains coming through this year.

29

It's too late. It'll be turning cold soon."

Liza stared at him, acutely aware of sweat trickling down her legs and between her breasts. Cold soon? *He must be crazy,* she thought.

Seeing her look of disbelief, Jake pointed to the mountains rising in the west. "See those mountains? Those are the Rockies. It'll be snowing up there in another month or so. Wagon trains have to get over those mountains before winter comes. Otherwise, they'll end up like the Donner Party. They were a group of people that split off from a wagon train and tried to make it across those mountains to California before the winter hit. But they left too late and got caught in the mountains in the middle of the winter. Those people who didn't freeze to death—" he hesitated, looking uncomfortable, then continued in a tentative voice—"well, the few who lived, survived because they ate each other."

Liza swayed; her stomach lurched. Seeing her pale face, Jake added hastily, "Well, they *were* already dead. Frozen to death, you see."

"Cannibalism?" Liza whispered weakly. "How horrible!"

"Maybe . . . maybe not," Jake answered solemnly. "It's hard to say what you or I might do if we were in that fix. The instinct to live is mighty strong, and this is mean country out here. Guess it's best not to judge," he added thoughtfully. "Anyway, since then, everyone is awful careful to get across those mountains before winter comes."

They had been talking as they walked and now stood beside the door of Jake's trading post. He took Liza's arm and led her into the dark building, saying,

"Give your eyes time to adjust."

Slowly, Liza was able to see the dim interior. The aisles were crowded with bags of flour, dried beans, coffee, cornmeal and barrels of salted meat. One wall, lined with shelves, was covered with tins of food, another wall with harnesses, halters, ropes, saddles and wagon wheels. Yet another section was crammed with tables loaded with clothing and yard goods. A group of colorful sunbonnets hung from a nearby pole, while an assortment of women's corsets dangled beside them. As she turned aside, Liza noticed a display of guns and knives of all makes and sizes. The opposite corner was filled with a variety of pots and pans, and right in the middle of them, sat a big brass bathtub.

Jake laughed at the look of astonishment on Liza's face. "You name it, I got it," he said proudly.

"But how do you ever find it?" Liza asked, laughing back.

"Well, if I don't know where it is, my wife does."

"You have a wife?" Liza asked in surprise.

"Yep, her name is Little Songbird." Jake waited for Liza's reaction, but when she only smiled sweetly at him, he sighed in relief.

Liza *was* shocked to learn Jake was married to an Indian, but she was no fool. She wasn't about to get into that controversy again. No wonder Jake was so adamant about Indians.

"Come on. My wife is back here," Jake said, leading her through the crowded aisles to a door at the back of the building.

Liza found herself in a clean, cozy kitchen, facing

31

the first Indian she had really ever seen up close. A short, dumpy woman, dressed in a plain calico dress, stood smiling shyly at her. Two braids of black, shining hair hung from her head, and two brown eyes studied Liza intently. Liza was both relieved and disappointed. Why, she didn't look at all savage.

"Little Songbird," Jake said, "this is the woman Alex was telling us about, Anne Garrett."

"She is beautiful," the Indian woman answered in an awed voice.

"Yes, she is," Jake replied, seriously looking at Liza again. "I don't rightly think Alex is expecting this." Then, seeing Liza's flushed face, he added, "But that ain't any of our business." Shrugging his shoulders, he looked from Liza then down at his wife. "Supper ready?"

"Yes, it's on the table now," the Indian woman answered.

Liza was captivated by her sweet, musical voice. She could understand why the woman was named Songbird.

After they had eaten their meal, Jake said to Liza, "Alex said he would meet you tomorrow at Elk Horn."

Liza was shocked. She had assumed the rancher would pick her up here. "My goodness! Where in the world is that?"

Jake laughed. "Now, don't you worry, Mrs. Garrett. We'll put you on the stage tomorrow. Old Joe is driving, and he knows where to drop you off. He often meets Alex at Elk Horn to deliver supplies for the ranch. Saves Alex the time and trouble of having to drive all the way into Fort Laramie."

Rising from the table, he continued, "But I'm sure you're tired and would like to get some rest. Little Songbird will show you to your room while I go back to the stage depot and pick up your trunks."

After Little Songbird had shown her to the bedroom and left, Liza looked into the mirror hanging on the wall—the first mirror she had seen since leaving St. Joe. What she saw shocked her. Her hair was matted and lifeless, her clothing limp, grimy and sweat stained. Her face was burnt from the hot wind and smudged with dirt, and there were dark circles under her eyes, testimony to her long, exhausting trip.

Liza's disappointment and resentment at not being met at the stage by Alex Cameron was replaced with relief. My God, she looked terrible! What would he think if he could see her now? What an awful first impression that would be! He was expecting a lady, not a filthy, bedraggled woman who looked like an overgrown street urchin.

A knock at the door interrupted Liza's thoughts. She turned and opened the door to find Jake standing there with her trunks.

After he had set them down by the bed, he asked, "Is there anything else I can get for you, Mrs. Garrett?"

Liza glanced up at the huge man and questioned in a hesitant voice, "Would a bath be too much trouble, Mr. Webster?"

Jake threw his shaggy head back and laughed. "Thought I saw you eyeing that tub out there. Yes, we'll see you get a nice, hot bath."

Later, Liza sat in the tub of water and scrubbed the

33

accumulated grime from her hair and body. Then, before she climbed in the big, comfortable bed—the first bed she had slept in since St. Joe—she rubbed her face and body with perfumed oil.

The next morning, she dressed in her prettiest blue suit, arranged her hair carefully, and pertly perched a small matching hat on it. She viewed herself long and critically before the mirror. Her newly-washed hair shone with red and gold highlights, and the dark circles under her eyes had disappeared, leaving nothing to mar the perfection of her beautiful, sparkling eyes. Even her skin didn't look so burnt, the oil having removed most of the redness and leaving a faint rosy flush in its place.

Satisfied with what she saw, Liza smiled smugly. "Now I'm ready for you, Mr. Alex Cameron," she muttered to herself.

Chapter 3

Liza was surprised when she felt the coach lumbering to a stop a few hours later. Being a seasoned traveler by this time, she had settled herself in for an all day ordeal. She had no idea where Elk Horn was, but she had imagined it would be a long trip.

The door banged open, and Joe, the grizzly old stage driver called up to her, "This is it, Mrs. Garrett. This is Elk Horn."

Liza climbed down from the stage and then looked around in astonishment. There were no buildings or anything, just the gently waving grass on the prairie and a few massive rocks. "You must be mistaken. There's nothing here," she said, turning to the old driver.

"Nope, this is it, all right." Joe spat tobacco juice on the ground beside him. "Met Mr. Cameron here myself too many times to be mistaken."

"But where is he?" Liza glanced apprehensively around the open prairie.

"Oh, he'll be here. Said he would and he will," the old-timer answered, scanning the horizon.

"You won't leave me here by myself?" Liza questioned with alarm.

The old man looked closely at the frightened girl and scratched his tobacco-stained beard. "I'll wait for a bit. But I can't wait too long, you know. Got to keep this stage on schedule."

Once again, the seasoned old-timer peered across the horizon, and then, spying something in the distance, smiled with relief. "There he comes now," he said, pointing to the south.

Liza squinted, desperately trying to see what he was looking at. She could barely see a wagon moving in their direction, but she certainly couldn't distinguish the driver's features. "How can you tell from this far away?"

"It's him all right," the old driver replied stubbornly, already climbing back on the stage.

"Wait!" Liza cried, panic-stricken. But before she could move, the driver had thrown her trunks off and the stage was moving away. She was left standing in a cloud of choking dust.

Liza stood, terrified as she watched the stage moving rapidly away from her. She turned, frantically searching for the wagon in the distance. It was getting closer and closer. *But it might not be Alex Cameron*, she thought. What if it was someone else, and she was stuck out there in the middle of the desolate prairie with a complete stranger? Liza waited, frozen to the spot, her heart thudding in her chest as the buckboard lumbered closer and closer.

Finally, the wagon stopped, and a man jumped

down, walking lazily toward her. The sun was to his back, throwing his face in a shadow, but Liza could see he was a big man. Tall, broad-shouldered, slim-hipped, he walked with an almost feline grace that belied his size. He approached her slowly, his spurs jingling at each step, the gun strapped to his muscular thigh slapping in cadence. He stopped a few feet from her, and although Liza couldn't see his face clearly, she could feel the heat of his gaze on her. Her heart rose in her throat.

"And just who in the hell are you?" a deep baritone voice asked roughly.

Liza jumped reflexively, her heart pounding in her chest. She struggled for control of her tongue and found, to her horror, that it seemed to be glued to the roof of her mouth. Finally, she blurted, "Anne Garrett couldn't come."

Towering over her, the man took a menacing step closer, bent down and glared into her face. "Well, now I know who you aren't," he drawled sarcastically. "But that still doesn't answer my question. Who are you, and what the hell are you doing here?"

Liza struggled for composure, determined not to appear more foolish than she already had. "My name is Elizabeth Wentworth," she replied, managing to sound much calmer than she actually felt. She peered into the shadowed face above her. "Are you Alex Cameron?"

Alex nodded curtly. *My God,* Liza thought, *even silent he's intimidating.* She chewed her lip nervously, not knowing where to begin. Gathering her courage, she said, "I was Anne's roommate in New

37

York, so I know of your agreement. But when she was killed, I came instead." *No*, Liza thought, *that doesn't make sense, either*. She wished he wasn't standing so close. His masculine presence seemed overpowering.

"So Mrs. Garrett is dead? And how did that happen?"

"She was run over by a carriage."

"And you traveled all this way to tell me *that?*" Alex asked in disbelief. "Haven't you ever heard of the mail?"

Totally frustrated, Liza mumbled, "The money . . ."

"Oh, I see," Alex responded, as he straightened to his full, imposing height. "You came to tell me Mr. Garrett is dead and to return my money."

Again, his words were edged with sarcasm, and Liza's fear was rapidly replaced with anger at this rude, arrogant man standing before her. "No!" she cried, stamping her small foot to emphasize her anger. "If you'll just wait a minute, I'll explain." This time, it was Liza who was leaning into his face and glaring.

Alex drew back with surprise, then gave a gentle, mocking laugh. "Oh, I see the little lady has a temper. All right, let's see if you *can* explain."

Liza glared at him, furious. This time, she was determined to tell her story completely and without interruption. Trying to make her voice just as haughty as his had been, she said, "As I informed you, Anne and I were roommates in New York. We were both looking for work when we saw your advertisement in the paper. As you know, Anne replied and you accepted. Then Anne was killed in

38

the carriage accident. But before she died, we agreed that I should come instead, since you still needed someone and I have all of the qualifications you wanted." *There, it's out,* Liza thought with relief.

"So you have come for the job?" Alex asked.

"That's right," Liza answered confidently.

"Wrong!" he spat.

Liza stood, utterly shocked, looking dumbly at him as he removed his hat. She gasped in surprise, for Alex Cameron was not at all what she had expected him to be. Before her stood a ruggedly handsome man in his late twenties or early thirties. As he pushed a lock of coal-black, wavy hair back from his forehead, Liza noticed his eyes, steel-grey and fringed with thick, unbelievably long black lashes. Her eyes flicked down to his mouth—full, sensual, yet stubborn and tight set—on to his firm, arrogant jaw, fringed with thick sideburns. Fascinated, her gaze continued to drift down the strong column of his tanned neck to his broad chest—sprinkled with black, softly curling hair at the vee of his shirt—then across his taut abdomen and slim hips, to stare finally at the muscular thighs of a man apparently accustomed to long hours in the saddle.

"Seen enough?" Alex asked cockily.

Startled, Liza blushed furiously. She looked up to see him watching her closely, one dark eyebrow cocked, an amused smile on his face.

"Now, it's *my* turn," he said in a silky voice, his eyes boldly raking her from head to toe and then back up, to linger at her breasts, and then again at her lips, before returning to her eyes. Casually, as if he were considering her a piece of merchandise, he walked completely around her until he stood arrogantly before her again, his smoky eyes looking deep into hers. Liza shivered, coloring even more hotly. She felt stripped, naked before this frightening, intensely disturbing man.

"Now," Alex said lazily, "let's just go through that list of qualifications again. If I remember correctly, Mrs. Garrett wrote that she was a loving, matronly woman with a good command of the English language, experienced in child raising, and capable of basic tutoring. Am I right?"

"Yes," Liza answered nervously.

"And you claim to have the same qualifications?" he asked in a challenging tone of voice.

Liza's chin rose stubbornly. "Yes, I do."

His eyes boldly caressed Liza's mouth as he said quietly, "Well, you may be loving enough." Liza blushed hotly. Then abruptly, he added coldly, "But you sure as hell *aren't* any matron."

Liza trembled, but Alex shrugged indifferently and continued, "But you do have an excellent command of the English language. In fact, I detect an English accent, do I not?"

Liza nodded.

Alex cocked his head, looking at her thoughtfully. "How much experience *have* you had in raising children?"

"Well, actually none, but—"

"Humph!" Alex interjected gruffly. "I thought not."

Again, Liza's anger rose. Her eyes flashed as she retorted, "Mr. Cameron, for your information, my father was a schoolmaster in England, and I was his assistant. I can assure you I am perfectly capable of handling small children and tutoring them. As you said, I *do* have a good command of the English language. I like children, and yes, I can . . . I can be very loving." Her stare bravely challenged his. "So as far as I can see, your only real objection is my age, and I fail to see what that has to do with anything."

Alex stared at the young woman standing before him, her lovely eyes flashing dangerously. *Dammit,* he thought irritably, *every time I think I have her whipped, she comes right back for more.* Alex was well aware of the imposing figure he cut; he had used it to his advantage before, and on much more dangerous foes than Elizabeth Wentworth. He had been absolutely shocked when he had driven up and found this beautiful, delicate creature standing here in the middle of this godforsaken prairie. And beautiful she was, Alex admitted, his silver eyes assessing her. That hair! Never had he seen hair that glorious shade of red. He wondered how long it was and if it was really as soft as it looked. And those eyes, with their thick, long lashes. Were they dark blue or violet? His perusal drifted to her wide, sensuous mouth. *Delicious,* he mused, *made for kissing.* He looked at her firm, stubborn, little chin and down her sweetly arched neck to her soft, rounded breasts. *Beautiful,* he thought, feeling a familiar tightening in his loins. He struggled for control, thinking angrily, *What in the hell is a girl like her doing here anyway? She belongs in a drawing room back East, with a rich husband to pamper her.* The seed of suspicion planted itself in his mind and grew.

Alex caught Liza's arm and shook her roughly.

41

"Who are you hiding from?"

Shocked at his sudden violence, Liza stammered, "What . . . what do you mean?"

"A husband, perhaps?"

"A husband?" Liza questioned, bewildered. "Why, I'm not married. I've never been married."

He drew her closer to his big body, his face leaning into hers. "Then the law?" he asked with a sneer.

"The law?" Liza was even more astonished. "What would they possibly want with me?"

He released her abruptly, almost throwing her away from him, and Liza stumbled. "A beautiful woman like you doesn't come to this godforsaken country unless she's running from something or someone," he accused. "Do you actually expect me to believe that you couldn't find a job in New York City, that you're so desperate for work you'd travel thousands of miles?"

Liza fought back tears of frustration. *Damn him!* she thought furiously. Was there no end to his insults? "Mr. Cameron," she said, her voice trembling, "I don't care if you believe me or not. What I told you is the truth. I've just recently come to this country, and Anne was the only friend I had on this side of the Atlantic. I tried to find a job in New York City, but since I don't have any experience or references, no one would hire me, despite my qualifications. And I still say I'm qualified for your job," she added firmly. "I don't understand your objections."

"I'll tell you why I object. Because this country eats up little girls like you!" Alex thundered.

Liza drew herself up to her full five feet, five inches

and replied haughtily, "I am *not* a little girl."

Alex's eyes arrogantly raked her body, causing Liza to blush furiously again. "So I've noticed."

"You're impossible!" Liza cried and turned her back on him.

Alex stared at her rigid back, beginning to feel a little weary. Why was he standing out here arguing with the little chit anyway? he wondered in disgust. "If you can't find work here in America, then why don't you go back to England?"

Liza whirled to face him. "Because there is no one to go back to, and I don't have any money!"

Alex was becoming more and more frustrated. "What about your family?"

"I just told you I have no one. My parents died last January, and my brother died on the trip over," Liza answered, her voice breaking.

Alex frowned. Either she was telling the truth or she was the best damned actress in the world. But he had seen the naked pain in her eyes and seriously doubted that anyone could be that good an actress. Even so, a delicate, gently-reared girl like her had no business in a raw land like this.

"All right, I believe you," Alex relented. "But you still can't stay here." Liza looked like she was going to argue, but Alex stopped her. "The answer is still *no!*"

Liza's shoulders drooped wearily. *I've lost,* she thought. *I gambled and lost. Now I have to go back and start all over.*

Liza's dejected look tore at some chord buried deep inside Alex. He had a sudden urge to take this delicate girl in his arms and comfort her, protect her.

43

The urge surprised Alex, for he was not by nature a tender man. Without even thinking, he found himself saying in a kindly voice, "I'll tell you what I'll do. I'll pay your fare back and write you a letter of recommendation. No one will have to know that I never actually hired you."

Liza looked at him in astonishment. After all his rudeness and insults, did he really think she would take anything from him? Did he actually think it necessary to bribe her to leave? "No, thank you, Mr. Cameron," she answered hotly. "I'll manage quite well without your help. And I assure you, you'll be paid back every cent of the money you sent to Anne."

Alex was briefly stunned by her angry retort. Then, seeing her walk briskly away, he called to her back, "Where are you going?"

"To catch the next stage back to Fort Laramie," Liza replied over her shoulder.

Alex's look turned to one of astonishment, before he recovered and laughed. "Then you're in for a long wait, little lady. The next stage going to Fort Laramie is next Tuesday."

Liza stopped in her tracks, then whirled, a shocked expression on her face. "Why, that's . . . that's . . ."

"That's right," Alex answered. "Four days away."

"But . . . but . . ."

"There's more traffic going west. Therefore, the stages travel in that direction every other day." He shrugged. "But not many people are going east, so the stages going that way have a bi-weekly schedule. Tuesdays and Thursdays."

Liza felt sick. She couldn't believe her ears. No stagecoach for four days? Whatever would she do?

She looked about the prairie in total confusion. Then she turned and peered down the rutted road, as if willing a stage to appear.

"You'll just have to come to the ranch, and I'll bring you back Tuesday to catch the next stage," Alex said calmly.

Liza thought about spending the next four days in the company of this arrogant, strangely disturbing man and decided against it. "No, thank you," she replied coldly. "I'll just wait here."

Alex stared at her, momentarily stunned by her answer. "Are you crazy? You're going to stay here with no food or water? A lone woman in the middle of this?" He waved his hand across the desolate landscape.

"Yes, I am," Liza replied stubbornly.

Alex was furious. Never in his life had he met such an obstinate, willful woman. First, arguing to go with him, and now, arguing against it. *Damn her and her stupid pride!* he thought angrily.

"Look, Miss Wentworth," he said, his voice low and threatening, "it's hot as hell out here, and I'm getting tired of sparring with you. You damn well *are* going to the ranch—and that's that!"

Before Liza knew what was happening, she was lifted by a pair of strong, muscular arms, carried to the buckboard and rudely deposited on the hard wooden seat. When Liza looked as if she might jump out, Alex commanded, "Don't try it!" Then he threw both trunks in the back of the wagon and lithely jumped in beside her.

For several miles, Liza sat frozen, staring straight ahead and seeing nothing. Then she heard a soft

45

chuckle. "You can relax now, Miss Wentworth. Now that we understand one another, I promise I won't bite you."

Liza looked up to see Alex's eyes twinkling, his mouth curved in amusement. *He's a psychopath!* she thought, *violent one minute, charming the next.* Liza didn't relax, but quickly found that she had another, more immediate problem to contend with—holding on to the bouncing wagon.

She tried to steady herself by grabbing the seat, but if she tried to grasp the side next to Alex, her hand touched his hard, muscular thigh much too intimately. If she held on with only one hand, she lurched against him every time the buckboard hit a chuckhole. After a while, Liza began to suspect that he was deliberately hitting every hole just to taunt her.

"Can't we go a little slower?" she asked.

"No, we've a long way to go, and we lost a lot of time back there arguing."

"Well, for heaven's sake!" Liza spat. "How much farther is it?"

"About an hour-and-a-half drive from here," Alex answered, ignoring her show of temper.

"To the ranch?"

"No, to the ranch house. Actually, we're on the ranch itself right now. We have been ever since we left Elk Horn."

Liza's gaze swept over the wide expanse of rolling prairie. "All this is your ranch?"

"Yes," Alex answered nonchalantly.

"Just how big is your ranch?" Liza asked in an astonished voice.

He laughed. "Big enough."

Liza continued to survey the landscape, still trying to fathom anything this big belonging to one man. She had seen some of the larger estates in England, but certainly nothing to compare to this. Then she noticed that something was missing. "Just what do you raise on your ranch?"

"Cattle, some horses. But you won't see any cattle here. They're on the south range now, being fattened up for the winter. The grass is better there. As for the horses, I just sold most of my herd to the army at Fort Laramie. The only horses left on the ranch are those we use for the ranch itself and my breeding stock."

Alex didn't mind Liza's questions about the ranch. He had worked very hard at making it a success. He was proud of it, and it was his one and only love. Besides, for some strange reason, he wanted to impress this prim, beautiful Englishwoman. But, much to Alex's disappointment, Liza didn't ask any more questions, and so, for a while, they rode in silence.

As the wagon rumbled across the sea of knee-high grass, Liza was fascinated with Alex's hands. Slender, but large and powerful, they handled the reins with a light ease. Liza found herself wondering what they would feel like on her. Shocked by her own thoughts, she flushed deeply while thinking, *Stupid, you know how they feel. They hurt.* Unconsciously, she rubbed her arm where Alex had squeezed it earlier.

The motion was not lost on Alex. "I'm sorry if I hurt your arm," he apologized, and then, seeing her still-flushed face, stopped the team abruptly, put his hand under her chin to tilt it up, and looked closely at her face, his own filled with concern.

"Take off that stupid hat!" he demanded as he grabbed the offending object and tossed it into the back of the buckboard.

"What . . . what?" Liza stammered in surprise.

"Here, put this on," he said, as he slammed his hat on her head. "The last thing I need on my hands is a woman with a sunstroke."

"But I'm all right," she objected.

"The hell you are! Your face is beet-red, and that's the first sign of sunstroke." Then, looking at her closer, he reached toward her neck, and Liza drew back in alarm. "Does that jacket come off?"

"Yes, but—"

"You've got something on under it, don't you?"

"Yes, a shirtwaist," Liza answered hesitantly.

"Then take the jacket off. I'm used to this heat, but if you aren't, it can kill you."

Liza started to refuse, but then thought it would be more embarrassing to try to explain the true reason her face was red. She couldn't possibly tell him the shocking things she had been thinking. Reluctantly, she removed the jacket and watched as Alex placed it in the back of the wagon with her hat.

"Isn't that better?" he asked, turning back around.

Liza had to admit she did feel better. She had been miserably hot. While this was her prettiest traveling suit, it was also her warmest. *Besides, a lot of good it did to dress up for him,* she thought. "Yes, this is much cooler." Liza smiled sweetly up at him.

Alex stared at her, bewitched. It was the first time he had seen her smile, and he was totally captivated. Was he mistaken, or had he seen a fleeting dimple

48

there in her cheek?

"I assure you, Mr. Cameron, I'm fine," Liza said, mistaking Alex's stare.

The spell was broken, much to Alex's relief. But not long after they had resumed their lumbering journey across the prairie, Alex realized that while Liza was more comfortable, he certainly wasn't. Her shirtwaist was damp enough to cling provocatively to Liza's soft curves, and Alex found that he couldn't keep his eyes off her breasts, rising and falling, seemingly beckoning to him. In an effort to distract himself, he sat up straighter, and then spied a lock of Liza's hair which had come loose. The breeze was playing with it, and Alex fought the urge to take it in his hand and wrap it around his fingers. A sweet, womanly scent came from her, and Alex breathed it in hungrily.

To his distress, Alex felt his heat rising, his manhood hardening. Abruptly, he stopped the wagon, jumped out and walked a few steps away, deliberately keeping his back to Liza and desperately fighting to control his body's reaction. What in the hell was wrong with him? He was acting like he'd never seen a beautiful woman before, and he had seen plenty of them back East. And, he'd never had trouble controlling himself before. Dammit, the girl had him acting like some stupid schoolboy! He stood for several minutes, staring off into the horizon and waiting for his blood to cool.

"Is something wrong?" Liza asked from the buckboard.

"No, I'm just looking," Alex lied with a low groan, his back still to her.

49

"Looking at what?"

"Looking to see if I can see the ranch house from here," Alex quickly fabricated.

"Well, can you?" Liza asked, her voice querulous.

Alex scanned the horizon and, to his surprise, was able to see the ranch buildings. Feeling more controlled, he sauntered back to the wagon. "Yes, look over there." He pointed south.

Liza was pleased to see a cluster of buildings in the distance. "But that doesn't look far."

"Farther than you think," Alex remarked as he climbed back into the buckboard and picked up the reins. "See those mountains over there?" He nodded to the west. "They're over a hundred miles away."

"You can't be serious," Liza said in a disbelieving voice. "Why, they look much closer than that."

"No, they're not. The air out here has an unusual clarity about it that makes everything appear much closer than it actually is," Alex explained. "Unfortunately, that misconception has led many an unsuspecting person to his death." He nodded toward the mountains again. "There's a desert west of here. Many a trapper, miner and wagon train have made the mistake of thinking the mountains and water were much closer than they actually were. Therefore, they didn't stock up on water as they should have, and found themselves in the middle of that desert with no water, and the mountains just as far away as they look from here."

"Were you born here?" Liza asked, relaxing for the first time and enjoying herself.

"No. As a matter of fact, I can't think of any white man that was. But my father was one of the first white

50

settlers. I was only a boy when we moved from Illinois. We had a nice, prosperous farm there, with good, rich soil."

Liza gazed about the barren landscape. Grass stretched from horizon to horizon, hardly a tree in sight. "Then why did your father move out here?"

"I don't know," Alex answered, remembering painfully. "Wanderlust, a dream perhaps. All I know is, we sold our farm, packed up our most precious valuables, and left for Oregon. That was our original destination. A man named William Sublett was taking a wagon train of Methodist missionaries to Oregon, and my father joined the train."

"Then why did you settle in the Nebraska Territory?"

"For several reasons. First, my father didn't like the way the trip was going." Alex chuckled. "Have you ever traveled with a bunch of missionaries? Too much squabbling, my father said. He always was an independent cuss." His expression sobered. "But mostly, it was because of my mother. She was frail, and by the time we reached here, her health was so poor that my father was afraid she wouldn't survive the trip over the mountains." The last was said with a touch of sadness, and Liza decided to ask no further questions.

Looking up into the sky, she spied two birds soaring majestically, high above them. For a good while, Liza watched in awe as they climbed higher and higher, performing a graceful ballet in the sky.

"Wambili," Alex said softly, watching the flight also. Seeing Liza's confused look, he explained, "That's Indian for eagle. It means cloud bird."

51

Liza gazed back up at the sight above her. "Yes, they do seem to touch the clouds, don't they?" she whispered.

"The Indian admires the eagle for its keen sight, its strength, and its marvelous power of flight. That's why they wear eagle feathers. Each feather worn is a symbol of some brave act."

"Then they're not just worn for decoration?" Liza asked in surprise.

"No, they're not. But the Indian can be just as vain as a white man. He'll wear bear-tooth necklaces, arm bracelets, intricately beaded buckskins for adornment—but never eagle feathers. Those have to be earned. And sometimes earning them is easier than finding them out here. Occasionally, the Indians will find an eagle feather lying on the prairie, but usually, he has to go into the mountains and climb into their nests to get them. Then he has to hope the nest is abandoned, or at least, hope the eagles won't come back while he's there." He chuckled. "We weren't that lucky."

Liza looked at him, her eyes questioning.

"When we were boys, Tanazin—an Indian friend of mine—and I decided to raid an eagle nest. We climbed for almost half a day before we reached the nest, and when we got there, it was empty. Not an eagle in sight. But before we could get our feathers and run, the eagles came back." He chuckled again. "Those eagles were mad as hell, and there is nothing that can be angrier than an irate eagle. Believe me, we had quite a fight on our hands. That's how I got this," he finished, indicating a long, thin scar on his forearm.

"But, certainly, a little bird like that couldn't be all that dangerous."

"Little! My God, do you realize that a full-grown eagle has an eight-foot wing span, and those wings are powerful. If he hits you with his wing in just the right way, he can break an arm or a leg. He's three feet long, from beak to tail, with wicked talons, two or three inches long and razor sharp. Why, their nests alone are five feet in diameter. No, I consider myself lucky to have gotten off so lightly."

"But you did get your feathers?" Liza asked, amazed that this man had actually fought an angry eagle.

"Only one . . . but it was magnificent—straight from the tail. I still have it, but," he added, laughing, "you can be sure the next time I take a notion to get an eagle feather, I'll buy one from a trading post, like any other sensible white man."

Liza laughed at Alex's candid admission, then took one long, last look at the birds high above them. But her mind wasn't on the eagles. *So, it's true*, she thought. *He is the personal friend of an Indian, has been since boyhood. What a strange man.*

When they rode into the ranch yard some time later, Alex began pointing out the various buildings: the barn, the corral, the wagon shed and the smokehouse. Nodding toward a long, low building, he said, "That's the bunkhouse. That's where the ranch hands stay when they're not on the range."

"How many hands do you have?" Liza thought that it must take an army to run a ranch this size.

"It varies. You see, ranching in this part of the country is seasonal work. With our severe winters, outdoor work is limited. So I don't really need many men in the winter. Actually, I wouldn't mind keeping a few hands year around, but the men that hire out as ranch hands in this remote area are mostly drifters. They come in the spring and then leave in the fall. Sometimes the same men come back, sometimes they don't.''

As they drew up to a large building in the center, Alex announced, "This is the ranch house.''

Liza's eyes widened in surprise. Before her stood a large log building, two-storied, with huge stone fireplaces at each side. The upper story jutted out several feet in the front to form the roof of a porch that ran the entire length of the house. The roof was supported with massive logs, and between those logs were smaller ones forming a railing around the entire porch. Liza was both surprised and pleased with the house. She had become accustomed to the rough-planked or log buildings that she had seen recently, but most of them had seemed thrown together, crude structures at best. This building was impressive, well planned and well built.

Before Liza could comment, Alex was helping her down from the buckboard. He handed Liza her hat and jacket. "I suppose you want these back now.''

"Thank you,'' Liza said, slightly embarrassed as she took off his hat and gave it back to him.

Alex gave Liza's hair a fleeting, admiring glance and then said gruffly, "Well, come on in.''

Before they could ascend the massive stone steps, however, they were met by a plump, short Indian woman. Liza regarded the woman curiously. She was dressed in a soft, beaded tunic and skirt made of some kind of animal skin, her feet enclosed in strange footwear that Liza knew were called mocassins. Around her neck hung a necklace of small bones and teeth. A long braid of grey hair framed each side of a broad, leathery, wrinkled face in which sat a pair of piercing black eyes. Liza continued staring, wide-eyed, utterly fascinated.

Alex grinned at her expression. "This is Bright Star. She's been with us for years."

Liza smiled tentatively at the Indian woman, and then she noticed a pair of small hands clutching the woman's skirts, and a small head, covered with golden curls, bobbing from behind her.

"Andy, come here," Alex commanded gently.

Shyly, the figure of a small boy emerged from behind the Indian woman, his intelligent brown eyes bright with curiosity. Alex stooped and put his arm gently around the boy, bringing him to stand before Liza.

"He must look like his mother," Liza blurted, thinking how different Alex's son looked from him.

Alex frowned, baffled at Liza's words, for Andy was the spitting image of his father. Then Alex realized what Liza was thinking. "No," he answered, laughing lightly, "Andy isn't my son. I'm not married. He's my nephew."

"Oh, I see," Liza replied, feeling relieved for some strange reason.

"He looks exactly like my brother, Rob," Alex informed her. Seeing Liza's questioning look, he added, "Rob took after my mother, while I look more like my father."

"Is your brother here?" Liza asked, looking around.

"No, he isn't!" Alex snapped. "And don't even ask

about the boy's mother," he warned in a hard voice.

Liza was shocked by his tone of voice.

"Look," Alex said more calmly, "I'd rather not talk about Andy's parents, and certainly not in front of him. Andy is my nephew biologically, but as far as I'm concerned, he's my son now."

Liza looked down at the small boy, his face apprehensive as he watched the two adults above him. *Poor little tyke,* she thought. *He's lost his parents, too.* Liza smiled her most winning smile and said quietly, "Hello, Andy."

The little boy's response was instantaneous, his frown replaced by a captivating grin, his eyes twinkling.

"Andy, this is—" Alex started. He hesitated and frowned, then looked at Liza intently. "I think Elizabeth Wentworth is a little hard for a young boy to say. Don't you have a nickname?" He grinned. "Betsy or Lizzy perhaps?"

Liza bridled at the use of the nicknames so commonly used for her name. How passionately she hated them both. She hesitated to tell this hard, arrogant man her nickname, used only by those close to her. But anything was better than being called Lizzy or Betsy, she decided with a shudder. "Liza," she answered, barely above a whisper.

Alex bent forward, peering closely at her face, and for a minute, Liza thought he had not heard her. Then she heard him repeating her name softly, "Liza."

Liza shivered. She had never heard her name said like that. With his deep, rich voice and soft western drawl, Alex had made the word sound more like an

56

endearment. Startled, she looked up to find Alex's warm, smoky eyes openly admiring her, and she blushed.

"Yes," Alex said, his voice strangely husky, "that name fits."

Abruptly, he pulled his gaze from her face and drew the boy closer. "Andy, this is Liza. She'll be staying with us for a few days." The last was said with a stern look at Liza, a look that warned her not to challenge his words.

Alex continued, his words directed to Liza, "Andy is a little shy. He hasn't been around a white woman since he was a baby. He doesn't lack for love though. Bright Star certainly gives him enough of that. But he's growing up not knowing his own culture and language, and I'm too busy with the ranch to spend as much time with him as I'd like. That's why I placed the advertisement."

Liza nodded, still smiling at the little boy, who seemed to be fascinated with her.

Alex continued, ignoring the rapt attention Liza and Andy were giving one another. "For that reason, you may find his English a little lacking for a four-year-old, but it doesn't mean he's not smart. He simply hasn't had much exposure to the language."

"I can tell he's intelligent," Liza commented.

"Oh? And how can you tell that? Considering he hasn't said a word," Alex retorted sarcastically.

"Why, by his eyes. If you remember, Mr. Cameron, I told you I've taught children before, and I can tell by a child's eyes whether he's intelligent or not. His eyes are either bright and alert or—"

"All right!" Alex interrupted sharply. "Then

57

there's no need for me to explain anything, and since I've got work to do, I'll just leave you with Andy and Bright Star. She speaks a little English, too. I'm sure the three of you will manage just fine."

Alex said something in a strange, guttural language to the Indian woman, then turned and strode angrily to the buckboard. He lifted Liza's trunks out of the back of the wagon and dumped them at the feet of the three astonished onlookers. Vaulting into the buckboard, he drove away in a flurry of choking dust.

"Brazen hussy," Alex mumbled to himself, irrationally infuriated. Soft and teasing one minute, and then lecturing him like some straight-laced school teacher the next. Then he laughed to himself, thinking ruefully, that wasn't what he was so angry about, and he knew it. She had him hot for her, and there wasn't a damned thing he could do about it. She was first-class stuff, a real lady, and not some cheap tart he could take for a quick tumble. So he had better keep his distance. Yes, Alex mused, he had better stay away from that tempting little delicacy.

Watching Alex drive away, Liza wondered what she had said to make him so angry. Goodness, he certaily was volatile. She turned to see Bright Star and Andy looking equally baffled, and not knowing what to say, she smiled nervously and shrugged her shoulders eloquently. Much to Liza's surprise, Bright Star broke into a wide grin as she returned Liza's shrug in a more exaggerated manner. Liza laughed, thinking that at least that exchange had been understood.

"Come," Bright Star said, motioning to the house, and Liza followed the two up the steps.

The hallway was dim, but she could see a broad

staircase in front of her and a hallway running to the back of the house on one side. She peeked into a doorway at her left and looked into a large parlor. A massive stone fireplace sat opposite her, covering almost the entire wall.

An assortment of comfortable-looking couches and chairs filled the room. Several bookcases, some stacked with books and one with a collection of rocks and other objects, lined one wall. Tables of various sizes stood about the room, and in one corner, a large desk resided. The smoothly-planked shiny floors were covered with bearskin rugs, and the walls were decorated with colorful Indian blankets. Liza was amazed, totally unexpected by this luxury.

Andy stood beaming up at her and then tugged her hand excitedly. Taking Liza into the room opposite the parlor, he led her into the dining room, furnished with a beautiful table and chairs. Against the wall, opposite another fireplace, was a matching china cabinet, filled with delicate china and exquisite crystal. Liza gasped in open admiration.

Caught up in his game, Andy giggled and pulled Liza from the dining room and down the hallway to the back of the house. The door there opened into a bright, spacious kitchen where yet another massive fireplace lined the back wall. Before Liza could respond, a door opened behind her, and she turned to see a wiry old man gaping at her in astonishment, his arms holding a bulging sack of potatoes.

Surprised with each other's unexpected appearance, they both stood staring. Then Liza regained her composure and smiled. "Hello. I'm Liza Wentworth."

The old man studied her, a puzzled expression on

his face. Liza realized that he had been expecting Anne and knew she would have to offer some explanation. But the last thing she wanted to tell anyone here was that Alex had refused her offered services. So she lied nervously, "I was a friend of Anne Garrett's, and I just happened to be passing through. I stopped by to tell Mr. Cameron that Anne won't be coming. She was killed in an accident over a month ago." Liza desperately hoped that the old man wouldn't question her story, knowing that it was flagrantly unbelievable.

"Humph," the old man mumbled to himself, guessing that wasn't all the story and wondering what it was. His eyes searched her face warily. "That's a shame. Alex was counting heavily on her to help him with little Andy here. I guess he was disappointed." His watery, blue eyes studied Liza curiously.

Liza couldn't think of a thing to say, so she just smiled her most innocent smile.

"Well, ain't none of my business," the old man said, shrugging his shoulders. "My name is Hiram. I'm the cook and general handyman around here."

"Hiram what?" Liza asked, thinking it was discourteous to address the older man by his first name.

"Just Hiram," the old man answered curtly, carrying the heavy sack to the table.

As he walked, Liza saw that he limped, and glancing down, she noticed that one of his legs was much shorter than the other. Then, realizing that she was staring, she raised her eyes quickly, hoping no one had noticed her rudeness.

"You hungry?" The old man scratched his grey beard.

"Well," Liza began tentatively.

"Reckon you are," Hiram said, not waiting for her answer. "Probably ain't ate since breakfast." He turned to the table and picked up a potato and his paring knife. "Supper will be ready in about an hour. It ain't gonna be fancy, though," he added irritably. "I don't cook fancy. Just plain wholesome food."

"I'm sure it will be delicious," Liza answered diplomatically. "May I help?"

"My God, no!" Hiram ejaculated with a horrified look on his face. "I ain't gonna have no woman messing around in my kitchen!" Seeing Liza's shocked expression, he apologized sheepishly, "Sorry, missy, but I like to do these things myself. You just sit there at the table with little Andy. This won't take long."

Liza sat down next to the little boy, who had been watching them solemnly. She glanced around the room and noticed that the Indian woman had disappeared. "Where did Bright Star go?"

"Got stuff to do, I reckon," Hiram answered. He tied a dishcloth around his middle and started mixing the cornbread in a large bowl. Shaking his grey head in disgust, he thought, *Ain't right for an Injun to be raising a fine boy like Andy.* Then, gazing at Liza, his look calculating, he mused, she sure was a fine-looking filly. Reminded him of that little roan he had before his accident. And he'd bet she was a lot of woman, too. Just what little Andy needed and, for that matter, Alex, too. Hiram didn't know why Alex didn't just up and get himself a wife, instead of

61

messing around with all this governess foolishness. Governess. Now, if that didn't beat all!

"Have you been here long?" Liza asked, interrupting Hiram's musings.

"Yep, guess I have. Worked for Alex's pa before he died, and now for Alex."

"Alex's father is dead?" Liza asked, unaware that she had used Cameron's first name.

"Yep. His ma, too. But she died a long time ago, when Alex and Rob were still boys."

"Then, his mother, father, brother and sister-in-law are all dead? Is there any other family here?"

Hiram raised one bushy eyebrow in surprise. So Alex hadn't told her about that sister-in-law of his, he thought. The little slut! Well, it was just as well. Some things were best forgotten. "Nope," he answered, "just him, the boy, Bright Star and myself. We all live here in the house, and come winters, Manuel—Alex's foreman—stays here, too. But you won't be seeing him. He's out on the south range now."

Liza nodded, remembering that Alex had said something about the south range.

"When are you leaving?" Hiram asked abruptly.

"Tuesday, on the next stage to Fort Laramie."

"You'll have to have Alex show you the ranch before you go. He's got a right pretty place here."

"Oh, I'm sure he wouldn't want to bother with me," Liza answered bitterly, then added quickly, "I mean, I'm sure he's much too busy."

"Humph!" the old man grunted to himself, not missing the bitterness in Liza's voice. Now what in the hell had the little gal meant by that? he wondered, his curiosity aroused again.

As if he sensed her discomfort, Hiram began entertaining Liza with stories about the West as he prepared the meal and they ate. In turn, Liza told Hiram about some of the more amusing incidents on her trip. They seemed to have reached an unspoken agreement—personal questions were taboo.

After the dishes were cleared from the table and washed, Hiram asked Liza if she wanted to bathe. Liza was surprised when he led her to the storeroom and pointed to a big brass bathtub sitting among the sacks of supplies. "We don't use it much in the summers," Hiram informed her. "There's a stream out back where we bathe, but I don't suppose a little lady like you would want to do that. So while you are here, anytime you want to use it, there's water in those barrels and soap and towels up on those shelves. Don't worry about emptying it. I'll do that for you."

"Thank you, and if you don't mind, I think I'd like to take a bath right now. I feel a little grimy after that hot, dusty ride."

"Sure thing! I'll pour some water in the tub for you."

Later, when Liza sat in the tub surrounded by sacks of flour, dried beans and coffee, she laughed, thinking what strange bathrooms these Westerners had. But the water was the same, and cleansing herself of all that dirt and dried sweat felt wonderful.

She found Hiram and Andy waiting for her when she walked from the bathroom. "I'll show you to your room now," Hiram said.

Liza felt a twinge of guilt for having dallied at her

bath so long. "I'm sorry. I didn't realize you were waiting for me to finish. I hope I haven't kept you from your chores."

"You didn't keep me from nothin'. I ain't got no set time schedule."

Liza followed Hiram from the kitchen. Andy fell in beside her, gazing up at her with mute fascination. Liza winced as she saw Hiram struggling painfully to get her trunks up the stairs with his crippled leg, but she knew that his pride would be hurt if she objected or tried to help him.

When they reached her room, she was pleased to find it as well furnished and comfortable as the rest of the house. A small vase of wild flowers sat on a table by the rocking chair near the window. Liza thought it a particularly nice gesture and wondered who had placed it there.

"Guess you'll be comfortable here," Hiram remarked, his breath still coming in short gasps from his struggle to get the heavy trunks up the stairs.

"Yes, this is lovely," Liza answered. Then looking him directly in the eye, she smiled and said, "Thank you for everything, Hiram."

Embarrassed, a flush rose on the old man's face. Trying to hide his discomfiture, he grumbled, "Well, come on, Andy," pulling the reluctant little boy with him to the door. "This little lady wants to get some rest." Stopping at the door, he eyed her speculatively for a moment and then grinned. "We'll be seeing you in the morning, Miss Liza."

Chapter 4

The next morning, Liza's first awareness was of a wonderfully soft bed and crisp, clean-smelling sheets. She stretched lazily, then opened her eyes. Temporarily disoriented, she looked about the strange room in confusion. Then she remembered where she was—in Alex Cameron's home—and a little thrill ran through her.

She gazed about the comfortable, sun-drenched room for a few moments, then picked up her watch from the small table beside her bed and looked at it. My God, it was almost noon. Ashamed of herself for having slept so late, she jumped from the bed, slipped off her gown and took a quick sponge bath. But she didn't hurry dressing. That she did with special care, refusing to admit to herself that she was doing it in hopes of running into Alex.

When Liza descended the stairs, she found the house completely deserted. Not only was Alex not there—eating his lunch as she had hoped to find him—but there wasn't a soul around. For a while, she wandered through the empty house, then decided on a walk outside.

She found the small stream at the back of the house, nestled in the cottonwoods. A deep pool of cool, clear water was situated to one side, perfect for bathing, and Liza could understand why they preferred it to the dim, musty-smelling storeroom. Leaving the pool behind, she strolled around the outbuildings and into the barn where she found Hiram grooming a pretty little pinto mare.

"Afternoon, Miss Liza," the old-timer said cheerfully.

Liza blushed in embarrassment at his reminder of the time. "I'm sorry I slept so late."

"Don't wonder that you did. You must have been plump worn out after that long trip of yours. I left something out for you to eat in the kitchen. Did you find it?"

"Yes, thank you, but I wasn't hungry."

"Humph!" Hiram snorted. "Skinny little thing like you could use some fattening up."

Liza laughed softly, taking no offense at his words. She knew that he grumbled a lot, but she also sensed that he was inherently kind and wouldn't knowingly hurt a thing. "What a pretty mare," she commented as she stroked the slim neck of the horse.

"You wouldn't have done that a month ago," Hiram remarked.

"Why not?"

"'Cause a month ago, you'd have got your arm bit off, that's why. This here is a mustang, and she ain't been broke over a month."

"A mustang? Is that a particular breed of horse?"

66

"Nope. Mustangs are wild horses. They roam in big herds all over these plains. Alex captures them, breaks them in, and then sells them to the army. Except these little mares here." He motioned to several other horses standing in nearby stalls. "He's saving them for breeding stock. Planning to cross them with that big black stallion of his, being as he's first-class horseflesh."

"Are you saying he's trying to produce a new breed of horses?" Liza asked in amazement.

Hiram hobbled over to one of the mares and slipped a feed bag over her head. "Yep, that's right. He's trying to get a breed that combines the endurance and speed of the mustang with the size, looks and brains of his horse. You see, most mustangs are small, mangy-looking, kinda ornery critters. These here mares are unusually good looking."

"I see," Liza said, fascinated. She was still stroking the mare when the little horse nickered softly and nuzzled Liza's neck playfully.

"Why, would you look at that!" Hiram said in awe. "Mustangs are usually kinda standoffish. You must have a way with animals."

"Yes, I like animals, and they seem to like me," Liza admitted.

"Sure enough, that's true," Hiram answered. "Animals know if you like them or not. They're a lot smarter than people. Just wait until I tell Alex about that little mare nuzzling up to you like that. Why, he'll never be—"

"No!" Liza interjected with alarm. "Maybe you'd better not tell Mr. Cameron I was here." Seeing the

67

old man's puzzled expression, she added, "Please?"

"Okay, don't get upset. I won't say nothin'."

Liza could tell Hiram was mystified by her outburst, and she felt uncomfortable with the old man's questioning eyes on her. She excused herself and hurried back to the house.

Why had she said that? Liza wondered. Why had her reaction to Alex's name been so violent? Ever since she had met the tall, ruggedly handsome man, her emotions had been in turmoil. She seemed strangely attracted to him and yet repelled at the same time. Perhaps because his reactions to her seemed so ambivalent—one minute charming her, the next insulting her. But Liza had to admit that she had been disappointed when he didn't return last night, and the main reason for her stroll had been in hopes of "accidently" running into him. He seemed to be avoiding her. Maybe that was it, she decided. Her female pride was wounded by his indifference.

When Liza returned to the house, Bright Star and Andy had returned. When he saw her, the little boy squealed in delight and ran to her, calling excitedly, "Liza, Liza!"

Liza was pleased to hear him say her name, and she bent and hugged him. At first, Andy looked shocked, then pleased, and in a few minutes, he was in her lap, raptly listening to fairy tales.

Liza had been afraid that Bright Star would resent Andy's attention to her. Glancing up from her storytelling, she saw the Indian woman leaning against the wall, her arms crossed over her chest, grinning broadly. Liza was relieved, and by the time she was through with her tales, she wondered just how much English the Indian woman understood, for Bright Star had seemed to enjoy the stories as much as Andy.

After their evening meal, Bright Star hurried an objecting Andy off to bed, and Hiram excused himself to do his outside chores. Liza wandered aimlessly about the house, and finally, bored to tears, she retired.

For a good while, she lay in bed tossing and turning in a futile attempt to go to sleep. She glanced out the window, admiring the beautiful full moon. Maybe if she took a walk in the fresh air, she'd be able to sleep, she decided, as she climbed from the bed. She pondered over dressing completely, then shook her head, thinking there wasn't a soul around to see her. She slipped into her dressing robe and crept quietly down the stairs.

As she stepped lightly onto the porch, she sighed at the breaktaking view. The moon bathed the whole landscape in a soft silver light. A gentle cool breeze played with her hair as she stepped across the path and gazed up at the sky. A million twinkling stars filled the heavens, winking down at her teasingly. They looked close enough to touch, she thought in amazement, unconsciously lifting her slim arm upward.

"Yes, they do look close enough to touch, don't they?" a deep, husky voice asked from behind her. Liza froze, then jerked her arm down guiltily, embarrassed at being caught in such a childish act.

"I've done the same thing many times," Alex continued in a soft voice, "thinking I had only to reach up and I could touch one."

Alex didn't want to frighten her off. He had purposely avoided her last night and today, but now that she was here, he didn't want her to leave. When she had suddenly stepped onto the porch, he had thought he was dreaming. She was a vision of loveliness, looking almost ethereal with her slim, graceful body bathed in moonlight and her thick, wavy hair falling softly over her shoulders and back. He had actually held his breath for a minute, afraid he would break the spell and she would disappear.

"I didn't know you were here," Liza said defensively as she turned to face him.

"I often come out here for a smoke before I go to bed. It helps me to relax," Alex said, moving slowly from the shadows of the porch to where Liza stood.

Seeing her tense, Alex moved away from her to lean casually on one of the log supports. Careful, he warned himself. She was as skittish as a frightened filly. He had to take it slow or she'd bolt. He gazed up at the sky as he spoke, "I know this land isn't much to look at in the sunlight, but there is absolutely nothing that can compare with it on a night like this."

Alex's soft western drawl was lulling Liza, and she relaxed, looking out at the tranquil scene. "It is beautiful," she admitted in an awed voice.

Why, I'm standing out here in only my gown and robe in the middle of the night, talking to a man that is almost a complete stranger, Liza thought, a little shocked at her own behavior. *I really should leave. But I don't want to,* she admitted inwardly. And so, Liza stood watching the moon as it climbed slowly in the sky, enjoying the companionable silence.

It was she who finally broke the silence between them. "You have a beautiful home, Mr. Cameron."

"No, please call me Alex," he said as he turned to face her, his smoky-grey eyes caressing her. "And thank you."

Seeing his look, Liza froze, but when he made no move toward her, she relaxed again. "I was surprised at how well built your home is. Most of the buildings out here seem to be thrown up with no forethought at all."

"Yes, I know," Alex replied with a gentle laugh. "My father planned this house carefully and then built it with just as much care. It took five years to build, but he wanted it to be perfect. He was building it for my mother."

"I imagine she was very proud of it."

"She died a year before he finished it," Alex answered, a touch of sadness in his voice.

"That's a shame," Liza said, her voice filled with compassion.

For a while, Alex gazed out at the night, seemingly lost in his thoughts and unaware of her presence. Liza stood quietly, feeling awkward and uncomfortable, as if she were intruding on something personal.

Abruptly, Alex broke the silence. "These logs came from the Medicine Bow Mountains, west of here. They're fir trees, and they'll probably last a hundred years."

"From the mountains?" Liza asked in surprise. "But how did your father ever get them down here?"

"That's a long story," Alex replied, fumbling in his shirt pocket for a long, thin cigar. Liza waited

71

while he lit it and leisurely drew on it.

For several minutes, Alex stood smoking and collecting his thoughts, then said, "Shortly after my father decided to settle here, he found a lone Indian out on the prairie. The man had been bitten by a rattlesnake and was close to death. My father stayed out there with him for a week and nursed him back to health. Black Hawk turned out to be the chief of one of the largest and most powerful Dakota tribes. He was so grateful to my father for saving his life, that he couldn't seem to do enough for my father in return. When my father mentioned he wanted to build a log cabin, Black Hawk took him to the Medicine Bow Mountains and showed him the Douglas firs. They were magnificent specimens, some of them well over a hundred years old. Actually, the logs in this house came from the younger, smaller trees."

"It must have been an awesome job," Liza commented, "bringing that many logs from that far a distance."

"It was. That summer and every summer for the next three years, my father and twenty or thirty of Black Hawk's braves went into the mountains, cut the trees and brought them back here, some on my father's wagon and some pulled behind Indian ponies. The Indians helped my father place the logs and then left until the next summer. My father could never have built this home without the help of Black Hawk and his braves."

"But how did you get all that heavy, beautiful furniture here? That must have taken a whole wagon train."

Alex laughed. "Many, many wagon trains."

Seeing Liza's confused look, he explained, "Actually, the furniture was my contribution. After my mother died, my father seemed to lose interest in the house. We had a huge home, with only the smattering of furniture we had brought west with us. It wasn't until my father died and I came home from college back East that I started my project."

Liza was surprised that Alex had attended college, but then she remembered his letter, certainly not the product of an uneducated person. "Then you brought the furniture back with you," she surmised.

"No, only the glass for the windows," Alex corrected her. "I brought that back from Independence by wagon myself, and believe me, I pampered it all the way. The rest of the furniture, I bought at Fort Laramie."

"Fort Laramie?" She hadn't seen any furniture stores in the small settlement. Even Jake Webster, whose store seemed to have everything under the sun, hadn't had any furniture in it.

Alex waited for a minute, deliberately enjoying Liza's puzzlement, before he continued, "I bought this furniture from people traveling on the wagon trains to California and Oregon. You see, almost every family brought their most prized possessions with them, but by the time they reached Fort Laramie, they realized that they needed the space in their wagons for things more necessary for survival. They were more than happy to trade a piece of furniture for a side of smoked beef. So that's how I got my furniture. Every time a wagon train would come through, I'd load up my beef and come back from Fort Laramie with a load of household goods. That's what I meant when I said many, many wagon trains."

"You took their most prized possessions?" Liza asked in an accusing voice.

"Yes, I did," Alex answered, irked by her tone of voice. "But they got something in return. My God, Liza, the whole trail from here to California and Oregon is littered with furniture people had to throw away to lighten their wagons so they could get them over the mountains or across the desert. Not too many years ago, I saw a grand piano someone had thrown away out in the desert. Can you imagine, a beautiful grand piano just sitting there rotting in the sun?"

Liza thought about the wagon trains struggling across the mountains and deserts and formed a mental picture of the women standing beside the wagon and crying as the men dumped their valued possessions in the dust. "I'm sorry. I didn't realize. It is sad, isn't it?"

"Yes, it is. But at least I know what I traded them may well have saved their lives."

Liza stood for a while, her mind occupied with thoughts of the wagon trains and all the problems they must have faced.

"Would you like to see the ranch?" Alex asked, breaking into her musing.

"Oh, I'm . . . I'm sure you're much too . . . much too busy." Liza wasn't sure she trusted herself alone with him. She was more than a little alarmed at her growing attraction to this rugged Westerner.

"It won't be any trouble," Alex answered. "Tomorrow is Sunday, and I don't do much on Sundays.

I could hitch up the buckboard and take you for a drive." Seeing Liza's hesitation, he said, "But then, maybe you're tired of bumpy wagon drives."

"Yes, I am," Liza admitted, much to Alex's disappointment. "Couldn't we go on horses?" she asked, thinking how much she would enjoy a horseback ride.

Alex laughed. "I'm afraid that's impossible. I don't have any sidesaddles."

"Sidesaddles? Why, I've never ridden on a sidesaddle in my life. I doubt that I could stay on one."

"Then how?" Alex asked, his brow furrowed.

Liza was enjoying seeing him confused for a change. "Why, astride, of course."

"Astride?" Alex questioned, staring at her skirts. "You ride astride?"

"I used to, in a pair of my brother's old britches."

"I see," Alex replied, eyeing her figure.

Liza began to feel uncomfortable as Alex stood gazing at her, his eyes seeming to take in every curve of her body. She felt flushed and strangely thrilled. The feeling was not unpleasant, and Liza was worried about what she had gotten herself into. "A buckboard will be . . . will be fine," she said nervously.

Alex barely nodded as his gaze slowly caressed her face. He moved closer, and Liza could feel the heat coming from him and smell the odor of smoke and leather. She stood frozen, her heart pounding in her chest, as he picked up one small hand in his large, roughened one and began to lightly stroke the soft, sensitive skin of her wrist with his thumb. A warm, tingling sensation ran up her arm. His eyes seemed to

75

devour her lips, and as he bent his head, Liza thought, *He's going to kiss me,* and desperately wanted it to happen.

Abruptly, Alex straightened, dropped her hand, and stepped back from her. "Tomorrow, then," he said, his voice unusually low and husky.

For a minute, Liza reeled in confusion and disappointment. Her legs were weak and trembly, and her heart raced wildly. Finally gaining her senses, she barely whispered, "Yes, tomorrow." Then she whirled, almost running from the porch.

Alex stood on the porch, trying to control the shuddering of his own body. Dammit, he thought, why in the hell hadn't he kissed her? Shaking his head, he knew the answer. Because if he had taken her in his arms, nothing, nothing could have stopped him from going all the way. What kind of spell had she cast on him that the minute he was around her he lost control? There was a natural sensuality about her, he admitted, and the fact that she was an innocent only made her more desirable—and more dangerous. Perhaps it would be better if he found some excuse to cancel the ride tomorrow.

But the thought of being with Liza became more and more tantalizing. Finally, Alex muttered, "Like hell I will!" Purposefully, he strode into the house, his mind intent on a plan.

Liza had lain in her bed for hours, tossing and turning in a turmoil of frustration and bewilderment, before she finally fell into a restless, fitful sleep. When she awakened the next morning, she decided that she would make some excuse to Alex. As much as she would enjoy a ride, she feared the emotional entanglement he seemed to be drawing her into. A gentle knock at the door interrupted her thoughts, and Liza, thinking that it was Hiram coming to see if she was awake, hastily threw on her robe and opened the door.

Alex stood in the doorway, an amused smile on his rugged, handsome face. "Good morning," he said, thinking that Liza looked beautiful with her sleepy eyes and her long golden-red hair hanging about her shoulders in disarray. "If we're going for a ride this morning, I think we had better get started."

"I—" Liza began. But before she could think of an excuse, Alex pushed a bundle into her arms.

Casually leaning his shoulder against the door-jamb and crossing his arms over his broad chest, he grinned. "I didn't want you to be disappointed about not getting a horseback ride, so I looked in the attic until I found these." He pointed to the bundle. "They're some of Rob's old clothes, but I think they'll fit."

Liza unwound the bundle, and a pair of musty worn boots fell out. The other garments were a pair of pants and a shirt. She raised her eyes, intent on excusing herself, and saw Alex watching her closely, a mocking smile on his face.

"You haven't changed your mind, have you?" he asked, openly challenging her.

Liza bridled. He thought she was afraid and was daring her to agree to the ride. But Liza, never one to refuse a dare, answered, "Of course not, and thank you for the clothes, Mr. Cameron."

"Alex," he corrected. "Remember?" he asked, a taunting look in his silver eyes.

"Yes, of course," Liza answered nervously.

"Say it," he demanded, his voice husky. "Say 'Alex.'" His eyes bored into hers as he leaned toward her.

Liza felt smothered by his nearness. "Alex," she whispered.

He stood staring at her face for a long moment, then, with an appealing, lopsided grin, asked, "Now that wasn't so hard, was it?" Before Liza could respond, he turned, walking from the room, throwing over his shoulder "I'll saddle the horses while you're dressing."

Liza studied the shirt and pants in her hands doubtfully and then thought recklessly, *All right, Mr. Cameron. No one dares me!* Excitedly, she scrambled out of her bed clothes and into the worn garments.

The clothes were tight, much tighter than her brother's had ever been. She tried tucking the shirt into the pants; but that seemed to emphasize her breasts, so she decided to leave it out. The boots were a little large, but that problem was solved by stuffing several handkerchiefs into the toes. After she had brushed her hair and tied it back with a small ribbon, she twisted and turned before the small dresser mirror, trying to see herself. She wished that she could tell what the pants looked like, but all she could see was the shirt hanging a few inches below her waist. *Oh, bother!* she thought irritably. It wasn't like she was going to a fashion parade or something so she turned and hurried from the room.

Alex waited outside the house with the horses when Liza emerged, tripping lightly down the steps. He sucked in his breath as he caught sight of her, the tight pants hugging her slim, beautifully shaped legs like a second skin, the shirt straining across her full breasts so snugly he could almost see the outline of her nipples. Her complexion, flushed with excitement, glowed radiantly, and her golden-red curls bounced with every step she took. Dammit, he thought with a groan, he knew this was a mistake.

"Would you like some breakfast before we leave?" Alex asked, sounding much calmer than he felt.

"No, thank you. I'm not hungry."

Well, I sure as hell am, Alex thought ruefully, but said instead, "I've got something packed here if we do get hungry later," patting his saddlebags. "Well, come on, let's get started," he said gruffly, leading her to her horse.

"Oh, I was hoping that I might get the little pinto mare," Liza said disappointedly when she saw her horse.

"What pinto mare?"

Liza flushed, then explained, "I saw her yesterday in the barn while I was walking around. I hope you don't mind?"

"No, but I think this gelding is a better choice," Alex replied, laughing to himself as he eyed his big stallion. "Under the circumstances, he'll be much easier to handle."

Before Liza could ask what circumstances, Alex was helping her mount. Liza blushed hotly when he placed her leg in the stirrup, his hand cupping her knee intimately. "How does that feel? Do the stirrups need more adjusting?'' he asked, his smoky eyes gazing up at her.

Liza found it suddenly difficult to breathe. ''No, they're fine,'' she managed to answer.

When Alex turned to mount his horse, Liza let out a sigh of relief. Sitting in his saddle, he turned to her. ''What would you like to see first?''

''I don't know,'' Liza answered, her excitement returning at the prospect of a ride. ''You're the guide.''

''Well, you've seen most of what there is to see of the north range, so I guess it's the south range this time.''

They rode in silence, Liza thoroughly enjoying the feel of being in the saddle again and of the wind blowing through her hair. Hill after hill of lush, green grass stretched before them, waving in the gentle breeze, the sky an azure blue dome above them. Liza laughed outright in sheer pleasure, the sound tinkling on the clear, dry air.

But Alex wasn't enjoying his ride. He was tense and miserable. When he rode behind Liza, he could see the curves of her firm, lovely buttocks and her long, sun-kissed hair swinging freely. If he rode beside her, he found himself staring openly at her breasts bouncing teasingly. He finally settled with riding slightly ahead of her, thinking irritably that she was nothing but a tease.

They rode over the prairie like this for a good while, Liza delighted, Alex mumbling darkly to himself. Finally, they crested an unusually high hill and stopped to gaze into a lush valley below them. A huge herd of cattle grazed leisurely, and in the distance, Liza saw a small cluster of wagons. She looked about her in awe, astonished at the size of the herd.

"The south range," Alex said lazily, and before Liza could comment, he added, "Let's ride over to that hill over there. There's a small tree where we can get out of this sun and have a bite to eat."

As Alex galloped away, Liza marveled at the ease with which he handled his big horse, for the two seemed to merge into one. She had noticed that he rarely used his reins, but seemed to guide and control the animal with his knees. No wonder his thighs were so muscular, she mused, blushing at the thought, and kneed her own mount, following him.

When they reached the tree, Liza dismounted and sat down, leaning against the tree trunk and gazing down at the valley. Alex tethered the horses and brought his canteen and saddlebags to where she sat. He crouched before her, offering her the canteen, and Liza drank greedily, a small trickle of water running down her chin and into the valley between her breasts. Alex watched it with envy.

After he had taken a long drink, he wet a handkerchief and handed it to her. "Maybe this will cool you off a little. I seem to have forgotten my hat today."

Liza glanced up at his thick, black hair, the breeze ruffling it softly, and took the handkerchief from him. Leaning back, she patted her neck delicately. Briefly, she became aware of Alex's hungry gaze on the arch of her neck, then dropping to her breasts. Alarmed, she abruptly handed the handkerchief back to him and pulled her long legs up before her, crossing her arms over her knees to shield her breasts from his view.

Frustrated, Alex sat on the ground beside her and pulled the saddlebags to him. "Well, let's see what Hiram packed for us," he muttered, as he pulled out cheese, dried beef and a hunk of flat bread. "It's no feast, but it will have to do."

Liza chewed the tough food with gusto, thinking that it tasted delicious. "Are all of those cattle yours?" she asked when they had finished eating.

"Yep," Alex answered, stretching out on his back beside her, his head cradled in his arms.

"How many do you have?"

"Around ten thousand head," he answered, plucking a blade of grass and chewing on it absently.

"Ten thousand!" Liza gasped. "How big a herd did your father have when he came out here?"

Alex laughed, rolling on his side to raise himself on one elbow so he could face her. "Actually, he didn't have a herd at all, just a milk cow. In fact, he originally tried farming, but that didn't work. The soil is rich enough, but it's too dry out here to raise crops without irrigating. He sort of drifted into cattle."

Alex sat up, wrapping an arm around one long leg as he gazed out at the herd of cattle. "At first, he made his living catching mustangs, breaking them and selling them at the trading post. You see, Fort William wasn't an army post then. It didn't become Fort Laramie until the army purchased it back in forty-nine and renamed it."

"But who bought horses way out here in this wilderness if the army wasn't here?"

"Fur trappers and miners. Then, later on, when the Oregon Trail was opened in forty, the people on the wagon trains. Almost every train had lost some horses from broken legs or snakebite." He chuckled. "My father also did a thriving business on axle grease."

"Where did he get the grease?"

"There are natural oil seeps out here," he answered, motioning vaguely about the landscape. "The Indians have used the oil for years as an ointment. Mixed with flour, it becomes an excellent axle grease."

Liza laughed. "Your father was certainly ingenious."

"Yes, he was clever all right. You had to be, to survive here."

"But how did he get into cattle, then?" Liza persisted.

"As I said, he sort of drifted into it. When he was out looking for mustangs, he'd occasionally come across a longhorn—cattle that had drifted north from Mexico. Then as the number of trains increased, he started finding stray cattle that had broken loose, or had been cut loose if the going got too rough." He grinned. "Of course, Black Hawk did his share, too. The Indians would find strays on the prairie, and since they didn't like the taste of tame meat, they would bring them to my father." He chuckled. "I'm not so sure they were all strays, though."

"You mean the Indians stole them?" Liza asked, shocked.

"Yes, I'm quite sure a few were stolen. But, Liza, the Indians don't consider stealing wrong. They think it's an act of courage to steal something and get away with it, much braver than fighting or killing someone. That's why they're such big horse thieves."

"But your father knew they were stolen," Liza objected.

"No, suspected," Alex corrected. "Besides, what could he do about it? First of all, he couldn't insult the Indians by refusing their gifts, and second, he couldn't chase all over the country looking for the man they had stolen them from. So he just kept them."

"And the herd grew this big," Liza said in amazement.

"Well, actually bigger. I sell some cattle every now and then. But right now, I'm trying to hold off selling too many, trying to let the herd build because of the war between the states."

Liza remembered the talk she had heard back in New York City about the growing unrest between the North and the South. "Then you think there will be war?"

"Yes, both sides will keep bickering until that's the only solution," Alex answered bitterly. "The only question is when. They've been at each other's throats for years. When I was back East in college, I heard both sides of the story." He scowled, then spat, "Damn fools! They're both wrong!"

Liza gasped at his venomous words. "How can you say that?" she asked in a righteous tone. "Certainly, the North is right. Slavery is terrible!"

"Slavery!" Alex cried, sitting up. "My God, Liza, do you actually think that's what the issue is?"

"What, then?" Liza asked, adding, "And stop

yelling at me."

Alex grinned sheepishly. "I'm sorry. I didn't mean to yell. It's just that it's so frustrating to know this war is coming and that no one can stop it. I guess the real causes are the same old ones that cause every war—greed and jealousy. Each wants to break the back of the other. What it boils down to is a power struggle over who will run the country, the North or the South. We here in the West are caught in the middle. Both the North and the South are trying to lure us to their side."

"Then which side will you fight on?"

"Neither. I won't fight against the North or the South. It's *their* disagreement. Let *them* fight it out. I've seen enough senseless killing out here to last me a lifetime, and I won't kill for another man's cause. Not when that cause is based on selfishness."

"Selfishness?" Liza spat. "Then why are you saving your cattle? Because they'll bring a better price when the war comes?" she asked angrily. "Why, you're no better than they are, looking out after your own selfish interests."

"No, Liza," Alex said, glaring at her. "I can sell this entire herd anytime and get a damn good price for it. I don't need a war to make a profit. I'm saving this herd becuase the Northern Army is going to need meat badly, and I hope my support will help shorten the war, because it's going to be a long, bloody one before it's over."

"But you just said you wouldn't take sides," Liza objected.

"No, Liza," Alex said quietly, "I said I wouldn't fight against either. But I didn't say I wouldn't support the one that has to win. If the South is successful in seceding, this country will be split in two. The next thing you know, the West will split off. Then we'll be split into several small, weak countries, vulnerable to every European power. No, this country has got to stay united. Otherwise, it will cease to exist, and we'll all lose in the end. I don't support the North, as a segment of the country, but the Union itself."

This was one argument that Liza had never heard, and it made sense. She felt ashamed of herself for jumping to conclusions and accusing Alex of being a profiteer. "I'm sorry I insulted you."

"That's all right. You're not the first person to question my motives. At least you didn't accuse me of being a coward because I said I wouldn't fight."

"But you said you wouldn't kill for another man's cause. Surely it's more cowardly to fight for a cause you don't believe in, than to stand up for your own beliefs."

Alex was surprised at her reaction to his beliefs, and strangely touched. "Thank you, Liza. You're the first person to understand how I feel."

Liza gazed up at him, marveling at the different facets of this strange, complex man.

For a long while, they sat silently gazing at the landscape, each acutely aware of the other. Eventually, Alex rose and said, "We'd better go or we'll be late for supper, and then I'll never hear the end of Hiram's grumbling."

Liza got up and brushed the grass from the seat of her pants while Alex watched admiringly. "Alex, what happened to Hiram's leg?"

"Grizzly bear," Alex answered as he carried his saddlebags and canteen to his horse. "He was out prospecting for gold when he got caught by the bear. Hiram finally managed to kill it, but not before the bear mauled his leg badly. I don't know how he ever managed to get himself to Fort Williams, and they would have amputated if he hadn't put up such a fuss. I understand he threatened to blow off any man's head who tried to touch him. The leg finally healed, but as you can see, he limps badly. I think he still has a lot of pain, and that's why he's so grumpy all of the time."

"I don't think he's grumpy," Liza said as he helped her to mount.

"You don't? Well, I guess he's just trying to impress you." *The old geeser,* he thought. *He's not immune to her charms, either.*

Alex mounted, and as they rode, he continued his story. "There wasn't much Hiram could do out here, since he can't ride a horse. My father hired him as a cook and general handyman, and as you can see, he gets around pretty good. He's really invaluable to me, good with the animals, and I've never seen a man who can fix a wagon the way he can. Of course, he had a tendency to be a little bossy," Alex added, chuckling, "and I have to straighten him out on who's boss."

Liza laughed, feeling relaxed, amazed at how much she had enjoyed her ride and Alex's company.

A while later, Alex asked, "How did your parents die?"

"They both died in an influenza epidemic," Liza answered, her happiness disappearing.

"And your brother?" Alex inquired gently.

"He was swept overboard during a storm at sea on our way to America," Liza answered, painfully remembering.

"I'm sorry. I didn't mean to bring up unhappy memories," Alex said. "I'm serious about that reference, though. If it would be of any help."

To Liza, Alex's well-intended offer seemed like a slap in the face. So, she thought bitterly, he was still anxious to be rid of her. She fought back tears of disappointment. And here she had thought that he was beginning to trust her. What a silly, naive little fool she'd been, she thought. "No, thank you, Mr. Cameron," she said in an icy voice, her back rigid. "That would be dishonest."

"All right, if you prefer," Alex answered, wondering what he had said to get her dander up this time.

When they rode up to the ranch house some time later, Liza was still upset and tried to dismount before Alex could help her. In her haste to get away from him, she lost her balance and fell into his arms, their bodies touching intimately from chest to thigh. A warmness flooded over her as Alex slowly let her body slide along his, and she was acutely aware of his hard, muscular chest, abdomen and thighs. When she finally touched ground, her legs buckled with weakness, and she clutched his broad shoulders for support.

Liza looked up into Alex's face and saw his eyes were smoldering with desire. Tightening his arms about her, he lowered his head until his lips touched hers, nibbling at the sensitive corners, and then moving over hers in an achingly sweet kiss. His lips

88

left hers to lightly nip her earlobe, her throat, back to the corners of her mouth, and finally returning to capture her mouth with his. The kiss deepened and become more demanding. The tip of his tongue teased her lips, and Liza instinctively opened to him as his tongue caressed and explored the sweetness of her mouth.

Liza melted into him, her breasts crushed against his hard chest, their hearts pounding in unison. Alex's hands stroked her back, caressed her hips, and finally cupped her small, tight buttocks, lifting her and arching her hips against his groin. Liza felt his long hardness, hot and throbbing, even through the layers of their clothing. For a minute, she thrilled at this intimate touch. Then, reality returned, and with it, alarm. She struggled and frantically tore her mouth from his, gasping, "No!" as she twisted out of his embrace.

Alex glared down at her, his breathing labored, acutely conscious of his manhood straining at his pants. For a moment, they stood facing one another, each trying to force the other to his will by sheer eye contact. Finally, as Alex stepped toward her to take her in his arms again, Liza whirled and ran, stumbling into the house.

Alex glared angrily at the door where Liza had disappeared. *Damned teasing little bitch!* he thought, furious. She had wanted it as much as he did, only she got more than she bargained for. Savagely, he grabbed his horse's reins, and as the frightened animal shied away from him nervously, Alex hissed, "Dammit, cut that out! I've had enough foolishness for one day!"

Liza ran up to her room, her heart pounding in her chest, her legs trembling, and threw herself on her bed. She lightly touched her mouth where Alex's had been only a few moments before. Why did she feel this way? She had been kissed before and had felt only disgusted or repulsed. Why, when this man kissed her, did she feel so peculiar? All warm and weak and trembly. And then Anne's words came to her in a sudden rush: *Some day, when the right man comes along, you will ache for his kiss and his touch.*

No! Not Alex! She'd never fall in love with that rude, arrogant, violent man.

A knock interrupted Liza's thoughts, and her heart beat even more wildly for fear it was Alex. "Liza?" Hiram's voice questioned softly.

Liza jumped up and ran to the mirror for a quick look. Her hair was mussed, her face still flushed. "Just a minute," she called, smoothing her hair back. Opening the door, she saw Hiram standing with a tray of food in his hands, a look of concern on his wrinkled face.

"I thought you might like a tray in your room since we've already eaten and Alex said he wasn't hungry," Hiram explained. The old man studied Liza, noting her flushed face and mussed appearance. *Wonder what happened?* he thought, puzzled. First, Alex thundered in like a mustang with a bee under his tail, and now Liza looked so flustered and upset. Damn, he sure wished these two young'uns could get along.

"Thank you, Hiram," Liza said as she took the tray from him.

"Did you have a nice ride?"

"The ranch is lovely," Liza answered, setting the tray on the dresser. The old man stood, shifting from side to side awkwardly, wishing that she would tell him what had happened. Liza looked at him and repeated, "Thank you for the tray, Hiram." Knowing that he was being dismissed, Hiram turned and limped dejectedly from the room.

Liza didn't feel hngry, so she undressed and put on her robe, throwing the borrowed clothing Alex had brought her into a corner of the room. Then she sat in the rocking chair, moodily looking out at the growing dusk. She sensed, rather than heard, the door open and whirled defensively to see who was intruding on her privacy.

A blond, curly head peeped around the corner of the door as Andy shyly entered the room. "Liza sick?" His beautiful brown eyes were filled with concern.

"No, I'm just tired from my ride."

"Too tired? No story?" the little boy asked, his look wistful.

Liza smiled. "Oh, no, I'm not too tired for that. Come and sit on my lap."

Andy ran across the room and crawled onto Liza's lap, looking up at her with excited eyes. Liza noticed a slight motion at the door and said calmly, "Please come in, Bright Star." The old Indian woman entered the room, a sheepish grin on her wrinkled face. "Sit on the bed," Liza said, motioning. Then, with two pairs of dark eyes on her expectantly, Liza began her story.

As Alex stormed down the hall, he noticed that Liza's door was open and, looking into the room, saw Andy sitting on Liza's lap, his arms around her neck, his blond head nestled on her breasts. He felt irrationally jealous of the little boy, and his rage at Liza grew. He stepped into the room and said angrily, "Andy, it's past your bedtime."

All three were startled by the unexpected interruption. Andy, seeing the thunderous look on Alex's face, scampered off Liza's lap, and he and Bright Star hastily left the room.

Alex's steely eyes bored into Liza. She shuddered at their dangerous look. His voice was hard and cold, his fury barely contained. "It won't work, Miss Wentworth."

"What won't work?" Liza questioned, confused.

"First you tried to seduce me, and then when you decided you didn't like the results, you used your wiles on the boy."

"Seduce you?" Liza asked in an incredulous voice.

"Yes!" Alex answered hotly. "Don't you think I know about women like you? Well, I certainly met enough of your kind back East. Soft and teasing, making promises that you have no intention of keeping." His eyes raked her boldly. "Well, it won't work. You're still leaving Tuesday, and until then, stay away from the boy!"

Suddenly, Liza understood his accusations. He thought that she had deliberately tried to entice him, and then Andy, in hopes that he would let her stay. Liza was furious. She leaped from the chair. "Why, you conceited, arrogant bastard!" Recklessly grasping the vase of flowers sitting on the table by her, she threw it at him.

Shocked by her outburst, Alex almost forgot to duck. The vase, aimed with deadly accuracy, barely missed his head and crashed against the wall behind him. He looked dumbly at the shattered glass on the floor and then up at Liza standing hands on hips, her violet eyes flashing dangerously.

"What makes you think I want to stay here?" Liza screamed. "No! No amount of money could keep me here. I can't wait to get out of here and away from *you!* And you can be sure, I'll pay you back every cent I owe you!"

"That's fine with me!" Alex roared back, finally regaining his senses. Furious, he turned to leave, but at the door, he whirled and said, "And stay away from the barn tomorrow. We're going to be busy there, and you'll just get in the way." Then he stormed through the door, slamming it behind him.

Liza stood, shaking with rage, for several minutes before she threw herself on the bed and sobbed uncontrollably. Then, totally exhausted, she fell asleep.

When she awakened the next morning, Liza was still furious with Alex—and in a rebellious mood. After she had taken a quick sponge bath, she dressed quickly and walked downstairs defiantly but, much to her frustration, discovered the house was empty. She found the breakfast Hiram had left out for her and ate quickly.

For several hours, she sat in a big overstuffed chair and tried to read, but she was unable to concentrate on the book. The more she thought of Alex's insults the night before, the angrier she became. What right did he have to tell her what she could or couldn't do? She wasn't his prisoner! Incensed, she slammed the book aside and stormed outside, impetuously heading for the barn in open defiance.

But when she reached the barn, it was deserted. Even the pretty mares she had admired on her previous visit were gone from their stalls. For several minutes, Liza stood, frowning in frustration, before she became aware of a noise coming from behind the barn. She walked to the back of the barn and pushed open a door that opened into the corral.

Liza's attention was immediately drawn to the sight of a little mare being held on a double lead rein by two ranch hands. The frightened mare was sidling nervously, rearing and pawing. Liza quickly glanced to see what she was frightened of. Alex's big black stallion arrogantly approached the mare while Alex and another ranch hand tried to hold the huge animal in check. One look at the stallion's male organ told Liza what she had accidently stumbled onto—a mating. She gasped in surprise and shock.

The stallion gently nuzzled the mare's rump, but the pinto ducked her head, whinnied shrilly and lashed out at him with both sharp hooves. The stallion checked, puzzled, and then reached out to her again. This time the mare lashed viciously at him with her teeth, but the stallion had had enough. Rolling his lips back over his teeth, he charged the mare, pinning her to the fence, and then he snorted, reared and, fitting his forelegs over her shoulders, mounted her.

Liza watched the mating with a mixture of fear, shock, fascination—and strange excitement. She felt her heart race, the palms of her hands wet with perspiration, and a warmness low in her belly. Suddenly, a shadow crossed her, and she was vaguely aware of Alex standing before her.

"What in the hell are you doing here?" he demanded as he slammed the door to the corral shut behind him.

Liza didn't answer—couldn't answer—her tongue thick and unresponsive.

Alex stared at Liza, her breasts rising and falling in short, excited breaths, her face flushed, her eyes glazed. She had tempted and teased him for days, and now, thoroughly aroused himself, his control snapped. He seized her shoulders roughly, throwing her to the straw-covered floor, holding her down as he covered her mouth with his in a long, punishing kiss.

Liza lay stunned, still in a state of shock from what she had witnessed. She was barely aware of Alex's demanding kisses or his hands fondling her breasts. But when she felt his warm hand on her naked thigh, she started to struggle, pushing his hand away, trying to squirm out from under him.

Alex caught both her wrists in one big hand and held them above her head as he continued to kiss her throat. When Liza became aware of his lips on her bare breasts, she whispered frantically, "No!" trying to twist away.

Alex threw one powerful leg over hers, holding her thrashing body. He raised his head and looked down into her wide, frightened eyes. "You're just like that little mare out there, aren't you, Liza?" he snarled. Then, nuzzling her neck, his voice strangely hoarse, he muttered, "Teasing, taunting, pretending you don't want it, when all the time you really do." He grasped her chin, his fingers biting into her cheeks, forcing her to look into his smoldering eyes. "Well, I'm tired of playing games with you, Liza. No more games!"

As Alex's mouth descended on hers, his tongue plundering, Liza began to fight him in earnest. Before, she had been confused and frightened by her newly awakened feelings, but now she was angry. He wanted to force her and no man would ever force her. She twisted and kicked furiously. In an effort to control her thrashing body, Alex lost control of her hands, and she clawed him, savagely raking his face and neck. She almost succeeding in getting away from him, but Alex caught her by her long hair, roughly yanking her back down. This time, he subdued her by laying his big body over hers, his hands capturing her wrists again and pinning them above her head. Realizing the futility of trying to fight his superior strength, Liza ceased to struggle, a tortured sob escaping her throat.

Alex looked down into Liza's face. Her lips were trembling, and her eyes were tightly shut, their long lashes lying like fans across her pale cheeks. *God, how beautiful she is, and how I want her,* he thought. He watched as a single tear escaped her eye and trickled down her temple, feeling a sudden pang of guilt. For a moment, his need to possess her struggled with his conscience. Then, abruptly, he released her and rose to stand over her. "Cover yourself!" he demanded.

Liza opened her eyes and looked up, confused. Then, realizing her state of undress, she quickly sat up, frantically pushing her skirts back down, fumbling with the buttons on her open bodice. She glanced up to see Alex standing over her, his face flushed and scowling, his shirt open from the struggle. His broad chest lay bared to her eyes, the black hairs glistening with perspiration, the muscles straining to control his rapid breathing. She looked down to see the huge bulge in his pants and then, terrified, back up into his face.

"Don't worry, Liza," Alex said, his voice still hoarse and gasping. "I won't rape you. I like my women warm and willing."

He bent and cupped her chin, jerking it up and forcing Liza to look him in the eye. His voice was hard and threatening. "But, it's a good thing you're leaving tomorrow, Liza. Because ... so help me God ... if you stay one more day, I won't be responsible for my actions!" With that, he shoved her away, turned and strode angrily from the barn.

After Alex had left, Liza sat trembling for a few minutes, trying to regain her composure. Finally, she stood on shaky legs and made her way to her room. Closing the door behind her, she walked to the dresser and looked into the small mirror. Her hair was mussed, wisps of straw still clinging to it. Her face was tear-stained, her mouth swollen from Alex's demanding kisses. Her breasts still ached; in fact, she ached all over. But not from her recent struggles, she knew. She ached for him. Liza gasped at her own admission, Anne's words pounding over and over in her ears: *And you will ache for his kiss and his touch.*

She sat on the bed, thinking dismally that Alex was right. She had wanted him. She still wanted him, she admitted. But he didn't care about her, only her body. *My God,* Liza cried silently, *why did I have to fall in love with a man who doesn't love me back?*

Her head snapped up. Did she love him? she wondered. What was love? How did she know it was real love? Again, Anne's words returned to her: *Your heart will tell you so. Listen to your heart.*

"No!" Liza cried and threw herself down on the bed, burying her head in the pillow and trying to block out Anne's words.

Liza wasn't the only one who was miserable. Alex was nursing his own battered emotions. He had walked angrily away to the stream at the back of the house. Kneeling, he splashed cool water over his face and neck. The raw scratches, where Liza had clawed him, burned like fire. *Damn her!* he thought, still furious and frustrated. For a minute there, she had fought like a wildcat, with a strength that had amazed him. Frowning, he ran one hand through his wet hair, wondering what in the devil was wrong with him. He had never acted so irrationally! What was it about her that made him behave like an animal?

He sat, puzzling over his actions. He had never had any trouble getting a woman. If anything, it had always been too easy. His rugged good looks and strong male sensuality had drawn women like a magnet. More often, he was the pursued, rather than the pursuer. Perhaps that was it. All the others were easy conquests, and Liza offered more of a challenge. Alex shook his head in disagreement. No, it was more than that. From the minute he had seen her standing in the middle of the prairie, he had wanted her, and his need had only grown. She was beautiful, but much more than that she was proud, spirited and intelligent.

Intelligent! Alex snorted to himself. Since when did he look for intelligence in a woman? Frowning, Alex admitted that he had enjoyed talking to her, telling her more about himself than he had ever told some of his friends. Alex couldn't ever remember talking to a woman seriously. He grinned. He had even enjoyed arguing with her. That was the trouble, he admitted ruefully. He enjoyed her too much, in too many ways. It was a good thing she was leaving tomorrow.

Alex felt a deep pang of regret, stunning him with its intensity. Then he consoled himself, thinking, *You'll forget her. Out of sight, out of mind.*

Chapter 5

Wanting to have plenty of time to pack and dress for her trip, Liza arose early the next morning. She looked at herself closely in the small mirror. Her eyes were still red and swollen from crying herself to sleep the night before. For someone who rarely cried, she had been doing an awful lot of it lately.

For hours the night before, Liza had lain awake and examined her confused emotions. She had finally acknowledged defeat and admitted to herself that she had fallen in love with Alex. The rest of the night had been spent in trying to resign herself to her fate. She would leave, and hopefully, someday she would forget him.

But knowing that she had to see him this morning, she was apprehensive. My God, how could she face him? she thought, panic rising. How could she sit beside him and pretend that nothing had ever happened? How could she possibly hide her feelings from him?

A knock sounded at the door, and Hiram called

out, "Liza? Are you well enough to travel this morning?"

Poor Hiram, Liza thought. He had tried to get her to accept a supper tray the night before, but she had refused to even open the door, saying she was ill and didn't want to eat.

She walked across the room and opened the door. "Good morning, Hiram. Yes, I'm fine this morning, thank you."

Hiram looked at the young woman closely. She didn't look fine to him; she looked like she'd been crying. Damn that Alex! What did he do to her anyway? Trying to hide his thoughts, he said cheerfully, "We'll have time for a nice breakfast before we leave. Alex asked me to take you to the stage. You don't mind, do you?"

Relief at not having to face Alex swept over her. "Oh, no."

"Well, I'll just get your trunks now. Save me the trip later," the old man mumbled.

After they had eaten, and while Hiram was loading her trunks on the buckboard, Liza said good-bye to Bright Star and Andy. Despite all of her resolves, Liza cried when she told the little boy, looking so confused and hurt, good-bye.

Throughout the long trip to Elk Horn, Hiram tried repeatedly to draw Liza into a conversation; but she was obviously preoccupied with her thoughts, and he finally gave up. *Damn,* he thought, *I had such high hopes for those two.*

Liza was caught up in a whirlwind of emotions, fear of what lay ahead of her, regret at what lay behind, and more overwhelming than all, a profound sense of loss. She didn't even notice that they had reached their destination until she heard Hiram ask, "Do you want to get down and stretch your legs a bit?"

Liza glanced around her, surprised that they had already reached Elk Horn. She gazed up the road as if expecting to see the stage coach. "Should be here any minute," Hiram said, seeing her glance.

"Yes, I think I will stretch my legs," Liza said. "It will be a long stage ride until nightfall." She climbed from the buckboard and wandered aimlessly about the prairie, then finally sat down on a rock that was shaded by a scrubby tree.

Hiram continued to pace restlessly, limping painfully back and forth. Several times, he stopped to peer down the road and then at his watch. "About an hour late," he said finally, shaking his head. "Never saw it that late before."

"Do you think something is wrong?" Liza asked, beginning to feel apprehensive.

"Don't know. But it don't seem right," Hiram mumbled. He looked down the road again, his eyes growing large with alarm.

"What's wrong?" Liza asked, squinting to see what he was looking at in the distance. A thin, ominous line of dark smoke rose from the prairie.

"That's smoke!" Hiram cried, a wild look in his eyes. "Come on, let's get out of here," he said, pulling Liza to the wagon by her arm.

"What's burning?" Liza asked as he hurried her into the buckboard.

"Afraid it's the stagecoach," Hiram answered, jumping in behind her and whipping the horses to a gallop.

"The stagecoach?" Liza gasped, holding on to the lurching wagon for dear life. "But, why—"

"Injuns!" Hiram answered in an excited voice. "Dad-blasted Injuns, I'll bet!"

"Indians?" Liza asked, glancing fearfully behind them, expecting to see a hoard of howling savages following them. Apparently, Hiram was just as terrified, for he drove the horses at a mad gallop across the prairie. Liza had all she could do to keep from being thrown off the wildly bouncing buckboard on that long, agonizing drive back to the ranch.

As they entered the ranch yard, still going at breakneck speed, Alex saw them from the barn and ran to meet them. Catching the horses' bridles and trying to calm the excited, trembling animals, he called to Hiram, "What in the hell is wrong with you, old man?"

"Stage didn't come. Saw smoke. Injuns, I think," Hiram gasped, almost as winded as the horses.

Alex glanced quickly at Liza and saw her pale, frightened face. "Take Liza into the house, Hiram," he said calmly. "I'll take some of the men and investigate." He turned and walked back toward the barn.

Even more terrified, Liza leaped to her feet and cried out, "Be careful!"

Alex turned and looked at her with surprise. After their last disastrous meeting, he had expected her to hate him. After all, he had almost raped her. For that reason, he had asked Hiram to take her to the stage, too ashamed to face her. A surge of joy swept through him, and a grin broke out on his face. He nodded his head, and without a word, he turned and strode

103

rapidly away.

My God, Liza thought, *why did I say that? I was determined to hide my feelings from him, and then I practically blurt them out for everyone to see. But what if he should be killed?* The thought renewed her panic.

Hiram saw the fear in Liza's eyes and reassured her. "Don't worry about him. Alex can take care of himself."

Liza stared at Alex's retreating back, her heart showing in her eyes. Kindly, Hiram forced her from the buckboard and into the house.

All that afternoon and evening, Hiram hovered over Liza, trying to distract her from her worries. But Liza's sense of impending doom couldn't be stilled. Even after he had left her in her room that night, she was terrified that Alex might be killed. Hadn't everyone she loved been taken away from her by death? she asked herself. First, her parents, then Dan, and finally Anne, they had all been claimed. *Please, dear God,* she prayed, *don't take him, too.*

Later that night, when she heard the horses galloping up to the house, she ran to the window, anxiously watching. An expression of sheer joy spread over her face when she saw Alex dismount and hand his reins to one of the ranch hands. Turning, she rushed from the room, totally unaware that her only covering was her thin nightgown.

Below her, Hiram stood talking to Alex. "Well?" the old man asked.

"Indians," Alex answered wearily. "A raiding party of Kiowas." Alex took off his hat and threw it down on the table. Then he unstrapped his gunbelt and laid it carefully beside it.

104

"Everyone dead?" Hiram asked, anxious for the grim facts.

"Yes," Alex answered numbly, "driver, guard and three passengers. The Indians cut the horses loose and then set fire to the coach. I sent a man to Fort Laramie, but I doubt that the army will catch up with them." He rubbed his aching neck and arched it back, then noticed Liza standing at the top of the stairs.

"Were they scalped?" Hiram asked impatiently, still wanting to hear all the grizzly details.

"Shut up, old man," Alex answered, motioning to Liza. Hiram turned in surprise toward the girl.

"I'll tell you in the morning," Alex said, indicating that Hiram should leave.

Hiram looked up at Liza and then at Alex. The two seemed to be devouring each other with their eyes. *I knew it, I knew it,* he thought gleefully. Grinning with immense satisfaction, he limped from the hall.

Alex's eyes bored into Liza's, seemingly pinning her to the spot, as he slowly climbed the stairs and walked over to her. Placing one finger under her chin, he raised her head gently, his roughened thumb sensuously stroking her jawline. Looking deeply into her eyes, he asked tenderly, "Are you all right, Liza?"

Liza trembled in response to his touch. Seeing her tear-stained face and feeling her tremble, Alex mistook her reaction for fear and said, "There's nothing to be afraid of. You're safe here. The Indians are probably miles away by now." Looking closer at her face and seeing her exhaustion, he added, "What you need is a good night's sleep."

Gently, he led her into her room and set her down

105

on the bed. Liza stared up at him as if her eyes couldn't get enough of him. Alex stood silently for a few minutes, his silvery eyes shimmering with emotion. He bent, running one finger over her full, bottom lip. Slowly, he lowered his head and kissed her lips, gently, tenderly. "Good night, Liza," he whispered.

He walked to the door, but before he left the room, he turned and said quietly, "Liza, I don't want to frighten you, but the Indians may not be gone from this area. Just in case, stay close to the house, and if you see anything suspicious, anything at all, get in the house—fast." His eyes bored into her. "Understand?" Then he smiled. "Please, no more rebellion."

Liza smiled and nodded her head in silent agreement.

Alex stared at her, paralyzed by a pair of soft violet eyes. Shaking himself, he turned and closed the door behind him. He forced himself to walk down the hall and into his room, where he threw himself across his bed. He lay on his back, one arm thrown over his eyes, and visualized Liza as he had seen her standing at the top of the stairs, her gown clinging to her round, tantalizing curves, her hair in glorious disarray, her full lips trembling, her beautiful eyes misty with tears. A groan escaped Alex's lips as he muttered, "How much torture can a man stand?"

The next day, Liza stood outside the house, watching Andy throw pebbles. "Watch, Liza," Andy called as he threw a pebble at a small clump of bushes. A startled rabbit hopped from the bushes and ran across the ranch yard. "Look, a rabbit!" Andy squealed and ran off following the small animal.

Liza remembered Alex's warning to stay close to the house, and called out to the little boy, "No, Andy, come back!" But Andy was too engrossed in the chase, so Liza raced after him, stumbling over her long skirts, calling for him to come back.

Suddenly, a horrible, piercing scream rent the air, and Liza glanced back to see a band of howling Indians galloping around the corner of the barn. Another quick look in Andy's direction made Liza's heart leap in fear. A lone Indian rode toward the boy, and before Liza could move, he swooped down from his horse and grabbed him. Andy screamed and thrashed wildly, and the Indian was having a hard time controlling both the small boy and his nervous horse. Without even thinking, Liza ran to them and caught Andy's legs, jerking on them, trying to pull him away from his captor. For a moment, she and the Indian fought a silent tug-of-war over the boy, while the Indian's horse shied excitedly, trying to rear.

Andy's body was released abruptly, and he and Liza both fell to the ground in a heap. The frightened horse reared and pawed at the air, his sharp hooves barely missing the two people huddled on the ground.

Trying to crawl away and dragging Andy with her, Liza felt a strong arm snake around her waist, and she was lifted up in front of the Indian. Liza clawed wildly at the arm that held her in a tight, breath-taking vise. She kicked frantically, hoping that if nothing else, she could unseat them both. The Indian grunted a low, guttural curse, tightened his knees about the horse, and raised his fist, which was the last thing Liza saw before her head exploded, and then, total darkness.

Alex had run from the barn when he heard the war cry and barely had time to dive to the ground to escape the hail of arrows as the band of Indians rushed by. Rolling from the dirt, he fired his Colt at the fleeing Indians, and one pitched forward from his horse. Then Alex heard Andy's scream and turned to watch in frozen horror the tableau taking place in the distance.

Hiram hobbled up to him, pointing his gun at the Indian who held Liza before him. "No!" Alex cried, pushing the gun down. "You might hit her!" Both men watched helplessly as Liza suddenly slumped forward and the Indian rode off to join his companions in the distance.

"See if Andy's all right," Alex brusquely told Hiram and turned to stride rapidly into the barn. By the time the old man returned, wheezing and limping badly, Alex was already saddling his horse.

"He's okay. Just scared to death," Hiram said. "You going after them?"

"Not yet!" Alex answered, tightening the cinch viciously.

"But they've got Liza!"

Alex turned, grasped Hiram's shoulders, and roughly shook him. "Dammit, old man, I know they've got her," he answered in an agonized voice.

It was the tone of Alex's voice rather than the shaking that calmed Hiram. "But . . . but . . ." he sputtered.

"If I try to follow them now, they'll kill her for sure. You know that. I've got to lag far enough behind them that they won't know I'm following. Make them think they're safe, and then, when they

108

don't expect it, try to rescue her," Alex explained patiently.

"But where are you going now?" the old man whined.

"To Tanaźin," Alex replied, turning to pick up his saddlebags.

"What are you going to that dad-blasted Injun for?" Hiram questioned, his voice scornful.

"Dammit!" Alex swore, slamming his saddlebags across his horse. "Stop acting like a hysterical old woman and think! In the first place, there were seven Indians in that raiding party, and if I'm not mistaken, there're another couple up in the hills, protecting those horses they stole yesterday. Do you really think I'm stupid enough to take on those kinds of odds?" Alex asked angrily.

"But, the army—"

"The army?" Alex spat contemptuously. "When was the last time they brought a captive back alive?"

Alex looked down at the old man and saw the fear in his eyes. Gently laying his hand on Hiram's shoulder, he said, "If I went to the fort, I'd lose too much time. And you know how important that is. I've got to pick up their trail while it's still fresh. Besides, who's the best Indian tracker you know?" He waited while the old man absorbed this and then continued, "That's right. Another Indian. With Tanaźin and his braves, I'll have someone to help track those Kiowas down and capture Liza back when we find them."

"But what if Tanaźin won't help? He's an Injun, too."

"Those Indians are Kiowas, old enemies of the

109

Dakotas. Besides, even if they weren't, I know Tanaźin would help me," Alex assured the old man.

Alex led his horse from the barn with Hiram hobbling along beside him. "I don't know how long I'll be gone. Tell Manuel I said to take over the ranch. I'll honor any decisions he makes," Alex instructed.

Hiram nodded in resignation. But as Alex mounted and started to ride away, Hiram's bony hand reached up and grasped Alex's thigh, his fingers biting into the muscles painfully. Alex looked down into his face. The old man's eyes were filled with tears, his weathered face contorted with pain. "You bring that little gal back, you hear?" Hiram said. "Bring that little gal back," he repeated with a sob.

Alex's chest muscles contracted suddenly as a flicker of fear ran through him. Laying his hand on Hiram's shoulder and gently squeezing it to reassure him, he answered, "I'll bring her back, old man. I promise. If it's the last thing I do, I'll bring her back."

Then, wheeling his horse abruptly, he rode away, traveling north, the opposite direction from which the Indian raiding party had ridden.

The first thing Liza was aware of when she regained consciousness was a terrible, throbbing headache. Opening her eyes, she saw the ground rushing past her and, turning her head to the side, the naked thigh of her captor. She struggled slightly and felt the Indian's hand shove her firmly against the galloping horse's back. Bile rose in her throat, and she gulped frantically to keep from vomiting.

Shortly thereafter, the Indian stopped and roughly pulled Liza from the horse. Ignoring her feeble attempts to struggle, he tied her hands before her, the rawhide biting into her small, delicate wrists. Then, with a grunt, he flung her astride the horse, mounted the horse behind her and galloped off at a fierce pace. Liza, her head pounding painfully, frantically grasped the animal's mane to hold on.

Later, Liza couldn't remember much of that day of wild flight. Her head throbbing with pain, her heart pounding with fear, she had fought bouts of nausea and dizziness the entire ride. When they had finally stopped late that night, she was only semi-conscious.

The Indian harshly jerked Liza from the heaving, sweaty horse, shoved her toward a small tree and pushed her down. As Liza looked up at him with terror-filled eyes, the savage offered her a waterskin, motioning for her to drink. She was terribly thirsty, but feeling nauseous, she shook her head. Angrily, her captor grabbed her hair, twisting her head back and held the waterskin to her mouth, forcing her to either drink or drown. Then he offered her a thin, dry piece of meat, and Liza, afraid to refuse the second time, nibbled at it reluctantly. Surprisingly, the salty meat seemed to settle her stomach.

When she finished eating, her captor reached down and untied her hands. Liza sobbed a small cry of relief as she rubbed her raw wrists, but before she knew what was happening, the Indian pushed her callously against the tree and tied her hands behind it. She looked up at him, thinking to object, but seeing the hard look in his black eyes, she dropped her head on her chest, a lone tear trickling down her cheek.

Liza lay watching the Indians eat, her heart thudding wildly in her chest, terrified of what would happen next. From all of the horrible stories she had heard, Indians raped their women captives. She held her breath as she watched the Indians—one by one—lie down, roll over and fall asleep. Not until the last man was snoring restfully, did Liza relax and close her eyes. Her last thought before she fell into an exhausted sleep was of Alex, as she sobbed softly, "Oh, Alex, help me."

From then on, Liza's days as an Indian captive were much the same. She remained tied at all times, whether they walked, rode or slept. When the Indians walked their horses over terrain obviously too rough for riding, Liza was forced to walk with a rawhide tether around her neck, and if she stumbled or fell, her captor jerked it impatiently, causing it to bite painfully into her throat. Her flimsy shoes had been ripped and torn the second day, and now Liza walked barefoot, her tender feet blistered and bleeding. She even relished the thought of riding, although the insides of her legs were raw from riding astride without a saddle and she hated the feel of the nearly naked Indian behind her. Her face was sunburned, her lips dry and cracked from exposure, and her wrists were festering where the rawhide had rubbed them. But from somewhere, Liza found the strength to keep up without complaining, knowing that if she didn't, the Indians would have no compunctions about killing her.

She had given up the fear of rape after the second night, deciding that those parts of the tales she had heard were simply not ture. In fact, instead of lusting after her, the Indians ignored her. Even her captor, who seemed to be personally responsible for her survival, paid little attention to her except for giving her water, feeding her and taking her off periodically for her nature calls. As a whole, the Indians seemed to be much more excited about the horses they had captured than her.

Then she shivered in revulsion, remembering the one Indian who had not ignored her. Several times she had seen him staring at her, his black eyes hot, glittering with lust. Scarface, she had named him, his face being horribly disfigured by an ugly, puckered scar that ran from his forehead to his chin, and she was thankful that he was not her captor.

She had long ago given up any hope of rescue. The second day, she had hoped all day to see a column of blue-coated soldiers swooping down on the Indians to help her. But then she had noticed, first with confusion, and then with heart-sinking realization, the Indians deliberately obliterating their trail. That had been the purpose of those long, tedious trips into the rocks and down the middle of a stream, and Liza, aware of the hopelessness of her situation, had wept bitterly. From then on, her only thoughts were of surviving this trip. She refused even to contemplate what her fate might be after it was over.

The fourth night of her captivity, Liza sat tied to a tree, wearily watching the Indians sitting cross-legged around the campfire, laughing and talking while they ate. She had become accustomed to their near nakedness, the only clothing they wore being a brief breechcloth and moccasins. Even their speech didn't seem as abrasive to her now, although she still

113

couldn't understand any of what they said. She glanced up and saw Scarface staring at her, his back to the other Indians. His eyes raked her, an obscene, one-sided leer on his face. Liza gasped, looking wildly about for her captor, as Scarface laughed contemptuously, turned and walked away. Eventually, long after the camp was quiet, she drifted into an exhausted sleep.

Liza was suddenly awakened by a rag being roughly stuffed into her mouth. Terrified, she opened her eyes to see Scarface squatting beside her, his face even more horribly contorted by his lust. He threw himself on her, pinning her to the ground, and shoved her skirts up, ripping her fragile underwear away. When he pushed her thighs open, Liza twisted and kicked frantically, feeling him viciously jabbing at her as he struggled to hold her hips in place. She finally managed to expel the filthy cloth from her mouth, drew in a deep breath of blessedly fresh air and screamed. Suddenly, Scarface was pulled from her by the other Indians.

Terrified, Liza didn't realize for several minutes that the Indians' curses were not aimed at her, but at Scarface. She watched in disbelief as the Indians shook their fists and grunted angrily at her attacker, who cowered away in fear. Only once did Scarface answer them back, and he was answered in turn with a swift, violent kick to his abdomen by one of his furious companions. Bending over, holding his stomach in agony, Scarface was dragged from the scene by two of the braves.

Liza cowered herself as the Indians turned and looked at her contemptuously. Then, abruptly, they turned away in disgust and left her to lay, trembling and sobbing, the rest of the night.

The next day, Liza was relieved to find the Indians were again ignoring her, but when she saw Scarface looking at her, she was even more terrified than before. His look of lust had been replaced with one of pure, naked hatred. *He'll kill me the first opportunity he gets,* Liza thought. That night, she fought desperately to stay awake, forcing her eyelids open, pinching herself, but finally, her weary body surrendered to sleep.

She was awakened by a slight noise. Sitting up, she looked frantically over the camp and saw that all seemed quiet and still. Then she heard the sound again—behind her.

"Liza," Alex whispered softly. "For Christ's sake, don't move," he added quickly, his voice low and intense. "Put your head back and pretend to sleep."

Liza's heart leaped with happiness. He had come! Alex had come for her after all. Dropping her head, relaxing against the tree, she closed her eyes, but she was unable to keep from smiling.

"That's better," Alex whispered from behind her. "Now, don't move. I'm going to cut your hands free, but don't move them yet. Stay just as you are." Liza felt a knife sawing at the rawhide bonds around her wrists and then the sudden release of her hands.

"Don't move until I say so," Alex whispered. "In a few minutes, Tanaźin and his braves will ride in, and all hell will break loose. When I say, *now*, jump up quickly and run with me."

Liza nodded, glancing beneath lowered lids at the Indians sleeping soundly by the campfire. One rolled

115

over suddenly; Liza tensed with fear. Then she sighed in relief when she heard his soft snore.

Suddenly, a piercing, blood-curdling scream sliced through the silent night. *"Huka hey, huka hey!"* the ancient Dakota war cry sounded, as a new, strange band of Indians swooped down on the campsite.

"Now!" Alex yelled.

Liza scrambled to her feet, and Alex grabbed her hand, running with her, pulling her away from the campsite. Liza felt a painful tug on her hair and turned to face Scarface, his ugly features twisted with hate, his black eyes glittering with blood-lust, his war club raised. A gunshot shattered the night, so close it nearly deafened her, and as Liza watched in horror, Scarface's chest seemed to explode, blood, tissue and pieces of bone splattering her face and dress.

"Come on, Liza!" Alex yelled, holding his smoking Colt in one hand as he shoved her away from the bloody carnage with the other. Another Indian leaped from a clump of bushes, his knife gleaming wickedly in the moonlight, but before Alex could fire his gun again, a second Indian swooped down on the first and buried his war club in his enemy's skull with a sickening crunching noise.

Liza lurched and fell to her knees, gagging.

"Damn!" Alex swore, lifting her and shoving her forward again.

As they raced through the darkened woods, Liza felt a sharp stab in her foot, followed by another pain. Limping painfully, she tried to run, but only stumbled and fell again. Exasperated, Alex slipped his gun into his holster and swooped her up in his arms, running with her.

Alex sped silently through the moon-dappled woods, away from the dying screams and triumphant yells of the bloody fight behind them. Finally, he reached a clearing where an Indian stood holding two horses. Alex pushed Liza quickly up on his horse and mounted behind her as two other Indians rode into the clearing. Riding his horse up to them, one of the Indians said something to Alex in a soft, guttural voice.

"Damn!" Alex cursed. "What rotten luck."

"What's wrong?" Liza asked anxiously.

"One of the Kiowas got away," Alex answered. "Tanaźin thinks their main camp isn't far from here. That means we've got to make a run for it. Sorry, Liza, but we've got a long, hard ride ahead of us."

Alex kneed his horse sharply, and they galloped off with the other Indians following closely behind. They rode, as Alex had predicted, long and hard.

As they raced through the night, careening around trees and boulders, the air rushing past them, Liza's foot began to throb painfully. Maybe she had been bitten. As the pain became more intense, she thought to ask Alex to stop and look at it, but then remembering what they were fleeing from, Liza decided to keep quiet, bearing the pain in silence. But the longer they rode, the worse Liza felt. She began to feel dizzy and nauseous, her head throbbing just as painfully as her foot.

Finally, near morning, they stopped at a small stream to water their horses. As Alex lifted his arms to help her dismount, Liza reeled drunkenly, her eyes blurred. Smiling a small, almost apologetic smile, Liza collapsed into his arms.

117

Chapter 6

Liza regained consciousness slowly. First, she was aware of lying on a soft fur and being covered with a rough blanket, and then, as she opened her eyes, she realized that she was in a tent of some sort. She gazed slowly about her and then gasped as her eyes fell on a young Indian woman sitting a few feet from her. At her gasp, the Indian girl rose and hurried from the tent.

Liza huddled weakly into her covers, tears streaming down her face, thinking bitterly it was all a dream. Alex hadn't rescued her after all. She had just dreamt it. She was still a captive of the Indians.

The flap on the tent opened, and a tall, large man bent to enter. Terrified, Liza cowered into the side of the tepee.

"Liza, are you awake?" a husky voice asked gently.

"Alex!" Liza cried with relief, catching one of his big hands in hers. "Is it really you?" she questioned, afraid to let go of his hand for fear he would disappear.

118

Alex laughed. "Yes, it's really me, and if being captured by Indians will make you so happy to see me, I'll have to see what I can do about getting you abducted every day," he teased.

Embarrassed, Liza dropped his hand and explained, "When I woke up and saw the Indian girl, I thought I was still a captive. That I had only dreamed you'd rescued me."

Alex laughed again. "I can see why. In fact, I was afraid you might think that. That's why I told Wahcawin to come and get me as soon as you woke up. We're in Tanaźin's camp now. You're safe. No one will harm you here."

Liza looked about the tepee, trying to orient herself and remember how she had gotten there. She frowned. "I can't remember arriving here. Was I asleep?"

"No, you've been unconscious for five days."

"Unconscious?" Liza asked, stunned.

"Yes," Alex answered, then added irritably, "Why in the hell didn't you tell me about the thorn, Liza. I know you must have felt it."

Liza remembered the terrible pain in her foot and leg. "Is that what it was, a thorn? I thought I had been bitten by something. I didn't tell you, because I didn't want to bother you. I mean, it seemed more important that we escape."

"I admire your bravery, Liza, but this is one time I wish you had been less brave. Apparently, that thorn was poisonous. If we had gotten it out sooner, you might have saved yourself a lot of pain and misery, and us a lot of worry."

"You mean a little thorn made me *that* sick?" Liza

119

asked incredulously.

"Apparently so," Alex answered. "At first, I thought you had just fainted from exhaustion, but when I couldn't wake you up, I was baffled. You seemed to be fine when I rescued you. It was Tanaźin who noticed the thorn in your foot. We tried to treat it as best we could, considering we were on the run, but when you didn't get any better, Tanaźin suggested we bring you to his camp, where his wife could treat you, instead of taking you back to the ranch."

"Was that Indian girl here with me·Tanaźin's wife?"

"Yes, Wańcawin. She has the healing gift, and she's been treating you with herbs and putting poultices on your foot ever since we got here yesterday. You may have Tanaźin to thank for your rescue, but you have Wańcawin to thank for your life."

Liza felt guilty. "Oh, Alex, when I woke up and saw her here, I was terrified. She must think me terribly ungrateful."

"Don't worry," Alex assured her. "I'm sure she understands. She would be just as frightened if she woke up in a white man's house. She tells me your foot looks much better. Let's have a look."

Before Liza could object, Alex lifted the blanket from her leg. Examining the foot closely and then running one finger lightly over her leg, he observed, "It looks much less swollen, and thank God, the red streaks on your leg are gone." Placing her leg back down gently and covering it, he asked, "How does it feel?"

Liza blushed at his intimate touch. "It's still a little

120

sore," she admitted.

"Well, Waḣcawin is preparing another poultice for it right now. Also some broth. Are you hungry?"

"Not really, only thirsty."

Quietly, the Indian girl entered the tepee, carrying two bowls. Smiling, she handed one to Alex; the other she set on the ground by Liza.

Lifting Liza gently by the shoulders, Alex tipped the bowl to her lips. "Here, drink this broth. It will satisfy your thirsty and give you some strength."

Liza took several swallows of the hot liquid. Shocked at how weak she felt, she turned her head away, whispering, "No more."

"Come on, Liza, all of it," Alex said firmly. "You wouldn't want to displease Waḣcawin after all she's done for you, would you?" he cajoled.

Liza glanced up at the pretty Indian girl standing above her. Waḣcawin was smiling, her brown eyes soft and compassionate. Liza weakly pushed Alex's hands away, took the bowl in her own hands and drank all of it. Her head dropped back down, the small act having totally exhausted her.

Alex shot a worried look to Waḣcawin, who smiled reassuringly back at him. Taking the other bowl, the Indian girl uncovered Liza's foot and began to pack a foul-smelling concoction around it.

"What's that?" Liza asked.

"A poultice of herbs and roots," Alex answered. "It helps draw out the poison."

Liza wrinkled her nose. "It smells awful." Alex chuckled at her complaint.

When Waḣcawin was through applying the poultice, she washed her hands and handed Alex

121

another small bowl. Alex bent and lifted Liza's head again. "Now you must drink this."

"What's it for?" Liza asked, already feeling well enough to be irritable.

"To help you sleep."

"But I just woke up!" Liza objected.

"Doctor's orders," Alex said, chuckling. "Waȟcawin insists you must rest. We'll awaken you periodically to eat, but in the meanwhile, you sleep."

He forced the bitter brew down her throat as Liza sputtered and tried weakly to fight him. Her head felt fuzzy before she even laid it down. Still, she managed to give Alex a resentful glare, bringing a laugh to his lips. *He's enjoying this*, she thought. *Why, he's nothing but a big bully.* Then she closed her eyes and drifted into a peaceful slumber.

Several times during the day, Liza was awakened by either Alex or Waȟcawin to drink the rich broth, followed by the bitter brew. That night, Liza lay sleeping soundly in her drugged state. She didn't hear Alex when he came in, stripped down to his pants and laid down on the pallet across from her. Later in the night, Liza awakened briefly and groggily gazed at Alex sleeping only a few feet away from her. She closed her eyes and smiled, thinking what a lovely dream she was having.

The next morning, Liza woke up feeling refreshed and much stronger. She was alone, and as she struggled to sit up, the blanket fell away from her. She gasped in shock, quickly pulling the blanket up to cover herself. Why, she was naked!

Alex picked this inopportune moment to enter the tepee.

122

"Where are my clothes?" Liza demanded, huddling in the corner, holding the blanket against her body.

Alex looked down into a pair of violet eyes flashing dangerously. "Well," he said sarcastically, "I see you're feeling better this morning. Well enough to be bad tempered."

"Bad tempered?" Liza spat. "I'm bad tempered because I want my clothes." Looking wildly around the tepee, she repeated, "Where are my clothes?"

Alex grinned, hooked his thumbs in his belt and rocked back on his heels. "If you're talking about those filthy rags you had on when we got here, we burnt them."

"Burnt them?" Liza gasped. "But what am I going to wear?"

Alex laughed, enjoying himself and vastly relieved that Liza was obviously feeling better. "When you're ready to get up, then I'll find you some clothes."

"I want to get up now!" Liza demanded.

"Nope," Alex answered firmly. "Wahcawin says you are to stay off that foot one more day."

"And I suppose you're going to keep me drugged all day again," she asked bitterly.

"No, no more sleeping medicine. But you are going to stay off that foot," he added in a hard, warning voice. "Tomorrow, if your foot still looks good, you can get up, and I'll find you some clothes." Then he grinned wickedly. "But I'm tempted to keep you naked, since I've finally found the secret to controlling you."

"How . . . how dare you!"

123

Alex threw his head back and laughed. Liza glared at him. Still chuckling, he said, "Well, if I had left you wrapped in just a blanket, I bet you wouldn't have been outside and captured by the Indians, now would you?"

Liza frowned. "Alex, I didn't disobey you. Andy was chasing a rabbit, and I was trying to catch him."

Suddenly serious, Alex squatted before her. "I know, Liza. That was a very brave thing you did, trying to rescue him from the Indian, but very foolish of you, too."

"Is Andy all right?" Liza asked, feeling guilty that she had completely forgotten to ask about the little boy.

"He's fine. He was a little frightened, but fine." Then he cupped her chin in his hand and looked deeply into her eyes. "Did the Indians hurt you?"

Liza, thinking that he was asking her if she had been raped, blushed and ducked her head. "No," she whispered, "they didn't do *that* to me."

Alex read her thoughts and laughed bitterly. "Well, rape was one thing I didn't have to worry about them doing to you, at least not until they reached their camp."

Liza looked at him with surprise. "How did you know they wouldn't—" she hesitated.

"Rape you?" Alex finished for her. "Because, Indians take a vow of celibacy anytime they go on a raiding or hunting party. They believe the sexual act robs them of the strength needed to obtain their goal, and that vow lasts until the task is finished and they are back in their camp. Any man who breaks his vow brings dishonor on the whole party."

124

Liza turned her head away. So that's how it was. That explained why the other Indians were so angry with Scarface when he had tried to rape her. And she wouldn't have been safe from rape after all, as she had assumed. They had been saving *that* until they reached the main camp. She shivered at the realization.

Alex noticed Liza's shiver and remembered her incoherent ramblings while she was delirious. He knew the Indians had done something to frighten her badly and wished she would tell him, instead of locking it up inside her. "I asked if they hurt you, Liza?" he said gently.

Liza wondered for one brief moment if she should tell Alex about Scarface's attack, and then decided against it. "No, they were harsh and rough, but not cruel," she answered evasively. "No, they didn't hurt me."

Something in Liza's voice told Alex she wasn't being completely honest with him, but he was reluctant to push her too hard. Seeing her uneasiness, he decided to change the subject.

"Tanazin asked me if I would go hunting with him today. Would you mind if I left you here? You wouldn't be afraid of staying with Wańcawin, would you?"

"No," Liza answered, relieved to be off the subject of her captivity and its unpleasant, frightening memories. "I wouldn't mind at all. She's really very kind." Then curious, she asked, "What does Wańcawin mean in English?"

"Flower Woman."

"Yes, she is like a flower—pretty, sweet and

125

delicate," Liza muttered, thinking aloud.

"Yes, she is," Alex agreed. "She's Tanaźin's favorite wife."

"Favorite wife!" Liza gasped, shocked. "For goodness sake, how many does he have?"

Alex grinned. "Three."

"Why, that's terrible!" Liza cried, outraged.

"No, it isn't," Alex answered calmly. He silenced her objection with an upraised hand. "Don't condemn the Indians until you understand their reasons, Liza. They live a very warlike existence, resulting in a constant shortage of men. Taking more than one wife is their way of providing for and protecting the excess women."

"And Tanaźin loves them all?" Liza asked in amazement.

Alex smiled, wondering at Liza's reference to "loves them." Did she mean the emotion, or the physical act? Deciding she meant the former, he answered, "Yes, he loves them all, but not necessarily equally." Seeing Liza's confusion, he said, "Tanaźin respects and feels kindly toward all his wives, but only Waȟcawin does he love deeply. She is his *wakanka*, his true wife. I suspect this is true with most Indians who have more than one wife. There is one who is special to him and therefore more loved."

"But aren't the others jealous?"

"No, the Indian husband is absolute ruler of his house. He would never tolerate a disruptive wife. If that were the case, he would divorce her, send her back to her family."

The discussion was brought to an abrupt halt as Waȟcawin, smiling shyly, entered the lodge. She and Alex had a brief conversation in the Dakota tongue,

126

and then Alex turned to Liza. "Wahcawin tells me she has a surprise for you today. Are you sure you don't mind that I go hunting with Tanaźin?"

"No, I'll be fine," Liza answered, smiling up at the comely Indian girl.

The surprise turned out to be a bath. True, it was only a sponge bath, accomplished with the use of a large bowl of water, a piece of a pulpy, yellowish plant for soap and her blanket for a towel, but Liza felt much more refreshed when it was over. And there was no doubt that she was cleaner, judging from the filthy water when she had finished.

Then Wahcawin combed the matted tangles from Liza's hair with a crude wooden comb, after she had sprinkled a strange powder into it. When the Indian girl was finished, Liza's hair lay in soft, golden-red waves across her shoulders and back. Liza was amazed at how clean it felt. Taking a strand and sniffing at it delicately, she realized that it even smelled clean. For lack of words, Liza looked up at the Indian girl and smiled her gratitude.

Wahcawin touched Liza's hair lightly, murmuring, *"Awanyake waśte."*

Seeing her obvious admiration, Liza knew it must be a compliment of some sort. "Thank you."

"Iśtima?" Wahcawin asked.

Liza frowned. "What?"

"Iśtima." Wahcawin folded her hands by the side of her head and closed her eyes.

"No," Liza answered, shaking her head, "I'm not sleepy."

"Iśtima," Wahcawin said firmly, this time a command.

When Liza awakened from her nap, she was alone

127

in the tepee, so she slipped from the blanket and limped around the small enclosure for a few minutes. She was still a little light-headed, but most of the pain was gone from her foot. When she laid back down on the blanket, she continued to move her foot, flexing it, rotating it, trying to get the stiffness out. She smiled to herself, wondering what Alex would say if he knew of her little rebellion. *Control me by keeping me naked,* she thought hotly. *Well, we'll just see about that!*

After Waĥcawin left for the night, Liza lay staring at the small fire in the center of the tepee, wondering when Alex had returned to the Indian camp. She felt both hurt and irritated that he had not come by to see how she had fared during his absence. For a long time, she lay contemplating everything Alex had told her about the Indians that morning. Despite all the logical reasons Alex had given her, she still found polygamy distasteful. She wondered how her new friend, Waĥcawin, really felt about it. Why, she wouldn't share Alex with another woman, she thought hotly, and then blushed at her own audacity. Forcing her thoughts to less disturbing channels, she closed her eyes and drifted off to sleep.

Liza barely awakened when Alex returned to the lodge later that night. She watched in a half-sleep, half-conscious state as he removed his boots and socks, then his shirt. When he reached for his belt, she suddenly became fully awake.

"What are you doing?" she cried in alarm.

Alex turned, a surprised look on his face. "Oh, so you're awake after all. I'm getting ready for bed," he said matter-of-factly as he pulled the belt off and sat

128

down on the pallet across from her. "How are you feeling?"

Liza stared at his broad naked chest covered with crisp black curls. She had seen a man's chest before—her brother's, the Indians'—but Alex's was much more muscular and obviously masculine. The sight both excited and unnerved her. "You can't sleep here!" she blurted in a shrill voice.

One dark eyebrow arched. "Well, you must be okay. I see you have your temper back," Alex answered in a sarcastic voice.

Angrily, Liza sat up, the blanket momentarily falling away from her. Quickly, she snatched it up, but not before Alex got a tantalizing glimpse of full, creamy breasts. Groaning to himself, he laid down on his back, forcing himself to stare at the ceiling of the tepee.

Liza was even more alarmed. She had seen the fleeting look of admiration and hunger in Alex's eyes when he looked at her breasts. It had given her a peculiar, warm feeling. "You can't sleep here," she repeated weakly.

Alex expelled an exasperated sigh. Casually laying on his back, his arms folded under his head and still staring at the ceiling, he said, "We're lucky to have a tepee to ourselves. We could be in Tanaźin's tepee, with him and his wives. But Tanaźin, in respect for your privacy, set this up for us." Turning his head and looking across at her, he continued, "I've been here every night since we arrived. Don't you think the Indians might think it a little strange that I suddenly decided to sleep outside?"

"But I was sick then," Liza said defensively.

129

Alex again sighed deeply. He knew what she was afraid of. It *had* been different when she was ill. Then he had only felt concern and compassion for her. But now that she was well again and looking so damned beautiful, his desire for her was even stronger than ever. Still, it wouldn't do to offend Tanaźin.

Alex rolled over with his back to her. "Liza, I'm tired, and I don't feel like arguing with you. I'm going to sleep here, and if you think you're big enough and strong enough to push me out that flap—you can just try!"

Alex could feel Liza's hot glare on his back. Finally, he rolled to face her. She lay on one arm, tightly clutching the blanket against her with the other, her golden-red hair falling softly about her shoulders, her violet eyes wide with alarm.

He frowned. "There's nothing to be afraid of, Liza. I haven't ravished you yet, and I don't intend to now. I promise I won't touch you"—his voice dropped to a low husky timbre—"until you want me to."

Liza gasped, her heart thumping wildly in her chest. Quickly she turned, laying with her back to him, squeezing her eyes tightly shut and biting on her small fist. *But I do want him to,* she admitted to herself, more frightened of her own hunger than his.

For a long while, Liza lay awake, tense and nervous. It wasn't until she heard Alex's deep, regular breathing and knew that he was asleep that she finally fell into an uneasy slumber.

Several hours later, Liza's nightmare began. Reliving her terrifying experience with Scarface, she felt him holding her down, his cruel fingers biting into the soft, tender flesh of her thighs, his frantic, obscene jabbing and prodding. She finally managed to scream, fighting at the hands holding her.

"Liza," Alex whispered, alarmed. "Liza, wake up. It's only a nightmare."

Slowly, Liza emerged from the grip of her dream, realizing that it was Alex's hands she had been pushing away. She threw herself against his big, warm chest, wrapping her arms tightly around him, trembling violently and sobbing hysterically.

Alex held her, gently rocking her, his big hands stroking her hair and back as he mumbled words of reassurance.

For a long while after her sobbing had ceased, Liza was content to lie in Alex's arms while he comforted her. She felt so warm and safe. Then, insidiously, Alex's movements changed from comforting strokes to sensuous caresses, his lips dropping featherlike kisses softly on her hair. She was acutely conscious of her naked breasts pressed against his equally naked chest, his hands running up and down her back lightly, sending small shivers tingling down her spine.

Liza looked up at Alex, his grey eyes now fiery with desire. He bent his head and touched his lips to hers, kissing her slowly, savoring her lips. She melted into him.

Gently, Alex lowered her to the pallet, their lips still locked in that sweet, aching kiss. Liza felt his heart thumping wildly in his chest, seemingly in unison with her own. She was vaguely aware of his hand caressing her breast, massaging it lightly, his thumb gently stroking the sensitive peak. Suddenly, she was frightened, and she tried to push him away,

131

whispering weakly, "No!"

Alex caught her hands, held them above her head lightly and looked down into her face. His voice husky and intense, he said, "Stop it, Liza. Stop fighting it." Taking her chin in his free hand, he forced her to look into his eyes. "We've both known for some time this was going to happen. You can't stop it . . . I can't stop it. It was inevitable."

Liza looked up into Alex's ruggedly handsome face. He was waiting, watching her intently, those smoky grey eyes willing her to admit to the truth. She knew that the decision was hers. *This is the man I love,* she thought. *And I do want him.* With a little sob, she slowly lifted her arms and slipped them around his neck.

Alex recognized Liza's action for what it was—her surrender. His heart leaped in his chest, a moan escaping his lips as he buried his head in the silky flesh of her throat. "Oh, Liza," he muttered hoarsely, "do you have any idea of how much I've wanted you?" His lips nibbled at her earlobe, sending delicious shivers through her. "Do you, sweetheart?" he whispered, pulling her to him fiercely.

Then he was kissing her as his hands caressed her. Tender, teasing kisses pressed on her neck, across her jawline, her chin, then he stopped to nibble at the corner of her mouth, before moving up to her forehead and eyelids and then down over her cheek. Excited and tormented, Liza turned her head to capture his lips with her own. But this kiss was not gentle. It was a deep, demanding, hungry kiss, and when Alex's tongue entered her mouth to taste her sweetness, Liza met it, at first tentatively, then

132

eagerly. A low groan escaped from Alex's throat as he tore his mouth away.

"Who taught you to kiss like that?" he demanded hoarsely, looking down at her passion-dulled eyes, his own filled with astonishment.

"You just did," Liza muttered, still dazed from the fiery kiss.

"My God," he groaned. "Then, no more of those kisses, sweetheart. Not yet, anyway. Otherwise it will be over before it even starts."

Liza looked up into his smiling face, puzzled by his words. Alex chuckled and nuzzled her neck. "Don't worry, sweet. I'm in control now." Then he was kissing her again. This time his head descended slowly down her neck, dropping love bites across her shoulders and down to her breasts—where he lingered—his tongue lazily teasing one rosy peak, then the other.

Liza suddenly found it hard to breathe, a strange burning sensation in her lower abdomen. Alex continued his sensuous assault at her breasts, his mouth, tongue and hands exciting her until she was writhing beneath him, begging him.

"Alex . . . I want . . ." Liza gasped. "I want . . ." She shook her head in frustration, not knowing what she wanted.

Alex kissed her mouth. "Not yet, sweetheart," he whispered. He moved away, tugged impatiently on his pants and kicked them away. Then he pulled Liza back into his embrace, holding her tightly, closely watching the reaction on her face.

Liza could feel every inch of his big, muscular body, but she was mostly aware of the long, hard length of his manhood, hot and throbbing against her. Both excited and frightened, a small whimper escaped her throat.

"Don't be afraid, sweetheart," Alex whispered. "It's only me. Don't ever be afraid of me."

He kissed and caressed her, slowly building the pitch of her excitement, his mouth and hands seemingly everywhere and leaving a trail of fire in their wake. His hand slipped between her thighs, slowly inching upward until he touched the softness between her legs, seeking until he found that tiny bud, then gently stroking.

Liza's eyes flew open as a heat suffused her, burning all the way to her toes. Her breath caught in her throat as the sweet ripples began, quickly becoming powerful waves of sensation. She arched her back, pressing herself even closer to those skillful fingers as a moan rose in her throat.

Feeling her wetness bathing his fingers, Alex knew that she was as ready for him as she would ever be. He had deliberately held back, wanting her to enjoy this first time, but now he couldn't control himself any longer. Every fiber of his being was screaming for release. Trembling with need, he lifted himself over her, positioning himself between her legs, still kissing and caressing her.

Liza felt the hard, throbbing tip of Alex's maleness against her thigh, and instinctively, she lurched toward him. Alex caught her hips, holding them tightly, whispering in her ear, "No, Liza. Let me."

Slowly and carefully, Alex entered her, and Liza could feel herself stretching to accommodate his rigid heat. As the pressure increased, he seemed to hesitate, and then Liza felt a sharp, piercing pain as he plunged deeply into her.

Reflexively, Liza pulled back and cried out. Alex quickly smothered the cry with his mouth, holding her shoulders tightly to keep her from pulling away, feeling her pain as if it were his own.

"No, Alex," Liza sobbed. "Stop, it hurts."

"Lay still, Liza," Alex moaned in her ear, his hands soothing her. "Lay still, sweetheart."

Liza was quieted by the tone of Alex's voice, for it sounded almost as anguished as hers had been. She lay beneath him while he continued to kiss and sooth her. Slowly, the pain subsided to be replaced with a dull ache, and then another sensation—an awareness of him filling her, hot and throbbing inside her. It was a strange, pleasant feeling. She frowned. "Is it over?"

Alex smiled at her innocence. "No, sweetheart, it hasn't even begun."

"But—"

"Sssh, sweet, don't talk. Just let yourself relax and concentrate on what you're feeling."

Liza did as Alex told her, and as the pleasant pressure in her built, she began to arch her hips tentatively, instinctively trying to intensify that growing sensation.

Feeling her movements, Alex cupped her hips and lifted her to him. "Follow me, Liza," he whispered, guiding her as he moved slowly, then more rapidly in her velvety softness. As Liza caught the ancient rhythm, her hips undulating, Alex groaned in her ear, "That's it, sweet, that's it."

Liza caught Alex's broad shoulders tightly as he

135

thrust into her deeply, each powerful stroke lifting her higher and higher. A strange tension was growing in her, filling her so completely she feared her skin would burst. Suddenly, Alex stiffened and groaned, collapsing with his head buried in the crook of her throat.

This time, Liza *knew* it was over. Slowly, Alex's ragged breathing became more regular. He nuzzled his head in her neck and kissed her ear. "Oh, God, sweetheart, I'm sorry. I wanted it to be good for you, too. But it's been so long, and I wanted you so much."

He rolled from her and pulled her into the crook of his arm, laying her head on his shoulder and tenderly kissing her forehead. Lying there in Alex's powerful arms, his hands still caressing her, Liza felt warm and contented. She briefly puzzled over his words, but having never known sexual fulfillment, she could hardly miss it. She snuggled closer to his warm, muscular body and fell asleep.

Alex lay for a long while after Liza had fallen asleep, thinking. He was satisfied and strangely dissatisfied at the same time. His disappointment did not lay in Liza, for she had been everything he had ever dreamed of and more. Yet he realized that he had been unable to give her the pleasure she had given him. He gazed down at the slight blood stains on her thighs and thought bitterly, *Why did I have to hurt the one woman I ever really wanted to please?*

Liza had been Alex's first and only virgin. He was experienced, but he had deliberately avoided innocents, preferring his sexual encounters to be with experienced women, who expected no promises or commitments. He considered himself a good lover, if his partners' responses were any criteria to judge by. He frowned. Then why had he been such a dismal failure with Liza?

Damn, Alex thought, she had been tight, too tight. For a moment, he had thought it would be physically impossible to take her and then, he had felt the membrane give and, unable to stop himself, plunged in. That was when she had cried out and the spell he had so carefully woven had been broken. If he could have held back longer, he might have been able to bring her to that peak with him.

Alex looked down at the fragile beauty sleeping so peacefully in his arms. Despite the fact that he had hurt her, he felt a strange exhilaration at knowing that he had been the first. How he had wanted her, still wanted her, even more so. A puzzled frown crossed his face at the thought. Then, brushing it aside, he bent his head and kissed her forehead, whispering, "Next time, sweetheart. Next time, I promise you."

When Liza awakened later that night, she was still lying in Alex's arms, her head on his shoulder, her hand on the soft hair on his chest. Unable to resist the temptation, Liza moved her hand, marveling at the feel of the tight curls over the hardness of his muscles.

"You're finally awake," a deep voice said.

Liza jerked her hand back guiltily and looked up to see Alex watching her, an amused smile on his face.

"Is it morning?" she asked, raising up slightly and looking about, noticing with relief that Alex had covered their naked bodies with a blanket.

"No," Alex laughed lightly. "But it seems I've

137

been laying here for hours waiting for you to wake up."

"What for?" Liza asked innocently.

Alex chuckled, pulling her head down and burying his head in her neck, kissing her there and then on the particularly sensitive spot just below her ear. "Because I want you again," he whispered huskily in her ear.

A shiver of anticipation ran through her.

His mouth trailed across her cheek in a tingling caress before it met hers, kissing her tenderly at first, then hungrily and thoroughly. With his hands and mouth, he explored her secrets, once again delighting in the silky texture of her skin, her sweet taste, her intoxicating scent. Soon, Liza's blood coursed through her veins like liquid fire, her senses reeling. Her hands roved hungrily over the rippling muscles of his shoulders and back, her mouth over the strong column of his throat, tasting his saltiness there.

Through her drugged senses, she heard Alex whispering in her ear, his voice entreating, "Touch me, Liza. Touch me as I've touched you."

Liza hesitated, a little shocked at his request. Alex took her small hand and guided it down to him. Liza gasped at the size of him, seemingly enormous, but as Alex taught her the movements that brought him pleasure, she marveled at the velvety texture of his skin, fascinated by the feel of him throbbing and growing even larger in her hand. With almost a will of its own, her hand became bolder, stroking him sensuously as Alex groaned in her ear, "Oh, Liza. Oh, God, sweetheart."

Rolling her to her back, Alex rose over her. Liza

tensed, anticipating the pain, but as Alex slowly and very gently entered her, she was only aware of the sensation of him filling her. When he had completely buried himself inside her, Alex lay still for several minutes, letting Liza savor the feel of him as he relished the feel of her velvety heat surrounding him. Then he began to move, stroking her slowly, sensuously, as his hands caressed her. Against her lips, he muttered, "This time, sweetheart, all the way."

His mouth covered hers in a hot, searing, penetrating kiss that melted Liza's bones and seared her lungs, while his hands were everywhere, searching, teasing, exciting. Instead of the strange tension growing slowly inside her as it had before, it skyrocketed. She strained eagerly toward him, meeting each powerful, deep thrust with one of her own, climbing higher and higher and higher to some unknown peak, her body frenzied in anticipation of something she sensed, yet did not know. When she came to that crest, she burst over in a shattering explosion and cried out, as Alex groaned and convulsed against her in his own release, moaning over and over, "Liza, Liza . . ."

Liza clung to Alex's broad shoulders as she slowly descended, still trembling in the aftermath. "What happened?" she asked in a small, frightened voice.

Alex smiled knowingly and rolled from her. Leaning over her and pushing a wisp of damp hair from her face, he bent and kissed her forehead and then the tip of her nose. "What happened, sweetheart, is what's supposed to happen. Only it didn't the first time, because you were too frightened, and I

139

was too impatient."

"Then it's always like that?" Liza asked, both awed and astonished.

Alex frowned, the question hitting him in the gut like a physical blow. No, he realized, it had never been that way before for him. The satisfaction was there, but something more—much more. His thoughts made him uncomfortable. "It should be . . . if it's right," he said, his answer more honest than he was willing to admit.

He lay back, pulling her against him possessively, feeling a contentment that he had never felt before. As he drifted into a deep, peaceful sleep, he thought, *Strange how perfectly our bodies fit together, almost as if they were created for one another.*

Liza cuddled into Alex's embrace, smiling with satisfaction at her new knowledge. Now she really knew what Anne had meant when she said, *And you will ache for his kiss and his touch.*

Chapter 7

When Liza awakened the next morning, she was alone in the tepee. She snuggled into the fur pallet where Alex had lain, enjoying his lingering scent. She stretched, catlike, smiling sensuously as she remembered his lovemaking the night before.

When Alex entered the tepee a minute later, however, she quickly snatched up the blanket to cover her nakedness and blushed furiously. Alex smiled in amusement, strangely touched by her innocence, then shook his head regretfully, thinking how much he would like to climb back under that blanket with her.

"Well, sleepyhead," Alex said, "it's about time you woke up."

"What time is it?"

"Almost noon."

"Oh, my goodness!" Liza gasped. "I don't know why I slept so late."

"I do," Alex answered, a wicked gleam in his eyes. His voice turned husky as he said, "Because I kept you up half the night making love to you."

Liza blushed even more hotly; Alex chuckled. "Come on, Liza," he coaxed. "This is the day you've been looking forward to. Today you can get up. And look what I've brought you," he said as he held up a buckskin dress.

Liza's small nose wrinkled with distaste. "But that's an Indian dress."

"Of course it's an Indian dress," Alex answered with exasperation. "What other kind of dress would I find in an Indian camp?"

"I can't wear an Indian dress," Liza objected stubbornly.

"Suit yourself," Alex answered with a shrug and tossed the dress down beside her. "But it's either that dress, or that damned blanket you seem so fond of. However, Waħcawin might be a little hurt. It's her favorite dress, and she thought you would like it."

Liza felt childish and ashamed of herself. Why hadn't he just said Waħcawin had sent the dress. "I'll wear it." She picked up the dress and glared at him.

Alex grinned. "I have another surprise for you, if you're interested."

Liza looked up at him, curious but wary.

"Come now, sweetheart, wouldn't you like a bath, a real bath? I know a secluded little pool, just deep enough for bathing. Are you interested?"

Unable to resist, Liza smiled. "Oh, yes!"

"Then get your dress on and we'll be off."

Alex waited, but Liza made no effort to drop the protective blanket. Shaking his head in amusement, he said, "I'll wait outside while you change."

Liza slipped the Indian dress over her head. The

142

soft skin clung to her body seductively. Frowning as she looked down at it, she realized that she must be bigger in the bust than Waȟcawin, as it was decidedly tight across her breasts. Besides that, the dress barely came to her knees. Fingering the dress, she admitted that it was pretty with the intricate beading on the bodice. Well, it was certainly better than that blanket, she thought ruefully, as she pushed the flap back and stepped from the tepee.

Alex eyed her appreciatively, noting how the skin clung to every hollow and curve of her body. Tearing his eyes away, he looked up at her face. "Better bring the blanket to dry off with."

"Oh, yes," Liza answered, ducking back into the tepee and searching until she found both the blanket and the small piece of plant left over from yesterday's bath.

When she stepped back outside, Alex motioned to the piece of plant in her hand. "What's that?"

"Soap." Liza laughed, showing it to him.

"Yes, it's what the Indians use for soap. It's from the yucca plant." He bent and picked up one of Liza's feet. "Here, put these on." He slipped first one foot, then the other into the soft moccasins. "How do they feel?" he asked, standing up.

Liza moved her feet about, testing the feel. "Why, they're very comfortable," she remarked in surprise. "So soft."

"I hope so. I padded the soles with a double lining."

"You made these?" Liza asked in astonishment.

Alex nodded.

"But how did you know my size?"

"Simple. I just measured your foot," Alex replied, taking her arm and leading her away from the Indian camp.

Liza had to almost run to keep up with his long strides. "Alex," she panted, "what does *awanyake waśte* mean?"

Alex came to a dead halt, and Liza bumped into him. "Who said that to you?" he demanded, facing her, his silver eyes boring into her.

"Waȟcawin, when she was combing my hair," Liza answered nervously.

Alex reached up, took a strand of her long hair, and watched in amazement as it curled around his finger, seemingly with a life of its own. "Yes, it is," he said gently. Then, looking into Liza's eyes, he explained, "It means, good looking, handsome. You see, there is no Dakota word for beautiful, although I'm sure that's what she meant."

Liza blushed and turned, walking away from Alex. He watched her retreating back, wondering if it was possible that she didn't realize just how beautiful she was?

Catching up with her, he guided her through a thick, dark woods until they came to a small pool of crystal clear water surrounded by large, graceful willow trees.

"It's spring-fed, so it may be a little cold," Alex warned. "So don't stay in too long." He turned and started to walk away.

"Where are you going?" Liza asked, apprehensive at being left in this secluded spot by herself.

Alex turned, a wide grin spreading across his face. "Would you rather I stayed?"

A slow flush crept up Liza's face. "No, but . . ."

Alex laughed at her obvious dilemma, then pointed to a big rock behind the willows. "I'll be up there, keeping watch for you." His eyes were warm and teasing. "Don't worry, Liza, I promise I won't peek." Then he turned and strolled away with the graceful, catlike stride that was so much a part of him. "Holler when you're through!" he called back over his shoulder.

Liza laid the blanket on the ground and stripped off her dress and moccasins. Carrying her precious piece of yucca, she stepped cautiously into the water—then gasped in shock. The water was freezing cold. For a minute, she hesitated, but Liza was determined to have her bath. Gritting her teeth, she waded in farther and drenched herself, shivering from the cold. Hastily, she soaped her body with pulpy yucca, then waded in until she was almost waist-deep. Holding her long hair up to keep it from getting wet, she dunked to rinse. By this time, she was shivering violently from the cold and started to beat a hasty exit from the pool when she heard a slight noise. She glanced up and froze in her tracks.

A tall, muscular Indian stood by the water, watching her intently, his black eyes openly admiring her, his lips curved in a smile.

Instinctively, Liza crossed her bare breasts with her arms and stumbled back into the pool, her heart pounding erratically. Before she could scream, she heard Alex's voice. "Don't be frightened, Liza. He's a friend."

Glancing up, she saw Alex standing on the rock, his stance relaxed and casual, a smile on his face.

145

The Indian looked up at Alex and smiled broadly in recognition. He pointed to Liza, saying something in the Dakota language. For several minutes, Alex and the Indian carried on a conversation in the strange tongue, their voices deep and guttural, while Liza stood in the water shivering, her teeth chattering, her legs turning numb from the cold. Her brief moment of fear quickly turned to anger as the two men calmly talked. She glared up at Alex, who seemed to be totally ignoring her. She grew more and more furious. Besides being miserable standing stark-naked in the freezing water, it was obvious, from the Indian's occasional looks and gestures in her direction, that they were discussing her, and she couldn't understand a word they were saying. It was maddening! She strained her ears, hoping to get at least a vague notion of what they were saying.

The Indian turned and stared at her boldly, his look too warm for Liza's comfort. *"Awanyake waśte,"* he said, and Liza blushed, recognizing the compliment.

"Mitawin!" Alex answered.

Liza was shocked by Alex's abrupt answer. His voice had had a hard, warning tone to it. She glanced up, surprised to see him glaring at the Indian.

The Indian looked away from Liza, nodded and smiled up at Alex. Again, Liza couldn't understand anything of what he said.

Alex looked down at Liza, his eyes warm and caressing. He smiled as he answered kindly, *"Waśte, waśteśte."*

The Indian grinned, saying something to Alex. Then he turned, glancing once more in Liza's direction, and walked arrogantly away from the pool.

"You'd better get out now, Liza," Alex called. "I can see you're blue from cold from up here."

Liza glanced angrily at the rock, but Alex had disappeared. Quickly, she waded from the pool, mumbling hotly to herself. "You'd better get out now, Liza. I can see you're blue," she mimicked Alex's words sarcastically. *Damn right, I'm blue,* she thought. It was a wonder she hadn't turned into a block of ice while those two stood there discussing her like she was a horse for sale or something. Furious, she dried herself and slipped into the Indian dress and moccasins. She was dressed, still shaking partly from cold and partly from rage, when Alex entered the small clearing.

"My God! You are blue!" Alex said when he saw her. Reaching for her, he tried to pull her into his arms, but Liza pushed him away violently.

"Keep your hands off me!" she hissed.

Alex glared at her; a small muscle twitched in his jaw. Catching her shoulders, he roughly pulled her into his arms. "I don't know what in the hell is wrong with you now, but you're freezing. Let me warm you up first, and then, if you're determined to, we can argue later."

"You don't know what's wrong with me?" Liza screeched, twisting away from him. "I'm standing in that pool, freezing to death, while you and that . . . that savage," she sputtered, angrily motioning in the direction the bold Indian had disappeared, "calmly pass the time of day. And you don't know what's wrong with me?"

147

Alex chuckled. Damn, she was a little wildcat when she got her dander up! Stooping to pick up the blanket and tossing it over her shoulders, he said calmly, "Here, at least put this on until you warm up."

Liza twisted, deliberately shoving the blanket off, her violet eyes blazing. "You could have at least told him to go away."

"Go away?" Alex asked, astonished. Then he laughed. "I'm afraid not, sweetheart. That was Tanaźin, and this is *his* camp, *his* pool, *his* everything," he informed her, his hand sweeping the area. "I could hardly ask him to leave."

"But I was naked!" Liza screamed.

Alex grinned. "I think we were *all* very much aware of that fact."

Liza felt impotent with rage. "I hate you!" she spat and turned to flee.

But before she could take a step, Alex caught her and pulled her back into his arms. This time, his grip was tight and no amount of twisting could free her. Finally, Liza went limp, a sob of frustration escaping her lips.

"I know the experience unnerved you," Alex said quietly. "But Tanaźin wasn't spying on you. He just happened to come across you at an inopportune moment. If I had demanded that he leave, I would have insulted him," Alex explained patiently.

"But you were talking about me," Liza said in an accusing voice. "I know you were." A pair of violet eyes bore into his. "What did he say?"

Alex was silent. Angrily, Liza jabbed him with her elbow, causing him to grunt in surprise. "I said what did he say?" she demanded.

Alex cocked one dark eyebrow. "Are you sure you want to know?"

"Yes," Liza answered in a determined voice.

"Well, first he asked me if your hair was the same color all over, and I said yes."

Liza paled as she realized what hair Tanaźin had been referring to. She was speechless with shock.

Seeing her reaction, Alex said hastily, "Tanaźin didn't mean any disrespect, Liza. He was simply curious. Redheads are rare out here, particularly your shade of red hair." His gaze caressed her hair. "In fact, he was so impressed, he said he was going to call you Petra, which means little fire." He laughed gently, a teasing twinkle in his eyes. "I think it's very appropriate, considering your temper." Ignoring her glare at his last words, Alex bent his head and whispered in her ear, "Like me, he thinks you're very beautiful."

Liza ducked her head at Alex's compliment, a little thrill going through her. But she was still shocked at the Indian's bold question, curious or not. On the other hand, she was secretly pleased with her new Indian name, Petra.

"What does *mitawin* mean?" she asked, lifting her head.

Alex stiffened, a wary look in his eyes.

"Well?" Liza demanded impatiently.

Alex appeared decidedly uncomfortable as he answered, "My woman."

Seeing her eyes widen, and thinking that she was shocked, he added hastily, "As I said, Tanaźin thinks you are very beautiful, and Indians have a way of

149

taking what they desire. But he respects me. If he thinks you belong to me . . ." His voice trailed off as he shrugged his shoulders.

Liza felt sick with disappointment. For one brief minute, she had hoped Alex was making a commitment, but he had only said it to protect her. Just where did she stand with him? she wondered. Pushing away from him, she turned and walked away, not wanting him to see the hurt in her eyes.

Alex frowned as Liza stalked off. *Now what in the hell did I say wrong?* he wondered.

"What else did he say?" Liza asked, trying to sound casual.

Alex shook his head. "Let's just forget it."

Liza whirled to face him. "No! I want to know everything he said."

"Everything?" Alex challenged.

"Everything!" Liza retorted hotly.

Alex was becoming angry. He resented Liza pushing him into this awkward position. He knew damned well she would be even more shocked at Tanaźin's last explicit question. He looked down at Liza, standing before him and glaring up at him, and had the urge to punish this beautiful spitfire. "All right, Liza, if you insist upon knowing. He asked me how the sex act was between us."

Liza gasped and her knees buckled, but Alex caught her, cupping her hips, forcing them into his suggestively. His eyes bored into her as he continued, "And I said *waśte, waśteśte.*"

The feel of Liza in his arms, her supple body against his, completely dissipated Alex's anger. He bent his head and whispered against her trembling

150

lips, "That means, good, very good." He nuzzled her throat. "And then Tanaźin wished us much joy in one another's bodies."

"How dare you!"

Alex stiffened; his eyes flashed. "Don't ever dare me, Liza," he threatened.

Liza trembled, tears threatening behind her eyes. She felt betrayed. "You had no right. No right to discuss something so private, so intimate with—with that Indian!"

"Dammit, Liza," Alex said irritably. "Indians didn't invent sex. As a matter of fact, they have a damned sight more healthy attitude toward it than the white man. They don't hide it away as if it were something dirty, or snicker about it, or make vulgar jokes about it. To the Indian, sex is just as natural an act as eating or sleeping. Therefore, they discuss it openly, and naturally."

"You had no right to discuss me with another man!"

Catching her arms, Alex shook her lightly. "Dammit, you're not listening to me. Tanaźin isn't just another man. He's an Indian! He thinks of sex differently than we do. I would have never dreamed of having the same conversation with a white man. We wouldn't have gotten past the first question, because I would have known he meant it as an insult to you, and I would have clobbered him. That's the difference, Liza. The Indian and the white man have an entirely different attitude toward sex. When I discussed our relationship with Tanaźin, I was using *his* attitude toward it. And when he wished us joy in each other's bodies, he was serious. He meant it as a blessing, not an insult."

"You agree with a lot of the things the Indians think, don't you, Alex?" Liza asked, still feeling resentful.

"Yes, I do. Sometimes, I think I'm more Indian than white. A lot of what they believe makes good sense. They approach things more honestly and openly than the white man. Their whole culture is based on honor—"

"Honor?" Liza interjected angrily. "They burn, steal, rape, kill and torture. Do you consider that honorable? Why, you admitted yourself, they're very warlike." Her voice had risen to an almost hysterical pitch.

"Stop it, Liza!" Alex demanded harshly. "Yes, they do all of those things, but so does the white man." He glared down at her. "You consider England a civilized country, don't you? A nation of honorable men?"

"Why, yes, of course," Liza answered indignantly.

"And just how peaceful are they?" Alex asked in an accusing voice. "How many years in your nation's long history has England known peace? How many years, when England wasn't involved in a war somewhere in the world? Hell, when you weren't fighting another country, you were busy fighting each other. At least the Dakota tribes don't fight among themselves—warlike or not!"

Liza sputtered.

Alex ignored her protest and continued, "And do you think those honorable Englishmen fighting in those wars didn't burn, rape, kill and torture their enemies? You say the Indians steal? Yes, they may be big horse thieves, but they don't steal whole countries, as our so-called civilized nations do.''

"You don't think much of the English, do you?'' Liza asked bitterly.

"Liza, I'm not condemning your countrymen. I only used them as an example. The point I'm trying to make is that the white man considers himself civilized, and yet, when the Indian does the same thing the white man does, he's considered a savage. You see, Liza, the Indian doesn't do all those things simply because he's an Indian, but because he's human. It's a weakness he shares with his fellow man.''

Liza's mind was reeling with the new concepts Alex had presented to her, ideas she had never before considered. As much as she hated to admit it, there was something almost hypocritical about the white man's attitude. Too often, he claimed to believe one thing, then turned around and did the very opposite. She knew of men back in England, respected leaders of the community, who cheated on their wives, stole from their business associates, and goaded by their own hatreds and greed, encouraged war and all its ugly brutalities. She suspected there was a bit of the savage still lurking in all men's souls. Only, what Alex had just said was true; the Indian was more open and honest about his nature.

Alex had no way of knowing Liza's thoughts, but he was acutely aware of her withdrawal. What in the hell had made him go off on that tirade? But it angered him to see the Indian criticized unjustly. And yet, how could he expect Liza to understand the Indian, when people who had lived around them all

153

their lives didn't understand them? *You fool*, he castigated himself. *All you've done is alienate her.*

Liza finally broke the silence. "Alex, I've heard you call this tribe Dakota. They must be a small tribe. I don't think I've ever heard of them."

Alex laughed, feeling almost ridiculously happy that she was talking to him again. "No, they aren't a small tribe. In fact, the Dakota is one of the largest Indian nations on the North American continent. You've heard of them, I'm sure. Only, you've heard of them by their white man's name, Sioux. Teton Sioux, to be exact."

"Sioux?" Liza asked in surprise. "Of course I've heard of them. Is Sioux the English name for Dakota?"

"No, it's a French word that means little snake or enemy. Dakota is the Indian name. It means the allied ones."

Liza frowned. "It's all so confusing. Why so many different names?"

"Because when the white man came out here, he renamed everything. With his usual arrogance, he named the hills, the rivers, the mountains, even the Indian tribes, not considering or caring that they already had names." He laughed. "But the Indians aren't any better. Look at how Tanaźin renamed you Petra."

"And what does Tanaźin call you?"

"Iśtahota," Alex answered. "It means grey eyes."

Liza glanced up at Alex's eyes. Such beautiful, strange eyes, she thought. They changed in shades of grey with his moods: sometimes the color of finely tempered steel, sometimes the color of shimmering silver, sometimes the color of a stormy sky, and sometimes—like when he was making love—the color of smoke. Quickly Liza looked away, embarrassed by her own thoughts.

Directing her mind into less disturbing channels, she asked, "And you and Tanaźin have been friends since you were boys?"

Alex frowned, contemplating Liza's question. "Actually, we're closer than friends, more like brothers. It's strange, but I've always felt closer to Tanaźin than I did to my own brother. From the minute Tanaźin and I met, it's been that way for both of us. Everytime my father came to visit Black Hawk, I'd tag along to see Tanaźin. Then I started staying over a couple of days and finally a week at a time. The year before I left for college, I spent the entire summer with him."

His voice dropped to a quiet, almost dreamy timbre. "I'll never forget that summer as long as I live. We pitched our summer camp along with the Cheyenne, the Dakota's allies. The very next day, we found the buffalo herd. It was enormous. And then the excitement that followed before the hunt—"

"You went on a buffalo hunt?" Liza interjected in an accusing voice, remembering her horror at the carnage she had seen on her trip west.

"Yes and no," Alex answered. "I was with the scouting party that sighted the herd, but no, I wasn't chosen as a hunter. Only the best hunters are chosen for the hunting party. There's too much at stake. The buffalo hunt is where the Indian gets his food supply for the entire winter." He laughed, saying ruefully, "I'm afraid I'm not very good with a bow and arrow."

Liza realized that there was a big difference in the Indian hunting buffalo for food, and the white man killing them for mere sport. She felt ashamed of herself for even thinking that Alex might be like those men, killing needlessly. "But you can shoot a gun," she objected.

Alex shook his head. "No, the Dakotas don't use guns on buffalo hunts. They're too noisy, particularly a lot of guns going off at once. They're afraid the noise will attract an enemy tribe or stampede the herd, scattering it. But the most important reason that guns aren't used is that it's impossible to tell using guns which brave made the kill. Musket balls can't be individually marked, but arrows can, using different colored feathers or notches. And the hunter who makes the kill is entitled to the hide. When you stop to consider how many things the Indian uses the hide for, you can understand why it's necessary to know who made the kill."

As they continued walking toward their tepee, Liza thought of how Alex not only spoke the Indians' tongue fluently, but he had actually lived with them. She studied him from the corner of her eyes, noting his animallike, lithe walk, the proud tilt of his head, the fearless glint in his eyes. Yes, it was true, she thought, in many ways he was more Indian than white. Not only did he think like an Indian, but he actually possessed some of their characteristics, and oddly enough, rather than detracting, they only added to his considerable masculine appeal.

That night, Alex and Liza were invited to a feast to celebrate her rescue and the Indians' successful raid on the Kiowas. As they strolled to the center of the camp where the festivities would take place, Liza noticed that the village, peaceful and serene that afternoon, had taken on an almost carnival atmosphere.

The excited crowd thickened as they entered the center of the village. Several large campfires added their light to that of the brilliant full moon above. Alex guided Liza through the crowd skillfully, bringing them to stand before Tanaźin.

The muscular chief looked down at Liza, his dark eyes first appraising and then frankly admiring. His voice was a deep rumble when he spoke, but all Liza recognized was the word "Petra."

"Tanaźin welcomes you, Little Fire," Alex interpreted for her.

Liza smiled shyly at the chief, and then, remembering their last encounter, blushed furiously. Tanaźin noticed her flush and smiled, a glint of amusement in his dark eyes. Turning, he called something to Waȟcawin, who was standing a few yards away. The Indian girl nodded and hurried away. When the chief turned back, it was Alex he addressed, much to Liza's relief.

As Alex and Tanaźin talked, Liza studied them below lowered lashes, thinking the two were enough alike to be brothers. Both were tall and darkly handsome, yet strongly masculine. Their movements were graceful, their stance proud, almost arrogant, and both possessed an aura of power and self-assurance. Though no Indian blood ran in Alex's veins, there was no doubt in Liza's mind that these two *were* bonded in some special way. They were soul brothers.

Waȟcawin returned with two bowls of food, offering one to Liza and the other to Alex. Accepting his bowl, Alex thanked the Indian girl, then turned to Liza. "Let's find someplace where we can sit down to eat."

As they weaved their way through the crowd, dodging children who were chasing each other, Liza noticed a group of grey-haired Indian women crouched in a small circle. The old women seemed oblivious to the noise and confusion around them, concentrating on the ground between them. Curious, Liza craned her neck to see.

Alex laughed. "They're gambling, the Indians' favorite pastime. But let me warn you, Liza, don't ever gamble with an Indian. They cheat something awful. What's more, they expect you to cheat in return. To them, that's part of the game."

After they had eaten, Liza was startled by the sudden noise of drums beating. The Indians crowded around them, pushing, shoving, babbling excitedly. Alex took Liza's arm and helped her up. "The warriors' dance is starting. Let's see if we can get a little closer so you can see better."

Alex shouldered his way through the crowd until they stood at the edge of the circle surrounding the dancers. Fascinated, Liza watched the braves as they performed, some almost frenzied in their enthusiasm. Alex explained that the dance was an ancient form of storytelling, each warrior relating his personal acts of bravery in pantomime. Liza thought there was a primitive beauty about the dancers, their movements in perfect unison to the rhythm of the pounding drums, their almost-naked, painted bodies glistening in the firelight, casting long eerie shadows over the ground.

But as the dancing continued for an hour, and then another, Liza grew weary. "How long does this go on?"

"All night," Alex answered. "Are you ready to leave?"

"Won't Tanazin be offended if we leave early?"

"No. He knows I plan on leaving early for the ranch tomorrow."

Still doubtful, Liza's eyes swept the crowd until she spied the chief sitting with a group of warriors at the back of the crowd. Several women milled around behind the men.

"Alex, are Tanazin's other wives here tonight?" Liza asked, her curiosity aroused.

Alex's eyes scanned the faces, and then he nodded. "Yes, see the rather tall woman standing right behind Tanazin? She's his first wife."

Liza stared boldly at the woman. She was older than Wahcawin and not nearly as pretty, with a hard look about her mouth. Deciding that this woman was no threat to her new friend, Liza asked, "And his other wife?"

"She's the woman Wahcawin is standing next to."

Liza saw her friend standing by a short, dumpy Indian girl. Her face was broader and her features coarser than the other Indian woman. She was smiling at something Wahcawin had said. Liza glanced down her body to further evaluate her and gasped. The Indian girl was pregnant, probably near term.

Feeling a strong sense of betrayal for Waȟcawin, Liza turned to Alex, saying in an outraged voice, "She's going to have a baby."

"Yes. I think she's due almost any day now."

"But you said Tanaźin loved Waȟcawin. That she was his true wife," Liza cried, her voice accusing.

"Dammit, Liza, a man doesn't have to love a woman to have sex with her," Alex answered irritably.

Liza flinched, feeling the harsh words like a slap in the face.

Regretting his impatience, Alex explained, "Tanaźin's second wife is Cheyenne. She was a widow when Tanaźin married her. Her first husband was a good friend of Tanaźin's, and he and their baby were both killed in a Kiowa raid. More than anything in the world, she has wanted another child. Tanaźin is her husband, and he's fond of her. Could he deny her that wish? Besides, they're all pleased about the baby. If you don't believe me, just look."

Liza glanced back and watched as Waȟcawin smiled and gently helped the Cheyenne woman lower her bulky, awkward body to a blanket on the ground. Then Tanaźin's first wife, her mouth surprisingly softer, handed a bowl of food down to the pregnant woman.

Liza shook her head in disbelief and looked over to Tanaźin. The handsome, arrogant chief was watching his wives, a benevolent look on his face.

Then Waȟcawin turned and moved away from the other two women. Gracefully, she walked toward Tanaźin, her hips swaying with a natural provocativeness. Liza observed Tanaźin as Waȟcawin approached him. He rose, smiling gently, his eyes warm with love—and then blazing hot with open, naked desire. Liza ducked her head in embarrassment.

"Now do you see what I mean?" Alex asked in a low voice.

Taking her small hand, Alex led her away from the festivities. Liza walked like one in a trance, Alex's words pounding in her head like a litany, *A man doesn't have to love a woman to have sex with her.* Over and over, her mind repeated the hateful words. She felt sick. *Oh, you fool, you fool,* she thought. *Just because you love him, you assumed his love-making last night meant he loved you in return. Not once did he tell you he loved you, much less make a commitment. Why, he hasn't even asked you to stay. You're a stupid, naive little girl,* Liza thought bitterly. *You gave yourself to a man who feels nothing for you but lust. To him, you're just another casual lover passing through his life.* Liza blinked back tears, a tightness constricting her throat.

Her pride fought to the surface of her emotions. She'd never let him know how she felt about him, and she'd never let him touch her again. Never again! she vowed.

Alex was aware of Liza's tension, but was puzzled by it. He frowned down at her, wondering if she was still upset over the relationship of Tanaźin and his wives. Something was definitely bothering her. He fought the urge to take her in his arms and comfort her. He smiled ruefully to himself. He had been fighting that urge all night. Many times he had

161

wanted to touch her, kiss her, but knowing that the Indians disapproved of public affection, he had controlled himself. He could hardly wait until they were alone again and he could hold her.

Lifting the flap to the tepee, he said, "Wait here and let me light a fire first. You might stumble over something." In a few minutes he returned, holding the flap up for her. After Liza had entered the tepee, he knelt at the opening and crossed two sticks in front of it. Seeing her puzzled look, he grinned. "That's the Indian way of saying, do not disturb."

Liza knew that Alex intended to make love to her, and her heart thudded in her throat; her mouth felt suddenly dry. "No, Alex," she muttered.

Alex looked up at her, surprised at her words. Then he frowned and rose. "Are you playing games with me, Liza?"

"No," she answered, her voice trembling despite her resolve. "Last night was a mistake."

One dark eyebrow arched, and a small muscle worked furiously in his jaw. "A mistake, Liza?" he asked in an icy voice. A cold fury built inside him. Last night, she had given herself, utterly, completely, and tonight— The teasing little bitch! Did she really think she could give herself to him so wholeheartedly one night and then reject him the next? Dammit, he would have her, possess her so totally she would never dare refuse him again. He would put his brand on her for life!

"No, Liza," Alex's voice was adamant as he moved menacingly toward her, "last night was no mistake." His steely eyes bored into her, pinning her where she stood. He slowly lifted his hand to her face, smiling in satisfaction as he saw her flinch, and then lightly ran his finger over her full bottom lip.

Liza's heart pounded rapidly. She felt trapped by the aura of intense power exuding from him. Alex smugly watched the frantic pulse beat in her throat, knowing that it wasn't caused by fear. His hand dropped to cup her breast, caressing it, his thumb teasing the nipple to a hard bud.

Liza felt weak, a hot tingling sensation rushing over her. In one last, desperate attempt to hold to her reserve, she stepped back. Strong arms closed around her as Alex pulled her to him, holding her arms down at her sides.

His eyes glittered. "And just so there will be no doubt in your mind . . ." He bent his head to her throat and lightly ran his tongue over it, tracing the racing pulse beat up to her ear, circling it, then gently probing it. Liza shivered in response. Alex smiled knowingly. He nibbled at the corners of her mouth, his tongue teasing and flickering like a fiery dart, but as Liza moved her head to meet his lips, he moved away, kissing her temple, forehead and eyelids.

Slowly lowering her to the fur pallet, he trailed hot kisses across her face and throat, deliberately ignoring Liza's silent plea to kiss her mouth. His hand caressed her breasts, hips and thighs, slowly inching her dress up. Then, lifting her, he pulled it over her head in one swift movement. Liza raised her arms to embrace him, but Alex shook his head and took both small wrists in his big hand, holding them firmly over her head.

Liza's senses reeled wildly as Alex continued his slow, determined assault. He nipped at her sensitive breasts, then licked the little stings away, his tongue

163

rolling around one tender peak and then the other. Liza gasped in pleasure. Raising his head, Alex softly taunted, "Does that feel like a mistake, Liza?" His eyes burned into her. "Or this?" His hand slipped between her thighs, his fingers sensuously stroking her.

"Alex," Liza moaned, arching her hips to his hand.

Alex smiled, two fingers slipping inside her as his thumb still teased and stroked that small bud, until Liza was gasping and twisting her hips beneath his skillful manipulations, moaning incoherently.

His hot breath fanned her lips. "What did you say, sweet?" Again, he pulled away before Liza's lips could touch his, and she sobbed in frustration.

Releasing her wrists, he rose and stripped quickly. Liza watched through passion-drugged eyes, thinking that he looked like a magnificent pagan god, tall and superbly muscled, his eyes glittering with fierce determination. Sinking to the pallet, he pulled her to him, letting her feel the throbbing heat of his eager organ against her, while his hands and tongue stroked and caressed, teased and tantalized with maddening purpose.

She was a victim on his altar of desire, his tongue and hands his instruments of exquisite, almost painful pleasure. "Alex, please!" Liza pleaded weakly, feeling as if she would go insane if he didn't give her release soon. Every nerve in her body was burning, drawn taut with need.

Rolling her onto her back, he positioned himself over her as she opened her legs eagerly. She gave a happy cry as she felt the hard, moist tip of him against her and then brushing with promise against the soft curls between her legs. She arched her hips to meet him, but Alex pulled away. Liza sobbed.

"Tell me what you want, sweetheart," he whispered huskily against her ear.

"I want you."

Alex smiled down at her, his silver eyes glittering. "No, sweet, that won't do. You'll have to be more explicit."

Liza was writhing beneath him. She felt his manhood brushing her thigh, teasing, taunting, so close and yet. . . . It was a tortured sob that escaped her lips. "I want you inside me."

Alex smiled, his heart soaring, exultant in his victory. His mouth crashed down on hers in a deep, savage, penetrating kiss, his tongue insistent, plundering her sweetness. He spread her thighs and fiercely plunged into her, still determined to brand her as his. Gentleness and tenderness now forgotten, Alex strove in deep, demanding thrusts, to possess her completely and totally.

Liza sensed his intent, and she fought him for her own possession, answering each powerful thrust with one of her own, her legs squeezing his slim hips as she ground her pelvis against his, her hands clawing at his back, her mouth biting at his neck and shoulders.

It was a mating that was half loving and half battle, until sheer passion drowned out everything. In savage, naked abandon, they swept to dizzy, spiraling heights, higher and higher, until they crested in a violent, all-consuming, fiery explosion.

Shuddering uncontrollably, they lay still entwined, their ragged breaths rasping in the air. "My God!" Alex gasped in awe as Liza cried quietly.

Alex cradled her, soothed her, kissed her tears away, until she fell asleep in his arms, and then he lay for a long while trying to understand and sort out the maelstrom of emotions that besieged him. The experience had shaken him to the core. He had never experienced such a tempetuous, white-hot climax, and he wasn't sure he ever wanted to again. The intensity of it had been almost frightening, a terrifying feeling that his body and soul were splitting and might never be reunited again. He had suspected a deep passion in Liza and had only meant to discover it. He had the uncomfortable feeling that he had awakened a sleeping tiger.

Alex shook his head, trying to clear his thoughts. He gazed down at the girl sleeping in his arms. Before, she had been a wild thing, stunning him with her passion. But now she looked so small and vulnerable. He wondered at his own overpowering feelings of protectiveness and possessiveness. She had aroused emotions in him that he had never felt in any of his encounters with other women, feelings he hadn't thought he was even capable of. She seemed to hold him by some strange, invisible bond.

"Oh, God," he moaned. "What have I gotten myself into?"

His mind wandered to the day when the next stagecoach would arrive. What then? Would he let her walk out of his life like nothing had ever happened? He felt his heart lurch and a strange tightening in his chest. Pulling her to him in a fierce embrace, he muttered, "No, not yet."

As he drifted off to sleep, his subconscious mind spoke with a determination of its own, "Not ever!"

Chapter 8

Alex greeted Liza the next morning in a light, teasing mood that left her no time for reflection and feeling even more confused and disconcerted. She had surrendered to him again, despite all of her fierce resolves, and try as she might, she could not place the blame totally on Alex. It had been her own treacherous body that had betrayed her.

Alex rushed her through breakfast and then through the camp to Tanaźin's tent, where Alex's black stallion stood already saddled. "Tanaźin offered me another horse," he said, "but I refused. Thunder carried us both for several days, so a few more won't matter." He bent and grinned at her. "Besides, I enjoy holding you in my arms."

Liza colored and turned her head away from him. Her eyes settled on Tanaźin and Wahcawin standing in front of their tepee. Wahcawin's face had a soft, rosy glow that made her look even lovelier than usual. Alex apparently noticed also, for he bent and whispered into Liza's ear. "She looks well-loved,

167

doesn't she?"

Liza gasped at his remark and glared at Alex, who laughed at her outraged look.

Alex said his good-byes to the Indian couple and led Liza to their horse. Liza turned back suddenly and found herself in Alex's arms. "So anxious, sweetheart?" he asked, a teasing glimmer in his eyes.

"Stop it, Alex," Liza retorted. "Be serious for a minute. I want to know how you say thank you in Indian."

A dark eyebrow arched in surprise. *"Pila maye,"* he answered.

"Say it slower," Liza requested.

Alex repeated the words and smiled at Liza's intense concentration. She ducked under his arm and went to stand in front of Tanaźin and Wahcawin. Facing Tanaźin, she said quietly, *"Pila maye."* The handsome chief looked surprised and then smiled broadly. Turning to Wahcawin, Liza repeated the words, but somehow "thank you" seemed inadequate for the woman who had saved her life. Impetuously, Liza hugged the girl and lightly kissed her cheek. Wahcawin stiffened, and when Liza backed away, she saw the shocked look on the Indian girl's face.

Alex stepped forward and said a few words in the Dakota tongue. Tanaźin and Wahcawin smiled. Liza stood by, feeling awkward.

As they walked back to Alex's horse, Liza asked, "What did I do wrong?"

Alex chuckled. "Indians don't kiss, Liza."

"Not even men and women?" Liza asked in astonishment.

"No." Glancing down at her, a warm look in his eyes, he said, "It's a shame, isn't it? They don't know what they're missing."

"Oh, Alex, I made a fool of myself," Liza fumed.

"No, I explained that it was the white man's way of showing affection. They were both pleased."

He lifted her on his horse and mounted behind her. Riding through the Indian camp, Liza felt a strange sadness at leaving. It seemed so quiet and peaceful.

As they rode across a small stream, Liza watched a group of Indian women scouring their pots, their children playing and splashing in the water around them. One Indian woman caught Liza's eye. Standing in knee-high water, she lowered her baby into the stream. At first, Liza thought the woman meant to bathe the baby, but she dropped him in the water and made no effort to retrieve him. Liza cried out, "Stop, Alex! That Indian is drowning her baby!"

Alex chuckled. "No, sweetheart. She's teaching him to swim. Just watch." The baby's head surfaced, the little hands furiously dog-paddling. "Indians teach their children to swim early," Alex explained.

"But he's only a baby," Liza objected.

"The Indians believe babies already know how to swim, having spent many months in the baby-water inside their mothers. Therefore, the babies are taught early how to swim, before they forget and become fearful of the water."

Liza looked up at Alex, her look clearly disbelieving.

He shrugged. "It works. Just look."

Liza watched as the baby paddled around his mother, a happy, almost ecstatic look on his face.

When his mother picked him up, the baby cried out in objection and struggled to get back in the water. Liza laughed. "I would have never believed it if I hadn't seen it with my own eyes."

As they crested the hill overlooking the Indian camp, Liza said, "Alex, turn around. I want to see the village one more time before we leave." Looking down at it, she said wistfully, "Somehow, I hate to leave it."

"I know. I always feel the same way every time I leave."

They sat watching the peaceful village for a few minutes. Then Alex nudged his horse, and they rode away.

"How far is it to the ranch?" Liza asked.

"Only a couple of hours if we take the short cut. But the terrain is pretty rough that way, so we're going the long way around."

As they rode, Liza was silent and withdrawn, reflecting upon her gloomy future and feeling more and more despondent. Alex didn't notice, being occupied with his own thoughts.

It was mid-afternoon when Alex stopped beside a small stream surrounded by graceful willows and rustling cottonwoods. "This looks like a good place to camp," Alex said, looking about him.

Liza was alarmed. She didn't want to spend another night alone with Alex. After last night, she didn't trust herself. "Can't we reach the ranch by nightfall?"

Alex swung lazily off the horse. "We could if we rode hard. But considering your recent illness, I think it would be foolish to push it. You'd be exhausted. Besides, Thunder is carrying double."

He helped her dismount. "Why don't you sit down while I take care of Thunder and set up camp."

Liza wandered over to the stream and stood staring down at it, wondering if she could fight off Alex's advances or if her body would betray her again if he tried to make love to her. In due time, she heard his steps behind her, but she deliberately kept her back to him, trying desperately to control her turbulent emotions.

"Liza, we need to talk," Alex said quietly. Slowly, he turned her to face him. "But first, there are some things I want to tell you. Promise me you won't interrupt."

Liza nodded, puzzled by his serious mood.

Alex led her to a fallen tree and motioned for her to sit down. He hunkered beside the stream, picked up a small stone and absently threw it into the water.

"First of all I want to tell you about my mother," Alex began. "As I've already told you, we had a nice, prosperous farm in Illinois, and my mother was happy there. She was a frail woman for farmwork, but we could afford household help, so she managed quite well. We lived close to several other farms, and she enjoyed visiting back and forth with the other women."

Alex sighed deeply. "I never knew what made my father decide to sell out and move west. I was only nine at the time. But I do know that my mother begged him not to. The trip was hard, even for women much stronger than my mother. We were the first wagon train to Oregon, so we had to blaze our own trail. That made the trip take even longer, and

171

by the time we reached Fort William, my mother was too ill to continue. I still don't know what made my father decide to settle in this godforsaken country instead of going back East, but he did. My mother never adjusted to the harshness of the land. The winters were particularly hard on her. But more than anything else, I think the isolation, the loneliness, was what killed her. She just gave up and slowly died."

Alex sat down on the ground beside her, staring off into space for a few minutes before he continued. "This land isn't any place for a delicate woman, Liza. Even the strong, hardy ones have a hard go of it. Sometimes, during the winters, we're snowbound for weeks at a time. A lot of women can't take that. They go crazy. Some women, like my mother, just can't take the loneliness."

Alex looked at Liza and saw her frowning. He smiled, "I know this doesn't make much sense to you now, but it will. Just be patient with me for a few minutes longer."

Liza nodded, pleased that he was opening up to her, even if she didn't know what he was leading up to.

Alex looked off, trying to decide where to continue. Finally, he said, "I was away at college when my father was killed. He was thrown while trying to break a wild mustang. He died instantly from a broken neck. I was still in a state of shock when I came home to take over the ranch. I certainly wasn't prepared for my brother Rob. He had changed while I was away. Oh, we had never been close. Maybe if we had been, things would have turned out differently.

172

He was lazy and irresponsible, totally disinterested in the ranch and prone to taking off on wild flings. I was only twenty-one at the time myself, so I couldn't handle him. No one could. He'd take money from the cash box and disappear for days at a time, sometimes weeks. God, Liza, I'd go crazy worrying about him. When he'd return, I'd ask him where he'd been, and he'd just laugh and say, 'drinking and whoring.' We'd argue about it, and he'd sulk around for a couple of weeks; and then the next thing I knew, he'd be gone again."

Alex took a small cigar from his pocket and lit it. For a few minutes, he sat smoking in silence, and Liza's heart went out to him. What a big responsibility for such a young man, she thought. Having to deal with a huge ranch and a wild, rebellious brother.

Alex broke the silence. "That went on for two years. Then, one day, Rob came home with a wife—a girl from one of the wagon trains passing through Fort Laramie. I was skeptical. They couldn't have known each other for long, and they were both so young. For a few months, things were great. They seemed to be crazy about each other. Rob even started taking an interest in the ranch. After a while, I thought maybe marriage was just what Rob needed to settle down. Marilee was a pretty little thing, and she seemed happy and contented. Then everything fell apart. Marilee got bored and restless. She started nagging and whining at Rob. They began arguing, and Rob got to sneaking off to Rita's place, a local brothel. He'd come home still half-drunk and reeking of cheap perfume. Of course, this just made Marilee angrier, and the whole thing would start all over."

Alex stopped and ran a hand through his thick hair. "By that time, Marilee was pregnant, and they both felt trapped. Their arguments got more and more violent. That's when I brought Bright Star to the ranch. She had lost her husband and had no family to look after her, and she was an experienced midwife. My original plan was that she come for a few months, to help Marilee with the baby, but she ended up staying permanently."

Alex threw the cigar away, rose and paced restlessly for a few minutes. Liza waited patiently, aching to take him in her arms and comfort him.

"I had hoped the baby would bring Rob and Marilee back together, but I was a fool to think that it would," Alex continued in a bitter voice. "Poor little tyke. They both ignored him. Rob got worse and started leaving for days and weeks at a time again. Marilee whined and complained constantly. When Andy was two months old, she decided to stop nursing him. Said it was ruining her figure. God, I don't know what I would have done without Bright Star. She sent to Tanazin's camp for one of their goats, and then she rigged up a feeding bag out of a deer bladder and a piece of cloth. Andy grew up on goat's milk, and the only real mother he's ever known is Bright Star."

Alex kicked angrily at a stone, sending it skittering across the ground and making Liza jump. "Marilee started flirting and hanging around with the ranch hands. I didn't think she was serious. I just figured she was trying to get even with Rob. Then one day, she ran off with one of the hands. Rob didn't even

174

bother to go after her. I think he was relieved she had left."

Alex sat down next to Liza again, saying in a weary voice, "A few months later, Rob got into a fight with some drifter in a saloon in Fort Laramie. Those who witnessed it said Rob picked a fight with the man; but the guy had a knife, and Rob was killed."

"And Marilee?" Liza asked, unable to keep silent any longer. "What happened to her?"

"I don't honestly know. We never heard a word from her. She could be dead for all I know. Frankly, I don't give a damn."

Alex walked to the bank of the stream and stood there for a few minutes, silent and brooding. With his back to Liza, he finally said, "Because I know how hard this country can be on a woman, and because of what happened between Rob and Marilee, I swore that I would never marry."

Liza felt his words like a physical blow, and tears came to her eyes.

Alex turned to face her, his look intense as he said gently, "Liza, I don't want you to leave." Striding to her, he lifted her to stand before him and gazed down warmly at her. "There's something between us, Liza. I know you feel it, too, or you would have never given yourself to me as you did. And it's not just lust or passion. It's something more."

At Alex's admission, Liza's defenses crumbled. Burying her head in her hands, she sobbed, "Oh, Alex, I love you." It was more a confession than a declaration.

Alex smiled at her words, his heart thudding wildly in his chest. He pulled her gently into his

175

arms, kissing her forehead. "How can you be sure it's love, Liza? Maybe it's just infatuation."

Liza pulled away from him angrily. She walked away and stood rigidly with her back to him.

Alex was feeling frustrated and a little irritated himself. He had been trying to keep a cool head about him. "Liza, I know what you want. You want me to tell you that I love you. That I'll love you forever. Hell, Liza, nothing lasts forever!"

Alex saw the slump of her shoulders and immediately regretted his harsh words. He walked up to stand behind her. This time his voice as gentle. "Liza, I could lie to you and promise undying love. But I'm trying to be honest with you. I've never felt this way before. How do I know how long it will last? A week? A month? A year? A lifetime? Rob and Marilee thought they were in love, too, but you see how long it lasted for them."

Liza whirled. "I'm not Marilee!" she spat angrily.

"I know. And I'm not Rob, either. But I still can't promise how long my love—if that's what these feelings are—will last. It's new and fragile for both of us. It needs time to grow and strengthen."

turned and walked away. "Just what is it you want from me, Alex?" she asked wearily.

"I want you to stay with me. Live with me. But I don't want a platonic relationship. After the last two nights, I could never accept that."

Again, Liza turned around, her look furious, her eyes glittering in rage. "I won't be your mistress, Alex!"

Alex winced, then paled. "No, I don't mean that. I don't want to buy your body. I don't want to use you.

176

That's not the kind of relationship I want."

"Then what?"

"I want you to live with me to give us time to get to know one another better. To give us time to see if our love is going to grow or fade away. And give yourself time to see if you can stand living in this country, too. It's hard on women. I don't want it to kill you, like it did my moither. Then, if it doesn't work out, we won't be trapped together for life and hating each other because we are."

"Are you suggesting a trial marriage? Why, I've never heard of anything so . . . so outrageous! Is that another of your *Indian* customs?"

Alex flinched at Liza's last words. "No, Liza, it's not an Indian custom. It's not even an American custom. As a matter of fact, it's an old custom that originated on the British Isles. Have you ever heard of handfasting?"

Liza had. Handfasting was an old middle-English custom, originating in the thirteenth century and practiced for hundreds of years thereafter. It was a trial marriage, where the couple agreed to live together for a given period of time, solemnizing their agreement with the clasping of hands. Strangely, it was a custom that was accepted by society, even sanctioned by the kirk, providing it didn't exceed the time limit. If, during that time, the couple decided not to marry and separated, no one thought any less of them.

"That custom isn't practiced anymore," Liza said. "Except, perhaps, in the most remote areas."

"And isn't that where we are? In a remote area?"

Seeing she was about to object, Alex raised his

hand to silence her. "No, Liza, hear me out. We both admit that we have strong feelings for one another, but that's no reason to jump into something as serious and binding as marriage. Under ordinary circumstances, I would court you until we got to know one another better. But that's impossible out here. It's not like you live right up the road on the next farm, or the closest village."

At Alex's last words, Liza recalled the small settlement at Fort Laramie. Perhaps she could find a job there, and Alex could court her properly. But then she remembered that there were only two trading posts, and with winter coming on, and no more wagon trains passing through, they wouldn't have a need for any help. No, the settlement was out, unless she was willing to work in a saloon, which she wasn't. Then her eyes lit up as another possibility occurred to her.

"Maybe I could get a teaching position at the fort itself?"

"Liza, you said yourself that you couldn't get a job teaching in New York because you don't have any references. What makes you think the army would hire you without them? Besides, they already have a teacher at Fort Laramie, a male tutor who's been there for years."

"Then maybe one of the officers' wives could use a maid?"

"No, Liza. The only women allowed on the post are the officers' wives. Except for the washerwomen. And believe me, the enlisted men's wives snatch up those jobs as soon as they become available. That's the only way they can live on the post with their husbands."

Liza was defeated. She knew she had to face up to her choices. She could either accept Alex's suggestion, or go back East and never see him again. The last thought was almost more than she could bear, plunging her into despair. She loved Alex with her whole heart and soul, and knew she would never love another. Without him, she would be an empty shell, only going through the motions of living.

"Just how long would this . . . this probationary period last?"

Alex felt weak with relief. He had been terrified that she would out-and-out refuse. And if she had, he didn't know what he would have done. "I believe the time set by the church for handfasting was one year. That way, you could stay through one winter and see how you feel about living in this country."

Liza knew Alex was afraid that she was too delicate and fragile to take this harsh country, but she knew she was stronger than he thought. No, what concerned her was his doubting the strength and endurance of his love, for there was no doubt in her mind that he did love her. "And after the year is up?"

"If we both feel the same way we do now, we'll be married, just like any handfasted couple."

Marriage. Yes, that's what she wanted. To know that she would belong to Alex, and him to her, for the rest of their lives. No, longer than that—forever.

"And if it doesn't work out?" Liza forced herself to ask.

"We'll agree if either of us feels it won't work, we'll simply tell the other."

Liza turned away from him. "Then I could leave anytime I wanted to?"

If Liza could have seen Alex's face at that moment,

179

she wouldn't have had any reservations. His face turned ghostly ashen, a pained look in his eyes. He finally managed to answer, "Yes, if that's what you want."

She would be gambling, Liza realized. Waging everything, her pride, her love, her self-respect, on Alex continuing to love her. But then, she remembered her only other alternative, and what the stakes were—marriage to Alex, a lifetime of living with the man she loved. Was she bold enough; did she love him enough to gamble all?

Alex was on the verge of promising Liza they would be married as soon as the next priest or preacher passed through the area, even though a hasty marriage was still against his better judgment, when Liza turned to face him. The smile on her face made his heart slam against his chest. He held his breath.

"All right, Alex," Liza said in a calm voice. "For one year."

Alex held out his large hands, and Liza placed her small ones in them, both realizing the import of that simple grasp.

"Oh, God," Alex groaned, pulling her into his arms in a fierce embrace. "I hope it works out for us, sweetheart," he mumbled in a voice thick with emotion.

Liza smiled and, with savage determination, fiercely vowed, *It will, darling. It's going to work, because I'm going to make it work. Our love is going to last—forever!*

Chapter 9

When Liza and Alex rode up to the ranch the next morning, they received a warm and enthusiastic welcome. Seeing Liza, Andy squealed in delight and threw himself into her arms, hanging tightly to her neck. Hiram hopped around them, repeatedly slapping Alex on the back. "I knew you could do it! I knew you could do it!" Even Bright Star, grinning broadly, seemed happy to see Liza.

When everyone calmed down, Alex took Liza's arm and motioned to a man rapidly approaching them from the barn. "Liza, I want you to meet someone."

Liza saw a dark-headed man striding toward them. He was of medium height, but his slimness made him appear taller.

"Liza, this is Manuel Ruiz, my foreman," Alex said when the man stood before them. Liza looked into a pair of warm, brown eyes.

"My pleasure, señorita," Manuel answered with a little bow, his slim lips curved into a smile.

"Was there any trouble while I was gone?" Alex asked the swarthy-faced man.

Manuel arched a delicate eyebrow and fingered his black mustache lightly. "A little," he admitted, shrugging.

Alex frowned. "I'll be with you in a minute."

Taking Liza's arm, he led her into the house. "I'd better check out a few things here at the ranch. I probably won't be back until dark. Will you be all right?"

Liza laughed. "I'm sure Hiram will take care of me." She glanced at the old man, who was occupied with shooing Andy and Bright Star away, admonishing them with "Too much excitement. She needs to rest."

Alex bent and kissed her on the cheek. "I'll see you tonight, sweetheart," he whispered, his voice warm with meaning.

Liza colored, embarrassed that Hiram had witnessed the scene. Hiram grinned broadly, saying after Alex had left, "I'm sure glad you two young'uns are getting along better. Now, come into the kitchen. I've got lunch ready, and then you can take a nice nap."

Liza released herself to Hiram's anxious ministrations for the rest of the day, thinking that he was much like an old mother hen taking care of her chick. After eating, she was whisked to bed for a nap. Awaking feeling refreshed, she bathed, savoring the hot water and real soap, and washed her hair for the first time in weeks. When she finally forced herself out of the tub, she was horrified at how dirty the water was.

That night, after they had eaten, Liza told Hiram

of her experience, leaving out the attempted rape and, of course, the intimacies she and Alex had shared. When she told him of what she had seen and learned in the Indian village, she was surprised to discover that Hiram knew almost as little as she about Indian customs and beliefs.

"Don't cotton to them, myself," he grumbled in explanation. "Don't much care what they do, as long as they leave me alone."

Later, alone in her room, preparing herself for bed and Alex's return, she felt nervous and awkward. Before this, their lovemaking had been spontaneous, and not something planned. She searched her trunk for a nightgown, finally picking one with voluminous gathering, because of the delicate embroidery at the neck and over the bodice. She was brushing her hair when the door flew open with a loud bang.

Startled by the unexpected noise, she flew to her feet and saw Alex standing in the doorway. He was bare-chested, a towel flung carelessly around his neck, the dark hair on his chest and head glistening with beads of water from his recent bath. He looked angry.

"Have you changed your mind already, Liza?" he asked, his voice biting.

"What do you mean?" Liza asked, trembling beneath his glowering expression.

"I'm asking you if you've changed your mind about our agreement?" Alex retorted angrily.

"Why . . . why, no, I haven't."

"Then what in the hell are you doing in here?"

"It's my room," Liza answered, still confused by his sudden anger.

183

"Not anymore, it isn't," Alex snarled. In three quick strides, he reached her and swept her up in his arms, carrying her out of the room, down the hall and into his bedroom. Kicking the door shut behind him with his heel, he flung them both on the bed, pinning her down with his big body half over hers. His steely eyes bored into her as he said in a determined voice that brooked no argument, "This is where you belong now. In my room, in my bed and in my arms."

Their eyes met. Alex's didn't waver. Liza chewed her lip nervously. "Alex, don't you think it would be better if I stayed in my room? What will the others—"

"Dammit, Liza! I'm not going to sneak to your room like some thief in the night. I'm not going to dirty our love that way. I'm not ashamed of it. Are you?"

Liza swallowed hard at the dangerous gleam in his eyes, then said hesitantly, "No, but don't you think that's being too blatant?"

Alex laughed, his anger dissolving. "No, sweetheart, it's called honesty. Do you think for a minute that we're going to be able to hide our relationship from the others? Once more, I don't want to hide it. I want it out in the open."

"Then you've told them about our agreement?"

Alex had never concerned himself about others' opinions of him or his actions. He lived by his own code. And he certainly wasn't going to start explaining himself now. "No, I didn't. It's our own personal agreement. It's none of their goddamned business!" Seeing the shocked look on Liza's face, he said, "Bright Star couldn't care less, and Andy is too young to know any better. As for Hiram and Manuel, they will probably assume we're going to get married." Taking her chin, he lifted her face gently. "Liza, it's not unusual in these parts for a man and woman to live together until a priest or minister wanders through and can marry them."

"There isn't a minister at Fort Laramie?" Liza asked in surprise.

"No, the army doesn't assign chaplains to outlying posts such as Fort Laramie. There used to be one at Fort Kearney, farther east, but he transferred somewhere else. So you see, Hiram and Manuel will just assume we're waiting for Father William to make his yearly rounds."

"Father William?"

"He's the missionary priest assigned to this general area. His primary duties are to convert the Indians to Christianity and provide spiritual care for those who already are Christians, but he makes his services available to anyone who wants them, regardless of their religion. He usually spends the winter with one of the Indian tribes, and then, during the spring and summer, he circulates through the area performing marriages and baptisms, saying mass and blessing graves." Alex frowned as his eyes searched her face. "Liza, is that what's bothering you? Do you feel guilty about what we're doing?"

Liza considered the question. Surprisingly, she had not felt guilt. Her love for Alex seemed so good, so right, and somehow, she couldn't see God condemning her for it. Besides, they had made a commitment to one another when they had hand-fasted, even if it was an irregular one.

She shook her head, whispering, "No, I don't feel guilty."

Alex sighed in relief. "Good. I'm glad. I would

never want that." Then he smiled. "Relax, sweet-heart, I'm not going to eat you." His eyes warmed as they swept over her. "On second thought, you look so good, I just might do that." He lightly bit at her chin, growling in mock ferocity. His hands tangled in the folds of her gown. Scowling, he raised a handful of material as if he had just realized that it was there. "What's this?" he asked in disgust.

She laughed. "Why, my nightgown."

"Take it off!"

Liza was shocked at his fierce demand. She shook her head. "No."

"Liza, it's one thing to make love to you inside a tent. It's quite another to try and make love to you from outside one."

"But it keeps me warm."

Alex grinned, a raffish gleam in his eyes. "I'll keep you warm. Take it off."

Their eyes locked in silent combat. Neither wavered.

"Liza," Alex said in exasperation, "we slept naked in each other's arms in the Indian camp, and last night, we made love in the open under the stars. Have you forgotten that?"

Liza shivered, remembering Alex's tender, yet passionate lovemaking the night before. "No," she answered, feeling weak at just the memory.

"Then why do you need a gown all of the sudden?" he asked in irritation. "Is it because you've stepped back into the white man's world and you feel the need to resume the white man's stupid, prudish ideas about sex?"

Liza remained silent, not answering because she

186

didn't know the answer herself.

Alex shook her lightly. "Dammit, Liza, you're not going to hide from me. Not behind that door in your room—or behind this ridiculous gown!" He rose quickly from the bed, pulling her with him. "Now, take it off!"

When Liza made no move, Alex reached his hand to the neckline menacingly, and Liza gasped at his silent threat. His voice low and determined, he said, "Either you take that gown off—or I'll rip it off! And I can assure you that when I'm finished, you won't have enough left for a decent dust rag."

Liza looked up and saw his eyes burn angrily. There was no doubt in her mind that he would do just as he had threatened. Her legs trembling, her hands shaking, she fumbled awkwardly with the buttons of the gown. She glanced up at Alex, her eyes pleading, but his jaw was set stubbornly, his look adamant.

The gown fell to the floor. Alex's breath caught in his throat, his gaze warm and soft as it caressed her. Lifting her chin in his big hand, his finger gently stroked the wild, erratic pulse in her throat. "You're beautiful, Liza," he said in a husky voice. "Why are you ashamed of your beauty?"

Quickly, he shrugged his pants off and pulled her down on the bed, his hands soothing her. "Don't hide from me, Liza," he whispered in her ear, his lips nibbling her throat. "I want to fall asleep with you in my arms, and awake beside you in the morning. If I wake up in the night, I want to be able to reach out and touch you. *You*, Liza, not a piece of material."

Then his mouth and hands were seeking, tantalizing, arousing until Liza was swept up in a whirlwind of passion. Afterward, they slept in a tangle of brown and white limbs, drenched in their own sweat, totally exhausted and satiated.

Later, Liza awakened slightly, barely aware of Alex slipping from the bed. Through half-closed eyes, she watched him as he lit the lamp by the bed, walked to the dresser and poured water into a basin sitting there. As he shaved, Liza's eyes feasted on him, his dark hair curling at the back of his neck, his powerful shoulder and back muscles, his slim hips, firm buttocks and long muscular legs. He had an animal beauty about him, she thought dreamily, and then as he turned, she shut her eyes tightly, not wanting to be caught openly admiring him.

Alex walked quietly across the room and sat on the bed beside Liza. Picking up a strand of her long hair, he tickled her nose with it. "Stop playing possum, Liza. I know you're awake. I saw you watching me in the mirror."

Liza flushed hotly, feeling like a child who had been caught with her hand in the cookie jar. Alex chuckled. "It's all right, sweetheart. I don't mind. I want you to enjoy looking at me, just as I enjoy looking at you."

To avoid his eyes, Liza glanced out the window. The sun was barely rising. "Do you always get up this early?" she asked, her voice husky with sleep.

"Yes, but there's no need for you to." Lifting her chin to force her to look him in the eye, he said, "I want you to promise me you'll move your things in here today."

Liza nodded silently, her hand lightly, sensuously

188

stroking his shoulder. Alex gazed down at Liza, her hair tousled, her face flushed, her lips still swollen from his passionate kisses the night before, and he felt that familiar stirring in his loins. She gazed back, her eyes sleepy and seductive. He gave a shaky laugh. "If you don't stop looking at me like that, sweetheart, I'll be forced to crawl back in bed with you. Then I'll have to listen to Hiram's tirade because my eggs got cold."

He bent and brushed her lips, then pulling the cover down, dropped a light kiss on one rose-tipped breast. With a little groan of regret, he rose, dressed quickly and slipped from the room.

Over the next several days, Liza's life drifted into a routine. Mornings, she would visit with Hiram in the kitchen, but the protocol he had established that first day still held. She could visit, but any effort to help was firmly rebuked. Her afternoon hours were spent reading or wandering about the house or yard. Andy was in and out of the house with Bright Star, so her only contact with the little boy was limited to bedtime stories. Then her rapturous nights were spent in Alex's arms.

By the afternoon of the fourth day, Liza was totally bored and restless. She was not used to such aimless days; she longed for activity. Irritably, she wondered where Hiram had gone. Probably in the barn tending the horses, she thought. Then the idea of a horseback ride occurred to her. That was just what she needed to relieve her boredom, and surely, Hiram would let her take a short ride if she stayed close to the house. Excited, she rushed upstairs and searched through her trunks until she found the clothes that Alex had loaned her a few weeks earlier.

Dressing quickly and then tripping lightly down the stairs, she walked toward the barn, her hips swaying with unconscious provocativeness.

Off to one side, Manuel stood by a wagon. He glanced up and saw her, his eyes showing first surprise, then appreciation, and finally, widening in alarm as Liza strolled by with a smile and wave. "No, señorita!" he called. Liza, caught up in her excitement at the prospect of a ride, didn't even hear him.

Turning at the barn, she walked a few steps before she became aware of someone watching her. She whirled and found herself facing four dirty, bearded men. Their hot, lust-filled eyes raked her, seemingly undressing her where she stood.

The largest and hairiest, his eyes glittering, rasped to the others, "Hot damn! I'm gonna have me a piece of that."

Slowly, menacingly, the four men circled her and moved toward her. One man stroked his groin obscenely, his mouth gaping, saliva dribbling down his chin as they closed in on her. Liza stood frozen to the spot, too terrified to move or scream.

A strong hand closed over her arm, and Liza cried out in surprise and fear, having not even seen the fifth man. She was shoved roughly into the barn with such haste that Liza stumbled. "What in the hell are you doing here?" Alex demanded angrily, swinging her around to face him. Liza had never seen him this angry, his eyes hard, his jaw rigid, his face blood-red.

"Oh, Alex!" she cried, weak with relief.

"Dammit, answer me!" he said, shaking her roughly.

"I came to see Hiram," she answered, still trembling after her unnerving experience.

"Dressed like *that?*" Alex snarled, his eyes sweeping over her.

Liza's fear was quickly replaced with anger. "What's wrong with the way I'm dressed?"

"Wrong?" Alex snapped. "You sashay around here with your breasts bobbing, and swinging that seductive little butt of yours in front of everyone, and you don't know what's wrong?"

"I've worn these clothes before. You didn't object then," Liza retorted.

"That was different!"

"Why? Why was it different?"

"Because it was only in front of me. And if I remember correctly, I wasn't very successful at keeping my hands off you either." One hand cupped her bottom insultingly.

Liza backed away and glared at him.

"Dammit, Liza! Didn't you see the way those men were staring at you? Do you have any idea of how close you came to being raped?"

Liza lifted her chin and shot him an icy look.

"Damn little fool," Alex growled. "Can't you even do what you're told."

Liza stood rigid with cold fury. Her voice was icy, sending shivers up his spine. "Don't you *ever* talk to me that way again." She pushed past him, her head held proudly. "We made an agreement, Alex. But that doesn't give you the right to tell me where I can go, what I can do, and certainly not what I can or can't wear." Her eyes smoldered with anger. "You don't own me, Alex Cameron. *No* man owns me.

Not ever!"

Liza turned and walked from the barn and through the group of men standing outside, her carriage proud, haughty, almost regal. The looks of lust on the men's faces turned to expressions of disbelief, and then mouth-gaping awe.

It wasn't until she closed the door behind her in their bedroom that Liza reacted. Trembling violently, a sob escaped her throat as she spat, "That bloody bastard!"

Angrily, she pulled a chair before the dresser and stood on it, viewing herself in the mirror. Her reflection caused her to gasp in shock. The material of the shirt stretched tightly over her breasts, outlining them in bold relief, its thinness allowing the darker areas of her nipples to plainly show through. She turned to view her backside. The tight pants fit her snugly, the creases at the bottom and the cleft between her buttocks clearly visible. She looked as if her lower half had been dyed blue. My God, she thought, even naked, she couldn't have been more blatantly exposed. Weakly, she stepped down from the chair and sat on the edge of the bed.

A noise at the door caught her attention. Looking up, she saw Alex standing in the doorway. He hesitated, his eyes shifting nervously. "I . . . I've come to apologize."

Liza stared at him in amazement. She doubted that this arrogant, stubborn man had ever apologized to anyone for anything.

"I was wrong to treat you like that," he continued.

He looked uncomfortable and awkward, and Liza, well aware of what this apology was costing his pride, felt sorry for him. Besides, she was never one to hold a grudge.

"I was wrong also, Alex," she answered tentatively. "I didn't realize what I looked like in the outfit until a few minutes ago. If I had, I would have never worn them."

"Forget the clothes," Alex said impatiently. "I was just frightened and angry, not really at you, but at those men. But that didn't give me the right to manhandle you."

"You were frightened?" Liza asked in disbelief.

"My God, yes," he answered, his voice trembling slightly. "No, to be honest with you, I was scared to death. Thank God Manuel saw you and came and got me. Even then, I wasn't sure we could hold them off."

Liza was baffled. "Manuel? What's he got to do with it?"

Alex sighed deeply in exasperation. "Liza, you actually believe my appearance on the scene stopped those men?" He shook his head. "No, Manuel was holding a gun on them the whole time we were in the barn. That's what stopped them."

Suddenly, Liza realized how close she *had* come. Her face drained of all color, and she shuddered, remembering Scarface's attempted rape.

Alarmed by her appearance, Alex rushed to her and took her in his arms. "Are you all right?"

"I didn't realize," Liza replied in a weak voice.

"I know. But, Liza, at the risk of making you angry with me again, I must impress upon you how important it is for you to be more careful. I'm not telling you to stay away from the barn or not go riding alone for just the fun of it; I have good

193

reasons." He lifted her chin so that she could see his serious, intent face. "This isn't England. Most of the men I hire are drifters, barely civilized men at best, and no doubt many of them are running from the law for no telling what heinous crime. Men like that take what they want and worry about the consequences later."

"I'll never wear those clothes again," Liza vowed.

Alex shook his head, exasperated. "Liza, I don't think you understand. It wasn't just the clothes. Even properly dressed, it's likely the same thing would have happened. You're a beautiful woman. To make matters worse, you have a seductiveness about you that tempts a man, and some men don't even try to exercise any control."

"You think I'm a flirt?" Liza asked indignantly.

"At one time I did, but since I've come to know you better, Liza, I've realized that you're totally unaware of your desirability. That's why it's so much more dangerous for you. I've got to impress upon you how you affect men, so that you can protect yourself."

Liza was still struggling with what he was telling her. "You think I'm seductive?" she asked incredulously.

Alex grinned. "Seductive as hell," he answered, then continued more seriously, "Liza, there is nothing more dangerous for a woman than to be both beautiful and innocently seductive."

"I didn't know I was," Liza answered defensively.

"That's my whole point."

Liza felt uncomfortable, almost as if he had told her she had warts on her nose.

194

Seeing her expression, Alex chuckled and kissed her forehead lightly. "Will you be all right by yourself? I still have a lot to do, but if you'd prefer I stay with you . . ."

"No, that's not necessary," Liza answered.

"Well, there's no more danger of those men bothering you. Manuel and I sent them on their way. They're gone."

Liza nodded silently.

"I'll see you tonight," Alex called over his shoulder as he walked out of the room.

Liza sat for a long time in a quandry over what Alex had said. He had called her beautiful before. Liza thought he exaggerated, although it pleased her to hear him say it. But seductive? She had thought only loose women possessed that trait, and yet, he had said it almost as if it were a compliment. Annoyed, she shook her head and vowed that she would eliminate this "seductive" trait from herself, not having the slightest idea of what made her so.

Later that afternoon, Liza asked Hiram if he thought it would be safe for her to bathe in the pool behind the house.

"I don't mind filling the tub for you," Hiram answered.

"I know, but I'm tired of sitting in that dark, stuffy storeroom. Besides, I'd enjoy a little swim. But not if you think it wouldn't be safe," she added hastily.

"Don't know why not," he answered thoughtfully. "There ain't nobody around, and it's not that far from the house. If you see anything suspicious, you just scream like hell, and I'll come running."

Delighted, Liza rushed off with soap and towel in

hand. She undressed, threw her clothes across a bush and waded into the pleasantly cool water. The pool was just wide enough for a short swim and up to her neck in the deepest part. She swam back and forth a few times and then floated lazily, watching the fluffy clouds in the sky above her.

A twig cracked, and Liza was instantly alert. She swam to one side of the pool and hid under a willow branch hanging in the water, her heart hammering in her chest. It must be just an animal, she thought, hating to call Hiram for no reason. She watched the bushes that fringed the pool with indrawn breath, ready to scream.

Alex stepped into the clearing. He looked about frowning. Hiram had told him she was down here. "Liza, where are you?"

"Under here," Liza answered timidly. "I didn't know it was you," she explained, feeling foolish.

"I'm glad you took my talk seriously." He gazed at her for a moment, then said, "That water looks good. I think I'll join you."

Liza watched as Alex stripped off his clothing, silently admiring his male beauty as it was revealed to her inch by inch. Then as he walked toward her in all of his masculine glory, she noticed the devilish twinkle in his eyes, a look that she sensed boded her no good.

"What are you up to?" she asked suspiciously.

Alex didn't answer. He laughed, then dove into the pool with a loud splash that made Liza jump before his hands caught her hips, pulling her under water with him. Liza emerged, spitting water and sputtering oaths, her long, wet hair tangled about her.

Pushing the snarled mass from her face, she asked, "Are you trying to drown me?"

Alex only laughed and dunked her again. This time, she came up fighting for balance, frantically grabbing Alex's muscular shoulders for support. Alex lifted her lightly from the bottom of the pool, holding her against him, facing her at eye level. "Can you swim?"

Liza pushed the wet hair from her face. "Well, it's a little late to ask," she answered irritably, "but yes."

"I don't believe you," he baited.

"Well, just put me down and I'll show you," she retorted indignantly.

He pulled her into a tighter embrace, his eyes warm with desire. "I'll find out some other time." His mouth covered hers in a long, searching kiss. Alex finally pulled his lips away, asking in a husky voice, "Where did you leave the soap?"

Her breathing too uneven to speak, Liza pointed to the bank. Nodding, Alex waded to the side of the pool, still holding Liza tightly to him. When he reached ankle depth, he dropped her gently to her feet and reached for the soap. He dipped the soap in the water and turned her, pushing her long hair out of the way as he began to soap her shoulders and back.

"What are you doing?" Liza asked, still too weak from Alex's kiss to even move.

"I'm going to bathe you."

"But I can—"

"Hush, sweetheart," Alex interjected. "You talk too much."

He lathered her back, stopping to kiss her spine at the rise of her buttocks. "You've got a dimple there," he said, his voice husky. His hands soaped her hips and buttocks in tantalizing strokes. Then he knelt and washed her graceful legs, kissing her once more on the sensitive skin behind one knee. "Another dimple," he muttered. Turning her, he stood and bathed her front, lingering a long time on her breasts, teasing and caressing, then down over her abdomen and thighs, making love to her with his skillful hands and hot stares.

Again, he knelt to minister to her legs, washing one dainty foot, then the other. As he rose, his hand trailed maddeningly slowly along her leg, up her inner thigh, to stroke lightly the silky softness between her legs, his fingers seeking, exploring.

Liza felt warm and tingly all over, her breath coming in short gasps.

Alex handed the soap to her, smiling, his eyes hot and commanding. "Now it's your turn," he said, turning his back to her.

Liza hesitated for only a moment and then soaped his back and shoulders, once again marveling at the rippling muscles, her hands trembling with excitement. She proceeded downward over his taut buttocks and long muscular legs. He turned, and Liza lathered his broad chest, acutely aware of his smile and his eyes watching her every move. Her hands swept over his hard, flat abdomen, and then she gasped at the sight of his obvious arousal. Quickly, she knelt and ducked her head, trying to appear engrossed in washing his legs to hide her mixed emotions of excitement and embarrassment.

"I think you missed something," Alex taunted.

Liza blushed, her whole body turning fiery red. It

was one thing to touch him there in the dark, but quite another to wash him there in broad daylight, particularly with him watching everything she was doing so closely.

Alex chuckled and lifted her to her feet, slipping one arm under her knees and carrying her into the deepest part of the pool to rinse the soap from their bodies.

His warm breath fanned her face as he whispered against her lips, "Did you know that the Dakota warrior washes his woman before he makes love to her the first time?" His tongue seductively traced her lower lip, and Liza shivered in response.

As he carried her to the bank of the pool, an intent expression on his face, Liza objected weakly, "No, Alex. Not here. Someone might see us."

"No one will see us," Alex answered, as he laid her down on the grass.

"But it's broad daylight!"

"I fail to see what that has to do with it," he whispered huskily, his lips nibbling at her ear, his hands gently searching with consummate skill. Then, before she could object further, his mouth was on hers, his tongue seeking and ravishing the honeyed sweetness of her mouth.

Later, Liza lay in his arms, their legs still entwined, watching the shadows around the pool deepen as the sun dipped in the sky. "Alex, I want to talk to you."

"Go ahead, sweetheart. I'm listening," he answered, his hands stroking her shoulders and back.

"No, not like this. Let's get dressed first," Liza replied, wondering how in the world she could carry on a serious conversation wrapped in Alex's arms and both of them still naked. It unnerved her—to say nothing of the distraction.

Alex laughed, making Liza wonder if he could read her thoughts. He rolled over and picked up his pants. When they were dressed, he grinned. "Now, what's so important that you had to interrupt our pleasant interlude?"

"Alex, be serious!" Liza rebuked him gently.

A dark eyebrow arched in surprise. Pulling her down to sit on the ground beside him, he said, "All right, shoot."

Liza nervously fingered the folds in her skirt. She didn't know how to approach this without making him angry. Gathering her courage, she said, "Alex, you said you didn't want me to be your mistress, yet that's how I feel."

Alex frowned. "You can't possibly think that I'm just using you."

"No." Liza hesitated, then continued, "At least, not consciously. But that does seem to be my only purpose." Seeing his thundering look, she quickly added, "Don't interrupt, please."

Alex's jaw tightened. He nodded curtly for her to continue.

"I'm not used to being pampered and waited on," Liza explained. "At home, I helped my mother with the care of the house and even had chores of my own to do. But Hiram and Bright Star won't let me lift a finger, and I don't see you until late at night."

"I'm sorry, Liza, but this is a busy time for the ranch. Later, I'll be able to spend more time with you."

"Alex, I don't expect you to entertain me," Liza retorted with exasperation. "For heaven's sake, I don't expect anyone to entertain me. I know everyone is busy and has work to do. That's just it. I don't have anything to do except—" She blushed. Looking at him, her eyes imploring his understanding, she explained, "I'm bored, Alex. That's why I went to the barn today. I thought a ride would relieve my restlessness."

"I guess I never considered that," Alex admitted thoughtfully. "I've been so busy myself." He shook his dark head. "I doubt that Hiram or Bright Star will relent, either. They're both very possessive about their chores. How much do you know about the care of horses?"

"A little, but not much," Liza answered, wondering what he was thinking.

"Do you still like that little pinto mare?"

"Yes," Liza answered, afraid to give in to her rising hopes.

"Then, she's yours."

"Oh, Alex, thank you!" Liza cried, throwing herself into his arms and hugging him tightly.

Smiling indulgently, he pushed her from him. "But it's not going to be all fun. You'll have to learn how to take care of her. Everything. From now on, she'll be your responsibility. Hiram will teach you."

Liza nodded eagerly.

"I know you like to ride astride," Alex continued. "I'd like to make a suggestion. I was thinking if you made yourself a riding skirt—"

Liza's eyes lit up. Before Alex could even finish his sentence, she interjected, "Now that you mention it, I

201

do remember seeing some of those at St. Joes when I was shopping. I thought they were so clever. I can take one of my skirts, slit the center seam and make pants out of it."

"I was going to suggest a riding skirt made from tanned buffalo hides. It would be much more durable and give your legs more protection. I have some hides you can have. Bright Star can sew them for you if you show her what you want."

"That would be wonderful!"

"But you're going to have to obey my rules about riding," Alex added emphatically, his look stern. "You'll have to limit your riding to the ranch yard. Otherwise, you'll have to wait until I can take you for a ride." Lifting her chin, his eyes bored into hers. "Understand?"

Liza was disappointed with the edict, but still, the idea of her own horse was exciting. She nodded in agreement, then said, "Oh, Alex, I've never had my own horse before. I'm thrilled. And I'll take good care of her, I promise." Then she added cautiously, "But that's not what I had in mind."

Alex frowned. "Just what *do* you want?"

"I want your permission to tutor Andy."

Seeing his frown deepen, Liza said defensively, "I'm really a very good tutor, Alex, despite what you think."

Alex shook his head. "That's not why I'm frowning, Liza. It's just that Andy is still so young for actual tutoring. I was thinking of that for later. Besides, that wasn't part of our agreement."

"And just what was our agreement?" Liza asked hotly. "That I be available anytime you want me?

202

Damn!" She stamped her foot angrily. "You're still treating me like a mistress, offering gifts to placate me." She lifted her head proudly. "I love you, Alex. You don't have to buy it." Tears welled in her eyes as she said, "You can keep your damn horse!" Turning, she ran from the clearing.

Alex caught up with her easily with his long strides. He grabbed her shoulders and forced her to face him, looking down at her in disbelief. "You're serious, aren't you?"

"Yes, I'm serious! That's what I've been trying to tell you, only you're too thick-skulled to realize it. I'm bored, Alex. I need something to do—something important, so that I can contribute, too. You don't need me to take care of your horse. Hiram, or any of your ranch hands, can do that. The only thing you need me for is to satisfy your—your lust!"

"Lust?" Alex bellowed in rage.

Liza saw the wounded look on his face and started sobbing in frustration. "Oh, Alex, I'm sorry. I didn't mean that. I know that's not all it is. I need you that way just as much as you need me. But I need more. I have to feel I'm doing something important, too."

Alex sighed, wondering at the complexity of this girl. Outwardly, she appeared very fragile, the kind of woman that needed pampering, but he was beginning to discover that beneath that delicate feminine exterior there was a core of steel. To be honest, he had to admit that he was overly possessive of her, not wanting to share her with others. He felt a little twinge of jealousy toward his nephew, although he realized that it was irrational. And true, he had never stopped to think of what she was doing to pass her time while he was away from her, or to wonder if she was content with her new life. "All right, Liza. If that's what you want. But I still think Andy's a little too young for tutoring."

Liza could hardly believe her ears. "Oh, thank you, Alex. And Andy's not too young to start learning his letters. I know he's still too young for any long sessions; his attention span is still too short for that. An hour or two a day is all he is capable of. But I think he will enjoy it, and I know I will."

Alex nodded, still feeling that ridiculous twinge of jealousy. "I guess we could set up your old bedroom as a classroom."

"That would be perfect."

"Is there anything else?" Alex asked, his look penetrating, his voice suspicious.

"Well, as a matter of fact, I've noticed that Andy has outgrown most of his clothes."

"Again?" Alex snorted. "I just bought him new clothes a few months ago."

"That's just it," Liza answered. "It's silly to buy new clothes. They're outrageously expensive, particularly for a child growing as fast as Andy is. I could sew him—"

"No!" Alex interjected. "You can tutor him if you insist, but there's no need for you to sew for him. I can afford to buy his clothes."

Liza was surprised at his anger, but decided to leave well enough alone. She shrugged her shoulders in defeat.

"Is that all?" Alex asked, his voice wary.

"Yes, that's all," Liza answered, thinking, *For the time being anyway.* A couple of hours tutoring and a few hours a day caring for her new horse certainly wasn't going to keep her occupied, but she would find other things and insidiously add them later. She had no intention of giving up her active, productive life because Alex felt some strange need to pamper her.

As they walked back to the ranch house, Alex said, "I'll be leaving tomorrow, Liza. We've got to start moving the herd closer to the ranch house so that Manuel and I can watch them this winter."

"Is winter that close?" Liza asked, amazed. The air was chilly now when the sun set, but still, she couldn't imagine winter just around the corner.

"No, it will be another six weeks to two months before we have our first snow, but the men will start getting restless soon and wandering off. We want to get the cattle moved before too many of the hands leave."

"How long will you be gone?" Liza asked, feeling a twinge of disappointment.

"About a week or ten days."

"So long?"

"Yes, by the time we round up the strays, it will probably take that long." He looked at her warmly. "Will you miss me?"

Liza colored, admitting quietly, "Yes." Thank God she had had this talk with Alex before he left, she thought. Another ten monotonous days, coupled with Alex being gone, and she would have been stark raving mad by the time he returned.

"Just think of how sweet our reunion will be," Alex said, pulling her closer to him.

Chapter 10

The following days were much busier than Liza had expected. The morning Alex departed, she gathered the supplies she had bought in St. Joe and, with Andy in tow, walked to her old bedroom.

The little boy was reluctant, wanting to play outside instead. "If you learn your letters, then you can learn words, and the next thing you know, you can read your own fairytales."

"Really?" Andy asked in awe.

"Yes, Andy. You've seen all of your uncle's books downstairs in the parlor, haven't you?" The little blond head nodded solemnly. "Well those are full of stories. Just think of how much fun that would be."

Andy's eyes were bright with excitement. "Teach me."

Liza made the lessons as much like a game as possible. The little boy was enthusiastic and eager, and Liza had a hard time limiting the sessions to two hours. She was amazed at his intelligence. If he kept up at this pace, he would be reading within a year.

She was glad she had thought to bring a primary reader with her.

Her afternoons were spent in the barn with Hiram and her new pinto mare. The first day, she just stood admiring the little horse and stroking her neck, talking to her gently.

"What are you gonna name her?" Hiram asked Liza.

Liza looked the mare over. She was basically white, with irregular brown and black markings over her body and neck. Liza fingered a black marking on the horse's forehead. "Star, I think."

Hiram guffawed. "So you saw that little star on her forehead, too? Yep, that's a good name for her."

"Shouldn't I be doing something for her?"

"Nope, not today," Hiram answered. "Just pet her and talk to her. Let her get used to your voice and your touch. Tomorrow I'll start teaching you how to take care of her."

And teach her he did. First, the proper amount and mixture of grain and oats. Then he gave Liza instructions on watering and how to rub the mare down after a ride. He lectured her on the care of the tender hooves and any small injuries the horse might receive. He taught her how to put the bridle on without injuring Star's delicate mouth. "Learn how to guide her with your knees," he said. "Sawing on those reins hurts their mouths. And keep your saddle blanket washed and soft so that it won't rub sores on her back. Always check it for burrs," he added.

When they reached the lesson on saddling, Hiram moved to pick it up for her. "No, let me," Liza objected. "I have to learn for myself." She struggled with the saddle, much heavier and bulkier than the English saddle she was accustomed to, and grinned in satisfaction when she finally got it on the mare's back. As she went to buckle the cinch, Hiram snorted, "Too loose."

Liza looked down at the cinch. It certainly looked tight enough to her.

"Give her a good swat on her haunch," the old man said.

"Why?"

"Just do it. You'll see," he answered irritably.

Liza did as Hiram had told her and heard a loud whoosh as the mare let out her breath. A good two-inch slack appeared in the cinch. Liza looked down at it in disbelief.

"A lot of horses try that trick," Hiram said, chuckling at Liza's expression. "Blow up their bellies, and then when you mount them, you find yourself laying on the ground staring up at their undersides."

Liza laughed and tightened the cinch. The mare looked back at her with a sheepish look. "No more of that," Liza scolded.

Then she learned the importance of exercising her mount, having to walk and run the pinto around the corral by the reins, since her riding skirt was not finished yet. Hiram sat on the fence, grinning and watching the laughing girl and whinnying horse, not knowing who was the most pleased with the other.

Later, Liza asked how to care for the saddle. Hiram frowned. "I don't think Alex meant for you to do that, too."

"Oh, yes," Liza insisted, her violet eyes sparkling. "He said everything."

Hiram grinned crookedly, thinking, *Yep, this little gal has got grit.* "Tomorrow, then," he grunted.

The next night, Bright Star brought a buffalo skin to Liza. Between motions and sketchings, Liza made the Indian woman understand what she wanted. After they had measured Liza, the Indian woman cut the skin with a wicked-looking knife, using it with amazing skill and deft expertise. But, after the skirt was cut out, a large amount of skin still remained. Motioning to Bright Star, Liza drew a quick sketch of a vest she had seen in St. Joe. The old woman nodded enthusiastically, took the pencil from her and added a fringe. Liza clapped her hands in delight. "Yes, Bright Star, that will be perfect."

Again, a good deal of skin was left. Liza stared at it, perplexed, and then grinned. "Pants? Andy?" Bright Star smiled and rushed from the room, returning with an old pair of Andy's pants to use for a pattern.

After they had demolished the buffalo skin, Bright Star sat down and began sewing. She used a heavy, hooklike instrument, puncturing the skin and pulling through the sinew used as thread. Liza saw that it was going to be a painstaking task. After a while, Liza gently took the skirt from Bright Star and started sewing herself. It was even harder than it looked. Patiently, the old woman guided Liza's hands, showing her the proper angle to hold her wrist to get the most momentum. The Indian watched and instructed until she was sure Liza knew what she was doing, and then she left the room.

Liza sighed deeply. She hoped that she hadn't hurt

Bright Star's feelings, but she wouldn't feel right sitting around doing nothing while the old woman labored over her skirt. But at the rate she was going, she wouldn't be finished with it until next spring.

Liza looked up, surprised when Bright Star returned carrying another hook. Taking the skirt from her, Bright Star handed her the vest instead. Then she sat across from her and started sewing on the skirt. Liza smiled gratefully, thinking ruefully that she might be able to finish the vest by the time Bright Star finished the skirt.

They were still sewing when Andy entered the room, looking disappointed when he saw they were already occupied. Quickly, Liza whisked the small pants away and hid them under a pillow. Gesturing to the bed, Liza said, "Come on, Andy. I can tell stories and sew at the same time." Liza didn't miss Bright Star's grin.

Liza looked down at her sewing and laughed, thinking that if anyone had told her a year ago she would be sitting with an Indian, sewing on a buffalo skin, she would have told them they were crazy. Now, if only Alex were here, her life would be perfect, she thought wistfully.

Although, Liza's days were filled with new and exciting tasks, her nights were sheer torture. The first night after Alex's departure, she donned her nightgown and climbed into bed, but the gown that had felt so comfortable only a few weeks ago seemed to choke her, the voluminous skirt wrapping around her legs and making her feel trapped. Irritably, she removed it, throwing it across the room, muttering, "Alex was right. It *is* a tent."

Then, lying nude beneath the sheets, she tossed and turned, her nakedness serving to remind her of her nights in Alex's arms. He had awakened a deep need in her and then left her to deal with longings that couldn't be satisfied. "Damn you, Alex!" she cursed in frustration, hitting the pillow viciously, twisting and turning until she finally fell into an exhausted sleep.

On the fifth night, before going to bed, Liza took a hot bath and forced herself to drink a warm glass of milk, determined to rid herself of her nagging thoughts. For a change, she fell asleep quickly, only to be tormented by her dreams. Alex's hands were caressing her, his lips seeking the sensitive softness of her breasts. She moaned, pulling his head closer, muttering his name in her sleep, and felt the promising brush of his erection against her thigh.

Slowly, she emerged from her dream into reality. Someone *was* in bed with her. A man! Terrified, Liza began to fight and claw, kicking out with a vengeance. The man struggled back and ground out hoarsely, "My God, Liza. What in the hell is wrong with you?"

Liza froze, still trembling all over from her fright. "Alex?" she asked unbelievingly, blinking in the dark, straining to see.

The bed dipped, a match flared and the lamp was lit. Alex stood by the bed glaring down at her, a vicious claw mark down his face and chest.

Seeing the ugly scratch, Liza stammered, "I'm . . . I'm sorry. I . . . I didn't know it was you."

"Well, what other man comes crawling into your bed at night?" he demanded. "Hell, you seemed willing enough at first. You even said my name."

Liza blushed. "I thought it was a dream."

Alex looked at her, disbelieving at first, then he grinned. "So you've been plagued by those devils, too?"

Lying beside her, he pulled her back into his arms. "Here I galloped half the night just to spend a few hours with you, and you damn near claw me to death." He shook his head ruefully. "That's the last time I'll crawl into bed with you without announcing myself first. I'd sooner try to bed a wildcat."

"But I wasn't expecting you back so soon. You said you would be gone at least a week or ten days," she pointed out.

Alex grinned. "It will be. This is just a visit."

"A visit?" Liza asked in astonishment.

"Yes." His voice was gruff as he growled, "Dammit, Liza! What are you, a witch or something? You're tormenting me. I can't think of anything but you, how desirable you are. It's embarrassing to walk around with a bulge in my pants, having the men snickering around behind my back. Besides, it's damned uncomfortable riding a horse in that condition."

Liza tried to suppress her giggle, but was unsuccessful.

"It's not funny!" Alex retorted. "The days were bad enough, but the nights were sheer hell." He groaned in remembrance of his agony. "I finally decided if I wasn't going to get any sleep anyway, I might as well make the most of it."

Alex grinned, thinking to himself that it had not

212

really been his idea at all. Manuel, who had had the misfortune of being bedded down beside him, had finally had enough of Alex's twisting, turning and dark muttering. "Why don't you go to her, compadre?" he had suggested in his soft, Mexican accent. "Maybe that way, we can all get some sleep tonight, for a change."

"So here I am," Alex said, shrugging his shoulders.

"You mean you have to go back in the morning?"

"Yes, before daylight," Alex answered, rolling to his side so that he could look down at her face.

For the first time Liza noticed that his hair was wet. Fingering the glistening dark strands, she asked, "You've been to the pool?"

Alex grinned. "Sweetheart, if you could have smelled me, you sure wouldn't have let me in your bed."

Liza smiled, asking in a teasing voice, "Do you think it's worth it? Riding all that way?"

Alex's gaze grew warm, his look devouring. "Oh, it's worth it." Burying his head in the crook of her neck, he nibbled her throat, and as he pulled her into an almost painful embrace, he moaned, his voice agonized, "Oh, God, Liza, I need you."

Liza gloried in her sense of power. If he had uncovered deep-seated needs in her, she had done the same for him. For the first time since she had agreed to their arrangement, she had no doubts, no reservations. "I'm here, my darling," she whispered, her hands caressing the hard muscles on his back, her lips trailing tender kisses over his shoulder.

Alex lifted his head, an astonished expression on

213

his face, his heart pounding with sheer joy. This was the first time she had kissed him of her own volition. He had always had to arouse her passion first, before she would return his kisses and caresses. He wondered briefly what had caused this spontaneous loving, but he was too excited to ponder the reason for long.

His mouth closed over hers in a long, demanding kiss, his tongue plundering, her own answering ardently, until they were both trembling with intense excitement.

Pulling his mouth from hers, he dropped fiery kisses over her eyes and face, down her silky throat, to her breasts, where he dallied, his tongue slowly savoring one rosy nipple, then the other. His hands fondled and tantalized as his tongue traced her ribs down to her abdomen to circle and lightly explore her navel, darting and flickering. Raising himself above her, he positioned himself between her legs, stroking her inner thighs, his hot tongue tracing intricate patterns over her abdomen, lower and lower.

Liza was writhing in ecstasy, her body on fire where his lips had been, her blood coursing hotly through her veins. But when his mouth touched the nest of curls between her legs, she froze, shocked and frightened. "Alex, no!" she gasped.

Alex raised his head, his grey eyes smoldering with passion. "I love you, Liza," he said, his voice soft and thick with emotion. "Let me show you how much."

Holding her thighs apart, he buried his head in her softness, his tongue flicking, teasing, stroking, exploring her erotically. Liza felt a consuming

214

warmth spread over her as her legs parted with a will of their own. Slipping his hands under her buttocks, Alex lifted her to his hot, seeking, devouring mouth, wildly excited by her scent and the taste of her honeyed sweetness. Grasping the damp curls on his head, Liza moaned, thrashing her head from side to side as wave after wave of exquisite pleasure washed over her.

Then, as she was begging for release, her muscles taut with expectation, every nerve ending of her body on fire, he entered her, and Liza felt that plunge like a bolt of lightning. Alex gasped in his own reaction to their sudden, fiery union, then filled her completely, deeply, as he sighed in her ear, "Oh, God, Liza, you feel so good . . . so warm . . . so tight."

He began his strokes, skillful and sensual thrusts that searched and caressed every inch of her, increasing in rhythm until it seemed he was trying to crawl inside her. His hands and mouth were everywhere, fondling and arousing, as their bodies rocked in a primitive frenzy as old as time itself. Time and time again, he brought her to that trembling brink, only to retreat, leaving Liza gasping, clutching, pleading, until in a series of deep, powerful thrusts, he lifted her to the height of passion. Their cries of ecstasy intermingled as they were hurled into oblivion, spinning, careening wildly. Soaring, their souls touched, danced, kissed, entwined and then returned to their bodies as they floated back to earth.

Alex collapsed over her, their bodies still joined, their sweat mingling, and their breaths rasping in one another's ears. As their trembling subsided, he whispered in her ear, "My love. My sweet, sweet love."

He started to roll from her, but Liza gasped, "No!" and locked her knees tightly around his slim hips. Alex smiled and, holding her hips tightly against his, rolled to his side, bringing her with him, still inside her.

Liza caressed his back, her tongue lazily licking his shoulder. "You taste salty," she muttered sleepily.

"And you taste like honey," he answered quietly.

Liza blushed at his meaning and then drifted off to sleep, wrapped in his strong arms and the safe, warm cocoon of his love.

Alex lay awake, marveling at the depth of emotions Liza aroused in him. He had never made love to a woman with his mouth, had never wanted to. Women had explored him in such a fashion, had even hinted that he reciprocate, but he had always refused—until Liza. It was as if he wanted to explore and possess her in every possible way, and it seemed that his hunger for her was never totally satisfied.

Feeling himself hardening and growing inside her, Alex smiled ruefully. Nibbling softly on her ear, he whispered, "Wake up, sweetheart. There'll be no sleeping tonight."

A week later, Liza paced the room impatiently, waiting for Andy to appear for his lessons. When the little boy sheepishly stuck his head around the corner of the door, she gasped at the purple stain on his mouth.

"What have you been eating?" she questioned, alarmed.

"Berries." Andy grinned, holding out his hand, asking, "Do you want one?"

"Are you sure they're safe to eat?" Liza peered down at the purple mess in his hand.

"Yes, Bright Star said so. Take one," the boy offered, glad for the excuse to take her mind off his tardiness.

Liza looked down at the mass of crushed berries, finding it hard to find one still reasonably intact. Finally, taking one less demolished than the others, she popped it into her mouth. Why, it tasted like a blackberry, she thought. Sudden memories of her mother's blackberry pies and blackberry jam washed over her. An intense desire for something sweet filled her, for although Hiram cooked delicious, nutritious meals, he never baked.

"Where did you find them?"

"Down by the pool," the boy answered.

Liza frowned. She hadn't noticed any berry bushes there. "Show me," she requested, taking the little boy's hand.

"But what about lessons?" Andy asked, surprised.

"That can wait until tomorrow. Today, we'll have a nature lesson," Liza said, determined she would beg and plead until Hiram agreed to bake her a pie.

Grabbing a bucket by the back steps, Liza followed Andy to the pool. When they reached their destination, she looked around her. "I don't see any berry bushes," she said, disappointed.

"Over here," Andy said, walking away from the pool downstream to where several bushes grew tangled in the underbrush.

The berries were scarce, obviously the last of the season. As Liza moved toward the bushes, Andy stopped her. "Better take a stick."

"Why?"

Andy's brown eyes twinkled. "Snakes."

Liza shuddered, but even the thought of the repulsive reptiles couldn't discourage her from her purpose. After they had shaken the bushes carefully to scare away any snakes, Liza and Andy picked until the branches were bare. The bucket was only half-full.

"Do you know where there are any more?" Liza asked.

"Why do you want so many?" the little boy asked, bored with picking.

"To make pies."

"What's pie?" Andy asked.

Liza stared at him in disbelief. "You've never eaten pie?"

Andy shook his blond head.

"Why, it's delicious. Much better than just the berries by themselves, more like candy. But we need more berries than this," Liza said, looking around.

The promise of something that tasted like candy restored Andy's enthusiasm. He ran off, calling over his shoulder, "This way."

After they had picked a full bucket of berries, Liza and Andy trudged back to the house and into the kitchen, setting the bucket on the table.

"What do you want with all those berries?" Hiram asked gruffly, eyeing the bucket with distaste.

Liza felt her courage ebbing. Then, smiling her prettiest and most beguiling smile, she answered, "I thought you might like them for pies."

"Can't make pie," Hiram grunted. "Can't do no baking, just plain old cooking."

Liza's heart fell. She glanced down at Andy, whose disappointment mirrored her own. Seeing his look

218

renewed her resolve. "Oh, I'm afraid I promised Andy, and he'll be so disappointed. I used to help my mother bake pies sometimes. If I helped you, do you think we could figure it out together?"

Hiram glared at her suspiciously and then looked into Andy's big brown eyes watching him earnestly. He hesitated, then limped over to the bucket of berries. Bending over them, he muttered in disgust, "Looks mostly like hulls to me." He looked up to see two pair of pleading eyes, and his heart melted.

"Well, all right," he said, his voice overly gruff to hide his feelings. "Tell me what you need, and we'll see what we can do. Andy, you sit there at the table and keep out of the way."

A flurry of activity occurred in the kitchen. Several times, Liza pretended confusion and asked Hiram's opinion, hoping to soothe his ruffled feathers. When they were through, three beautifully-browned pies graced the table, their juices still bubbling beneath the flaky crusts.

That night, Alex came in for supper after everyone else had eaten. Liza kept him company while he ate, sipping a cup of tea. When Hiram proudly slid a piece of blackberry pie before him, Alex looked at it in surprise. He looked up at the old man. "I didn't know you could bake pie."

"Can't," Hiram answered, then grinned. "Liza baked it."

It was Liza's turn to be surprised. Instead of sounding resentful, as she had expected, Hiram had sounded almost proud of her.

Alex ate the pie greedily, as though he, too, had been craving sweets. When he finished, he looked at Liza with a new admiration. "I didn't know you

219

could cook, too."

Liza smiled nervously, glancing quickly at Hiram to see his reaction. Too much praise might not be a good thing. "Well, actually, I can't cook real meals like Hiram can. My mother always did that. I only helped her with the baking."

Alex cocked one dark eyebrow, giving her a quizzical look. Somehow, he knew she was lying. What puzzled him was why?

Hiram limped happily about his domain, chattering. "You should have seen Andy gobbling it up." He guffawed. "Had more on the outside than the inside. And Bright Star made a pig of herself. Ate two pieces," he said in a disapproving voice.

Alex chuckled. "I'm not surprised. Indians are notorious for having a sweet tooth."

Liza laughed, remembering her horror as she had watched the Indian woman spoon teaspoon after teaspoon of sugar into her tea.

Alex was still looking at Liza, his expression thoughtful. Without taking his eyes off her, he said, "Hiram, what ever happened to that honey Tanaźin brought us a couple of months ago?"

"It's up in the cabinet," Hiram answered. "Why?"

Alex leaned toward Liza, his eyes boring into hers as if defying her to lie to him. "Can you bake bread? I mean honest-to-God white bread."

Liza squirmed and glanced over at Hiram. The old man was standing with a glazed look in his eyes. "White bread and honey," he muttered wistfully. "I ain't had that since I was a boy."

Relieved that she wouldn't have to lie, she smiled and answered, "I suppose so."

"Will you bake some for us sometime?" Alex asked.

Liza looked into his warm, grey eyes and smiled. Then, directing her gaze to Hiram, she answered, "If Hiram will help me."

The old man bristled with self-importance. "You just tell me what you need and I'll get it for you."

Alex suppressed a laugh. "Come," he said, rising from the table and leading Liza from the kitchen toward the porch. Stopping before the door, he dropped a light shawl over her shoulders.

It had become a habit for Liza to join Alex on the porch every evening while he smoked. Leaning against one of the posts, Alex pulled her into his arms and kissed her lightly on the temple. "That pie was the best thing I've ever tasted," he said. He nibbled her throat. "Next to you, that is."

Alex lifted her head and looked at her closely. "You lied in there. Why?"

Liza hesitated.

"Come on, Liza," Alex commanded gently. "What's all this business about not knowing how to cook?"

"It's simple," Liza answered. "I didn't want to upset Hiram."

Alex frowned, then nodded. "Yes, I know what you mean. He's so possessive about that kitchen. Always was." He chuckled. "I remember when Bright Star first came and she tried to help him with the cooking. You never heard such a row in your life."

Liza laughed.

Thoughtfully, Alex said, "I can't figure it out. Do you think he feels threatened in some way?"

"I'm sure he does."

"But why?" Alex asked irritably. "Certainly, he can't think he'd lose his job. To be honest, I'd rather have him working in the barn full time. He's so good with the animals. I could always hire another cook."

"No, Alex! Don't do that!"

"Why not? He's getting too old to hold down both jobs. Sometimes it makes me feel guilty."

"Oh, Alex," Liza said, "you don't understand. Cooking isn't just a job to Hiram. It's much more than that. Feeding someone is a means of caring for them. It's a way of showing love. I think that's why Hiram is so protective of it. It's the only way he can show you and Andy how much he loves you. Probably the only way he feels comfortable with. Whatever you do, don't take it away from him. That would be like rejecting him and his love. And don't ever forget how important it is to him."

Alex looked down at her totally dumbfounded. Tightening his arms around her, he said, "Now, why didn't I think of that?"

Liza laughed. "Because you're a man, that's why."

A dark eyebrow arched. "Oh? And what does that have to do with it?"

"A man tries to reason everything out. He thinks with his head, and love can't be reasoned. It has to come from the heart. That's why, sometimes, a woman can see things more clearly than a man. She uses her instincts and her heart to guide her."

Alex gazed at her, perplexed. At times, she was an enigma to him, a puzzling mixture of child and woman. One minute, she was innocent and shy, taking childish pleasure in small, inconsequential things. Then the next minute, he would catch a tantalizing glimpse of the woman beneath, warm, compassionate, understanding.

"Alex," Liza said, breaking into his musing. "Where did Hiram come from?"

"I don't know. Would you believe, I've known him all these years, and yet I have no idea of where he came from or how he came to be in this godforsaken country. I don't even know his last name."

Liza looked at him in disbelief.

"It's true. I've tried to find out, but he always evades my questions. I know he's been out here for a long time. He's spent time as a trapper and a miner. He even scouted for some of the wagon trains before his accident. That I know from his stories. But why he's here I don't know, although I suspect, like most people out here, he ran from something."

"Why do you think that?" Liza asked.

"Liza, people who are contented and happy where they are don't come to this country. It's too raw, too desolate, too lonely. They come because they're trying to escape something, a tragic event in their lives, a situation they just can't live with, sometimes the law."

Liza gasped. "You don't think Hiram is running from the law?"

"No," Alex answered firmly. "That I'm sure of, but whatever it is, he's locked it deep inside him."

Liza sadly contemplated what Alex had told her. Her mind wandered to Manuel, the handsome Mexican who now shared Hiram's sleeping quarters and their meals. "And Manuel?" she asked curiously.

"It was a long time before I found out his story," Alex answered, fumbling in his pocket for a slim cigar and then lighting it. "You learn not to ask too many questions out here, but lying side by side at night under the stars has a way of making a man open up. I'd always wondered about him, too. He has an almost aristocratic air about him."

Liza nodded. She had noticed Manuel's refined gentlemanly manner and thought it strange. He was not at all like most of the men in this isolated territory.

Alex exhaled slowly, the smoke curling about them. "His father was a Spanish aristocrat of some sort, a don. He came by his ranch in Mexico by a Spanish land grant. It's a huge ranch, covering hundreds of square miles. He was a very wealthy and powerful man, but unfortunately, Manuel is not his legitimate son. Manuel's mother was an Indian house servant. The old don acknowledged Manuel as his bastard, and he was raised right along with his legitimate sons and given the same education and privileges—until the old don died. According to their code, bastards can't inherit. When his father died, Manuel could have stayed on as foreman for his half-brothers. He would have had a job for life. For some, that would have been enough, but not for Manuel. Apparently, he inherited the old don's pride, if not his money or holdings."

Alex continued, "He was a half-breed and a bastard to boot. He knew he could never overcome the prejudices of his own people, never be accepted for himself, so he moved on. It was Manuel who taught my father and myself cattle ranching. Before he came, we were just stumbling in the dark. He's still teaching me things."

"How long has he been here?" Liza asked, enthralled with the story.

Tossing the cigar away, he answered, "He came

224

while I was away at college. According to Hiram, he just wandered in one day and asked for a job. It didn't take my father long to recognize his skill and knowledge, or that he was a cut above the other drifters. He made him his foreman, and after my father died, I kept him on. He's invaluable to me."

"But it's so sad, so unfair," Liza said, misty-tyed. "It wasn't his fault."

"I know," Alex answered grimly. "It's always the innocent that suffer. He's one of the nicest people I know, and a damned good cattleman. But around here, he's respected, and strangely enough, accepted. Oh, sometimes, some of the ranch hands try to give him a little trouble, but don't let his gentle appearance fool you. He knows how to handle men, and he can be as tough as the rest of them."

"Manuel?" Liza asked incredulously. She couldn't imagine the soft-spoken, polite man handling an ugly bunch of ranch hands.

"Sweetheart, he's murder with that whip he carries. He doesn't even need a gun or knife." He shuddered slightly. "You won't catch me provoking that little Mexican."

"Maybe you shouldn't have told me, Alex. He might resent me knowing his past."

"No, I don't think so. Manuel seems genuinely fond of you. I don't think he'd mind." He pulled her closer to him. "Just so he doesn't get too fond of you. Don't think I don't know how charming he can be," he said gruffly.

"Don't you think you can trust me with your friends?" Liza teased, wiggling seductively against him.

Alex groaned in response. "Maybe, but the

question is, can I trust my friends with you?" He pulled her into a tight embrace, his mouth seeking hers in a fierce, possessive kiss. Cupping her chin and raising her head, his eyes devouring her, he said in a roughened voice, "That's just to remind you who you belong to."

Liza trembled, just a little frightened of his intense possessiveness. But then, she had to admit if any woman tried to take Alex from her, she would be just as fierce. Smiling provocatively, she moved closer to him in open invitation, and Alex sucked in his breath at the feel of her pressing against him. "It's getting cold out here. Let's go inside," she said in a low voice filled with promise.

Later, Liza awakened to find Alex gone from bed. Frowning, she slipped out and pulled on her dressing gown. She peered out the window, but could see no activity in the yard below her. Quietly, she walked across the room and down the stairs. A glow of light shone from under the kitchen door. She cracked the door and peeked into the room. Alex and Hiram sat at the kitchen table, each eating a large piece of her blackberry pie.

Silently, she shut the door and tiptoed down the hall. *Best-tasting thing next to me,* she thought. *Well, Mr. Cameron, don't think I didn't notice which one you had a second helping of.* She laughed to herself as she crept up the stairs.

Several days later, Liza was searching the kitchen cabinets for the tea cannister. Where could Hiram have put it? she wondered irritably, opening one door, then the other.

She had not been able to sleep, and although Alex often came in late at night, she was apprehensive. An unusually violent thunderstorm was playing havoc outside, and her nerves were taut from worrying about Alex. She jumped as a particularly loud clap of thunder shook the house.

Hearing the kitchen door slam behind her, she turned and saw Alex standing there, his hair plastered to his head from the rain, his coat dripping water to the floor, his boots caked with mud.

"Take off those muddy boots before you move one step!" Liza rebuked him, as a wave of relief washed over her.

Alex cocked one dark eyebrow. "Well, that's a hell of a way to greet me," he grumbled.

Liza looked at him. Raindrops glistened on his thick dark lashes. "Oh, Alex," she cried, "I didn't mean to speak so harshly. But I was worried about you. Where have you been?"

Alex grinned. "Come here, Liza. I want to show you something."

She walked to him, the skirt of her dressing gown rustling softly. Alex watched the sway of her hips appreciatively. Opening his coat slightly, he said, "Look what I found."

Liza peered into the open coat. A small black nose peeked out, and two inquisitive brown eyes stared at her. "A dog!" Liza said excitedly.

"Yep, he's a real dog. Not one of those tame coyotes that the Indians keep."

Taking the soft, furry animal from Alex, she held it before her. "Where did you find him?"

"Out on the prairie. Apparently, the little beggar strayed away from one of the wagon trains. No

227

telling how long he's been out there. Must be a pretty good hunter though, or he would have been dead by now."

Alex struggled with his muddy boots and removed his coat. Grabbing a towel hanging on a rack by the door, he began drying his face and hair. "Is there any coffee left?"

"I think so. Do you want something to eat?"

"No, just something to take the chill out of my bones."

Alex walked to the stove, poured a cup of the steaming brew from the pot sitting at the back of it, and sat down at the table. Stretching his long legs before him, he relaxed, watching Liza and the dog.

She stood with the little black and white, shaggy animal cuddled in her arms, the dog licking her face and neck avidly. "Watch it, boy," Alex growled with mock ferocity. "That's my territory you're infringing on now."

Liza laughed. "He's adorable, Alex. Should we wake up Andy?"

"My God, no!" Alex answered, bolting up to a sitting position. "I don't want to spend the rest of the night listening to an excited boy and a barking dog. He can see him in the morning."

The little dog gnawed on one of Liza's fingers. "Do you think he's hungry?"

Alex chuckled. "He shouldn't be. That's all the little beggar has done since we picked him up. Eat. He looks like he's going to pop a gut any minute."

Liza glanced down at the dog's distended abdomen and laughed.

Setting the cup down and pushing himself from the table, Alex rose. "Come on, Liza, let's go to bed. I want to get out of these wet clothes."

"What about the dog?"

"He can sleep here in the kitchen. It's nice and warm here. It's a damn sight better than what he's been used to."

Liza carried the dog to the fireplace and laid him down before it, petting him until he settled down.

As Alex and Liza walked across the room, the dog whined plaintively. Turning back to look at him, Liza said, "Oh, Alex, look at him. He looks so pitiful."

Alex laughed. "Don't let him fool you, Liza. Why do you think I call him little beggar?"

"But he'll be lonesome and frightened here all by himself," Liza objected.

"Hell, Liza," Alex replied irritably, "he's been out on that prairie by himself for months."

"I know, but this place is strange to him. Can't we take him to our room for tonight? He can sleep at the foot of the bed, and then tomorrow night, he can sleep with Andy."

Alex frowned.

"Please?" Liza begged.

Looking into a pair of pleading, violet eyes, Alex melted. "All right," he agreed reluctantly, "get the little beggar and let's go before I catch pneumonia."

While Alex was undressing, Liza pulled a small rug to the foot of the bed and laid the dog on it. Kneeling on the floor, she patted and crooned softly until the little animal fell asleep.

A pair of muscular arms encircled her waist as Alex pulled her up and brought her back against his hard body. His hand slid under her dressing robe and sensuously kneaded her abdomen as he buried his head in the crook of her neck, nibbling at the soft skin there.

Liza heard a low, warning growl and then . . .

"Damn!" Alex swore viciously, pushing Liza away. She turned to see him trying to shake off the little dog, which clung with fierce tenacity to his leg.

Quickly, Liza bent and pulled the animal from Alex's ankle.

"That little bastard bit me!" Alex shouted, giving the dog a murderous look.

Liza held the excited dog protectively in her arms. "Oh, Alex, he was only trying to protect me," Liza said, her voice pleading. "He thought you were going to hurt me."

"Where in the hell would he get a stupid idea like that?" Alex demanded.

"Oh, Alex, calm down. He's just a little dog. Here, put your arms around me." She stepped closer. "Once he sees that it's all right with me, he won't bother you anymore."

Reluctantly, shooting the dog another heated glare, Alex slipped his arms lightly around Liza. The dog looked up between them, one eye covered by a floppy ear, and wagged his tail.

"See?" Liza said in amusement.

Alex gave the dog a wary glance. "All right, but if that little bastard bites me again, I'll kill him." Tentatively, he bent his head and kissed Liza lightly on the lips, his eyes never leaving the dog.

"See? It's all right now," Liza said. Taking the dog back to the rug, she laid him down and walked to her side of the bed. Slipping off her robe, she crawled under the covers.

For several minutes, Alex stood glaring hotly down at the sleeping dog. Then he turned and walked to his side of the bed. Bending down to blow out the lamp, he hesitated, gave the dog one more suspicious glance, and then extinguished the lamp. Silently, he crawled in next to Liza.

Liza waited for Alex to begin his overtures to lovemaking. When he made no move toward her, she rolled on her side and lifted herself on one elbow to look at him. Alex lay on his back, his head pillowed on his folded arms, staring at the ceiling. Puzzled by his odd behavior, Liza moved closer to him, her thigh lightly brushing his groin. She felt his whole body tense.

"Don't do that, Liza," he ground out between clenched teeth.

Leaning over him to get a better look at his face, the tip of her breast trailed across his hard chest. Alex could not suppress the low groan that escaped his lips.

"Don't you want to make love to me?" Liza asked.

"Hell, yes!" Alex spat, but he continued to lay rigid, staring at the ceiling.

Liza frowned. "Then what's wrong?"

Alex gave a short, harsh laugh, but didn't change his position. "Well, I've been laying here thinking. If that little bastard gets that upset when I just kiss you, then what in the hell is he going to do when we really get going?" He shook his head. "Somehow, I don't relish the idea of an attack from the rear."

Liza giggled, rolled over and slipped from the bed. Moving across the room, she picked up the sleeping dog and carried him out, laying him down in the hallway outside their bedroom door.

Lying propped on one arm, Alex watched as she closed the door behind her and walked back to the bed. A jagged flash of lightning momentarily illuminated the room, and Alex got a brief, tantalizing glimpse of her lovely, naked body.

Stopping to stand by the bed beside Alex, Liza asked, "Is that better?"

"Hell, yes," Alex groaned as he placed his arm around her waist, pulling her down and rolling her beneath him.

The next morning, Liza slept late. She awakened slowly and stretched languidly, smiling to herself as she savored the memory of Alex's fiery lovemaking the night before. It was some time before she forced herself out of bed, dressed and descended the stairs.

Even before she opened the kitchen door, she heard Andy laughing and the frenzied barking of the dog. When the little boy saw her, he ran to her and excitedly pulled her into the room. "Look, Liza. Look what I've got. A dog!"

Liza smiled. "Yes, I know. I saw him last night. Do you like him?"

"Oh, yes!" Andy exclaimed, his brown eyes bright with happiness. "And he's smart, too," he added proudly. "Watch." He threw a small stick he was holding, and the little dog bounced after it.

"Here, doggie! Here, doggie!" Andy called as the dog carried the stick back to him and dropped it at his feet.

"What are you going to name him?" Liza asked.

Andy looked up at her, a puzzled look on his face. "You can't just call him doggie. You'll have to give him a name."

Andy frowned and looked down at the dog, perplexed. For a moment, he studied the animal, and then a smile crossed his face. He looked back up at Liza, his eyes sparkling, and said, "Little bastard."

Liza gasped.

Seeing her shocked look, Andy said defensively, "Well, that's what Uncle Alex calls him."

Liza fought hard to suppress a giggle. "I know," she said. Then, bending down, her arm around the boy's shoulders, she said, "But just between us, I don't think that's a very pretty name."

Andy frowned. "You don't?"

"No, I don't. Besides, a dog should have a short name. One that's easy for him to remember and for you to call him," Liza pointed out.

The small boy's brow furrowed as he looked down at the dog, which sat watching them avidly, his head cocked to one side, his tail wagging furiously. Andy lifted his head and said tentatively, "Happy?"

Relief washed over Liza. "Oh, I think that's a wonderful name!"

"You do?" Andy asked, surprised.

"Oh, yes! If I were a dog, I'd love to be called Happy."

Andy grinned broadly. He turned and ran from the room, calling over his shoulder, "Here, Happy! Here, Happy! Come on, boy!"

Liza watched as the door slammed behind the little boy and the dog. She began to giggle helplessly, muttering, "Little bastard, indeed."

Chapter 11

Liza sighed in contentment as she watched Alex lighting the fire in the big fireplace a few days later. The days were pleasantly cool now, but the nights were decidedly chilly, even in the house. This was the first fire in the parlor this year, and it was something of an occasion, with Hiram and Manuel joining them for a companionable evening.

As the kindling caught and flared, their attention was distracted by the sound of horses rapidly approaching the house. Hiram limped to the window and peered out into the dark. "Injuns!" he gasped.

Alex and Manuel rushed to the hall for their guns as a loud, demanding knock sounded on the door. The two men looked at one another in surprise. Frowning, Alex walked to the door, cautiously opened it a crack and then, seeing who it was, threw it open.

Liza's breath caught in her throat. Tanaźin stood in the doorway. Naked, except for his breechclout and moccasins, his face and chest slashed with paint, the lamp from the hallway bathed him in a subdued light, giving him the appearance of a magnificent bronze statue. Except no statue had eyes like that— black, hot, glittering with hate. Liza shivered.

As Alex and Tanaźin talked in low tones, Liza glanced beyond them to the ranch yard and saw a band of warriors quietly approaching the house on their horses. Both the men and their horses were slashed with paint. No one had to tell Liza this was not a casual visit. This was a war party. She shivered again, an icy fear clutching her heart.

Alex turned as Tanaźin retreated and was swallowed by the inky darkness. Facing the three watching him closely, Alex said, "Three of Tanaźin's tribe, a woman and her two children, were murdered today by four white men. We're going after them." Turning to Manuel, he asked, "Will you saddle Thunder for me?"

After Manuel had left, Alex reached for his gunbelt laying on the hall table, and then walked into the parlor to the gun cabinet that stood in one corner. Hiram and Liza followed him.

"How did it happen?" Hiram questioned.

Alex glanced at Liza and then dropped his gaze to concentrate on loading his powder horn. "Apparently, the woman wandered away from the camp in search of berries. She had her papoose and seven-year-old daughter with her. The men caught her unawares, raped her and the child, and slit their throats. Then they bashed in the baby's head against a tree trunk."

Liza's stomach lurched; her knees suddenly felt weak.

"How do they know it was white men?" Hiram

asked. "Could have been other Injuns."

"Because they did a shoddy job on the woman's throat," Alex answered. "She lived just long enough to identify them and give a detailed description of what they looked like." He gave Hiram a hard look. "Besides, you know Indians wouldn't have killed them. They would have taken them as captives. And Indians don't rape children!"

Liza struggled to a chair, fighting the nausea rising in her throat. She watched silently as Alex strapped on his gunbelt and tied the holster laces to his thigh. For the first time, she fully realized his intent.

"You're going to kill them," she said hoarsely, a new terror coursing through her.

Alex ignored her, searching the drawer for his pouch of balls and patches, then reaching for a rifle in the cabinet.

A mixture of fear and indignation raced through her. "Alex, you can't! You can't set yourself up as judge and jury. Let the law take care of it," she pleaded.

"What law?" Alex spat angrily. "Are you talking about the territorial marshal at Fort Kearney? Even if he would do anything—which I doubt—by the time he got on their trail, it would be winter. He'd never track them down."

"The . . . the army," Liza sputtered.

"The army?" Alex laughed harshly. "Liza, the army is here to protect the white man from the Indian." His look was hard, his voice caustic as he said, "No one protects the Indian from the white man. They'll hang a man out here for stealing a

236

horse, but they won't do a damn thing to him if he kills an Indian. As far as they're concerned, an Indian is less than an animal. If justice is to be done, then the Indian must do it himself."

"Then let the Indians handle it!" Liza shrieked. "It's not your problem."

Alex looked at her with disgust. Silently, he turned and walked back into the hall.

"Alex!" Liza screamed to his back. "If you do this, you'll be no better than those men—a murderer!"

Alex whirled, his jaw set, his eyes glittering. "Then that's what I'll be," he snarled.

Their eyes locked, violet and grey, in a fierce, silent struggle. For the first time, Alex became aware of Liza's pale, frightened face. Before, everything had been blocked from his consciousness by his blind fury. *She'll never understand,* he thought, as a wave of regret washed over him.

His anger gone, he said quietly, "Liza, I'm sorry—but this is something I have to do." He shook his head sadly. "Not even you can stop me." Grabbing his coat in his free hand, he turned and rushed from the house.

Frantic, Liza ran after him, catching his arm, screaming, "No, Alex!"

Roughly, he shook her off, took Thunder's reins from Manuel and swiftly mounted. Without even glancing in her direction, he whirled the horse around and galloped off, the band of Indians closing behind him.

Liza turned to Manuel and Hiram, tears streaming down her face, her eyes pleading. "Stop him," she whimpered weakly.

Hiram shrugged, turned and limped into the house. Liza's eyes sought Manuel's, her look entreating, but his look was just as cold and hard as Alex's had been. "A man must do what he must," he stated firmly, and then he, too, turned and walked away.

Liza stood alone in the cold, dark night, sobbing.

The next few days and nights were an agony for her. Hiram and Manuel, ever loyal to Alex, avoided her, their eyes heavy with reproach.

The first day, Liza raged in silent anger and righteous indignation. But as the next day and night passed slowly, with no sign of Alex's return, Liza's heated anger turned to cold fear. It gnawed at her, her mind creating visions of Alex being hunted down for murder, or worse yet, lying dead somewhere, killed by the very men he stalked. By the end of the third evening, she was sick with worry. She buried her pride and sought out Manuel.

She found him in the parlor, reading a book. When she walked in, he looked at her coldly, his eyes full of disapproval. She trembled and then sobbed, "Oh, Manuel, I'm so frightened."

Manuel's eyes slowly warmed and filled with compassion as he looked at the delicate, alarmingly pale girl standing before him. Deep, dark circles underlay her eyes, testimony of her sleepless nights. He was fiercely loyal to Alex, but he was also genuinely fond of this girl. It wasn't her fault, either, he thought sadly. Alex and Liza were from two different worlds. How could she be expected to understand, having been brought up as she was in her own orderly, sheltered civilization?

"Of what are you frightened?" he questioned quietly.

"What if something's happened to Alex? What if he's lying injured somewhere? What if he's dead?" she asked, her voice agonized.

The swarthy-faced man smiled knowingly. So, he thought, her love won out after all. Rising to his feet, he led her to the couch as she sobbed against him. "Sssh, chiquita," he muttered in a soothing voice. "He is all right. He is a tough hombre, your Alex. We would not expect him back so soon."

Liza allowed herself the luxury of being comforted, her sobs now coming from relief. "You're sure?" she asked, her voice childlike in its entreaty.

"I'm sure," Manuel replied, smiling down at her.

Liza looked into warm, compassionate eyes. "I'm so confused," she confessed.

Manuel smiled down at her. *Dios!* she was a beautiful woman. He gently brushed a tear from her cheek. "I know. This is all strange to you. But remember, chiquita, this is not England. You must not be so critical of things you do not understand. We often do things here that might not seem right to others, but they are necessary. Your Alex does not go simply to kill, but to seek justice. He doesn't do it because he wants to, but because he *has* to."

"But it's still wrong," Liza countered.

"Why? Because those murderers were not tried and sentenced by a white man's court?" He shook his head sadly. "No, Alex was right. No white jury would condemn those men. The same would be true in my country. Indians do not have rights under our laws. Perhaps, someday it will be different, but I think it will be a long time coming." His eyes searched her face as he waited for his words to sink in. "So, you see, three innocent people were murdered,

239

and the white man's law does nothing. No, it is left up to the Indian to seek his own brand of justice."

"But Alex is white. If he kills those men, he's just as guilty of murder as they are under the law."

"Ah, yes, the law," Manuel said with a deep sigh. "Legally, Alex is guilty. But morally?" His look was intense. "There is a higher law than man's law, Liza. Laws are not always morally right. Alex is not the kind of man to stand by and do nothing while innocents are brutally murdered, just because the law is weak. He has a higher judge to answer to. Too often, men turn their backs to injustices and excuse themselves, thinking it is not their concern. That is the coward's way out, and Alex is not a coward."

Liza shook her head in confusion.

"Let God do the judging, Liza," he said. "He is the ultimate judge of us all."

Liza looked up and smiled, thinking that Manuel was so kind, so understanding and wise. "You remind me of my father."

"Dios!" Manuel cried in mock horror. "A beautiful, young woman sits next to me and tells me I remind her of her father. Come, chiquita, I am not that much older than you. Think of what you have done to my masculine ego," he teased.

Liza laughed, her fears awnd doubts now eased. As she rose, Manuel caught one hand gently. The expression on his face was deadly earnest. "Remember, Liza, what Alex does is not an easy thing for a man to do. He will need you more than ever when he returns."

Now it was Manuel's eyes that were entreating, and Liza smiled in understanding. "I hope, someday, I find a friend as good and true as you are to Alex.''

A flush rose on the handsome man's swarthy face. He quickly averted his eyes and shrugged casually. Not wishing to embarrass him further, Liza turned and left the room.

Much later that night, Liza returned to the parlor in search of a book. She was curled up in a chair reading when Alex walked into the room. A wave of immense relief swept over her. Then, examining him closer, she was shocked by his appearance. He was filthy; his face, under the three-day growth of beard, was ashen grey with fatigue.

Alex gave Liza a quick, furtive glance and wearily walked to the decanter of whiskey sitting on a table. His back to her, he poured a large drink and tossed it down. Liza watched in growing alarm as he rapidly downed three more. She had never seen Alex drink this way. Occasionally he would have a drink, and then only one.

Finally, he turned, facing her defiantly, reeling slightly. He seemed to be waiting for something, as if he was steeling himself for an attack. Knowing that he expected it to come from her, Liza's heart went out to him.

She rose, smiling gently, and as she approached him, a surprised expression came over his face, a wary look in his eyes. She took his hand and raised it to her face, rubbing it against her cheek, kissing the scraped, bloody knuckles.

Stunned, Alex stared at her in disbelief. He had expected a tirade, sharp words or accusations, but certainly not this.

''Come, you're exhausted,'' Liza said, leading him

upstairs to their bedroom, supporting him as he reeled and stumbled from the whiskey he had consumed. He passed out the minute his head hit the pillow.

Liza struggled to get off his muddy boots and his reeking socks. She rolled his heavy, limp body from side to side until she managed to remove his shirt. Breathing hard from her exertions, she glanced down at the filthy, blood-splattered pants and set her energies to the task, but no amount of tugging and pulling could get them past his hips. Finally, giving up, she pulled the pants back up and covered him with a blanket. Sliding in the bed beside him, she snuggled up to his unconscious body and lightly kissed his stubbled cheek. Hugging him to her fiercely, she fell asleep.

Alex was still sleeping soundly the next day when Hiram and Manuel ascended the stairs. Anxious to hear Alex's story, they wanted Liza to awaken him. She stood, barring the door, her arms crossed and her violet eyes unwavering. "No!" she refused adamantly.

"But he'll be mad if we let him sleep all day," Hiram argued. "He'll want to see how things are coming along here at the ranch."

"To hell with the damned ranch!" Liza retorted, giving both men a fierce, determined look.

Hiram stared at her, utterly shocked at her language. Manuel chuckled, thinking she looked like a lioness guarding her cub. "Come, Hiram," Manuel said. "She's right. He needs his rest."

The men turned and walked away, Hiram grumbling under his breath, as Liza returned to her charge.

Alex was still asleep that night when Liza retired. Not once during the day had he moved, even to change position. Laying beside him, Liza anxiously touched his brow, fearing he might be ill, but it was cool. He muttered something in his sleep and rolled to her, pulling her possessively into his arms.

Much later that night, Liza awakened to find Alex gone from the bed. Glancing about the room, she saw him standing at the window and staring out into the dark, silent night. Tossing back the covers, she rose and walked up behind him. If he heard her, he gave no sign. Slowly, Liza's arms crept about his waist, and she felt him tense. She hesitated for a moment, then snuggled against his back.

"What day is it?" Alex asked harshly, his body rigid in her arms.

"Tuesday. You slept straight through," Liza answered, feeling a growing fear. What was wrong with him? Liza wondered. He seemed so cold, so withdrawn. Gently, she kissed his shoulder.

Alex's control broke. He moaned, turned and viciously threw her on the bed, his kiss brutal, his hands cruel and hurting as he made violent, savage love to her. Liza lay beneath him, her heart thudding in fear, fighting back tears as she submitted meekly. *He's exorcising his demons*, she thought. *He doesn't even know what he's doing*, she told herself over and over. She felt only relief when he finally convulsed over her and collapsed, his head buried between her breasts.

"Oh, my God, Liza. I'm sorry. Forgive me," he muttered, his voice anguished.

"Sssh, darling," she soothed, her hands stroking his head, his neck, his shoulders. "Tell me about it," she said tenderly.

For a few moments, Alex was silent, and when he spoke there was a haunted quality about his voice. "We caught up with the murderers the next afternoon. They never knew what hit them. Not one of them even got a shot off. When the warriors found the Indian woman's necklace on one of the men, they were even more enraged. It had been a wedding present from her husband." He hesitated, shuddering in remembrance. "The Indians mutilated them—horribly—and then left them there to rot. I rode back with Tanaźin until he and his braves turned off for their camp. Then I circled back and buried them."

Alex raised his head and looked deeply into Liza's eyes. "Don't misunderstand my motives, Liza. It wasn't because I thought that they deserved to be buried. They were murderers. They deserved what they got. They had killed before, and there was no doubt in my mind that they would have again. I kept thinking that the next time it could have been you and Andy who were their victims. I only buried them to hide the evidence. I was afraid an army patrol might find them, and then there would be reprisals against the Indians. I felt there had been enough killing, so I dragged their bodies into a ravine and started a rock slide. They're buried under tons of rock. No one will ever find them."

Alex's eyes bored into hers as he waited for her reaction, fully expecting her to condemn him for hiding the massacre. Liza remembered Manuel's words, *He will need you more than ever when he returns*. Tenderly, she stroked his stubbled cheek.

"You did the right thing, Alex. There has been enough killing."

Relief washed over Alex. He buried his face in her thick hair, savoring its smell, and pulled her into a tight embrace.

Liza continued soothing him, her hands stroking his broad back. "But, Alex, if Tanaźin didn't need your help, why did he ask you to go with him?"

Alex pulled away from her and sat on the side of the bed. "For several reasons. In the first place, the man whose wife and children were murdered helped rescue you from the Kiowas. In a way, I was obligated. But I think Tanaźin had another reason for wanting me along. Some of his braves hate the white man, many times rightly so. They push for raids against them. But Tanaźin is a peaceful man at heart. He encourages his people to try to live in harmony with the whites. I think he felt if I was present, he could show his braves that all white men aren't evil, that some white men believe in simple decency and equal justice for the Indian. I was a symbol, Liza. He didn't need me to track down and punish those men, but he did need me to show his braves that decent white men don't condone such behavior, either."

Alex leaned over Liza, his eyes searching her face. "Now, there's something I don't understand. You were angry with me when I left, and the whole time I was gone, I despaired. I thought you would never understand. I was afraid I had ruined everything we had built between us. What happened to change your mind?"

Liza wondered if she should tell him of her talk

245

with Manuel, but then decided against it. She smiled and moved closer to him. "I had a lot of time to think things over, Alex. This time, I was the one who was wrong. I was too quick to criticize. No one knows all the answers. We all have to do what we think is right."

Alex pulled her tighter into his embrace. "I love you, sweetheart—but I don't think I deserve you."

Chapter 12

Liza sank in the tub, sighing deeply as the hot water soothed her tired, aching muscles. Alex would be furious with her if he knew that she had spent the whole day scrubbing the upstairs floor, she thought. Then, glancing down at her raw, reddened knees, she frowned and reached for a bottle of bath oil sitting on a stool next to the tub. As she poured a small amount of oil into the water, the smell of violets wafted through the air. She frowned, hoping that she had not added too much. The scent was awfully strong. Then, shrugging her shoulders, she slipped lower into the water.

While she soaked, resting her head against the rim of the tub, she gazed about the kitchen. Her eyes locked on the fireplace, watching the play of colors in the flames. There were a lot of things she didn't like about winter, but at least it got her out of that stuffy, crowded storeroom. Using the fire as an excuse, now she could bathe in here.

Languidly, she raised one shapely, slender leg and

began to lather it.

"Beautiful," a deep, masculine voice said.

Liza jumped in surprise, jerked her leg down and bolted upright in the tub. Then, seeing who the intruder was, she said breathlessly, "Oh, Alex, you scared me to death."

He stood in the doorway, his broad shoulder leaning against the doorjamb, his warm eyes roaming over her, seemingly devouring her.

Liza blushed and sank lower in the tub. "What are you doing here?"

"Watching you." He grinned and pushed himself away from the door, striding lazily across the room. Standing over her, his eyes rested on her breasts, barely covered by the water. Liza shot him a hot look and covered the soft mounds with her arms.

Alex chuckled. "Do you need any help?"

"No!" Liza spat, resenting his intrusion and remembering all too well what had happened the last time Alex had helped her bathe.

Alex bent, and Liza could feel the warmth of his breath on her nape. A finger stroked her shoulder seductively. "You're sure? I could wash your back for you."

Liza tingled all over. "That's not necessary!"

"Well, in that case . . ." Alex said, sitting on a chair and casually pulling off his boots and socks.

"What do you think you're doing?"

"Taking off my clothes," Alex answered, removing his shirt. He grinned wickedly. "It looks so good, I've decided to join you."

"You can't!" Liza cried, as she watched him slip off his belt.

"Why not?" he asked, maddeningly calm as he unbuttoned his pants.

"Because the tub is too small. You won't fit!" Liza screeched.

"I'll fit," Alex replied obstinately, as he skimmed the pants down over his slim hips and kicked them off. Grinning broadly, he climbed into the tub and laid down over her, his muscular thighs straddling hers.

Liza gasped as she felt his manhood brush against her thigh. Alex chuckled and raised her arms, fitting them around his shoulders. His own arms locked in a tight embrace around her as he nuzzled the crook of her neck.

"Mmmm," he mumbled, "you smell good. Like violets. I like that."

Liza was truly irritated. There was a time and a place for everything. A sudden, wicked gleam came to her eyes. "You're sure you like the smell of violets?"

"Mmmm, yes," he muttered against her ear, kissing it.

Grinning impishly, Liza cautiously reached for the bottel of oil sitting next to the tub. Slowly, careful not to disturb him, she poured a large amount of oil in one hand and then began rubbing it sensuously over his back.

"Oh, God, that feels good," Alex groaned.

Liza lowered her voice to a deliberately seductive timbre. "Do you like that, darling? You're sure you don't want me to stop?"

"Oh, God, no," Alex answered, mouthing her shoulder.

This time Liza poured the entire bottle into her hand. She continued stroking and massaging the oil into the firm skin of Alex's back and lower to the crest of his buttocks. Alex was writhing beneath her hands. Abruptly, she stopped.

"Don't stop," Alex pleaded huskily.

"I have to," Liza replied innocently. "There isn't any more oil left."

Slowly, Alex lifted his head. Frowning, he looked at her warily. "What oil?"

Showing him the bottle and smiling sweetly, Liza answered, "Why, the violet bath oil, of course."

A look of disbelief and then sheer horror came over Alex's face. "You put violet oil on me?"

Liza pouted slightly, her eyes wide. "But you said you liked it."

"Dammit!" Alex exploded. His exit was absolutely frantic. The tub tilted dangerously as Liza struggled to keep it from overturning.

"What in the hell made you do a stupid thing like that?" Alex asked, furiously drying himself.

Liza was a consummate actress. Tears welled in her eyes; her lips trembled. "But you said you liked it."

Jerking his clothes on, Alex looked down at her suspiciously. "Dammit, Liza. What do you think everyone will think when I walk around smelling like a French whore?"

Liza couldn't restrain herself any longer. The laughter bubbled up and escaped her lips in a sudden outburst.

Alex glared down at her, his look murderous. Picking up his boots and socks, he snarled, "You know, for a grown woman, you've got a perverse sense of humor."

Turning, he walked angrily from the room, slamming the door behind him so violently the windows rattled. Liza laughed all the harder, making the tub rock precariously, spilling water all over the floor.

When Alex came in for supper that evening, Hiram, Manuel, and Liza were already seated at the table. Liza knew that Alex was still angry with her by the hard set of his jaw and the icy glance he gave her. The strong, sickening-sweet smell of violets preceeded him as he approached the table. Both Hiram and Manuel glanced up with astonished looks on their faces.

Alex was very aware of their expressions. He had bathed twice in the pool and still hadn't been able to get rid of the odor, and undoubtedly, the two would guess just how he had gotten it.

Alex gave the two men a hard, challenging glare, daring either to make any comment. Manuel, ever the gentleman and never the fool, quickly averted his eyes and pretended sudden interest in his food.

But not Hiram. That banty little man wouldn't think of passing up the opportunity to bait Alex. Sniffing the air in an exaggerated manner, he leaned across the table. "You smell something, Manuel?"

Liza watched as the swarthy Mexican tried to hide the amusement in his eyes. "Si, compadre," he answered, a small muscle twitching at the corner of his mouth. "For a minute there, I thought I might have smelled gardenias, but I must have been mistaken."

"Damn right, you're mistaken," Hiram replied,

sniffing the air again. "That's violets you smell. Yep, that's violets."

Alex leaned forward, his big body menacing. "Shut up, you old fool! Even your nose is getting senile."

Liza and Manuel averted their eyes. Hiram just shrugged, and all three began eating. Throughout the meal, Alex pushed his food angrily around his plate, glaring at them.

As usual, Hiram was the first to finish his meal. Nonchalantly, he pushed his chair back from the table, picked up his plate and limped toward the sink. When he reached Alex's side, he stopped, bent down and whispered in a voice loud enough for Manuel and Liza to hear, "Next time try jasmine. Violets don't suit you."

An ominous, deadly silence filled the room. It only lasted a moment, but to Liza it seemed a lifetime. Then Hiram started cackling hilariously, hopping about, slapping his good leg with his hand. Liza watched as the muscles in Manuel's throat jerked and his body quivered. Finally, he threw his head back and roared with laughter. Liza's control shattered, and she started giggling.

Alex stared at the three of them, his look thunderous. But when they all three totally ignored him, his expression turned incredulous, and finally, helpless. A small grin appeared on his face, then widened, until Alex's baritone laughter joined the others.

Several days later, they had their first snow. Liza

wasn't even aware it had snowed during the night, until she went downstairs and found Alex sitting at the kitchen table and drinking a cup of coffee.

"What are you doing here at this time of the morning?" she asked.

Alex laughed. "Woman, would you push me out into the snow?"

"Snow?" Liza cried in an excited voice. "It snowed?"

Alex nodded, his eyes twinkling with amusement.

Running to the door, Liza threw it open and then gasped at the wondrous sight. A mantle of white covered the landscape. "Oh, Alex, it's beautiful! We never had this much snow back in England."

Alex had followed her to the door. "This is just a little snow. In fact, it will all probably melt off in a few days. Wait until the real snow comes. Sometimes, you can't even see the tops of the fences. Believe me, by the time winter is over, you'll be thoroughly sick of it."

Liza gazed at the peaceful, serene scene for a few moments, the snowscape reminding her of pictures she had seen. She started to step out the door, but Alex restrained her by placing his hand on her arm. "Where are you going?"

"I want to go out in it."

"Without a wrap?"

Liza laughed, closed the door and started for the stairs.

"I'll get your cloak for you," Alex said. "Where is it?"

"In the back of my wardrobe."

Alex strode to the stairs and then lithely took them

two at a time. Liza watched, fascinated as always with his graceful movements. She waited impatiently for him to return, but when he descended with her wrap hung over one arm, he was frowning.

"Is something wrong?"

He shot her a strange look. "This doesn't look very warm, Liza."

Liza glanced at the cloak she had searched so diligently for when she had shopped in St. Joe. "It was the heaviest wrap I could find."

"I don't doubt that, but when winter really sets in, it won't be warm enough," he replied, throwing the garment over her shoulders.

"I doubt that I'll be outside that much," Liza answered. She was too excited to have her day ruined with a discussion about the inadequacies of her wrap. It was the warmest she had, and it would just have to do. Pulling the hood over her head, she opened the door and ran out. Alex grabbed his coat and followed.

For a long while, she stood wide-eyed, looking first one way and then the other. She picked up a handful of the powdery snow and let it sift through her fingers. Realizing that it was still snowing slightly, she lifted her head, letting the soft flakes caress her face, laughing with sheer joy, the sound tinkling through the crystal air. Then she ran through the snow, laughing and cavorting like a child.

Alex stood watching her in amusement. He saw her pick up a handful of snow, but didn't realize her intent until it was too late. The snowball hit him full in the face.

"Why, you sneaky little minx," he said, laughing. "If it's a battle you want, then you've got one."

Throwing snowballs back and forth at each other, they ran across the yard, Liza's light laughter mixing with Alex's deep one. Finally, Alex caught her by the shoulder, and they fell into the snow.

Laughing, they rolled over and over, finally coming to rest with Liza lying beneath Alex. She looked up into his smoky grey eyes as his arms enfolded her. He bent his head and kissed her, his lips playing at hers, teasing, thrilling, sending shivers of pleasure through her. His lips brushed her temple, his words a soft whisper near her ear as he asked, "Have you ever wondered what it would be like to make love in the snow?"

Liza could feel the cold creeping through her clothing. She laughed, "I don't think that would be a good idea. What if you got frostbite and your thing fell off? Then where would we be?"

One dark eyebrow cocked. *"Thing?"* Alex asked incredulously. "My God, Liza, how degrading."

Liza colored and ducked her head.

Alex's warm hand cupped her chin as he lifted her face. A small smile played on his lips. "I assume you are referring to that part of my body that gives us so much pleasure. In view of that, can't you think of something better to call it than *thing?*"

"What?" Liza asked timidly.

Alex laughed, then finally sobered. "Liza, didn't your mother tell you anything?"

Liza's resentment of Alex's attitude turned to cold fury. Too many times he had laughed at her naivete. She shot to her feet and glared down at Alex, who was watching her warily, a frown on his face. "Of course my mother told me things!" she said hotly. "And I'm sure, if I had married, she would have told me more before the wedding. I know that you think I'm prudish and that my sex education is sadly lacking. But Alex, middle-class English mothers don't discuss the male anatomy with their daughters, and I, too, am the product of my culture. I'm trying to be more open about sex—but don't push me!"

Alex rose and pulled her into his arms, rocking her slightly. Dropping a tender kiss on her head, he said huskily, "I've been a damned fool."

Liza looked up at him. "I don't mind being teased a little, Alex, but don't ridicule me. I can't be something I'm not. I'm not sure I can ever change."

Alex felt a twisting pain in his chest, and his voice trembled slightly as he said, "I don't want you to change, Liza. I love your innocence and naivete. They're so much a part of you. You wouldn't be the woman I love without them. I didn't realize that you felt I was ridiculing you."

Liza hung her head. "I suppose I'm being too sensitive about it."

"No, I think I've been insensitive. I won't laugh at you anymore, but I can't promise I won't smile. I won't be laughing at you, Liza, only showing my pleasure. So many women here in the West are hardened, their language coarse and outspoken. But you're so fresh, so sweet, and you have no idea how much that pleases me. I don't want you to ever change."

Noticing the bluish tinge of her lips, he said, "We'd better get you inside."

As they walked toward the door, Liza limped slightly. Alex glanced down and saw that she was only wearing shoes. "Damn!" he swore, swinging her up into his arms and carrying her to the house.

Liza looked up at him, surprised by his sudden action.

"I just realized that you don't have any boots on," Alex explained. "My God, Liza, do you want to get frostbite?"

"I don't have any boots," Liza answered irritably. "You didn't say a thing about boots on your list."

"You're right. My mistake. But you can't trudge around here in the snow until we find you some. Frostbite is a very serious thing out here, Liza. Sometimes, when it's really cold, it only takes several minutes for it to happen."

Back at the house, Alex massaged her feet to return the circulation to them. "I never realized your feet were so small. What size do you wear?"

"Size four."

He frowned. "That might be a problem. I doubt if even Jake Webster has boots that small. We may have to figure out something else for this winter. Do you have warm gloves and a scarf?"

Liza nodded, feeling disappointed. She hoped that she wouldn't have to spend the rest of the winter in the house for lack of proper footwear.

Seeing her brooding look, Alex said, "Don't worry about it, sweetheart. I'll work on it."

Later that night, as Liza was preparing for bed, Alex walked to her wardrobe and pulled out the violet ball gown. "I found this today when I was looking for your cloak. That must have been some party for such a beautiful ball gown," he said, remembering the pang of jealousy he had felt when he had wondered who her escort had been.

That explained why he had looked at her so strangely when he came down the stairs, Liza thought. Guilt for having spent his money so foolishly arose in her. For a moment, she considered letting Alex make his own assumptions, but then decided against it. "I've never worn it, Alex, except to try it on. I bought it in St. Joe in a moment of weakness."

It was Alex's turn to feel guilty. He gazed at the plain, simple dress she wore and frowned. She deserved to wear beautiful clothes and to be taken to places where she could wear them. She had given him so much, and he had nothing to give her in return.

Liza misinterpreted the scowl on Alex's face. "I know it was a waste of money and that I'll never use it—"

"Not necessarily," Alex interjected, his look brightening. "Will you put it on for me?"

Liza remembered how revealing the gown was and blushed.

"Please?" Alex entreated.

Liza took off her dress and, taking the ball gown from him, slipped it on. Alex buttoned the long row of tiny buttons at the back and then turned her around to face him.

As Alex stood openly admiring her, Liza nervously fingered the bodice, trying to pull it up so it wouldn't show her cleavage. "It's too low. I don't know why I even bought it."

Alex's eyes were warm as he gently brushed her

258

hands away. "It's a beautiful gown for a beautiful woman." His gaze caressed her breasts. "All ball gowns are cut low like that. It's just that you have such high, perfect breasts, Liza. Most women have either too much, or too little."

A warmness washed over Liza. *He means it*, she thought. *He really thinks I'm beautiful.* Her embarrassment turned to pride, and she stood erect, causing her breasts to jut out even more. Alex gaped at the sight, then reluctantly tore his gaze away as she gaily pirouetted in front of him.

"Do you really like it?" Liza asked, thoroughly enjoying his warm, appreciative gaze.

Alex laughed derisively. Sitting on the bed, he pulled her onto his lap. "I should think that would be obvious, sweetheart. I'm practically panting. But how would you like to go to a ball, so you can wear it?"

Liza looked up at him to see if he was teasing, but his face was serious. "But where could we go to a ball out here?"

"Every New Year's Eve, they have a big dance at Fort Laramie for the officers and their guests. I have a friend who's stationed there. He and I went to college together. He's from the East and very socially conscious. He's always begging me to come to the dance, telling me that I'm burying myself out here. I'm sure we could stay with him and his wife."

"But that would be in the middle of the winter. Could we travel in weather like that?"

Alex frowned. "That could be a problem, but we don't usually have blizzards until later in January. A lot would depend upon the weather, but if it's halfway decent at all, I don't see why not."

"In the snow?" Liza asked in disbelief.

"Yes, we put runners on the wagons every winter to convert them to sleighs. As long as the snow is not too deep for the horses to get through, we can make it. Of course, we'd have to leave here early in the morning to get there by mid-afternoon and then stay over the next day. I'm sure we wouldn't want to make the trip back the next morning, after we had been up dancing half the night."

"Oh, Alex, that would be wonderful!" Liza cried. She jumped from his lap and twirled about the room.

Alex felt that strange twisting pain in his chest again as he watched her. He was anxious to show her off. Grinning, he thought, *Just wait until those snobbish officers see her. Their eyes will pop out. And their prim, pompous wives will turn green with envy.*

In her excitement, Liza danced to the window. She stopped and gazed out at the snow falling against the windowpane, her mind reeling with fantasies of the dance. She envisioned herself dressed in her beautiful ball gown as Alex escorted her to introduce her to his friends. She froze. And just how would he introduce her? she wondered. *May I introduce Liza. We're handfasted, until we can decide if we want to marry or not.* Oh, she could just imagine the scandal that would cause among Alex's socially conscious eastern friends.

Dejectedly, her head fell against the windowpane, and a single tear trickled down her cheek. Angrily, she brushed it away.

Alex had been sitting on the bed watching her. He

260

wondered at her sudden change of mood. Rising, he walked over to her and stood behind her. "Is something wrong?"

Liza kept her back to him deliberately. Absently, she drew patterns on the pane with her finger. "Maybe we'd better not go."

"And why not?" Alex demanded, turning her to face him.

Liza kept her head averted. She didn't want him to see the tears in her eyes. Miserable, she wished that he had never found the ball gown. She had been so happy and contented before this.

Alex shook her lightly. "I said why not?"

Angry at being forced into this confrontation, Liza raised her head and spat, "And just how will we explain my presence?"

So that was it, Alex thought grimly. "Why not tell them the truth? That you came to tutor Andy and be his governess? Our relationship is none of their business."

Doubt was written all over Liza's face.

Alex sighed. "Liza, everyone at Fort Laramie knew that I was looking for a governess. Jake picked you up at the stage depot, remember? And, although I like the man, he has a tendency to be a big blabbermouth. I'm sure everyone at the fort knows you're here. But no one knows about our relationship. Only Manuel and Hiram know that, and you know how close-mouthed they are. Just because we go to a dance together, doesn't mean people are going to guess we're sleeping together. As far as they're concerned, I'll just be bringing my nephew's governess out for some holiday cheer."

261

Liza's heart was thudding with excitement again. "Do you really think so?"

"I know it," Alex assured her.

The snow melted, just as Alex had predicted. But two weeks later, a heavier one fell, and Liza knew this time it would stay. Wistfully, she stared out of the window, wishing she could go out.

That afternoon, when Alex returned from the barn, he was carrying something in his hands. Grinning, he led Liza to a chair and sat her down. Kneeling before her, he shook out a pair of animal skins. "Your new boots," he announced.

Liza looked down in astonishment. They looked much like the moccasins he had made for her, except they were longer and laced up the front.

"This is what the Indian women wear," he said as he removed her shoes and slipped on the boots.

Liza smiled, both surprised and pleased. The boots were lined with thick fur.

"I had to wait until I got some pelts from Tanaźin to line them with," Alex continued. "How do they feel?"

Liza wiggled her toes. The soft fur tickled her foot. "Wonderful."

Alex smiled and removed the boots. "Wear thick socks under them, mine if you ddn't bring any with you. Or, if you prefer, you can even wear shoes. But don't go out in the snow without them."

Liza nodded, watching as Alex slipped on her shoes. Then she gasped as his hand slid up under her dress and caressed her thigh. Shocked, she jerked her leg away and looked about the kitchen guiltily. "Stop that, Alex," she admonished. Then she laughed. "Don't you ever think of anything else?"

Alex sat back on his heels, grinning up at her. "Not when I'm around you."

But when Hiram entered the kitchen a second later and looked at him quizzically, Alex shot to his feet. "Just trying on Liza's new boots," he explained to the old man, a sheepish expression on his face.

Trying to appear casual, Alex strode from the room. After the door had closed softly behind him, Hiram guffawed and muttered, "Yeah, and I bet that ain't all."

Liza blushed fiery red, only confirming his suspicions.

Several days later, Liza had reason to be thankful for her new boots. She was struggling with a log, trying to get it into the house, when Alex and Manuel rode up.

"What in the hell are you doing?" Alex demanded, scowling down at her.

Liza dropped the log, a wave of relief rushing through her. Running to him, she said, "Oh, Alex, I'm so glad you're back. Hiram slipped on a patch of ice this morning when he came out to get firewood and hurt his bad leg. Bright Star and I managed to get him back in the house, but he won't let either of us look at it."

"Damn!" Alex swore, swinging down from his horse.

"You go ahead with Liza," Manuel said to Alex.

"I'll take care of the horses, and then I'll bring in the firewood." Alex nodded grimly, and he and Liza rushed into the house.

Liza was standing at the kitchen sink peeling potatoes when Alex emerged from the old man's room. His face was ashen.

Seeing his look, Liza asked, "Is it broken?"

"No," he answered. Then he lowered his voice so that Hiram couldn't hear. "It's just that I never realized how badly mangled his leg was. But it is badly bruised, already turning black and blue."

"We need to pack it in snow," Liza said. "It should have been done right away, but he wouldn't let us touch him."

"Don't you think hot packs would be better?" Alex asked.

"No," Manuel interjected from the kitchen table. "Liza's right. That's how we treat horses. Cold the first twenty-four hours, then hot packs." Rising from the table, he said, "I'll get the snow."

"All right," Alex answered, "but I'm afraid we've got a fight on our hands."

And battle it was. It took both Alex and Manuel to control the old man. They had to literally man-handle him amongst curses from all three, before Hiram finally bowed to the two younger men's superior strength and let them pack his injured leg in snow.

For the next several days, Liza took over the cooking, and Manuel assumed Hiram's chores in the barn. Liza was seasoning the stew one evening when Alex strode from Hiram's room shaking his head.

"Is Hiram's leg worse?" Liza asked anxiously.

264

"No," Alex admitted, his look perplexed. "That's what I can't understand. The bruises have almost completely disappeared, and yet he insists he doesn't feel like getting up." He sat wearily down at the table. "I never thought I would see the day when Hiram would lie quietly in bed. It's not that I begrudge him the rest, but he seems so listless, so depressed. Frankly, I'm worried about him."

Liza had noticed Hiram's despondency also and was troubled by it. But she had attributed it to his injury. Suddenly, she realized what was bothering the old man. She and Manuel had been doing such a good job with his chores that he didn't feel needed anymore. Silently she berated herself for a fool. Well, she decided, there was nothing to be done, but try and undo the damage.

Intently, she spooned Bright Star's and Andy's stew into bowls and placed them on a tray. "Would you mind taking this up to Bright Star and Andy for me? Andy has a little cold, so they're eating upstairs tonight."

Alex nodded, rose from the table and took the tray, his mind still wrestling with the puzzle of Hiram's illness. Before he left the room, he glanced back at Liza. She was pouring seasoning into the stew. "What about Hiram's tray?" he asked.

Liza jumped in surprise, then turned, a strange, almost guilty look on her face. "Oh, I thought you had left," she muttered lamely. "I'll take Hiram's tray to him." Alex thought her behavior peculiar, but shrugged and left the room.

When he returned to the kitchen, Hiram was already eating. After Alex had sat down, Liza set his plate of stew before him. "You fed Hiram?" he asked her.

Liza nodded silently. Then Alex heard the old man coughing violently. Starting to push himself up from the table, Alex said, "Damn, I hope he's not going to get a cold, too."

Liza placed a hand on his shoulder, restraining him. "No, he's all right. Sit down and eat your stew."

Liza's voice sounded strained to his ears, but Alex shrugged and took a big bite of stew. He gasped at the fiery taste, his eyes watering. Quickly, he swallowed and then began to cough, feeling his insides burning from his mouth to his stomach. Grabbing a glass of water, he frantically gulped it down, hoping to quench the fire. When he could finally talk, he glared at Liza, asking angrily, "What in the hell did you do to the stew?"

"Tastes fine to me," Manuel commented, looking at Alex as if he had lost his mind.

"Of course it tastes fine to you!" Alex retorted. "Hell you damn Mexicans eat so much hot, spicy food you don't even have any taste buds left, to say nothing of your cast-iron stomachs!"

If Manuel resented Alex's remark, he gave no sign of it. Calmly, he continued eating his stew.

Alex glared at Liza, who seemed to be deliberately moving closer to Hiram's door, and frowned in puzzlement.

"I'm sorry, Alex," Liza apologized in an unusually loud voice. "I told you I don't know how to cook as well as Hiram, and seasoning food correctly is an art. You have to remember I only did a little baking at home. I never cooked real meals before. I didn't realize how difficult it was, or how much work was involved. Oh, I'll be so glad when Hiram finally gets well."

Suddenly, all of the pieces of the puzzle fit together for Alex. That explained Liza's peculiar behavior before, he thought. She had guessed what was bothering the old man, and the little minx had deliberately over-spiced the stew. He smiled warmly at her. Never had he loved her as much as he did at that moment.

Manuel watched them curiously. Suddenly, he, too, realized Liza's ploy. "I know what you mean, Liza," he said loudly. "That sorrel mare kicked me today when I was trying to treat her sore leg. I guess I don't have Hiram's gentle touch. I'll be glad when he's well, too."

"Well, we'll just have to struggle through until Hiram's well enough to resume his chores," Alex added.

The three conspirators grinned at one another. Then Alex looked down at his plate regretfully, thinking it was a damn shame to ruin perfectly good stew.

The next morning, Hiram was bustling about the kitchen. His limp was decidedly more pronounced than usual, but no one mentioned it, or suggested that he go back to bed.

Chapter 13

One evening in early December, when they were all sitting in the parlor enjoying the fire, Liza brought up the subject of Christmas. "What do you do for Christmas?" she asked the three men.

Alex shrugged. "Not much. We all exchange presents, and Hiram always fixes a big meal. Of course, we all look forward to that."

Liza smiled. Since Hiram's accident, both Alex and Manuel made a point of occasionally complimenting the old man's cooking. Apparently, Hiram felt more secure, for he often asked Liza to bake something. He didn't seem to mind her baking as long as he was acknowledged as the "real cook."

"Maybe you can bake a cake, Liza," Hiram offered on cue.

"If you'd like," Liza answered sweetly. "What kind do you suggest?" She was still careful to ask either his help or his opinion.

"We'll look in the pantry and see what we can find," Hiram answered, his voice filled with self-importance.

Liza glanced at Alex and saw him quickly hide a smile with his hand as he pretended sudden interest in the fire.

She sighed deeply. "In England, we always had a yule log and wassail for Christmas."

The others looked at her curiously. "What's wassail?" Hiram asked.

"It's a drink," Liza answered. "Actually it's hot apple cider, that's been spiced. It always tasted so good because it was so warming."

"And the yule log?" Alex asked.

"It's a special log," Liza replied. "The biggest log you can find, because it's supposed to last the entire Christmas season." She laughed. "But we seldom found a tree that big. Several days before Christmas, my father would go out and chop down the tree. Then, on Christmas eve, we'd all go out in the sleigh and drag the log home. After it was lit, we'd drink wassail and have a party."

Alex studied Liza, wondering if she was feeling homesick. He frowned as he remembered how much sorrow she had experienced in the last year. Too much for one so young, he thought. He smiled. "That doesn't sound hard. I don't see why we can't do that, too."

"Can we?" Liza asked, her eyes sparkling with excitement.

Alex gazed at her with amazement. That such a small thing could make her happy was incomprehensible to him. He smiled to himself, thinking that the child was back. That fascinating child-woman enigma.

"We used to have a piñata," Manuel said.

Alex lifted an eyebrow in surprise. He had never

heard Manuel mention anything of his past in front of the others. He laughed and said, "All right, Manuel. We give up. What's a piñata?"

Manuel smiled, and when the Mexican smiled, he was a devastatingly handsome man. Alex glanced at Liza, who was watching Manuel raptly, and felt a twinge of jealousy.

"A piñata is made of layered paper and glue," Manuel explained. "You shape it in any form you want, usually an animal or a bird, anything you choose. Then you paint it and fill it with candy and nuts. On Christmas day, the piñata is hung from a rafter, and all the children are blindfolded and given a big stick. Each child gets his turn, and the object is to hit the piñata hard enough to break it so that all the candy and nuts fall out." He laughed. "Then all the children scramble for the treats."

Liza laughed. "That sounds like fun. Andy would love that."

Manuel grinned. "Sometimes, the adults would participate, too."

"All right," Alex said decisively. "We'll have a piñata for Christmas, too. What do you need to make one?" he asked Manuel.

"Old paper, flour for the glue, paint and of course, the nuts and candy."

"Well, there are plenty of old newspapers in the attic," Alex commented. "And flour is no problem. But paint?" He frowned.

"I know!" Liza cried. "Bright Star can make some. The Indians are always painting things. Surely, she knows how."

"Of course," Manuel agreed. "I'll ask her."

For a few moments, everyone was quiet, lost in their own thoughts. Abruptly, the silence was broken. "We used to have a Christmas tree," Hiram said, his voice unusually soft and wistful.

If Alex had been surprised at Manuel's revelation, he was absolutely shocked by Hiram's. Never once, had he heard the old man mention anything of his past before he came west. He stared at him with disbelief.

"I've heard of them," Liza said. "That's a German custom, isn't it?"

Hiram flushed and grunted, "Yep."

"What kind of a tree is a Christmas tree?" Alex asked.

"Ain't a kind of tree," the old man grumbled. "Any old evergreen will do. It's how you decorate it that makes it a Christmas tree. We used to string berries and popcorn and hang them on the branches. Sometimes, we put candles on it."

"Oh, Alex, Andy would love that, too," Liza said. "Think of all the fun he would have decorating the tree."

Alex laughed and answered ruefully, "And I bet he wouldn't be the only one decorating it. There'd be you, and Bright Star, and Hiram—"

"Not me!" Hiram interjected. "I'm gonna be too busy cooking."

Alex gazed at the old man, still amazed to discover that Hiram was of German origin. "Would a pine tree do?"

Hiram shrugged, pretending disinterest. "Don't know why not."

"Can you find one?" Liza asked Alex.

"I think so. There's a small smattering of pines not too far from here. It isn't any forest, but I think I can find one large enough to suit our purpose."

"Can Andy and I go with you when you go to get it?" Liza asked.

"I don't know how I can get around it," Alex groaned, and everyone laughed.

Soon, Manuel and Hiram drifted off to their beds, and Alex and Liza were left alone before the big fire. Liza studied Alex intently as he added another log to the roaring blaze. She was excited about their Christmas plans, but disappointed that there was nothing of Alex's childhood included.

"Alex, what did you used to do for Christmas when you were a child back in Illinois?"

Alex shrugged. "We had our gifts and Christmas dinner. Then on Christmas night, if the weather permitted, all of the farmers and their families would get together for a big Christmas dinner and dance. Everyone brought food, and after eating, the fiddles were brought out; and all the adults danced, while the children ran around playing games."

Liza frowned. Well, there was certainly no way they could do something like that. She had no idea how far away their nearest neighbor was. In all of her riding with Alex, she had never seen another ranch house, or even a cabin.

"But isn't there something special you remember?" she persisted. "Something that only your family did."

Alex sat watching the fire for a few moments, his look thoughtful. Then he smiled. "There is something that I remember now. When I was about six years old, we went for the usual barn dance at one of the neighboring farms. The farmer's older brother had just recently come to live with them, having retired from the sea after years and years of sailing on a whaler. He whiled his spare time away by carving figurines out of whales' teeth. That year, he had done a group of carvings depicting the nativity scene, and they were displayed on a small table off in one corner of the barn. He had carved Mary, Joseph and the Christ child. He had even done shepherds, wisemen and several small animals. I was fascinated with them." He laughed as he remembered. "I spent the entire evening watching them. I even refused to eat. They were so lifelike that I was afraid to take my eyes off them, for fear they would move and I would miss it. When we left that night, the old sailor gave them to me. He even put them into a beautifully carved box. I think that was the nicest Christmas present I ever received."

"What happened to them?" Liza asked.

"My mother kept them for me. They were really too beautiful to play with. Every year at Christmas time, she would bring them out and display them. I never really got over my fascination with them. But," he added sadly, "I never saw them again after we moved out here. They must have been left behind."

The longer Liza thought about what Alex had said, the more convinced she became that the carvings had not been left behind. She had a strange feeling, one that she really couldn't explain. "Where are the things your mother brought with her?" she heard herself asking.

"Most of it is still in the attic," he answered,

wondering why Liza looked so peculiar. Her face was pale, a strange intense gleam in her eyes.

"Then that's where the carvings are," Liza said with sudden insight.

"No, Liza. I've been through all that stuff countless times. They're not there."

"May I look?" Liza persisted.

Alex started to refuse. He was in no mood to rummage through all that junk. But Liza seemed so determined that he finally sighed in resignation. "All right. Come on."

The attic was crammed with boxes and crates. As Alex set the lamp down, Liza asked, "What did the box with the carvings in it look like?"

"It was about a foot long and six inches wide," Alex answered. Liza nodded, the strange feeling even more intense.

After an hour of careful searching, they had found nothing. "See, I told you," Alex said wearily. "The box isn't here."

Liza glanced about her in frustration. She had been so certain. Her eyes fell on an old trunk in one corner. "What's in that?" she asked, pointing to it.

"Just some of my mother's old clothes."

Liza walked to the trunk. "Do you mind if I open it?"

Alex shook his head, and as Liza lifted the lid, he mumbled, "I really should throw those clothes away. I'm sure they're rotten by now."

Liza rummaged through the dresses, musty with age, but could find no box. Disappointed, she sat back on her heels, staring down at them. Well, at least they could use the material for Christmas decorations. They weren't too rotten for that. A piece of red material at the bottom of the trunk caught her eye. Plowing through the dresses on top, she pulled it out to look at it closer.

As she started to unroll the red dress, a small object fell out. Both she and Alex stared at it. It was a small figurine of a shepherd. Quickly, Liza unrolled the dress to reveal the rest of the set.

"You found them," Alex said in amazement.

"Yes," Liza answered. They had yellowed with age, but they were exquisite. As Alex had said, they had an amazing, lifelike quality to them. "Oh, Alex, they *are* beautiful!"

Alex frowned, perplexed. "How did you know they were here? More women's intuition?"

How could Liza explain what she couldn't understand herself? It had not been simply intuition. It was as if some unseen force had prodded and guided her. She shivered and glanced about the damp, musty attic, almost expecting to see Alex's mother standing there.

"Something like that," she finally anwered. "I just couldn't see a mother throwing something away that meant so much to her son."

Alex nodded, accepting her explanation. "But why do you think she put them in the trunk with her dresses?"

"To save room, I suppose," Liza answered, baffled herself. Then, with that same sudden, unexplainable insight, she added, "Perhaps she didn't want your father to know that she had kept them."

Alex looked at her strangely. "That's right. Father could never understand my being so enthralled with

275

them. He thought they were silly." He studied her intently, even more perplexed. "But how could you know that?"

Again, there was no way Liza could explain. She shrugged. "Just a feeling."

Alex's close scrutiny was making Liza uncomfortable. She could never explain to Alex that she could almost feel his mother's presence in the room. "She must have loved you very much," she remarked. Again, the words came out with no thought, and Liza shivered.

Alex fingered the carving lovingly. "I suppose she did. But it's strange. I never stopped to think about it much until now."

Somehow, Liza sensed that had been Alex's mother's intention all along. To remind her son of how much she had loved him. Liza smiled, a warm feeling coming over her, glad that she had been the woman's instrument. "And now Andy has something to remember his grandmother by," Liza said, no longer frightened that the words came from Alex's mother and not her. *And someday, our children, too,* Liza added, the thought her own.

Alex was thinking the same thing. "Yes," he answered, "a gift from the past to the future."

As they walked silently from the attic, Alex pondered over the strange revelations this night had brought, first Manuel, then Hiram and now his mother. He was so occupied with his thoughts that he never noticed when Liza turned and smiled back into the room. It was just as well, for he wouldn't have been able to see the woman who smiled back.

*   *   *

The next few weeks before Christmas passed in a flurry of excited activity. Everyone in the household was busy with the preparations, either obviously or secretly.

Every afternoon, while Andy and Bright Star were napping, Liza would slip off to her bedroom to work on her Christmas presents. She had dug out her precious skeins of wool from her trunk, one of the few things she had brought with her from England. From the soft, heather-grey wool, she had knitted a sweater for Alex. It was bordered at the waist and cuffs with a red and blue geometric design. From the rest of the red and blue wool, she had knitted neck scarfs for Hiram and Manuel, and a cap and mittens for Andy. Then she had painstakingly sewed the buffalo skin pants for him but, knowing the little boy's disdain for gifts of clothing, had added a book on animals from all over the world, which she had picked up in St. Joe. Although he couldn't read yet, she thought he would enjoy looking at the pictures of the exotic animals: elephants, giraffes, camels, kangaroos.

She agonized over what to give Bright Star, for the Indian woman never wore any article of white man's clothing. Liza finally decided on a necklace of braided red and blue yarn and large colorful beads. When the necklace was finished, she studied it critically. It looked gaudy and cheap, and Liza almost cried in frustration. She could only hope that the Indian woman would realize that it was the thought that counted.

A week before Christmas, Alex took Liza and Andy to find the tree. As they approached the group of small pine trees, Andy jumped up and down excitedly, clapping his hands. Swinging his nephew down from the sleigh, Alex said, "All right, Andy, pick out the one you want."

"That one!" the little boy cried, pointing to the largest tree.

Alex groaned. "I should have known you'd pick the biggest one."

Liza looked at the tree critically. It was large, but much too bare. Her eyes searched until she found a smaller, thickly branched tree loaded with pine cones. Catching the small boy's arm, she said, "Andy, look at this one. How thick and pretty it is! And look at all those pine cones."

Andy looked at the tree and then back at the larger one. He frowned in indecision.

"Oh, look, Andy!" Liza cried. "There's even an abandoned bird nest in it."

Andy rushed over to the small pine and stared at the nest in awe. "This one! This one!" he cried, jumping up and down.

Alex grinned and whispered to Liza, "You're a born manipulator, sweetheart." Liza tried to look indignant, but giggled instead.

While Alex chopped down the tree, with Andy screeching with every swing of the ax, "Don't knock down the nest!" Liza gathered pine branches and pine cones.

After the tree had been carefully loaded into the wagon, Alex looked around at the remaining pines. "I'm afraid I don't see anything here that looks big enough for a yule log, Liza."

"That's all right," Liza answered. "I saw one in the woodpile that looks just the right size. We can just set it aside."

Alex laughed. "I bet I know which one, too. We've all been avoiding that particular log for years. No one wanted to break his back trying to lift it."

After the tree was set up in the parlor, everyone stood around admiring it. Particular interest was shown in the bird nest.

"Would you like for me to make some eggs for your nest?" Manuel asked Andy.

The little boy looked at him dubiously. "How can *you* make eggs? You're not a bird."

"Come on, I'll show you how," the Mexican said, grinning. "You can help me." The next day, three blue-speckled, papier-mâché eggs appeared in the nest.

Liza and Andy decorated the tree with bows made from the old red dress Liza had found in the attic, and Hiram showed them how to make stars and dolls from straw, which they hung on the tree with pieces of old yarn and ribbon. Bright Star contributed a bucket of berries, warning gravely as she handed them to Liza, "No eat." The two women strung them on thread and draped the garland over the tree.

When the tree was finished, Liza decorated the mantle, the front door, and the dining room table with the extra pine boughs and the remaining red bows. It was Hiram who suggested candles, which they nestled into the mantel and dining room decorations.

When Alex and Manuel returned that afternoon, they gazed about them in surprise. "I'll have to admit, it looks pretty good," Alex commented with a grin.

"No, amigo," Manuel corrected him. "It is beautiful."

That night, when everyone was seated in the parlor, Alex brought in the whale-tooth carvings. Clearing a small table by the fireplace, he placed them on it amidst more ohs and ahs.

"Where'd you get them?" Hiram asked.

Alex winked at Liza. "From my mother."

"I ain't never seen them before," the old man grumbled.

Then Alex told the story behind the carvings, and how he and Liza had found them in the attic.

"That sailor should have been a sculptor," Manuel remarked in admiration, and everyone agreed.

All except Andy, that is. The little boy had stood staring raptly at the carvings from the minute they had been placed on the table, totally oblivious to the conversation around him.

Liza smiled and walked over to him. She crouched beside him. "Those are from your grandmother, Andy," she said tenderly.

A puzzled look came over the boy's face. "Who's that?"

"She's your father's and Uncle Alex's mother. She's in heaven now with your father, but she wanted you to have these to remember her by." Liza hesitated and then added, "She wanted all of her grandchildren to enjoy them."

The little boy frowned, considering this new knowledge. "She must be a very nice lady."

"She is, Andy, and she loves you very much," Liza answered.

"From heaven?" Andy asked.

"From heaven," Liza confirmed.

Andy nodded solemnly, his attention back on the carvings. How easily children accepted the basic truths, Liza marveled.

When she rose and turned, she found all three men watching her. Alex's look was warm and full of emotion, Manuel's admiring, and unless she was mistaken, Hiram's eyes were misty. The old man shuffled his feet in embarrassment and, mumbling something about bed, left the room.

The remaining days until Christmas flew by. Liza raided Alex's mother's trunk for old material to wrap her presents in. She and Hiram consulted on the cake she would bake. The result was filled with apples, raisins, nuts and spices, and they both knew that it would be delicious.

Christmas Eve, everyone gathered in the parlor as the yule log was brought in and lit. Then Hiram proudly presented the group with a bowl of steaming wassail. Liza took a big swallow and gasped as the fiery liquid burned her throat. "You put liquor in this," she protested hoarsely.

"Hell, yes. Who ever heard of drinking plain old apple juice," Hiram grumbled.

Alex laughed. "Just consider it a hot toddy, Liza. Go ahead and drink it. It's good for you."

Liza laughed, but was careful to take only small sips at a time. Alex's eyebrow lifted in surprise when she asked for a second cup. But when she went for a third, he stopped her. "I don't think you should. You don't want a hangover on Christmas day." Liza giggled, feeling warm and a little tipsy.

The next morning, everyone was up early. As

Andy's excited squeals and Happy's barks echoed through the house, Alex groaned and rolled over, trying to bury his head beneath the pillow. "The one day in the year that I allow myself a holiday, you'd think I could sleep late," he grumbled.

Liza, already dressed and excited herself, pulled the covers from him. "Get up, sleepyhead. Christmas is no day to sleep late."

Alex rolled over with a growl and pulled her into bed with him. He nuzzled her throat, his hands busy with her buttons.

"Alex, stop that!" Liza cried indignantly, pushing his hands away.

"Just a Christmas present," Alex said, chuckling. Then he kissed her warmly. "Merry Christmas, sweetheart."

"Merry Christmas, darling," Liza replied, struggling from the bed and straightening her clothes. "But that's one Christmas present that will have to wait until later," she said, blushing prettily.

Reluctantly, Alex climbed from bed and dressed. When they entered the parlor, everyone was waiting for them. Andy prodded them with, "Hurry up! Hurry up!"

Presents were exchanged and unwrapped in a flurry of confusion and excitement. Liza sighed in relief when everyone seemed pleased with her gifts. She was particularly proud when Bright Star removed her old bear-claw necklace and slipped Liza's on instead, obviously happy with her simple gift. Even Happy was pleased with his gift from her—a big bone that he gnawed on noisily in one corner of the room.

Alex saved his gift to Liza till the last. "It was too big to wrap," he explained, leaving the room and returning with a beautiful fur cape. Placing it over Liza's shoulders, he said, "You might say this is a gift from Bright Star and me. I contributed the pelts, but it was she who sewed them together for me."

"Thank you, Bright Star," Liza said, still shocked by the gift and very much aware of how much work went into it.

The old woman nodded, smiling in return.

"Oh, Alex, it's just beautiful," Liza cried, fighting back tears of happiness. She had never had such a luxurious gift before. "Where did you get the furs?"

"From Tanaźin. That's silver mink, and it's rather rare."

"It must have cost a fortune!" Liza gasped.

Alex laughed. "No, but Tanaźin knows how to strike a bargain. He gets Thunder's first colt. He's been quite interested in my breeding experiment all along." Alex's eyes were warm with admiration as he looked at her. "Now you have something warm to wear. And I *do* expect you to wear it," he added firmly.

"But it's too beautiful to wear every day," Liza objected.

"As far as I know, furs don't wear out," Alex remarked. "Besides, it's the warmth that's important. I'd better not see you sticking your head outdoors without it," he warned gruffly.

"Yes, sir," Liza said in mock meekness. "Whatever you say."

Alex chuckled. "That will be the day!"

After a big meal of turkey, venison, an array of

vegetables, and Liza's homebaked bread and apple cake, everyone returned to the parlor. Alex sank to the couch and groaned. "I don't think I'll ever be able to eat another bite of food."

Later that afternoon, Manuel brought out his piñata. He had kept it a surprise, and everyone waited in anticipation as he unveiled it. It was shaped like a little grey burro, complete with red bridle and colorful baskets hanging on each side.

As Manuel blindfolded Andy and gave the excited little boy instructions, Liza thought that it was a shame to destroy something as beautiful as the piñata. When Andy broke it on the tenth swing, with Happy barking furiously and the adults yelling encouragement, Liza sighed in relief to see that only one haunch had been destroyed. She smiled when Andy, after scrambling for the candy and nuts, demanded that it be cut down and added to his pile of presents. Several times during the afternoon, Liza noticed the little boy talking to the burro just as seriously as he did to Happy, laying beside him and thumping his tail in perfect understanding.

That night, after an exhausted Andy and a weary Bright Star and Hiram had retired, Liza and Alex sat on the couch watching the fire in the fireplace. Manuel sat in a chair opposite them, one leg thrown casually over the arm of the chair, quietly strumming his guitar.

Liza sighed deeply, thinking what a wonderful Christmas it had been. Not once had she been homesick. Alex's thoughts were much the same as he pulled her closer to her and said, "It was a wonderful Christmas, Liza. The best I've ever had. And all because of you. Without you here, it would have been like all those others, sort of lonely." Lacking further words to express his feelings, he kissed her tenderly on the temple.

Liza glanced quickly at Manuel, a little embarrassed at Alex's show of affection, but the Mexican was staring moodily into the fire, absently playing his guitar.

Alex looked at him thoughtfully and then asked, "Can you play a waltz, Manuel?"

Manuel, startled from his thoughts, looked briefly confused, and then he said, "*Si, Sobre Las Olas.*"

"What does that mean?" Liza asked.

"Over the waves," he answered, beginning the lilting, swaying melody. "It is a very popular waltz in Mexico."

Alex rose and bowed gracefully before Liza. "May I have this dance?"

Liza flushed and protested, "Oh, Alex, not here."

Alex grinned down at her. "Come on, Liza. If we're going to a dance next week, don't you think it would be a good idea if we practiced a little? It's been a long time since I've danced. Not since college. I'd hate to embarrass you by stumbling all over you."

Liza laughed and rose. Alex took her in his arms and guided her across the room. He danced as he walked, lightly and gracefully, and soon Liza was lost in the swaying rhythm of the music. For a long time, they waltzed around the room, while Manuel played the music over and over. Alex pulled Liza closer to him, their bodies gliding in slow, seductive movements, dipping and swaying, as he waltzed her closer and closer to the door and finally into the hallway.

He bent and swept her up in his arms, his eyes warm with desire. Starting up the stairs, he muttered thickly, "And now it's time for that other Christmas present."

Liza was just as anxious as he for their love-making, but still a little shocked. She glanced back to the parlor where the soft music still continued. "But what will Manuel think when we just disappear?"

Alex embraced her tighter. "That I'm taking you upstairs to make passionate love to you." But before Liza could object, his mouth locked over hers in a hot, demanding kiss. Her resistance melted as he carried her up the stairs.

Below, Manuel never even noticed their departure. His thoughts were occupied elsewhere, remembering other Christmases—those happy Christmases of his early childhood when he had been too young to realize that he was a bastard, a half-breed, and an outcast.

Chapter 14

Six days later, Liza and Alex climbed into the sleigh for their trip to Fort Laramie. Although it was still very early, Liza could see that the day was going to be perfect, the sky cloudless as the rising sun caressed the snowy landscape.

"Hiram has promised us good weather," Alex said, as he tucked furs around Liza's legs. She was wearing her new fur cape, the fur-lined boots that Alex had made for her, and warm mittens. Alex had tucked a scarf about her face under the hood, and she was so bundled up, she could hardly move.

As Alex climbed in beside her, Liza grinned. He was just as bundled up as she. Under his heavy fur jacket, he had on the sweater that Liza had knitted for him, and he wore two pair of buckskin pants. *We look like two fat bears,* she thought, laughing to herself.

But as the trip progressed, Liza was grateful for Alex's caution. She realized now that it was much colder than she had thought. She looked at the two horses pulling the sleigh, their backs covered with heavy blankets. "Will the horses be warm enough?"

"They're better off than we are," Alex answered. "At least they're moving, and that generates heat."

As they neared the fort, Alex told Liza about his friends. "You'll like Kathleen and Tom. There's nothing pretentious about either of them." He chuckled. "Especially not Kathleen. You see, she's rather outspoken. Personally, I find her honesty refreshing, but sometimes I think she embarrasses Tom. Not that he loves her any the less for it. He worships the ground she walks on. Only, he doesn't know how to handle it. He comes from a wealthy, eastern family, very pompous, stern, rather forbidding people, and he grew up under a set of strict, rigid social rules. I think that's one reason Tom is so fascinated with Kathleen. She's just the opposite of everything he grew up with. She's warm, spontaneous, fun-loving." Alex glanced down at Liza, who was looking at him curiously. "You'll see what I mean when you meet her. I'm only trying to prepare you for her, so you won't be shocked by what she says."

Liza was beginning to wonder what she had gotten herself into. "How long have you known Tom?"

"We went to college together. Then he attended West Point for two years. You can't imagine how surprised and pleased I was when he was stationed out here six years ago."

"Isn't that rather long to be assigned to one post?"

"Yes, but Tom likes this country, and most of the officers don't. Therefore he didn't have any trouble getting reassigned here. Also, if he had gone back

East, he would still be a lieutenant, but by staying out here, he got promoted to captain. Promotions are hard to come by in peacetime, and since his family disinherited him, every promotion helps."

"Disinherited him?" Liza asked, shocked.

"Yes, his parents didn't approve of Kathleen," Alex replied with a deep scowl on his face. "They told him if he married her, they would cut him off, and they did just that."

"But why? Just because she's open and fun-loving?"

"No, because she's Irish," Alex answered bitterly. "We Americans have not shrugged off our old English prejudices. In this country, the Irish are looked down upon. The only people lower on our social scale are the Negro and Indian. Surely, you can't deny that there's a lot of prejudice in England against them?"

"No, but we've been enemies for hundreds of years." Thoughtfully, Liza added, "I thought everyone is supposed to be equal here."

Alex laughed harshly. "Not hardly. That equality exists in principle. I suppose that's why so many of the poor bastards come to America, thinking to get a fresh start and a new lease on life. Then they find out that things aren't much better here than in Ireland."

"But if she's Irish, and Tom came from a wealthy family, how did she meet him?" Liza asked, puzzled.

"Kathleen was a washerwoman for the army."

"You mean a laundress?"

"Yes. The army hires women to launder the soldiers' uniforms. They even do the officers' laundry. If you remember me telling you, washer-

289

women are the only women besides the officers' wives and families that are allowed to live on the post. Most of the washerwomen are the wives of the enlisted men. That means they can live on the post with their husbands, and the job gives the couple a much needed added income. You can see why the job is so easily filled."

"Then Kathleen was married before," Liza surmised.

"No, when a position became available in his company, an Irish friend told her about it. Fortunately, the company was just being transferred to Fort Laramie, and not many women were willing to move to an isolated post on the frontier. So she got the job."

"Then Tom met Kathleen at Fort Laramie?"

Alex laughed. "Yes. According to Tom, he went to pick up his laundry one day, and Kathleen was at the other end of it. For Tom, it was love at first sight."

Liza stared at him in disbelief.

Alex continued to chuckle. "Just wait until you meet Kathleen. Then you'll understand."

When Liza and Alex drove into the fort, Liza was surprised to find that it was much larger inside than it appeared from the outside. As they approached a row of white-washed cabins, a woman opened the door in one of them and, seeing them, squealed in delight, running out in the snow to meet them. Liza sat, stunned, as Alex jumped from the sleigh, picked up the woman and swung her around, placing a resounding kiss on her cheek.

"Stop that, you handsome rascal!" the woman said, giggling. When Alex set her back on her feet, she turned to face Liza.

Liza looked down at a young woman not much older than herself. She was shorter than Liza and much more voluptuous. Her chestnut hair had been pulled back in a bun, but rebellious curls had escaped around her face. A small, pointed face with a snub nose, generously sprinkled with freckles, looked up at her. The deep brown eyes were sparkling. "You must be Liza," the young woman said calmly.

Before Liza could answer, Alex reached up and swung her down from the sleigh. "Liza, this is Kathleen."

"How do you do," Liza responded.

"Ohhh, look at that luscious fur cape!" Kathleen cried in admiration.

Liza couldn't help but laugh. "Thank you. Alex gave it to me for Christmas," she informed the girl, who was stroking the fur.

"You'll be lucky if I don't steal it from you," Kathleen said, laughing. Then, realizing that she wore no wrap, Kathleen shivered. "Come on in. It's freezing out here."

Inside the cabin, Kathleen took Liza's cape and hung it up. When she reached for Alex's coat, he shook his head. "I'd better get the horses stabled first."

"No, wait a few minutes," Kathleen said. "Tom will be here any minute and go with you. At least have a cup of coffee first."

Kathleen led them to a table and chairs by the fireplace. As she poured cups of coffee for the three of them, she chattered happily. "Our cabin isn't very fancy—just this room and a bedroom—but it's better

291

than most. At least our fireplace doesn't smoke. I told Tom I'd put up with anything but a smoking fireplace."

Liza was beginning to see what Alex had meant about the warm and vivacious Irish girl. She found herself liking her immediately.

The door opened, and as the captain entered the cabin, Alex called with pleasure, "Tom!"

As the two men greeted each other enthusiastically, Liza studied Tom. He was shorter than Alex, stockily built, but all muscle. His head was covered with tight, blond curls, and when he turned, Liza noticed his eyes were a deep, vibrant blue.

As Alex led him toward her, Tom's look was openly admiring. "Tom, I'd like you to meet Liza," Alex said, his pride in her shimmering in his eyes.

"My pleasure," the captain said, his voice deep and cultured.

"How do you do," Liza replied, noting that Tom wasn't nearly as handsome as Alex—his nose a little too big, his jaw too square, all his features strongly masculine. But it was a likable face, one that suggested strength and authority.

"Stop staring, you big ox!" Kathleen admonished Tom, rudely poking her husband in the ribs. Her dimpled smile and twinkling blue eyes belied her irritation. Liza blushed as Alex and Tom laughed, the flustered captain a little nervously.

"I was just telling Kathleen that I should get the horses stabled before I do anything," Alex said to Tom.

"I agree," Tom answered. "They look half frozen out there."

292

The two men stepped outside, and a minute later, Alex returned with their trunk, asking Kathleen, "Where should I put this?"

"In there," Kathleen answered, pointing to the bedroom.

After Alex had left, Kathleen grinned at Liza. "Now that we got rid of them, we can enjoy ourselves." She took a pot from the fire and poured water into a teapot sitting on the table. After the tea had steeped, she pushed the coffee cups aside and poured tea for them.

Liza laughed. "You don't like coffee, either?"

Kathleen wrinkled her nose in distaste. "Can't stand the stuff. Tom insists he's going to make an American out of me yet, but if it means liking coffee, I'll never make the grade."

The two women sat drinking their tea, each carefully scrutinizing the other under lowered lashes. Then, as if simultaneously deciding that they liked what they saw, their eyes met, and they smiled.

"I'm Irish," Kathleen said, throwing the comment out as if it were a challenge.

Liza lifted her head proudly and replied, "I'm English."

The two women stared at one another across the table, and then they both laughed.

"Well, so much for the old Irish-English rivalry," Kathleen remarked, "Are you tired, Liza? Would you like to take a nap?"

"No, but I am worried about my gown. I'm afraid it must be wrinkled. It may need a little touch-up ironing before the dance."

"That's no problem," Kathleen said, rising from

the table. "Let's go see."

As Liza pulled the violet ball gown from the trunk, Kathleen gasped. "Oh, it's beautiful! Did Alex buy that for you, too?"

"No, I bought it in St. Joe." Placing it up against her, Liza asked, "You don't think it's too daring, do you? It's cut awfully low."

"Lord, no! It's no lower than mine." Kathleen pulled an apple-green, velvet gown from her wardrobe. "See?" The colors of the two gowns complemented one another beautifully.

"Oh, I can't wait until tonight," Kathleen said in an excited voice. "We're really going to set those old biddies back on their ears. I've been waiting for years to show them a thing or two. They think they're so high and mighty. Just wait until they see you. For once, they're going to see some real class. They'll be pea-green with envy." She clapped her hands, her brown eyes sparkling. "I know, we'll tell them you're a countess or something."

Liza laughed at the ridiculousness of Kathleen's suggestion. "Kathleen, I'm a governess. You can't expect them to believe something as outlandish as that."

"Why not?" Kathleen demanded. "You look like one. And you could be, and still be a governess, too. There were a lot of impoverished nobles running around back East when I was there."

"But it would be a lie," Liza objected.

"Oh, pooh!" Kathleen retorted, pouting slightly. She dimpled mischievously. "Can't we just sort of hint?"

Liza laughed. She was amazed at her feelings

toward the Irish girl. It was as if they had been friends for years. She decided the best way out was to change the subject. "Do you think the gown needs ironing?"

Kathleen looked at the dress. "Yes, it is a bit wrinkled. Here, let me have it. I'll have it ironed in no time."

Liza followed her back into the kitchen, objecting, "I can do it."

"Not nearly as fast as I can," Kathleen retorted. Her eyes challenged Liza's again. "Or didn't Alex tell you that I was a washerwoman for the army before I married Tom?"

"Yes, he told me," Liza answered, matter-of-factly.

"That didn't shock you?" Kathleen asked, astonished.

"No, why should it? I was a scullery maid back in New York." She laughed harshly, saying in a bitter voice, "At least you didn't get fired from your job."

Then Liza told Kathleen of her experiences back in New York City and how she came to be fired from her one and only job. As Liza talked, Kathleen ironed the gown in quick, professional strokes and listened sympathetically, every now and then nodding in agreement. Liza was surprised at herself, for this was something that she had not even told Alex. She still felt degraded by it, but somehow, she felt the Irish girl would understand.

When she finished the story, Kathleen remarked, "I know what you mean. I had a few of those jobs myself before the army hired me. It seemed to me that I spent more time trying to avoid their husbands with their filthy, pawing hands than I did working. It's a wonder that I survived with my virginity still intact."

Liza flushed at Kathleen's outspoken words.

Seeing her look, Kathleen cried, "Oh, Lord, I keep forgetting that you're a lady. You'll have to forgive me. I'm afraid I'm always blurting out something like that. That's one of the reasons the other officers' wives don't like me. They think I'm too outspoken, that I talk like a whore— Oops!" she said with a laugh. "See what I mean? It's a wonder Tom puts up with me."

Liza tried to make the girl feel more comfortable. "No, it's probably just me. I guess I'm pretty straight-laced when it comes to sex. At least, that's what Alex seems to think." Suddenly, Liza realized the implication of what she had said, and her face flushed scarlet. She looked at Kathleen, who seemed not the least bit shocked. "I guess you're not the only one who blurts out things."

Kathleen smiled warmly. "Don't be embarrassed because of me. Tom and I were lovers for two years before we married. Besides, I already guessed you and Alex were lovers before you said anything."

"How did you know that?"

Kathleen giggled. "Because I know Alex. I've never seen him look at a woman the way he does you, like he could eat you up. And I saw you looking at him." She shrugged. "I just put two and two together."

"It's that obvious?"

"No, not to others it wouldn't be," Kathleen assured her. "But remember, I told you Tom and I were lovers before we married. That's the way we used to look at each other." She laughed. "I've been there."

"Alex and I are secretly handfasted," Liza confided.

Kathleen nodded, familiar with the custom.

"Alex said everyone would just think I was his nephew's governess, that no one would guess our relationship, but if it's that obvious, maybe we shouldn't go to the dance."

"Nonsense! I told you it's not that obvious," Kathleen said in a firm voice. "Besides, those old biddies wouldn't recognize love if you waved it before them in blaring red." She gave Liza a penetrating look. "Do you really care what they think?"

Liza didn't care. Her love for Alex was so good, so right, that she couldn't be ashamed of it. "Not for myself, but I wouldn't want to embarrass Alex in front of his friends."

"Embarrass Alex?" Kathleen asked in astonishment. "Why, he's so proud of you, he's about to bust his buttons. Besides, they aren't his friends. He hates most of the officers and their wives almost as much as I do."

"Hates them?" Liza gasped, her expression shocked.

"Well, maybe those words are a little too strong," Kathleen admitted. "Dislikes them, I suppose. The officers are arrogant, haughty snobs, and their wives are nothing but a bunch of mean-mouthed gossips. They put themselves above others. Neither Alex nor I like that kind of people. Tom either, except he has to work with them." Kathleen's eyes suddenly filled with tears. "Personally, I don't give a damn what they think of me, but it's hard on Tom. He's always having to defend me." Abruptly, Kathleen started crying. "Oh, they're right. I'm not at all the proper wife for him."

Liza pulled Kathleen into her arms. "Don't be

silly. Alex told me Tom is crazy about you, that he worships the ground you walk on. If you two love each other, what does it matter what they think?''

"I didn't think it would matter, either. But no matter how hard I try, they just won't give up. They don't think I'm good enough for Tom, and they never will!" Kathleen said vehemently. "That's why it took two years for us to get married. The commanding officer wouldn't approve it. He thought Tom should marry some high-faluting society girl back East. He told Tom that it was important to have a proper wife, that he was an officer and a gentleman and should marry a lady, not some common washerwoman.''

"He called you that? A common washerwoman?" Liza asked angrily.

"I don't know if those were his exact words or not. But that's what he meant when he said I wasn't a lady. If Tom hadn't been so determined and stubborn, we still wouldn't be married.''

"But the personal lives of his officers shouldn't be any of his business!" Liza objected vehemently.

"But it is. That's the way the army is. They think they own you, body and soul. And if you don't do what they want you to, even in your personal life, you don't get promoted.''

"But Tom is a captain already," Liza pointed out.

"Only because he stayed out here. And, Liza, he stayed because of me. He knew that I'd never survive with those army wives back East. Oh, don't you see? I'm holding him back, and I'm afraid he'll regret marrying me someday," Kathleen said, her voice anguished.

"I don't think Tom will ever regret marrying you."

"Did you know that his family disinherited him because of me? Don't you think he'll regret that some day?" She was crying softly again.

"No, I don't, Kathleen," Liza said firmly. Then she told the Irish girl how her own mother had been disinherited because she married a mere schoolmaster.

"And she never regretted it?" Kathleen asked, astonished.

"Never!"

"But it's different with a man. He has to feel he's successful or he gets bitter," Kathleen pointed out wisely.

"Yes, that's true," Liza agreed. "But I think if Tom ever had to choose between you and the army, he'd choose you. The army isn't the only way for a man to make a living, or be successful in life. If he uses you as an excuse for his failures, then he's not much of a man."

"Now wait a minute!" Kathleen retorted, her eyes flashing. "You can't talk about Tom like that!" Then, seeing Liza's grin, she laughed. "You're sneaky."

"If you love him, you'll fight for him," Liza said.

"Love him? Ever since I laid eyes on that big ox, I've been crazy about him! But you're right. He is worth fighting for. And those old biddies aren't any match for a fighting Irishman," she said, raising her chin defiantly.

Liza laughed.

Kathleen was looking at Liza with a new respect and feeling a little awed. "You know, when Tom told me Alex was bringing you for the New Year's dance, I was dreading it. I thought you would be a snob like those other women." Puzzled, she asked, "Don't you think it's strange how we hit it off so well? I mean, we're really not anything alike."

"I think we're alike in many ways, Kathleen. We're both poor, we're both new to this country, and we each love a man and aren't afraid to admit it to the rest of the world." She winked. "And to tell you the truth, I think we're both just a little bit rebellious. To be honest with you, I always resented being told what to do. It made me even angrier to be told how to think, as if I didn't have a mind of my own."

Kathleen nodded in understanding, carrying Liza's ball gown back into the bedroom. After hanging it in the wardrobe beside hers, she turned to Liza. "I feel a little foolish, though, bawling like a baby, and you almost a complete stranger."

"That's funny. I don't feel like a stranger," Liza replied.

Kathleen smiled. "Neither do I. God, Liza, it's been so long since I've been able to talk to someone. I mean really talk," she added earnestly. "I try to pretend, for Tom's sake, that it doesn't bother me, but it does." Her eyes regained their mischievous sparkle. "Then you will help me show up those old biddies?"

"If it will make you happy," Liza replied. Surprisingly, she meant it. She had no intention of standing by and letting those other women intimidate Kathleen, and if they embarrassed Alex and Tom in the process—be damned!

The two young women looked at each other in

perfect understanding and then started laughing helplessly. Distracted, they didn't hear the outer door close.

"What's going on in there?" Tom called from the other room.

Kathleen winked at Liza and called back, "We've been nibbling at your whiskey."

"You've what?" Tom yelled back in a shocked voice. He looked into the room, not knowing what to expect. The two women lay crosswise on the bed, their bodies convulsing with laughter. Finally, Kathleen pushed herself off the bed and walked to her husband. "Oh, you big ox, the only thing we've had to drink is a cup of tea."

Tom noticed her red, swollen eyes and frowned with concern. Seeing his look, Kathleen lied quickly, "Oh, I never laughed so hard in my life. It even made me cry."

Liza was sitting on the bed watching the two. To reinforce Kathleen's explanation, she said, "Me, too," brushing an imaginary tear from her eye.

The relief on Tom's face was obvious. "Well, you two certainly seem to have hit it off. What's so funny?"

"Something you wouldn't understand, love," Kathleen replied smugly. "Women talk."

"Oh," Tom replied, feeling a little embarrassed.

"I suppose you two men are hungry?" Kathleen asked. She stood on tiptoe and sniffed at her husband's breath. "Uh-huh, been over to the tavern, haven't you?"

Tom flushed and grinned.

"Well, the least you two could have done is ask us if

301

we wanted to go, too," Kathleen said.

Tom looked aghast and glanced over at Liza apprehensively.

Kathleen giggled. "Don't worry, love. I don't shock Liza." She kissed him quickly on the cheek and flounced from the room.

Tom watched her go, then turned to Liza, obviously flustered. "She's more bark than bite," he offered in way of an explanation.

Liza smiled. "Don't apologize to me, Tom. I think she's wonderful. I wouldn't change her for the world."

Their eyes locked in silent, mutual understanding. Finally, Tom smiled. "She's very special to me. Things have been kind of rough on her lately."

Liza knew that her instincts had been correct. If it ever came to a choice between Kathleen and the army, Tom would choose his wife.

"I'm awfully glad you came," he added.

"So am I," Liza replied.

"What's going on in there?" This time it was Alex who called out. He had tried to keep his voice light, but everyone noticed the barely suppressed jealous timbre of his voice.

Tom and Liza smiled at each other and then walked from the room. "Nothing," Liza called ahead, "I just misplaced my shoe and Tom was helping me find it."

While the women were doing the dishes, the men went into the bedroom to change. When they emerged, Kathleen squealed in delight. "Would you look at that? I've never seen two such handsome men!"

302

Alex grinned in amusement and Tom colored hotly. And handsome they were; Tom in his blue dress uniform and Alex in his black evening clothes. Liza studied Alex from under lowered lashes. She had never seen him dressed in formal wear before. The black coat accented his broad, muscular shoulders and trim waist, and the white frilled shirt beneath it contrasted with his deep tan. He looked rakish and devilishly handsome. Liza shivered in response to his strong masculine magnetism.

Alex smiled at her, his eyes telling her he had guessed her thoughts. Liza felt a slow flush creep up her face, a flush she had absolutely no control over. She was vastly relieved when Kathleen pulled her into the bedroom, admonishing the two men, "Now, no peeking."

The two women dressed admist ohs and ahs and giggles, both feeling like young girls going to their first dance. First, Liza laced Kathleen as the Irish girl prodded her with "Tighter, Liza. Lace it tighter."

"But, Kathleen, you won't be able to breathe if I make it any tighter."

"Who cares," Kathleen said, laughing, "as long as I knock their eyes out!"

Then Kathleen laced Liza. "You don't even need a corset, you're so slender," she said enviously. "Oh, I hate you!" she cried in mock dislike.

The women arranged each other's hair. First, Kathleen's chestnut tresses were piled on top of her head with love-locks at each temple, and then Liza's hair was pulled back from her face and up to fall in a soft cascade of golden-red curls at the back of her head.

After the dresses were donned and buttoned, the two women stood admiring one another. "You look lovely, Kathleen," Liza said. The Irish woman did look exceptionally pretty. The apple-green dress clung to her ample curves, the color of her gown complementing her hair and peach coloring while giving her a vibrant glow.

"Oh, Liza, you're beautiful," Kathleen said in a hushed voice.

Liza flushed at what she thought was an extravagant compliment. But Kathleen's appraisal was just as accurate as Liza's had been. Liza *was* beautiful. The violet of the gown brought out the color of her eyes and her creamy, flawless complexion. The dress fit her graceful curves like a glove, accentuating their perfection. While Kathleen was teasingly provocative, Liza was devastatingly sensual.

"What's taking so long in there?" Alex called from the other room, breaking the women's rapt admiration of each other.

Kathleen laughed. "Let's go knock 'em dead."

When they entered the room, each man's breath caught in admiration. Alex's eyes warmed with open desire when he saw Liza, his look devouring her.

Tom watched Alex uncomfortably from the corner of his eye. Hell, he had admired the two women, too, but Alex looked as if he might ravish the poor English woman right on the spot. His eyes caught Kathleen's, and she giggled. Coughing to gain Alex's attention, he said in a loud voice, "Well, I guess we'd better go."

Reluctantly, Alex tore his eyes away from Liza and grinned at his friend. He reached for Liza's fur cape and threw it over her shoulders. As Kathleen and Tom disappeared through the open door, he pulled Liza back and kissed her nape, whispering, ''You're beautiful, sweetheart. I can think of better things to do than going to a dance.''

"Stop it, Alex,'' Liza scolded lightly, and then laughing, they joined Tom and Kathleen on the porch.

As they walked to the building where the dance was to be held, Liza and Kathleen were both caught up in an excited, carefree mood. They teased and bantered back and forth, leaving the two men feeling left out and rather puzzled. There seemed to be some sort of conspiracy between the two women, and Tom, knowing his wife's antics all too well, was frankly alarmed. Even Alex, realizing how stubborn and rebellious Liza could be when she set her mind to it, was beginning to feel uneasy.

When they entered the ballroom, after leaving their wraps at the door, an audible gasp was heard over the music. Alex grinned, well aware of the effect Kathleen and Liza had on the other guests. The officers' wives' eyes glittered with envy, and no wonder, considering the expressions on the men's faces. The officers' response to the sight of the two young women ranged from rapt admiration to outright, lustful leers.

Seeing the lustful looks, Alex began to feel uncomfortable again. ''Maybe this was a mistake,'' he mumbled to Tom.

The captain nodded glumly. ''I'm afraid we've got a battle on our hands,'' he answered as he glared at one of the officers who was blatantly staring at

Kathleen and Liza. The man colored under his hot gaze and averted his eyes.

Alex was doing a little murderous glaring of his own. Almost all of the officers present had heard of the rugged rancher's reputation with both his fists and his gun. The leering looks suddenly turned to gentlemanly smiles and nods.

"That's a little better," Alex mumbled.

"Yes," Tom muttered back, "but the battle has just begun." He nodded to the barrage of officers descending on them to ask Kathleen and Liza to dance.

The two men's evening was spent miserably as they watched, time and time again, Liza and Kathleen being claimed for dances by the ardent officers. The two women seemed to be enjoying themselves immensely, laughing and flirting outrageously, deliberately egging their admirers on. The officers' wives' glares were no less murderous than Tom's and Alex's.

Tom nodded to one furious woman glaring at her husband. The man was dancing with Kathleen, his eyes glued on the Irish woman's cleavage. Tom muttered glumly, "I'm afraid there's going to be quite a few rows tonight after the dance is over."

Alex didn't hear his friend's remark. His eyes were glued on Liza and the officer dancing with her. "If she doesn't stop that damn flirting, I'll wring her neck," he said, furious.

"Liza and Kathleen are only doing it to irritate the women," Tom pointed out.

Alex ignored him, his eyes darkening dangerously. "And if that bastard doesn't stop looking at her like

306

that—I'll kill him!"

Tom slashed Alex an alarmed look. He hadn't missed his friend's possessive attitude toward the beautiful English woman. And knowing Alex as well as he did, he would never make the mistake of crossing him. "Alex, Liza is a beautiful woman. You can't blame the men," he reasoned.

"I know she's beautiful, but I didn't come to this damned dance to watch other men fawning all over her," Alex shot back angrily. As he stepped forward, his eyes glittering with intent, Tom restrained him with a hand on his arm.

"What are you going to do?" Tom asked warily.

"Cut in," Alex hissed.

"You can't do that," Tom objected. "That would be considered an insult."

"Insult be damned! If we don't do something, we're going to have a riot on our hands."

Tom glanced around the ballroom. Several of the couples were already bickering openly. "I'm afraid you're right," he agreed reluctantly, and then sighing deeply, said, "Lead on, my friend."

Alex walked determinedly across the room, his jaw set firmly, his eyes smoldering, and tapped demandingly on the shoulder of the man dancing with Liza. The man whirled indignantly, about to object, but when he saw the fierce look on Alex's face, he paled and quickly bowed out.

Tom didn't have any trouble reclaiming his wayward wife. Of course, the fact that he outranked the man was a decided advantage.

Alex pulled Liza into his arms roughly and danced her away from the crowd. Liza let out a small gasp and protested, "Alex, you're holding me too close."

"If you're worried about causing a scandal, sweetheart, it's a little late for that," he retorted angrily, pulling her into an even more possessive embrace.

Liza glanced up at him in surprise. "You're jealous."

"Damned right!" Alex ground out. "But that's irrelevant. The point is, whether you realize it or not, you're in much more danger of being murdered here tonight than you ever were as an Indian captive. If you don't believe me, just look around."

Liza glanced at the other women. Their looks were no longer envious. Their eyes glittered with pure, unadulterated hatred. She shivered. "Oh, dear, I'm afraid we carried it a little too far."

The ludicrousness of the situation suddenly hit Alex. He chuckled. "Well, maybe if you behave yourself the rest of the night, you might get out in one piece."

Liza and Kathleen didn't have much choice in the matter. Anytime they were even remotely approached by one of the braver officers, Alex or Tom gave the man such a threatening look that the man invariably retreated.

The last dance was a waltz. Alex pulled Liza to him in a tight embrace. Shocked, Liza objected, but as the strange familiar magic between them began, she weakened, melting into him. Their bodies whirled and dipped across the dance floor, their eyes fused. Locked in their own world, they swayed in rhythm to the music, totally oblivious to the other people around them.

One by one, the dancing couples retired to the sidelines of the dance floor to watch them, some looking on with awe and admiration and some with open shock. Tom and Kathleen exchanged knowing looks.

In one corner of the room, the commandant of the fort stood watching the handsome dancing couple. He had been very much aware of the events of the night and had watched in secret amusement.

His scrawny, pinch-faced wife, standing beside him and watching Liza and Alex dance, hissed, "Look at that! It's indecent!"

The colonel watched as the couple, their bodies molded together, gracefully, sensuously glided across the room. They were young; they were beautiful, and they were very much in love.

"Stop them! Do something!" his wife demanded indignantly.

The older man had no intention of doing anything. To this day, he regretted his interference in trying to block the marriage between Tom and his delightful Irish lass, and that had been at his wife's insistence also. Besides, the young English woman reminded him of someone lost long ago, and he felt a deep pang of regret.

"Governess, my eye!" his wife spat. "Mistress is more like it. It's obscene."

Sighing deeply, the colonel turned to his wife. His eyes bored into her as he said coldly, "Sometimes, Grace, you are a monumental pain in the ass." He stood for a minute, savoring her look of shock and horror, and then whirled and strode from the room, signaling the end of the dance.

When the two couples returned to Tom's cabin, Alex pulled Liza back, saying to Tom and Kathleen, "We'll join you in a minute." Tom and Kathleen left them standing on the snow-covered porch.

Alex took Liza in his arms, groaning in her ear, "Oh, God, sweetheart, I'd give my right arm to be able to make love to you tonight." His mouth descended on hers in a hot, searing kiss, his tongue invading, then searching, her mouth. His arms snaked beneath her cape, wrapping tightly around her small waist as he molded her soft body to his hard one. The impassioned kiss continued for a long time.

Finally, he pulled away from her, his breathing ragged, his body trembling with need. Carefully, he set her away from him, his voice roughened with desire. "You'd better go in now, before I take you right here in the snow."

"What about you?" Liza muttered.

"I'll be in, in a minute," he answered, acutely aware of the bulge straining at his trousers. "When I've cooled off a bit. Tell them I'm having a smoke."

As Liza entered the cabin, still shaky herself, Kathleen jumped guiltily from her husband's lap. Obviously flustered, she smoothed her dress and patted ineffectively at her mussed hair. "Where's Alex?" she asked a little breathlessly.

"He's having a smoke," Liza answered, blushing at having stumbled in on them.

Having regained her composure, Kathleen walked to the door and said, "Well, for heaven's sake, he doesn't have to stand out there in the cold. He can smoke in here."

"Kathleen!" Tom called. Kathleen turned, puzzled

by his urgent tone of voice. "Maybe Alex wants some fresh air," Tom suggested diplomatically.

Kathleen stared dumbly at her husband, who was grinning and shaking his head slightly. Finally, the realization hit her. "Oh," she replied vacantly.

After the two women had retired, Tom removed his coat and boots. He was sitting in a comfortable chair by the fireplace and having a quiet drink when Alex came into the house.

"It looks like we're stuck in here tonight," Tom said. "Make yourself comfortable and have a drink." He motioned to the whiskey bottle standing on the table.

Alex stripped down to his shirt and pants and, taking his glass of whiskey with him, settled into the chair opposite Tom. For a while, the two men sat drinking in companionable silence.

Tom broke the silence. "That's some woman you've got there."

Alex's dark eyebrows rose in surprise. From his tone of voice, he knew that the captain had guessed his and Liza's relationship.

"Is it that obvious?" Alex asked.

Tom grinned. "Let's just say that anyone who doesn't know you wouldn't have guessed." He chuckled, adding, "Until that last dance, that is. Hell, you might as well have hung a sign around your necks in glaring red announcing that you're lovers."

Alex frowned, then aware of Tom's eyes on him, shrugged.

Tom glowered at him, feeling his old resentment rise. Hell, he thought irritably, Alex didn't give a damn what others thought, and the frustrating thing about it was that Alex got away with it. Ever since their college days together, Tom had envied Alex's ability to be coldly indifferent to other's opinions. It wasn't that Alex was anti-social. He could be devastatingly charming, if he chose. He was just too damned independent.

Alex had been something of an enigma to his college friends. While Tom and the others had always striven hard for social acceptance, Alex had maintained his cool, disinterested attitude. "Arrogant bastard" one of their mutual acquaintances had called him. But the man had been careful to hide his opinion from Alex, for the western man had a barely suppressed lethal savagery about him that had commanded respect. As a result, most of Alex's friends had admired, envied and feared him.

Of course, a few of their fellow classmates had not been that astute. Tom chuckled, remembering the time when four of Alex's classmates had decided to teach the arrogant Westerner a lesson. They had waylaid him in a dark alley one night. Alex had given them a swift, deadly demonstration of western fistfighting and left the four bleeding and bruised. From then on, Alex had been given a wide berth.

The captain smiled smugly, thinking of Alex's reaction to Liza's and Kathleen's antics at the dance. Instead of being cooly amused, as Tom would have expected, Alex had been furiously jealous. Tom had been surprised at the show of emotion, never having expected to see the day when his friend would be anything but indifferent to a woman.

That was another thing about Alex that had

312

irritated Tom and his other classmates. Women had seemed to be drawn to the darkly handsome man, with no noticeable effort on his part. "The women chase him like a bunch of bitches in heat," one of their classmates had complained bitterly. Well, Tom thought in secret satisfaction, he had finally seen the day when a woman had turned the tables on Alex. He wondered curiously just how deeply his friend's emotions had been touched. He decided to fish.

"To tell you the truth, Alex, I'm glad to see someone else besides myself behave like a fool over a woman," Tom said. "I enjoy the company."

"I'd hardly call what you feel for Kathleen behaving like a fool," Alex answered in a clipped, hard voice.

The comment, and the tone of Alex's voice, told the young captain all he needed to know. So, Tom mused, Alex no longer thought his feelings for Kathleen amusing. He studied Alex closely. This was no simple infatuation. He was deeply in love. A god had fallen from the heavens and had become mortal. Tom chuckled. "So that's how it is."

Alex glared at him, knowing full well what Tom meant, but offered no denial.

For a few moments, Tom sat and savored his revenge, but he knew better than to pursue the subject. Friend or not, Alex would resent any further probing. He decided, wisely, to change the subject. "I'm glad you came, Alex. There's something I've been wanting to discuss with you."

Alex's relief was obvious. "Oh? What's that?"

"My enlistment is up next year, and I'm thinking of resigning my commission."

"You must be joking. You can't do that," Alex replied in a shocked voice.

"And why not?" Tom retorted.

"Because there's a war coming, and the army is going to need good officers."

"That's not my problem," Tom answered coldly.

Alex stared at him in disbelief.

"Hell, if you can say it's not your problem, why can't I?" Tom said hotly. "Maybe I don't want to fight, either."

Alex glared at him. "I've told you my reasons."

"Oh, yes, I've heard all your reasons," Tom answered in a sarcastic tone of voice. "That's a bunch of bull, Alex, and you and I both know it."

A muscle in Alex's jaw twitched angrily. The two men glared at each other. Finally, Tom sighed heavily and said in a quiet voice, "Some day soon, our country is going to be at war. Not just the North, not just the South, but *our* country. If you're an American, it's your problem, yours and mine. And besides, you're not the kind of man to let someone else fight your battles for you."

Tom continued obstinately, well aware of Alex glowering at him. "It's going to be a long, bitter war. Hell, I'm not as stupid as some of my fellow officers who think we'll beat the South in a couple of months. They've been preparing for this war for years, stockpiling arms and munitions, buying ships. Do you realize most of our best military leaders are Southerners? If they go with the South, we'll be left floundering like a ship without a rudder. Besides, the South will be fighting the defensive side, and that's always a decided advantage. Hell, I'm not so

314

sure we'll even win it," Tom ended grimly.

Alex's angry expression was replaced with one of concern.

Tom stood and refilled their glasses. "Sure most of the fighting will be done in the East, but the whole country is going to feel this war, one way or the other." Handing Alex his drink, Tom looked him in the eye. "The old man called me into his office the other day."

A dark eyebrow rose, and Alex smiled mockingly. "I assume you're referring to your illustrious commandant," he said sarcastically.

"Hell, Alex, the colonel knows your opinion of him, and he admits that he's made some mistakes in his dealings with the Indians out here. He's an Easterner. He doesn't understand the Indian mind. But don't underestimate him. He's shrewd. If there's one thing he does understand, it's this coming war. That's why he wants to talk to you."

"To me?" Alex asked, surprised.

"Yes, as I said, he's smarter than you think. He believes, if the going gets rough, they'll try to stir up the Indians."

Alex frowned. "Do you think they would actually go that far?"

"Why not? It wouldn't be the first time the enemy used the Indians against us. Remember the War of 1812? The British made the Indians their allies and actually paid them a bounty for every white scalp the Indians brought them. Hell, Alex, we're talking about war! The South will be fighting to win and using any and every method possible. Even if they don't make the Indians their allies, just stirring them up would be enough. We can't fight a large-scale Indian war in the West and another war in the East." He shook his head. "No, there's no way we can fight two fronts at once. We'd lose for sure."

"But what does the colonel want to talk to me about?"

Tom sat down and took a long drink before answering, "He figures, sooner or later, you'll join up. And that would be a mistake." Tom grinned at his friend. "You'd make a terrible soldier, Alex. You're too stubborn and independent. I can't see you taking orders from some shave-tail lieutenant. Besides, you have skills and talents much more valuable to your country, and the colonel is smart enough to see them."

"Get to the point!" Alex snapped.

"He wants you to be his scout."

"He's got his damned Crows for that!" Alex spat.

Tom remained unruffled. "Civilian scout would be your official title."

Alex gave him a suspicious look. "And unofficially?"

"A trouble shooter, a diplomat of sorts," Tom answered. "The colonel needs a man who knows Indians, understands them, and, in turn, is trusted and respected by them."

Alex shot to his feet. "If you think I'm going to use my influence to talk the Indians into fighting for the North, you're crazy!"

"No, no," Tom soothed. "God, I hope it never comes to that." Motioning to his friend, he said, "Sit down. Hear me out before you jump to conclusions."

Alex returned to his seat, his expression still suspicious.

"All the colonel wants you to do is to try to keep the Indians neutral," Tom said. "Make them realize that the South would only be using them for their advantage. It won't be easy. The South will have their own men in there, wooing them. You'll be sitting on a powder keg. But hell, Alex, do you realize what a large-scale Indian war could mean? One blood bath for this country is enough, but two?"

Alex could see Tom's point. A full-scale Indian war in the middle of a civil war would be a catastrophe for the North. And what would it do to his friends, the Indians? Both would be the losers. He sighed. "I'm afraid the old man over-estimates me. I don't have that much influence with the Indians."

"Hell, Alex, if they can't trust you, who can they trust? You're a good friend of Tanazin's, and that alone will pull a lot of weight with the other tribes. You know Indians, and you understand them, probably better than any white man out here. You're the man for the job, but the question is, will you take it?"

"Don't you think Washington will send some-one?"

"Hell, this whole territory would be in flames before those stupid asses in Washington even know what's going on!" Tom spat. "You know how that goes. Too little, too late. Besides, can't you just imagine who they'd send? Some idiot who doesn't know a damned thing about Indians, and that would be even worse. That's why it would have to be unofficial. We'd be trying to keep the lid on from the very beginning."

"But what if the colonel is transferred? Won't they need him back East?"

Tom laughed harshly. "If the war department was smart, that's the first thing they'd do. He's a good officer, and that's the kind of fighting he understands. But who ever heard of the war department doing anything smart? Besides, he's made some enemies back East, enemies in high places. That's why he's here in the first place."

Alex's curiosity was aroused. "Enemies?"

"Yes, he fought in the Mexican War, and I understand he was a damned good officer. But you know that war wasn't the noblest war we ever fought. We wanted the rest of Texas and California, and we deliberately provoked a war with Mexico to get them. Besides that, it wasn't the best-fought war, either. The army made a lot of mistakes and blunders. The old man was disgusted with the whole thing and voiced his opinions loud and clear. Unfortunately, the superior officer he criticized the most, turned out to be the hero of the war. The army sent him here both to silence him and punish him."

Alex was impressed. "He does have powerful enemies."

"Yes. So he figures he'll be out here for a while. Maybe for the duration of the war. Who knows?"

Tom refilled their glasses. "You know, I have to admire the old man. He got a rotten deal. Most men would be bitter and sit back and let the men in Washington make fools of themselves. But he's smart enough to see what's coming, and he loves his country, despite everything."

"Maybe, he's not so bad after all," Alex said cautiously. "But do you think he'd listen to me?"

"Yes. As I said, he admits he doesn't understand

Indians. And remember, he won't be doing this for the glory, or even the recognition. His reasons are the same as yours. He loves his country and doesn't want to see any more blood spilled than absolutely necessary."

"Then that business about resigning your commission was all a ruse, wasn't it?"

Tom grinned. "Yes and no. I'll stick it out until the war is over, but I have decided that I don't want to make the army my career after all." His look was pensive. "You know, I had an instructor at the Point tell me that I'd never make it as a career man, that I was too stubborn, too intelligent, too sensitive. It made me mad as hell at the time, but he was right. I can't stand following through on some of these orders that come from Washington. There's no rhyme or reason for them, and some of them are just downright stupid. It's one thing to put your life on the line for someone else's stupidity, but it's quite another to risk the lives of your men, too."

Alex agreed. He could well understand Tom's dilemma. "Then it's not just because of Kathleen?"

"No, but that's part of it," Tom admitted. "Hell, it's bad enough putting up with all these stupid orders, but they think they own my private life and Kathleen's, too. I thought I grew up in a rigid social structure, but it's nothing compared to the army. I could probably put up with it myself, but I can't stand what it's doing to Kathleen. Those damned women! The whole lot of them couldn't equal her little finger."

"I agree," Alex said.

"But it's getting to her," Tom continued, his voice

319

almost anguished. "Some day they'll break her spirit, and I can't stand by and watch that." He looked at Alex intently. "I'm glad you brought Liza. Kathleen's been more like herself tonight than I've seen her in months."

"And you think Liza's the reason?"

"I know she is," Tom replied firmly. "Kathleen has found out she can be accepted by another woman as an equal. Considering that she believes Liza to be a high-class lady and much above her, that comes as a surprise and real boost to her ego. It's just what she needed."

Alex frowned. "I don't think Liza considers herself superior," he said defensively.

Tom chuckled. "No, you and I both know that, but not Kathleen. Can't you imagine what that revelation has done for her?"

Alex smiled. "Then I'm doubly glad I brought her. But, if you're not going to make a career out of the army, then what are you going to do?"

Tom's look was thoughtful. "I'm not sure. But I do know I want to be my own man, and I'd like to stay out West." He grinned. "What I'd really like to do is be a rancher like you."

"Out here?" Alex asked in surprise.

"Yes."

"What about Kathleen? This land is rough on women. A rancher's life isn't easy."

"Kathleen can take it," Tom answered confidently. "Hell, if you knew what she went through back in Ireland . . ." His voice trailed off. Then he laughed. "I'm the one who may not make the grade. I don't know a damned thing about ranching."

"Neither did my father," Alex answered, pleased with Tom's decision. "Manuel and I can help you. I even know a nice spread near my ranch that you can buy, if you're interested."

"You're not afraid of the competition?" Tom joked.

"Hell, no." Alex grinned. "I guess this country is big enough for the two of us."

"Damn! I wish this war that's coming was over with, and I could get on with my life," Tom said.

The two men sat for a long time staring morosely into the fire. Finally, Alex broke the silence. "I'll go see the colonel in the morning."

The next afternoon, when Alex returned from his talk with the colonel, Liza and Kathleen were sitting at the table talking.

"I have to pick up some supplies for the ranch from Jake," Alex said. "Do you two want to come along?"

"Do you want to go, Liza?" Kathleen asked. "I've invited Jake and Little Songbird for supper tonight, but if there's something you need, we can go."

"No, I don't need anything," Liza replied.

After Alex had left, Kathleen looked Liza directly in the eye and said, "Little Songbird is my best friend here at the fort."

Liza smiled.

"Doesn't that shock you?" Kathleen asked in surprise.

"No," Liza answered calmly. "Should it?"

"Well, it does everyone else. She's Indian, you know."

"Yes, I know," Liza answered, fully aware of why

321

Kathleen felt defensive for her friend. "But I have two Indian friends myself."

"Who?" Kathleen asked, surprised.

"Well, first there's Bright Star. She's been with Alex for years. She's practically raised little Andy. And then there's Wahcawin. She's Tanazin's wife."

"Tanazin's wife? How did you meet her?"

Liza told Kathleen of her abduction by the Kiowas, her rescue, and how Wahcawin had nursed her back to health. The Irish woman listened with rapt fascination. When Liza had finished her story, Kathleen cried, "My God, how exciting! Tell me," she said confidentially, "they say Tanazin is a handsome rascal. Is that true?"

Liza grinned. "Yes, but not as handsome as Alex."

"Hell, who else is?" Kathleen responded. Both women laughed.

"And you say his wife is pretty?" Kathleen asked, her eyes twinkling with curiosity.

"Yes, Wahcawin is lovely. But actually, she's his third wife."

Kathleen looked appropriately shocked, and Liza tried to explain the relationship of Tanazin and his wives as Alex had explained it to her.

"Not me!" Kathleen retorted. "I wouldn't share Tom with any other woman. My God, just the thought of Tom making love to another woman makes my blood boil. Why, I'd scratch her eyes out."

Liza blushed at Kathleen's frankness and then giggled. "I felt the same way, but maybe we're just being selfish."

"Selfish, my eye," Kathleen said. "Tom's my man, and I don't share him with anyone." Then Kathleen giggled, her look mischievous. "Of course, if you want to share Alex with me—"

"Not on your life!" Liza interjected.

Kathleen laughed. "Well, you can't blame a girl for trying." Her look turned thoughtful. "You know, I've often wondered about Alex. He's so . . . well, so masculine. He must be a great lover."

Liza was utterly shocked. For once, she couldn't think of a thing to say. Her face colored a deep crimson.

"There I go again!" Kathleen cried. "Putting my foot in my mouth." Liza laughed uncomfortably, wishing she could change the subject.

Kathleen did it for her. "Did you know Little Songbird is going to have a baby?"

"No, I didn't," Liza answered, relieved to be off the subject of Alex.

"Yes, and I'm so envious I don't know what to do," she said sadly.

"But why?"

"Because I've been trying so hard to get pregnant." Her eyes glittered with tears. "Oh, Liza, I want to give Tom a baby so badly. We've been married for over a year now, and there's still no sign. It seems I can't do anything right. God must be punishing me."

"Punishing you? What makes you think that?"

"Because the whole time Tom and I were lovers, I prayed I wouldn't get pregnant. God must be punishing me. Who ever heard of an Irish woman who can't get pregnant? My own mother had thirteen children."

"Don't be silly, Kathleen. God doesn't punish people like that."

"Then what's wrong with me?" Kathleen cried.

"Probably nothing," Liza replied firmly. "Maybe you're just trying too hard."

Kathleen blinked the threatening tears away and then grinned, her lower lip still trembling. "I only know of one way to get pregnant, and that's not hard."

Liza laughed. "Kathleen, you're impossible. I mean, maybe you should stop worrying about it. You're probably just tense, that's all. Many couples don't have children for several years. My own parents didn't."

A hopeful look came over Kathleen's face. "That might be so. Jake and Little Songbird have been married three years themselves."

"Is Tom worried about it?" Liza asked.

"Oh, no. He says he would just as soon wait for a while." She averted her eyes in a surprising show of shyness. "He says he enjoys having me all to himself."

"See, you're the only one worrying, and probably over nothing." Liza laughed. "Once you get started, you probably won't be able to stop."

Kathleen laughed, too. "Now, that's probably the truth. At least, I hope so," she quickly added.

That night, after Liza and Kathleen had retired, Alex and Tom again sat before the fire, talking quietly. Tom looked up in shock when Kathleen entered the room in only her nightgown, the soft material clinging to her ample curves.

He glanced nervously at Alex and then rose to divert his wife, but Kathleen pushed him aside and stood, hands on hips, before Alex. "Don't get me

324

wrong, Alex," Kathleen said. "I'm glad you and Liza came to visit. But I don't see why that has to mean I can't sleep with my husband."

Tom's shocked gasp filled the small room.

Alex's eyes glittered with amusement. "I agree, Kathleen. Where do you suggest I sleep?"

The woman grinned mischievously. "Well, I certainly wouldn't want to push you out in the cold." She tilted her head, her brown eyes sparkling. "I don't see anything wrong with the bedroom, do you?"

Alex's eyebrows rose in surprise. He glanced at Tom to see his reaction to Kathleen's suggestion for sleeping arrangements. The captain's eyes were lifted to heaven in a silent appeal.

Alex grinned and rose from the chair. "Anything to make my gracious, lovely hostess happy."

As he crossed the room to the bedroom, he heard Tom sternly admonishing, "Now, Kathleen—"

"Hush up, you big ox!" she hissed. Then, her voice low and seductive, she said, "I've been laying in that bed all this time, thinking of you...."

The door closed quietly behind him as Alex scanned the bedroom, his eyes squinting in the dim light coming from the small fire in the fireplace. He walked to the bed and gazed down at Liza, sleeping on her side with her back to him. Quickly, he undressed and slipped under the covers with her. As he pulled her to him, she snuggled closer in her sleep.

Liza was dreaming the most delicious dream. At least, she thought it was a dream. Suddenly, she was awake and alert. This was no dream! "Alex! What are you doing here?"

325

Alex chuckled. "I've been evicted, sweetheart, and have no place to go. Surely, you're not going to push me out in the snow."

"Get out of here! What will Kathleen and Tom think?"

Alex grinned. "As a matter of fact, it was Kathleen's idea. She said she saw no reason why she couldn't sleep with her husband just because we were here. She kindly suggested that I sleep in here."

"Oh, Alex," Liza said, giggling at Kathleen's outrageous suggestion, "you go right back out there." She shoved at his big body.

Alex didn't budge. Instead, he calmly folded his arms under his head. "No, I don't think that would be a good idea. Somehow, I got the impression our hosts were going to be occupied for a while, and I wouldn't want to embarrass them by walking in on them."

Liza glared down at him. Alex lay, grinning up at her. Finally, she laughed, shaking her head. "That Kathleen."

Alex's amusement turned to warm desire. "Yes," he answered huskily, "she's wonderful." Then a steely arm snaked out and pulled Liza down and under him. Swiftly, and with intent expertise, he silenced any further protests.

The next day, as they drove to the ranch, Alex told Liza of his discussion with Tom and of his subsequent talk with the colonel. As he talked, Liza felt a growing sense of fear and despair. When he had finished, Liza cried, "You can't! You said you wouldn't fight, you wouldn't kill for another man's cause."

"I know what I said, Liza, but I was wrong. Tom was right. It's going to be my war, too. I can't sit back and watch my country torn in two. And I certainly can't stand by and watch this territory turned into a battlefield. It's something I have to do."

Liza remembered the night Tanaźin and his braves had rode into the ranch yard. That night, Alex had said the same words. Yes, she thought sadly, and if he has to kill, a little part of him will die each time. Her heart felt like a block of ice in her chest, but she knew it was useless to argue.

Her hands trembled as they cupped his face. Alex's eyes pleaded silently for understanding. "Yes, Alex," she muttered.

And I'll be waiting for you to heal your wounds, both those of your body and your soul, she thought grimly. *In war, you men have your job, and we women have ours.*

Chapter 15

A week later, Alex sat behind the massive desk in the corner of the parlor, his head bent over the open ledger before him. Absently, he pushed a lock of hair back from his forehead and then moved his hand through his thick hair and down over his neck to one shoulder, massaging the aching muscle there. Glancing up and looking through the circle of light cast by the lamp, his gaze lingered on Liza, who was leaning against the window and watching the snow fall outside.

The fire picked up the red and gold highlights of her hair lying softly about her shoulders. Her dressing gown was pulled tightly around her, revealing every sweet, provocative curve of her body. Alex felt a stirring in his loins and regretfully lowered his eyes to the column of figures in the ledger.

Adding the figures for the third time, he glanced up, thinking irritably, *Now what in the hell is she doing?* Liza stood by a table, lightly fingering a small statuette. Her dressing gown gaped open, allowing Alex a tantalizing glimpse of a creamy breast. He squirmed uncomfortably in his chair.

"Why don't you go to bed, Liza?" Alex suggested. "I'll probably be up half the night with this."

"That's all right, Alex," Liza answered sweetly. "I'm not tired. I had a long nap this afternoon. I don't mind waiting up for you."

Alex stared at her full, seductive lips and felt his mouth go dry. Groaning, he buried his head in his hand and glared down at the ledger before him. Determined, he started adding the numbers again. This time a small noise distracted him, and he looked up to see Liza bending over the fireplace to add another log to the fire. The cloth of her gown stretched tightly over her shapely buttocks, outlining their perfection.

A snarl escaped Alex's throat as his hand slammed down on the desk top, causing the lamp to shake precariously. "Dammit, Liza, will you stop that!" he yelled.

Liza whirled, her violet eyes wide with astonishment, her face pale with alarm.

Instantly, Alex's anger vanished. Feeling contrite, he said gently, "I'm sorry, sweetheart, but you keep distracting me."

"But I only put another log on the fire," Liza said defensively, a touch of hurt in her voice.

Alex's eyes warmed. Smiling he said, "Come here, sweet."

Warily, Liza walked across the room to where Alex sat. As she approached, he pushed the chair away from the desk, then pulled her onto his lap. Lightly stroking the line of her jaw, he apologized. "I'm sorry I yelled at you, sweetheart. I know you're not doing it deliberately. Only, I'm feeling a little horny right now, and anything and everything you do distracts me."

Liza's brow furrowed. "Horny? Is that an Indian word?"

Alex chuckled. "No, but I'm sure they have an expression for it, too." Lowering his head, he nuzzled the silky skin of her throat.

"What does it mean?" Liza asked.

Alex nibbled her earlobe, his voice husky as he replied, "It means when you want it so badly, you can't think of anything else. You can't even sit still."

Liza knew without a doubt what "it" was. Her eyes twinkled, her lips curved into a mischievous smile. "Can a woman be horny, too?"

Shocked, Alex raised his head to look at her. Frowning, he shook his head, gently rebuking her. "You shouldn't say that word, Liza. It's really very vulgar." This time his mouth descended to the base of her throat, his lips dropping hot searing kisses downward toward the swell of her breasts.

"Well, can she?" Liza demanded obstinately.

But Alex was too absorbed in his fascinating exploration even to hear her question. Exasperated, Liza caught his ears and roughly jerked his head up. "Can she?"

Alex's eyes were glazed with desire. Totally frustrated, he muttered, "You pick the damndest time to ask questions. How in the hell would I know. Why?"

Liza smiled impishly; a dimple winked in her

330

cheek. Tilting her head, she answered, "Because I think I've been feeling a little horny, too."

Alex stared at her, both surprised and shocked. Slowly the meaning of her words registered on his passion-dulled brain. So that's why she had been restless. Why, the little minx was in no better shape than he was.

Liza felt his laugh deep in his chest long before it rumbled past his lips. Alex threw his head back and roared. Then he rose, carrying her to the door in swift, purposeful strides.

Liza nestled into Alex, laying her head against the strong, tanned column of his throat. "Where are we going?" she asked dreamily.

Alex's voice was low and seductive. "To bed, sweetheart." Then he chuckled. "Where else do two horny people belong?"

Later, much later, Liza lay beside Alex, watching him as he slept. His hair was tousled, his mouth relaxed, the tired lines on his face erased, making him look much younger.

Liza regretted that he had so little time to really relax. She had been amazed at the amount of work to be done on a ranch during the winter. She had assumed that once the snow was heavy on the ground, his outdoor work would be finished until spring. But that was not so. Every day, unless there was a blizzard, Alex and Manuel rode out to check on the herd. Often, they would find cattle trapped in an unusually high drift, and after much tugging and cursing, they would release the unfortunate animals. Alex constantly complained about the cattles' inability to dig down through the snow to the grass

331

beneath. "Stupid cows. We have to show it to them. Grass can be six inches from their noses, and they're too dumb to know it. Even a buffalo is smarter than that," he would rant.

Much of his and Manuel's time was spent tracking and killing the wolves that constantly menaced the herd. And when they were not occupied with the cattle, they were busy repairing the wagons and harnesses.

So every night, Alex would come home exhausted and still have his bookkeeping to do. It was a chore he apparently hated with a passion. "My books wouldn't be in this mess if I'd kept up with them in the first place," he had told Liza.

Liza sighed deeply, wishing there was something she could do to lighten his load. Since her activities were limited now because of the bad weather, she found she was often bored and restless. She wondered if there was anything she could do to help Alex. Her mind searched the possibilities until she lit on one with deadly intent. Smiling, she fell asleep.

When she awakened the next morning, Alex was gone from the bed. "Oh, no!" Liza cried as she threw off the covers and hastily pulled on her dressing gown. She caught Alex just as he was opening the front door.

"Alex, wait!" she called urgently.

He turned, a surprised look on his face. He watched in silent admiration as she hurried down the stairs, her long hair flying and her dressing gown flapping about her legs, offering a tantalizing glimpse of white thigh. He groaned. She tripped on the last step and fell into his arms.

Alex chuckled. "I thought I had finally satisfied you last night. Sweetheart, you're insatiable."

"Stop it," she answered irritably, thinking that here she had almost killed herself to catch him before he left, and all he could do was tease her. Besides, Alex had hit on a sensitive nerve. She was beginning to wonder if she wasn't a little wanton. "I have something I want to discuss with you."

Alex frowned. "Can't it wait until tonight? I heard wolves howling early this morning. I want to track them down before the snow covers their trail."

"This won't take long," Liza insisted. "Come into the parlor." Alex frowned, following her.

Turning to face him, she said, "I want to help you with your bookkeeping. That way, you won't be so tired in the evenings."

Alex grinned. "Are you complaining about my lovemaking? You seemed quite satisfied with it last night," he taunted.

Liza colored and then stamped her foot. "Dammit, Alex, I'm serious!"

Alex sobered quickly. Liza rarely cursed, and then only when she was really angry about something. But hell, she couldn't possibly be serious. Everyone knew women didn't know a damned thing about keeping books.

"Liza, bookkeeping isn't a game. It's serious work," Alex said patiently.

"I know that!" Liza replied angrily. She was beginning to resent his condescending attitude. "But I can do it just as well as you can."

"Honey," Alex said in a placating voice.

"I can!" Liza retorted. "I told you my father gave me extra tutoring, and arithmetic was my best subject. I bet I know more about it than you do!"

Alex's look was clearly doubtful.

"Try me," she challenged.

"All right!" Alex snapped. *She gets the damndest notions,* he thought, walking to the desk and picking up the ledger on it. Liza followed him and stood, her arms folded tightly across her chest, her eyes flashing.

"Don't you want a pencil and paper?" Alex asked.

"No, that's not necessary," Liza replied coldly. "Just read off the column you want added."

Alex laughed. "Oh, come on, Liza, you can't add without—"

"Just read it!" Liza interjected, her eyes glittering dangerously.

This is ridiculous, Alex thought. *But what the hell!* Slowly, he read the long column of figures. Before he had barely called off the last number, Liza named the sum for him. He stared down at the ledger in surprise.

Then he glared at her, saying in an accusing voice, "That was a trick. You knew I'd pick the column on the open page, so you memorized the answer."

Liza smiled smugly. "If you think so, then find another column, any column."

Alex leafed back through the ledger until he found a particularly difficult column. He remembered that he had labored over it for several hours before finally coming to an answer. He smiled arrogantly and slowly read off the column.

"Repeat the last two numbers," Liza requested.

Alex grinned, thinking that she was stalling for

time. He read off the numbers.

When Liza called off the correct sum, he stared at her, totally dumbfounded. "How did you do that?" he asked, a little awed.

Liza smiled. "I can't explain it. All I know is that I can add, subtract, multiply, and divide in my head. It just clicks off. My father couldn't understand it, either."

Alex nodded. "I knew a guy in college like that."

"Then you'll let me keep your books?" Liza asked, excited at the prospect of a new challenge.

Alex shook his head. "I don't know, Liza. Bookkeeping isn't just adding and subtracting. Things have to be entered from a bill of sale—"

"I can do it," Liza interrupted. "You can show me how."

"It's a lot of work, Liza. It takes a lot of time."

"I've got the time. I can work on them in the afternoons when Andy and Bright Star are napping. I never know what to do with myself then, anyway."

Alex hedged. "I've been thinking of hiring a man to keep my books for me."

Liza's eyes narrowed. "What is it that's bothering you, Alex? Is it because I'm a woman, and you don't think a woman can do the job as well as a man?"

Alex shuffled his feet, his look uncomfortable.

Liza glared at him. "Why is it that you men always think you have a monopoly on brains? Do you think intelligence comes automatically with your male equipment?" She motioned vaguely at his crotch.

Alex stood, absolutely stunned.

"For your information, Alex, women are just as smart as men, only we're expected to stand around

335

pretending to be stupid to feed your male egos. Tell me, Alex, why are men afraid of a woman who uses her brain? How does that threaten you? And how could it possibly detract from your strength? You pride yourself on being honest and fair, Alex. Always championing the underdog. But you're not being honest and fair with me. When it comes to women, you're nothing but a bigot!''

Alex was reeling under her accusations. His logic struggled with his male ego, and his frustration led to anger. "We'll discuss it tonight." Furious, he strode from the room.

All day long, Alex struggled with himself. Once he had finally admitted to himself that he did feel a little threatened by an intelligent woman, he was better able to sort out his feelings. He asked himself why? Did Liza's intelligence detract from her femininity? He grinned, thinking, *Certainly not!* Did it detract from his masculinity? The answer was an emphatic "no!" Slowly, he was able to admit that he hadn't been fair to her. His male ego still struggled, finding it difficult to give up its age-old, superior attitude. The idea of a man and woman being intellectually equal was a totally new concept. It would take some getting used to, Alex admitted. But it was a beginning.

When he returned to the house that evening, he went looking for Liza. "The bookkeeping job is all yours," he informed her.

"Oh, Alex, thank you," Liza cried when she recovered from her surprise. "I promise you, I'll do a good job. I won't let you down."

Alex grinned. "I know you'll do a good job, but

there's a catch."

Liza looked at him warily.

"I've decided if you're going to take on the bookkeeping job full-time, I'm going to pay you, just like I would a male bookkeeper."

Liza frowned. She opened her mouth to object.

Alex stopped her. "It's only fair."

"All right," Liza agreed reluctantly. Then she remembered all the times she had longed for her own money to buy small things for herself and gifts for others. She hated to ask Alex for it, and never had for that reason, although she knew he would never begrudge her. Her own money, earned by her own efforts. The thought gave her a heady sense of independence.

She nestled against Alex's warm, muscular body. "You're an exception, a wonderful man," she said lovingly.

"That's funny," Alex replied. "I was just thinking the same thing about you."

A month later, Liza sank into the downy comfort of a big chair in the parlor, smiling contentedly. How she loved these lazy, carefree evenings before the warm fire. Ever since she had taken over the bookkeeping, Alex was free to relax in the evenings, too. They had made it their habit to retire to the parlor for a few hours each night before bedtime. Sometimes they sat and talked quietly. Sometimes they were joined by Bright Star and Andy, and Alex would entertain them with stories of his experiences, which was what he was doing now.

She watched as Alex patiently answered one of Andy's questions, thinking that he would have made a good teacher himself. She studied the rugged rancher under lowered lashes. The lines of tension were gone from around his eyes and mouth, and his whole body seemed more relaxed now. Probably because he had been relieved of some of the work and stress, she realized with satisfaction.

Liza had been shocked at how much work the bookkeeping job really was. But Alex had been infinitely patient in teaching her and answering her questions. Instead of resenting her success with her new job, as Liza had feared he might, Alex was proud of her. Because of this new acceptance and appreciation of her, and the free time they now shared, their love had grown and deepened.

She forced herself from her thoughts to give Alex her full attention.

"A wonderland lies north and west of here," he was telling Andy. "John Colter, a fur trapper, discovered it in the early part of the century, and since then, it's become a favorite meeting place for the fur trappers. But the Indians have always known of it. They consider it an ancient sacred ground."

"What's it like?" Andy asked, excited. "Have you been there?"

"Yes, Tanázin and I went once. It's beautiful, like a fairyland."

"Did you see any fairies?" Andy asked, his eyes wide with wonder.

"No, but you could almost imagine them playing amongst the trees. The area consists of hundreds of miles of hills, plains and valleys, covered with beautiful forests and surrounded by magnificent, snow-capped mountain ranges."

"That doesn't sound so wonderful to me," Andy complained.

"But wait," Alex said, his voice dropping to a low, mysterious timbre. "Strange things can be seen in this area. In some places, boiling water shoots up in the air for hundreds of feet. They're called geysers."

Andy cocked his head, his look dubious. "How can water go straight up in the air?"

Alex explained, "The water lies beneath the surface of the ground, surrounded by hot rocks. The warmth from the rocks heats the water until it's boiling, and when the pressure becomes too intense, the water shoots into the air." Alex demonstrated with his hands.

Andy squealed in delight. "Like Liza's teakettle!"

"Sort of," Alex answered with a smile. "The area is sprinkled with hot springs, many of them boiling. The water in the springs holds limestone in solution, and as it cools, it forms terraces of delicate beauty and a variety of color, yellows, browns, pinks."

Andy's eyes were wide as Alex continued, "Several rivers run through the area, and Tanaźin and I counted thirty waterfalls. One fall was particularly beautiful. Actually, it was two falls in succession. First the upper falls, about a hundred feet high, and then a short distance away, the river makes another plunge of about three hundred feet. In its leap the water is dashed against the rocks, causing a fine spray, and the whole gorge below is filled with rainbows."

Liza listened, spellbound, as Alex continued. "At

one place we saw a pool of boiling clay. It looked like a big pot of yellow and red mush. We passed a hill from whose sides jets of steam issued with such force that we could hear it a mile away. Tanaźin said the Indians call it Roaring Mountain."

Alex's voice was almost hushed, and Liza had to strain to hear. "But the most beautiful, most awesome sight of all was the canyon. It must have been fifteen or twenty miles long and hundreds of feet deep. It's a stupendous chasm, its walls marvelously colored, as if some giant artist had painted them with every hue of color." Alex shook his head. "I can't possibly describe its beauty and grandeur." He looked at Liza, his smoky eyes gazing deeply into hers. "Someday, I'd like to take you there."

The spell was broken by Andy. "Is that where you got this?" The little boy held out the gold nugget that usually rested in the bookcase with Alex's eagle feather and other interesting rocks.

"No," Alex answered. "My father and I found that in the South Pass District of the Wind River when I was a boy."

"Near here?" Liza asked in surprise. She had always thought that the gold nugget had come from someplace else, like California.

"Yes," Alex answered.

"I didn't know there was gold around here," Liza remarked.

"Yes, gold was discovered in forty-two," Alex informed her. "But it wasn't a big strike and it quickly played out. Miners still stalk the area, but personally, I hope another strike never occurs again."

"Why not?" Liza asked.

"Because the miners tear up the land and muddy the rivers. Then there's always the influx of un-desirables that follow all gold strikes." He shook his head sadly. "Gold fever isn't a pretty thing, Liza. It turns men into animals. We've got enough problems here without that."

Andy was bored with the conversation. "Let's play horsey, Uncle Alex."

"Again?" Alex groaned, but good-naturedly rolled to the floor.

Liza watched in amusement as Alex crawled around on his hands and knees, trying to buck a squealing Andy off his back. Finally, Alex collapsed on the floor, vowing Andy had broken the horse's back. Bright Star led the reluctant buckaroo off to bed.

Alex pulled off his boots and socks, smiling at Liza warmly. "Come here, Liza."

Liza glanced quickly at the closed door.

Alex chuckled. "Don't worry. No one will inter-rupt us."

Liza grinned impishly. "What about your broken back?"

With lightning speed, Alex caught her and pulled her to the floor, rolling her beneath him on the bearskin rug. His tongue teased her ear, and his teeth nibbled at the delicate earlobe, sending small shivers of pleasure up her spine. "It will be a cold day in hell," he muttered in her ear, "when my back isn't up to making love to you."

"Wait!" Liza cried urgently. Before he could object, she wiggled from his arms and rose. As she

341

walked to the door, Alex jumped to his feet to stop her, but when she pushed the bolt on the door firmly shut, he stopped and grinned.

Liza turned and walked gracefully toward Alex, a strange, teasing smile on her lips. Alex reached for her, but she twisted away from him, saying huskily, "No!"

Alex watched, puzzled, then mesmerized, as she began to undress before him. Her movements were slow, deliberately provocative, as first the dress and then the petticoats fell to the floor. She laughed quietly as she kicked off her shoes. Standing before him, dressed only in her chemise and silk stockings, she turned away and, watching him over one shoulder, slowly slipped the garment down her body. Alex's mouth went dry, his heart thudding erratically in his chest as he watched the fascinating, erotic performance. He sucked in his breath when she turned to him, wearing only her silk stockings. Her eyes locked with his, she slowly slipped off one stocking, then the other. Her arms rose gracefully as she unpinned the bun at the back of her head, causing her breasts to jut out enticingly. Beads of perspiration broke out on Alex's forehead. As the heavy red-gold mass of hair tumbled about her shoulders, she again laughed huskily, the sound playing havoc on Alex's already aroused senses.

As she stood proudly before him, Alex stared at her, the firelight turning her skin to a warm, honey color. "You look like a goddess," he mumbled, reaching for her.

She danced away from his outstretched arms. "No, don't touch me," she whispered. Slowly, seductively she moved toward him. "Don't move. Let me."

Alex stood frozen to the spot as she unbuttoned his shirt and pushed it off his shoulders and down his arms. Deliberately, she brushed her naked breasts against his chest and laughed when she saw him clench his teeth. She traced the powerful muscles of his chest from one shoulder to one dark nipple, lazily circling it until she saw it harden. Leaning forward, she licked the hardened bud and heard Alex's moan of pleasure. Smiling with self-satisfaction, she unbuckled his belt and unbuttoned his pants, her hands lingering over and teasing the hard bulge beneath. Slowly, she slipped the pants over his hips and thighs, and as she lowered her body, her hair caught briefly around Alex's erection. The sensation was almost unbearable for Alex. He ground his teeth and clenched his hands.

Liza sat back on her heels and looked up at him boldly. Alex stood like a magnificent bronze statue, the firelight playing over his powerful muscles. The human male animal in its perfection, she thought, a shiver of anticipation running through her. She smiled seductively and beckoned to him.

As Alex lowered himself beside her, he reached for her again. For the third time, she pushed his hands away and admonished him, "Don't touch. Remember?"

Alex knew that she was teasing him, deliberately provoking his passion. But he was already wildly excited and seriously doubted that he could stand any more of this exquisite torture. He groaned as she pushed him back against the fur rug.

Kneeling beside him, Liza teased and taunted him with featherlike strokes. Her finger circled his ear and traced the frantic pulse down his throat, leaving a trail of fire in its wake. Her hands lightly explored his chest, across his abdomen, teasingly close to his groin, and down to his thighs, feeling the powerful muscles jerk in response to her touch. Still stroking one thigh, she lowered her head and dropped tiny kisses over his neck and chest and down his stomach, her tongue flicking and then circling his navel. His abdominal muscles contracted tightly.

"Liza," Alex gasped, his voice pleading, feeling he would explode at any minute.

She smiled up at him, shaking her head. Her hand moved from his thigh to stroke the velvety skin of his erection. One finger slowly traced the long, hot shaft from its base to the crown that glistened in the firelight. Alex moaned. She bent and placed feather-like kisses over it. Alex trembled violently, crying urgently, "Liza!"

Smiling, Liza lifted her body over his and lowered her hips, gradually enveloping him, slowly surrounding him inch by inch. Alex writhed in delicious agony beneath her, feeling her heat and the small spasms of her muscles clutching him.

Alex couldn't stand any more torture. He snarled, and one hand circled her neck, forcing her head down to his, as the other hand pushed her hips tightly against his. His kiss was fiercely demanding, and as his tongue plunged into her mouth, he arched against her, thrusting in deep, powerful strokes.

His mouth left hers to devour her neck, shoulders and breasts in tiny love-bites and greedy licks as now both hands held her firmly against him. The tempo increased; the rhapsody rose and built to unbearable heights until it finally burst into a violent, con-

344

suming crescendo.

They lay, still entwined, shuddering, the firelight dancing over their glistening bodies. For a while, Alex lay, just savoring the feel of their bodies still joined, and then, he gently rolled Liza from him. He gazed down at her, his look incredulous.

"Now, where did you learn that?" he demanded thickly. Shaking his head, he added, "And don't tell me I taught you."

Liza laughed. "But you did. Remember that night in the Indian camp when you seduced me? You teased and taunted me, until I thought I would go crazy."

Alex smiled, and then his look turned warm and tender. "You know, sweetheart, you're a puzzle to me. Just when I think I know you, you show me another facet of yourself. Tonight, the seductress." His eyes searched her face. "I wonder if I'll ever solve all of your mysteries."

Liza smiled, her look again seductive. "Did I please you?"

"Please me?" Alex laughed shakily. "Sweetheart, as much as I enjoyed that, you had better not do it too often. I'm afraid you've completely drained me."

"Oh, I doubt that," Liza replied. To prove her point, she brushed one silky thigh against his groin. His response was immediate.

Alex's facial expression was one of utter surprise. Then he grinned. "All right, my little seductress," he said huskily, "but this time, it's my turn. And remember the rules. No touching."

"Alex!"

Chapter 16

Spring awakened slowly that year, insidiously. The snow melted and turned the ground to mud; the warm sun beamed down benevolently and dried the mud. Then violent thunderstorms swept the area and turned the ground to mud again, the cycle repeating itself over and over.

The ranch work increased to a feverish pitch as the calving season began. Alex and Manuel were gone from dawn to dusk, flushing the herd from low areas subject to flooding and pulling trapped cattle from mud holes. They doubled their efforts against the wolves and other predators that threatened the particularly vulnerable newborn calves.

One night, Liza awakened to find Alex gone from bed. She crept to the window and peered out into the dark night. Lightning flashed in the distance, signaling the approach of yet another storm. She glanced below her and saw light shining from the half-open barn door.

Another mare was foaling, she thought excitedly.

Hurriedly, she pulled on her dressing gown and flew down the stairs. She stopped briefly at the door to throw a shawl over her shoulders and then ran across the ranch yard, her feet squishing in mud puddles, cold water splashing on her bare legs.

She slipped past the barn door and stood breathing heavily from her run, glancing about the barn. Alex stood to one side, washing his arms and bare chest in a bucket of water.

"Is it over?" she asked.

Alex turned in surprise and then smiled. "Yes, and isn't he a beauty?" He nodded to the stall across from him.

Liza blinked back tears of disappointment. "Why didn't you wake me?"

Alex frowned. "I'm sorry, Liza. I forgot."

"All the animals around me are giving birth, cows, horses, cats, but I've yet to see anything born," she complained. She glared at the white cat lying in the corner of the barn, her kittens nursing hungrily. "Even Snowball let me down," she said bitterly.

"You mean you've never seen anything give birth?" Alex asked in astonishment.

"Never."

Suddenly, Alex could understand Liza's anger at the cat. Liza had pampered Snowball throughout her entire pregnancy, and then the cat had slipped off to have her kittens and cheated Liza of the long-awaited experience. "It seems we've both let you down," he admitted. "I didn't realize that you had never seen anything born. I can see how disappointed you must be. I promise, I won't forget the next time."

"I suppose you think I'm being childish," Liza

said tentatively.

"No, not at all. Everyone should see something born at least once in their lifetime. It's a wonderful experience. As many births as I've watched, it still leaves me with a feeling of awe." He smiled and reached for her hand. "Come and see the new addition to my breeding stock."

The little chestnut foal was lying in the straw by his proud mother. As Liza approached, he looked at her quizzically. "Look, Alex, his eyes are open."

"Yes," Alex answered with a chuckle.

"But I thought animals' eyes stayed closed for a week or so. Snowball's kittens didn't open their eyes for ten days."

"Small animals, yes, but larger animals open their eyes shortly after birth."

Liza watched as the mare nuzzled her newborn and whickered softly. The little colt tried to rise, but collapsed weakly. Again the mare nudged her foal, encouraging him with gentle whinnies. Finally, the little horse struggled to his feet, wobbling precariously on his long, spindly legs. He took a few shaky steps as the mare prodded him toward her flank. The foal searched, and then, finding what he was looking for, nursed greedily.

"Oh, Alex, he's beautiful," Liza said, awed, her voice a mere whisper.

"Yes, he is. He'll make a handsome stallion."

"Is he the one that goes to Tanazin?" Liza asked, remembering Alex's agreement with the Indian chief in return for the mink pelts that resulted in her fur cape.

"No, our agreement was for Thunder's first colt.

348

He's that little black one back there." He motioned to the back of the barn. "Actually, this is Thunder's third colt this year."

Liza's eyes swept over the stalls of breeding mares. Remembering Alex's promise that she watch the next foaling, she asked, "Which one foals next?"

"That would be your pinto, Star. But I'm afraid that won't be for some time yet." Alex grinned. "I think it would be appropriate, however, since you were present at its conception, also."

Liza blushed as she remembered the horse-mating scene. Recalling it made her feel strangely excited.

Alex watched the pulse beat in her throat quicken. "I see you remember," he said, and his eyes warmed. "That reminds me of some unfinished business." His eyes bored into hers, and Liza watched, mesmerized, as he took off his boots and socks, and then his belt.

Her heart was pounding frantically in her chest. She remembered the day Alex had almost taken her by force in this very barn. She was aroused, but perversely, she didn't want to submit. She wanted to be mastered, conquered.

She looked Alex in the eye, her voice a hoarse whisper, "I won't surrender meekly."

Alex's thoughts had been running parallel to hers. He understood her game only too well. A muscle twitched in his cheek, and he nodded curtly.

For a long moment, their eyes remained locked, each waiting for the other to make the first move. Suddenly, Liza pivoted and ran for the door. In three swift strides, Alex caught her and spun her into his arms. She kicked, her hands clawing at his face and chest. He grunted in response and threw her over his shoulder, pinning her thrashing legs tightly against his hard chest. As he walked to the back of the barn, Liza beat on his back with her fists. He retaliated with a hardy slap to her buttocks.

Kneeling, Alex dropped her on the straw of an empty stall and, before she could move, pinned her with his big, powerful body. One hand quickly untied the sash of her robe, the other roaming demandingly over her body. Liza thrashed and kicked, squirmed and clawed, until she finally managed to roll away from him. Grabbing a fist-full of fiery hair, Alex yanked her back. Her robe was quickly disposed of, and once again, Alex pinned her down, this time straddling her thighs. With one hand, he caught both her small wrists and pulled her arms over her head. Liza twisted and squirmed beneath him, hissing epithets, as Alex nipped at her throat, breasts and belly. Liza strained her neck and sank her teeth into his muscular shoulder.

Alex swore as his mouth came crashing down on hers in a savage kiss. His free hand struggled with his buttons, and when he lifted his hips to shed his pants, Liza seized her opportunity. Wildly she bucked her hips, unseating him, and twisted out from under him, crawling away. Freed from his pants, Alex followed and, kneeling, caught her hips in a tight vise and pulled her back to him. In one swift, powerful thrust, he was inside her.

Liza gasped, not in pain, as she was ready for him, but in surprise.

The steely grip around her hips relaxed. "My God, did I hurt you?" Alex asked, his voice thick, but full of concern.

350

"No," Liza admitted. She could feel her buttocks against his hard abdomen, the backs of her thighs against his muscular ones, his manhood throbbing and hot inside her. The unusual position unnerved her. "But . . ."

Alex chuckled. "Sweetheart, there's still a hell of a lot you don't know about lovemaking."

The game was over, as Alex leaned forward to tenderly kiss and nibble at her sensitive nape. One hand rose to caress and tease her breasts, the other holding her firmly against him. He licked her shoulder blade and down her spine as his hand beneath slowly lowered to the soft, silky curls between her legs, his fingers stroking and teasing.

Liza's breath came in tiny gasps, her body tingling all over, her blood singing. Then he began to move inside her, at first slowly, seductively, and then boldly, powerfully, with increasing urgency, carrying them to reeling heights, spinning and whirling upward until Liza felt herself shattering. Quickly following her, Alex exploded, his seed a hot, searing jet deep within her.

They collapsed in the straw, Alex's body still over hers, their bodies drenched in sweat, their breaths labored. Alex's voice was tender; his warm breath fanned her ear, as he whispered, *"Micante, tecihila."*

Liza wondered at the words. Alex had said them before in the throes of passion. They were Indian, and from the tone of his voice, she knew that they were love words, an endearment of some sort. Twisting, she rolled over beneath him and looked up at his face. Her hand caressed his strong jaw. "What does *micante, tecihila* mean? You've said it before."

A strange look flicked briefly across his face. Then he smiled. One finger brushed her bruised, swollen lips. "Someday, I'll tell you."

Liza frowned, but before she could pursue the puzzle, Alex moved away from her and pulled on his pants. Handing Liza her robe, he said, "We'd better go before that storm outside breaks and we're stranded out here."

As they walked back to the house, Liza was oblivious to the thunder rolling and the jagged bolts of lightning all around them. She was occupied with wondering over Alex's secretive behavior. What did the mysterious words mean?

Spring progressed into summer. True to Alex's prediction, the drifters returned, sometimes alone, sometimes in twos or threes. A few had worked for Alex before, the others were strangers. Most were heavily bearded, dirty, rough-looking men, but one stood out from the others.

He was a tall, large, blond-headed man, surprisingly clean shaven. He might have been considered handsome, except for the hard, flinty look in his eyes and the cruel twist of his mouth. The men called him Lou.

Liza would have paid him no mind if he had not watched her constantly, his hot eyes raking her boldly. On two occasions, he had caught her unawares, once on the way to the pool and once in the barn. Both times, he had pretended surprise and been mockingly polite, but Liza had known these were no chance encounters. She had known that she was being deliberately stalked and had been terrified. She had considered telling Alex, but had no proof against the man. Not once had he attempted to touch her. For several weeks, she didn't see him, and her tension eased.

The work on the ranch had kept Alex busy as the cattle were rounded up, the young calves branded and then castrated, and the herd driven to their summer pasture.

When this was done, Liza had hoped Alex would have more free time, but then he had been gone for over three weeks on an expedition to capture mustangs. He had returned with over sixty horses, and now he and the other hands were trying to break them before the trip to Fort Kearney.

Liza had been disappointed when he had announced the planned trip and then had scolded herself for being so childish.

"I have a contract with the army," he had explained. "Each year, I take fifty or sixty horses and a hundred or so head of cattle. Manuel and I take turns, and this year it's my turn to take the drive."

"How long will you be gone?" Liza had asked, trying to keep the disappointment from her voice.

"About four to six weeks, depending upon what problems we run into. The horses are easy to drive, but the cattle can't be driven too fast, or they'll be nothing but skin and bones by the time we get them there."

The morning before the day the drive was to begin, Liza arose feeling tense and anxious. As she stood gazing out of the window, her hand strayed absently to her abdomen. *I must find some way to tell him today*, she thought. *Only, I wish he wasn't so busy, so preoccupied.*

For almost three months, Liza had known she was pregnant, but she had put off telling Alex, hoping he would make the final commitment she longed for. True, their agreed year of trial wasn't over yet, but Liza felt she was running out of time. Above all, she had not wanted to feel she had forced him into marriage.

If only we had some free time to ourselves, she thought. For, in truth, she had seen little of Alex the past few weeks. Often she was asleep when he came to bed, and the few times she had been awake, Alex had fallen into bed exhausted, exchanging only a few brief words with her before falling asleep. She felt a sudden, violent resentment toward the ranch that seemingly demanded all of his time and attention. The emotional turmoil had left her feeling insecure, tense and exhausted. *I'll tell him tonight*, she vowed, as she dressed for the day.

Once Liza was downstairs, her dilemma was forgotten as she was carried away in a frenzy of last-minute preparations. She was helping Hiram stock the chuck wagon when the old man mumbled, "Salt, we need more salt."

Liza glanced down at Hiram's leg. He was limping badly from scurrying back and forth from the kitchen to the wagon. "Let me get it," Liza said, restraining him gently with her hand. "Tell me where it is."

Liza hurried off to the smokehouse. Intent on her purpose, she didn't see the blond-headed man who had been watching her and had followed her around the back of the house.

She opened the smokehouse door and peered into its dim interior before she took a few tentative steps inside. A small noise alerted her, and she turned to see Lou standing in the doorway, blocking it.

Liza's heart thudded wildly in her chest, her mouth dry with fear.

"Well, good morning, Miz Cameron," Lou drawled sarcastically. His eyes glittered; his voice dropped to a low, menacing tone. "But then you aren't really his wife are you? Everyone knows you're just his fancy piece."

Liza's legs trembled. "Get out of my way," she demanded weakly.

Lou grinned wickedly. "I'm afraid not. You see, I've been waiting for this for a long time." His eyes raked her body in bold insult, making Liza shiver with terror. "I've been watching you switch that sweet, little tail of yours, and I've decided that I'd like a taste of it, too."

Fear finally galvanized Liza as she leaped forward and ducked under Lou's arm. His powerful, cruel hands caught her and slammed her against the door, his massive arms pinning hers to her side. She opened her mouth to scream as Lou's mouth closed over hers, his tongue invading, almost choking her. His hands pawed at her painfully as she kicked and twisted wildly.

Suddenly, Lou was wrenched from her and thrown to the ground. Alex stood between them, his face distorted in fury.

"Now, wait a minute," Lou gasped. "You've got this all wrong, Cameron. She's been making eyes at me all along, trying to get me to meet

355

her somewhere."

Liza gasped at his accusations.

"Get out of here," Alex said in a hard voice.

Liza stared at him in disbelief. Certainly, he couldn't believe Lou's wild accusations, she thought frantically. "Alex," she pleaded.

"I said get out of here," he repeated, turning his back on her, barely able to contain his anger at Lou until she had left.

"No!" Liza screeched hysterically, grabbing his arm.

Roughly, he shook off her hand and pushed her toward Hiram, who had just limped up to them. "Get her out of here," Alex ground out between clenched teeth.

Hiram looked at the pale, trembling girl, his eyes full of compassion. Putting one skinny arm around her, he led her away as she sobbed on his bony shoulder.

Alex turned to face Lou, who was grinning at him arrogantly. "I'm going to beat the hell out of you," Alex announced, his voice low and deceivingly calm.

Lou glanced quickly at Alex's clenched fists and then up into his eyes, burning with cold fury. He scrambled to his feet. "Now wait a minute," he said shakily. "I don't know what you're so mad about. She's only some little tramp you live with." He glanced frantically at the circle of men forming around them, as if seeking confirmation or support. Seeing none, he whined, "I figured if she'd give it to you, she could give me some, too."

As Alex stepped toward him with deadly intent, Lou cried out in one last desperate attempt. "What do you want to fight me for? She's just some cheap whore. Hell, you couldn't think much of her yourself, or you would have married her!"

A primitive, blood-curdling roar escaped from Alex's throat as he lunged for the man. The force of Alex's drive threw both men to the ground, where they rolled in the dirt, each swinging at the other with well-aimed blows.

Lou was a big man, an even match for Alex, and he had a reputation as a deadly fighter. But Alex's fury seemed to give him superhuman strength as he absorbed Lou's punishing blows with no outward effects. Frantic, Lou reached for the knife concealed in his boot.

Alex saw the glint of metal through a red haze of rage. Grabbing the hand with the knife, he cruelly twisted Lou's arm, totally unaware of the man's scream of pain in his ears. Pinning Lou to the ground, Alex unmercifully battered the man's face and head, his blows brutal and with deadly intent.

"Stop it! Stop it, Alex!" The frantic words came to Alex from far away as he struggled against the two men pulling him from Lou's still body beneath him.

"Stop it, Alex! You will kill him!" Manuel cried.

The Mexican pushed Alex away with a strength amazingly powerful for a man so much smaller. "See, he is unconscious," Manuel said, trying to calm his enraged friend.

Alex's chest heaved in painful gasps, his vision still blurred with rage. "I'll kill him!" he rasped.

"No, no, amigo," Manuel soothed as he wrestled Alex back. "Killing him will solve nothing. It is not him you are so furious with. It is yourself. Killing him won't change anything." Manuel's voice was gentle and entreating.

Alex glared at the unconscious body lying on the ground. Lou's face was battered and bruised, blood pouring from his nose and mouth. Alex felt suddenly sick but, curiously, still angry. "Get him off the ranch before I get back," he hissed. "Or I *will* kill him."

"Si, amigo, si," Manuel answered in a soothing voice.

Turning, Alex stumbled angrily to his horse. The men who had been watching the fight scattered warily out of his way. Still furious, he mounted and, sawing savagely on the horse's reins, galloped off in a flurry of dust.

Alex never knew how long he blindly raced his horse across the prairie that day. Slowly, he became aware of Thunder's heaving chest, the alarming blowing noises coming from the animal beneath him. Finally alert, he stopped and dismounted, looking at his horse, shocked at what he saw.

"Poor fellow," he mumbled. "And now, I've tried to kill you, too."

He led the exhausted animal into the shade of a small tree. Then he removed the saddle and rubbed him down with grass. When Thunder's breathing had returned to normal, Alex poured water from his canteen into a cupped hand and offered it to the thirsty horse. Only then did he assuage his own thirst.

He sat and leaned back against the tree, feeling his exhaustion for the first time. His head pounded as Manuel's words repeated themselves over and over in his mind, *It is not him you are so furious with. It is yourself.*

Yes, Alex finally admitted, Manuel was right on

target. He had been angry with Lou when he had found the man mauling Liza. The man deserved a good thrashing. But the killing rage had not come over him until Lou had said, "Hell, you can't think much of her yourself, or you would have married her."

He'd been a damned fool! And it had taken another man, the scum of the earth, to bring him to his senses. In his typical, arrogant fashion, he had ignored others' opinions, never stopping to consider what his and Liza's relationship was costing her in the way of her pride and self-respect, how much he might be hurting her. And she had given him everything, freely, asking nothing in return. Sure, he had told her he loved her, but he had withheld the one thing she needed and deserved the most, his name, the final, ultimate commitment. Without that, all else was meaningless.

There was their agreement. At the time they had made it, Alex had doubted Liza's endurance and, in its newness, the strength of their love. But those doubts had been laid to rest long ago. There was no need to wait the full year to make Liza his wife. Then, why hadn't he made a point of finding someone to marry them as soon as spring had come and the snow had melted?

He knew the answer. Basking in the warmth of Liza's love, he had allowed himself to become complaisant, acting as if it were his due, taking it for granted. Instead, he had directed his energies to the ranch, misplacing his priorities. Yes, he was an arrogant, selfish bastard—and a damned fool!

But, thank God, it wasn't too late to set things right. Surely, he could find someone to marry them on his trip to Fort Kearney and bring the man back with him.

A sense of immense relief washed over him. He rose and walked swiftly to his horse. The big animal shied, eyeing him warily. "It's all right, old boy," Alex said, patting the animal's neck. "Everything is all right now."

It was late at night when Alex reached the ranch. After he had stabled Thunder, he rushed into the house and up the stairs, taking them two at a time, his heart pounding in anticipation. He found Liza asleep on their bed.

A lamp was burning softly beside the bed, picking up the red and gold highlights of Liza's hair. As Alex looked down on her, he felt that familiar twisting ache in his chest. She looked so small, so delicate, so beautiful, he thought. He frowned. She was still dressed in her clothes, and her face was unusually pale, with dark circles beneath her eyes. She's exhausted, he realized, surprised and irritated with himself that he had not noticed before.

He felt a deep pang of disappointment. He had rushed home with thoughts of apology, followed by his promise to bring someone back with him to marry them, and then a joyous night of lovemaking. He fought the urge to awaken her. *No,* he rebuked himself, *for once, don't be selfish. She's exhausted, and right now, she needs her rest more than he does you.* Gently, he covered Liza with a blanket.

Reluctantly, he left the room and descended the stairs. He sat at his desk for hours agonizing over the note that he would leave her. How could he possibly put into words the things he felt: his need, his love, how he regretted his own stupidity. His final product was brief and to the point. He wrote: *Sweetheart, I know I haven't told you lately how much I need and love you, but I do—desperately! I've been a fool to postpone our wedding for so long, but I promise when I return from Fort Kearney, I'll bring someone back to marry us, even if I have to kidnap the man or force him at gunpoint. I can't wait to make you my wife. Alex.*

Alex looked down at the note in disgust and then glanced out the window. Seeing the sky was beginning to lighten and knowing that he was already running late, he cursed quietly. Again, he considered waking Liza and, once more, decided it would be selfish on his part.

Sighing, he opened the desk drawer, found the ball of twine and broke off a piece. Then he walked to the book shelf and picked up the gold nugget. He smiled as he slipped it into his pocket, thinking of the wedding ring it would make.

Back in the bedroom, he glanced about the room, wondering where to leave the note so Liza would be sure to find it. Carefully, he leaned it against the lamp, thinking that she couldn't possibly miss seeing it there.

He sat cautiously on the bed beside her and lifted her left hand gently. He placed it on his knee while he slipped the piece of twine around her finger and tied it. He looked down at her small, graceful hand and thought, *Soon it will be a gold one, sweetheart.* She stirred slightly as he slipped the string from her finger.

For a few moments, he sat and gazed at her, studying each feature as if to memorize it. Finally, he leaned forward and tenderly kissed her brow, whispering, *"Micante, tecihila."*

Then, with a deep sigh, he rose and left the room.

When Liza awakened that morning, the sunlight was streaming through the window. She blinked in confusion, vaguely wondering why she still had on her clothes, and then remembering, she was suddenly alert. Quickly, she glanced about the room, but Alex was not there.

She jumped from the bed and ran to the window, peering down at the empty ranch yard below her. Raising the window, she leaned out it and craned her neck, looking toward the barn.

"No!" she cried, choking back a sob. "No, he can't be gone!"

She flew from the room, completely forgetting the wide open window. A strong gust of wind blew in, billowed the curtains and caught the note by the lamp, lifting it, playing with it precariously, until the note dropped and fluttered under the dresser.

Liza raced out the front door and almost stumbled into Hiram, coming back from the barn. The old man looked at her in alarm.

"Are they gone?" she asked in a frantic voice.

Hiram scowled. The girl looked terrible, her face deathly pale, her eyes wild. He didn't have the heart to say the words. Reluctantly, he nodded.

Liza felt her world shattering. She stood by watching helplessly as all of her hopes and dreams seemed to explode and drift away in a puff of smoke. A ragged, pained sob tore from her throat as she ran back upstairs to her room.

She cried until there were no more tears, and then she lay numbly staring at the ceiling.

The previous afternoon, after Hiram had left her, Liza couldn't believe that it had happened, Lou's ugly accusations and then Alex's anger. That night, she had waited for Alex's return, thinking that he would realize his mistake, that he couldn't possibly think she was like Marilee, a cheap flirt. But Alex hadn't come, and she had cried herself to sleep. And now this morning, he had left without a sign or word, so angry with her that he had not even slept in the same bed with her. She remembered bitterly his last words to her, *Get out of here, Liza*, words said because he couldn't bear even to look at her. But he was angry, Liza argued with herself. Even if it was unjust of him, he loved her, and she knew he loved her. But he didn't trust her, another part of her argued back, and love without trust was meaningless.

For three weeks, Liza waited, hoping desperately when Alex's anger cooled he would send some word. She was tortured by remembered phrases Alex had said, *You want me to tell you I love you. Hell, Liza nothing lasts forever.* And, *By this time Marilee was pregnant, and they were both trapped.* And finally, *Get out of here, Liza.* The words pounded at her, ate at her.

Finally, Liza made her decision. By the time Alex returned, her pregnancy would be obvious. She no longer knew if he loved her or not, but her pride would not allow her to trap him into marriage. Nor could she marry a man who didn't trust her. She would leave, letting Alex think she had changed her mind, and he would never know that she carried his child. She could live with his hate, but never his pity or distrust.

It was her turn to write a note that read: *Alex, you said I could leave anytime I wanted to, and now I can see it won't work for us. I'm taking the money you paid me for my bookkeeping and going back East. Liza.*

Liza's eyes blurred with tears as she read the brisk, cold words. She knew that they would hurt Alex, even if he no longer loved her. But that was what she wanted. She wanted to sever all ties, leave no doubt in his mind.

She sobbed and buried her face in her hands. "Oh, God," she muttered. "I still love him. I always will."

That night, she sought out Hiram for the first time since Alex's departure. Several times, the old man had approached her, pleading for her to confide in him, his eyes anxious and full of concern. Liza had firmly rejected him each time. Now, as she approached him, the old man felt a surge of relief.

"Hiram, I have a favor to ask of you," Liza said, her voice surprisingly calm.

"Anything, Liza. You know I'd do anything for you," Hiram answered anxiously.

"I want you to take me to the stage tomorrow."

Hiram felt as if he'd been kicked by a mule. "You're leaving?" he gasped.

Liza struggled for control. "Yes, I'm leaving."

"Liza, don't do this to Alex," the old man pleaded. "I know he's hot-headed and stubborn, but he loves you."

Maybe he loves me, but he doesn't trust me, Liza

thought bitterly. "Not enough, Hiram. Maybe he loves me, but not enough."

"Liza, listen to me," Hiram said. "I'm gonna tell you something I ain't never told no one." His look was intense. "I loved a girl once, and she loved me, too. We had a quarrel. I can't even remember now what it was about. I was hot-headed, just like Alex, and I ran away mad." He shook his head sadly. "It took me two years to admit to my mistake." His eyes had a haunted look as he continued. "I went back for her, but she had married another man. I lost her because I ran, and I ain't never forgiven myself." His look was imploring. "Don't do this, Liza. Don't run away."

Liza gazed at the old man standing before her. His pain made her briefly forget her own. So that was why Hiram had come west, she thought sadly. "I'm sorry, Hiram. I'm so sorry for you," she said, her voice filled with compassion.

"But don't you see? You're making the same mistake."

"No, this is different. I have to go," Liza insisted.

"Wait until Alex comes back. Talk to him. You'll straighten it out. You'll see."

"You don't understand. I can't wait!"

"Then wait until Manuel comes back from the range this weekend. Talk to him."

"No!"

They stared at each other, Hiram's eyes begging, Liza's rejecting. Finally, Liza said in a deadly calm voice, "If you won't take me to the stage tomorrow, I'll saddle Star and go by myself."

Hiram saw the determined gleam in her eyes and

knew that this was no idle threat. Suddenly, he felt the weight of his years. He slumped his shoulders in resignation. "I'll take you."

"Thank you." The words were a mere whisper. "And, Hiram, would you give this to Alex when he comes back?" she asked, handing him an envelope with her note in it.

Hiram nodded glumly.

"And would you mind telling the others good-bye for me? You see, I can't bear—" Her voice broke, and she sobbed as she stumbled from the room.

Hiram stood staring after her. "Damn," he cursed under his breath. A single tear crept down his old, weathered cheek. Viciously, he swiped at it, muttering, "Damn stubborn young'uns!"

The trip to the stage the next day was an agony for Liza and Hiram. Both were acutely aware of the pain of their parting, and each tried to hide it under a cover of silence.

Hiram waved the stage down, mumbling obscenities when he was almost run over by the galloping horses.

"What in the hell do you think you're doing, old man?" the stage driver yelled down at Hiram. "Get out of the road!"

"Got a passenger for you," Hiram called up, motioning to Liza.

"You got money?" the driver asked suspiciously.

"Of course, I got money!" Hiram yelled back indignantly. "You must be new on this run."

"So what if I am?" the man on the stage retorted.

"'Cause if you weren't new, you'd know who I am, and you wouldn't be asking stupid questions!" Hiram was hopping from one foot to the other in his anger.

"Okay, okay, don't get so upset," the driver answered, trying to placate the old man. "Throw her trunks up and get her in the coach. I've got a schedule to keep up."

Hiram glared at the man, mumbling, "Smart-assed whipper-snapper." He wrestled Liza's trunks to the man and then handed him a few bills. "You mind your tongue," Hiram warned the driver. "That there is a real lady."

For the first time, the driver got a good look at Liza. His eyes widened as he said, "Wow, would you look at that! What's a woman like her doing out here in the middle of nowhere?"

"That ain't none of your damn business!" Hiram spat, his eyes flashing.

"Okay, okay, no need to be so touchy," the man soothed. "Get her on the stage then, so I can go."

Hiram climbed down from the stage and opened the door for Liza. For a moment, they looked at each other sadly, and then Liza hugged the old man and kissed his cheek. A ragged sob escaped her. Fearing that she would break down completely, she hurried into the coach and collapsed in a corner as the door closed behind her.

Liza didn't look back as the coach rolled away. If she had, she would have seen a broken, old man standing in a swirl of dust, sobbing as if his heart would break.

Chapter 17

Liza sat huddled in the corner of the stagecoach, totally unaware of the passage of time and distance. She existed in a void created by her pain and loss. Even after the stage had stopped that evening and all of the other passengers had departed, she sat staring vacantly into space.

A hand shook her roughly. "Hey, lady, you gotta git out now. Stage stops here for the night."

Liza looked up in confusion at the stage driver. She peered out the window and saw that it was almost dark. "Yes, thank you," she mumbled as the man backed out of the coach.

Wearily, she climbed from the stage and looked around her. The street was deserted except for a stable hand who was unhitching the exhausted horses from the coach. The boy looked at her curiously.

Liza studied the dusty, delapidated stage depot and remembered the horrible sleeping accommodations she had found in such places on her trip west. Thinking that she was too exhausted to face that, she

368

turned and called to the boy as he led the horses away, "Is there some place else I could find a room for the night?"

The boy kept walking away from her, the jingling of the horses' harnesses drowning out her call. Liza stood in the dusty, rutted street, small and forlorn, her depression and loneliness enveloping her.

"Well, now, look who just got in town," a voice drawled behind her.

Liza jumped in surprise and then turned to face the man grinning at her. She gasped. It was Lou. At least, she thought it was, and looked closer. His nose sat at a peculiar angle, and one eye sagged almost closed. A ragged, still-raw scar ran from his forehead to his jawline, and his grin revealed several missing teeth. She stared at his disfigurement and shuddered in revulsion.

Seeing her reaction to his face, Lou's grin turned to an ugly snarl. "I ain't so pretty since your boyfriend got ahold of me," he said, his voice bitter.

Alex had done that to him? Liza thought in surprise. For a brief minute, she felt compassion. "I'm sorry," she mumbled.

"I just bet you are," Lou said in a hard, sarcastic voice. "What happened? Did he throw you off the place, too?"

Feeling something menacing under Lou's seemingly calm exterior, Liza's fear returned. She glanced frantically about the empty street.

Lou saw her look and knew that she was on the verge of bolting. He hadn't believed his luck when he saw her standing alone in the middle of the street. Ever since the beating, he'd done nothing but dream

369

of revenge against this bitch and her lover. Now he had her, and someday, he'd get Alex, too.

Quickly, Lou bent and picked up Liza's trunks. "Come on. I know a place they'll put you up for the night." He turned and walked away rapidly.

Liza stood for a minute in shocked surprise. She hadn't expected Lou to help her. Something warned her not to trust him, but he had her trunks, and every stitch of clothing she owned was in them.

"Wait!" she called after him. But Lou continued walking down the street and then turned, disappearing around the corner of a building.

Liza ran after him, the semi-darkness distorting her vision. She hurriedly turned the corner after him and realized her mistake. This was no street. A hand closed over her mouth, and an arm held her captive, as Lou pulled her farther back into the shadows of the alley. He slammed her violently against the wall of the building beside them, pinning her with his body, and forced a gag into her mouth. Liza kicked and twisted, tears of fear and frustration burning in her eyes, as Lou cruelly twisted her arms behind her back and tied them.

Lou laughed. "I've been dreaming of the day I'd get my hands on you, Miss High and Mighty." Furious, he threw her against the building, his breath hot and reeking of whiskey against her averted face. "You little bitch! You're nothing but a slut. Do you hear me?" he asked, his voice rising as he shook her roughly. "A slut!"

Liza tried to twist away. Savagely, he cuffed her, and she reeled from the blow, fighting for consciousness.

370

Laughing, Lou threw her over his shoulder and carried her to the back of the alley, where his horse stood ready and waiting. Liza knew this was her last chance, and she struggled desperately to get away from him. Finally, she kicked his groin. Lou gasped in pain, cursed and viciously backhanded her. She collapsed at his feet.

Lou glared down at her, rubbing his throbbing groin. "Bitch! Slut!" he spat, kicking the inert woman on the ground. Then, lifting her, he threw her across the front of the horse. Mounting behind her, he turned the horse away from town and rode out into the dark, silent prairie.

When Liza first regained consciousness, she thought that she was an Indian captive again, but her memory quickly returned. She heard Lou's drunken laughter above her and was ten times more frightened than she had ever been when the Indians had abducted her.

"So, you've finally come to," Lou snarled. Stopping the horse and dismounting, he said, "This place is just as good as any." Roughly, he pulled her from the horse and threw her on the ground. Liza lay huddled on her side, looking up at him in terror.

He reached down and jerked the gag from her mouth. Instantly, Liza gasped for air. "Don't need that no more," he said. "You can scream your head off out here, and no one will hear you." He laughed—an ugly, spine-tingling laugh. "And you'll scream all right."

"Please don't hurt me," Liza begged. "I'm going to have a baby."

Lou's eyes glittered. "A baby? *His* bastard?" He

roared in laughter. "Oh, this is even better, his whore and his bastard!"

He pulled a whiskey bottle from his saddlebags and took a long swig from it. In the moonlight, Liza could see his face, and it was even more distorted now. His eyes had a wild look about them, his face full of hate and— He's insane! Liza realized, and a new terror rose in her.

He bent down and yanked on her hair, snapping her head back. Placing the whiskey bottle against her bruised mouth, he hissed, "Drink. Drink, dammit! You're gonna need it."

"No," Liza muttered, twisting her head away. The whiskey spilled over her face and bodice, the raw liquor burning her cut and swollen lips.

"Waste good whiskey, will you!" Lou slapped her and then lunged at her, trapping her beneath him. His eyes glowed with hatred as he said, "You know what I'm going to do to you, don't you? Then when I'm through usin' you, I'll slit your throat!"

Liza turned her head away, gagging.

Lou yanked her head back, "Then I'm gonna take your body and throw it at him and say, 'Here's your slut back.'" He threw his head back and laughed, a horrible, blood-curdling, insane laugh. The sound made the hair rise on her nape and sent a violent shudder through her.

Abruptly, his laughter stopped, the sudden silence even more ominous. His eyes burned with lust as he leered down at her, his mouth jerking convulsively at one corner. He grabbed the bodice of her dress and ripped it away. The small pouch with her hidden money in it flew to the side. Lou didn't even notice it as he pawed at her tender breasts, twisting and pinching them sadistically. He leaned down and brutally bit into one soft breast, and Liza screamed in agony.

"That's it, scream," he rasped. "I want you to scream." He rolled her over and untied her hands. "I want you screaming and fighting," he panted.

Liza lay motionless beneath him, stunned. "Fight, damn you!" he yelled, as he pawed her ruthlessly. Frenzied, he yanked up her skirts. Liza felt his hands digging into her thighs, and she began to fight him, twisting, clawing, kicking, heaving. He laughed—a hideous sound. Liza suddenly realized her fighting was only exciting him more, that he needed it to become sexually aroused. She went limp, pretending to faint.

"Damn you! Damn you!" he cried, shaking her.

Liza had flung her arm out and away from him when she had pretended to faint. Beneath her hand, she felt a large, jagged rock. Could she? she wondered.

"Wake up, bitch!" Lou yelled. Furious, he slapped her and then backhanded her. Liza felt herself reeling from the hard blow, dangerously close to unconsciousness. She moaned.

"That's it, that's it," Lou panted excitedly. Liza felt him lean away from her, fumbling with the buttons on his pants. Desperately, she fought the dizziness threatening to engulf her. It was now or never. Her hand closed over the rock, and summoning every bit of strength she had, she slammed it against Lou's head.

She heard a sickening thud and Lou's grunt as he

collapsed over her. For a few minutes, she lay gasping, fighting her dizziness and the waves of nausea washing over her. She felt something wet on her chest and weakly raised her hand to touch it. It felt warm and sticky. She raised her hand and stared at it dumbly. It was blood. That recognition prompted her to action.

Frantically, she twisted out from under Lou's limp, heavy body and weakly crawled away. Then she sat and stared at him. The wound on his temple was bleeding profusely, the blood puddling on the ground beneath his head. *My God*, Liza thought, *I've killed him!* She lurched away from the inert body, bile rising in her throat. Then she fell to her knees, vomiting. Eventually, she slumped weakly, sobbing hysterically.

Hearing a low moan, Liza jerked her head up and saw Lou's hand twitching. Terrified, she scampered away, stumbling, half crawling, until she reached the horse standing nearby. She struggled to pull herself into the saddle, her fear giving her the needed strength to mount. In one last surge of determination to escape, she kicked the horse, digging her heels into his flank. Surprised, the big animal galloped off.

For hours, the horse wandered aimlessly around the dark, lonely prairie, the woman on his back making no effort to guide him. Only when he stopped would Liza drag herself back from semi-consciousness to nudge him on. The horse was left to choose his own destination, which was fortunate. Instinctively, he headed for water.

It was still dark when the exhausted horse stopped and dropped his head to drink greedily from the water trough. The woman who lay slumped and unconscious across his back silently slipped to the ground. Whickering softly, the horse nuzzled her limp, crumbled body. When she didn't move, he wandered off to graze on the sweet grass nearby.

How long Liza lay on the dew-dampened ground that night, she never knew. She was discovered the next morning by a huge black man, who, after staring in disbelief at the battered woman, turned and ran back to the house nearby. Shortly, he returned with an excessively large, fleshy woman.

"My God!" the woman cried out as she knelt beside the unconscious Liza. "Sam, go and see if Will is still with Marie. If he is, tell him I said to get out here," she instructed the black man.

"Yes, Miz Rita," Sam answered, then trotted off.

Rita carefully scrutinized the young woman. Her face, swollen and horribly battered, was covered with blood from a cut high on her forehead. Her bodice was torn open, and dark bruises could be seen over her breasts, one particularly ugly bruise the result of a bite, the teeth marks still vividly red. Her neck and arms were black and blue and covered with scratches. Gently, Rita pulled the gaping bodice closed.

No one had to tell Rita what had happened. She knew the signs. The girl had been raped. "Son-of-a-bitch!" she swore angrily. But how, she wondered, did the woman get out here in the middle of nowhere? She glanced around and saw the horse grazing a short distance away. Carefully, she studied the horse and its saddle, looking for anything that might distinguish it and, thereby, its owner, but she could see nothing familiar about it.

"Dirty bastard!" she spat. "I'd like to get my hands on him for just one minute," she mumbled between clenched teeth.

Rita's attention was drawn to a stocky, middle-aged man lumbering across the yard, muttering darkly under his breath. "Dammit, Rita," the man said, "what in the hell is wrong with you, getting a man up at this ungodly hour of the morning?"

"Are you sober?" Rita asked the man calmly.

"Of course, I'm sober. Hell . . ." His voice trailed off as his watery, bloodshot eyes fell on Liza. His look was one of concern and then was quckly replaced with one of wariness. "Is this what you called me out here for?"

"I should think that would be obvious," Rita replied with a hint of sarcasm.

"Why me?" the man asked.

"Dammit, Will, we both know you're a doctor."

"I don't practice medicine anymore," Will replied stiffly.

"I know you don't!" Rita answered heatedly. "But you're still a doctor. Surely, you're not going to let this woman lay there and die? The least you could do is look her over and tell me if I should get the doctor from the fort."

Will was still reluctant. He glanced down at Liza and then at the determined expression on Rita's face. Wearily, he ran his fingers through his greying hair and then sighed in resignation. He bent and examined Liza.

"Well?" Rita demanded.

"There are no broken bones. As for other injuries, she will need to be examined more closely." The doctor looked up. "Can we get her moved into the house?"

Rita turned to the big black man, who stood watching curiously from a distance. "Sam, come here and carry her up to my room."

After the doctor had examined Liza thoroughly, Rita asked, "Well, Will, what do you think?"

Will looked down at Liza thoughtfully. "I don't think she has any internal injuries. Her pulse is regular and strong, although she probably has a small concussion." He bent and examined the cut on Liza's forehead. "I don't even think this requires stitching. It probably won't even leave a scar."

"She's been raped, hasn't she?" Rita asked.

The doctor rose, walked to the bureau and washed his hands in a basin of water. "Technically, no. I think attempted rape would be more accurate." He turned, drying his hands on a towel. "However, I want you to watch her closely for bleeding."

Rita looked at him, puzzled.

"She's pregnant," the doctor explained. "I'd estimate around four months."

"You think she'll miscarry?" Rita asked, a worried expression on her face.

Will shrugged. "It's hard to say. I've seen pregnant women who have fallen down a flight of stairs, off horses, and yes, beaten just as badly as this woman. Many of them continued their pregnancy with no ill effects. But one never knows. For that reason, it might not be a bad idea to keep her in bed for a few weeks, just to play it safe."

Rita nodded and studied the doctor curiously. The man standing before her was not the same ir-

377

responsible drunkard she knew. This man was poised and polished. Even his manner of speech was different.

"Will, I know it's none of my business, but . . ." Rita hesitated and then plunged on boldly, ". . . why did you stop practicing medicine?"

Will stiffened with resentment.

Rita laughed harshly. "Hell, Will, you'd think a madam would know better than to ask personal questions, wouldn't you? I'm sorry."

The doctor turned and stood with his back to her. For a few moments, he was silent, and then he spoke, his voice low and haunted. "There was a beautiful young woman, gay and happy, full of life and love. I made the wrong diagnosis, and—" a sob tore from his throat—"she died."

"Will," Rita said gently, "doctors ain't God. They're human, too. They can make mistakes just like anyone else. Surely, you know that."

"Oh, yes," Will answered bitterly, "they told us all that crap in medical school." He turned, his face distorted with anguish. "There's only one hitch. The young woman was my wife. If she'd gone to another doctor, she'd be alive today. I killed her, Rita. I killed the woman I loved." His pain-racked eyes bored into Rita's. Then he lurched for the door, muttering, "Oh, God, I need a drink."

Rita frowned as the door closed behind him. What a shame, she thought, and what a waste. A good man like that made one honest mistake and it torments him for the rest of his life. She turned to look down at the battered woman lying on the bed. While another man did something like this and gets away scot-free.

She walked to the dresser in the corner of the room and took out a large nightgown. As she dressed the limp woman in it, she chuckled. The gown all but swallowed the small form. Rita studied the young woman. With all the swelling on her face, it was impossible to tell whether she was pretty or not. *But that hair,* Rita thought admiringly, as she stroked a golden-red curl. *Now, if I had to be a redhead,* she thought, *why couldn't it have been that color, instead of this carrot-top I've got?* Gently, she covered Liza and then sat down heavily on a chair next to the bed, beginning her long vigil.

Liza regained consciousness that afternoon. She blinked her eyes, but her vision was too blurred to distinguish anything. Her head throbbed, and when she tried to turn it, a sharp pain shot up her neck. She moaned.

"No, honey, don't try to move," a kindly voice soothed. "You're safe now. No one can hurt you here." A gentle hand stroked her forehead. "Just rest."

Almost instantly, Liza fell into a normal, peaceful sleep.

It was evening the next time she awoke. Liza looked about the strange room curiously and then saw the massive woman standing by the side of the bed. Liza had never seen such a huge woman with orange-red, frizzy hair streaked with grey. For a moment or two, Liza stared in astonishment, and then she became aware of gentle, brown eyes watching her and a wide, generous mouth smiling down at her.

Embarrassed by her own rudeness, Liza dropped

her gaze. "Where am I?" she asked, wincing painfully when she moved her lips.

"Don't talk, honey. I know it hurts," Rita said with compassion. She considered telling the girl the truth, but decided against it. "You're about five miles from Fort Laramie. We found you this morning out by the water trough. Now, don't you worry about nothing. You're safe now. Just try to rest."

"Water," Liza muttered.

Gently, the big woman raised Liza's head and held a glass to her mouth, but Liza's lips were so swollen that most of the water ran down her chin and neck. "Wait a minute, honey," Rita said. Taking a spoon, she patiently spooned water into Liza's mouth until Liza nodded, her thirst appeased.

"Thank you," Liza mumbled, again feeling very drowsy.

"Now you just rest," Rita said quietly.

Before Liza drifted off to sleep, she noticed the big woman's dress. It was made of some shimmery material in a bright rose, the color clashing atrociously with the woman's reddish-orange hair. The last thing Liza thought was that this woman must be going to a party.

When Liza awakened the next morning, she was alone, but was finally alert for the first time since her attack. Her head still throbbed, and she still ached all over. Tentatively, she touched her swollen, tender lips and recalled the nightmare she had survived and shuddered.

Carefully raising her head, she curiously studied the room. It was furnished with heavy, ornate furniture. Red velvet curtains with gold tassels hung at the windows and covered the canopy above her. She wrinkled her nose in distaste.

Weakly, she laid back on the pillow and then gasped in astonishment. A full-length mirror hung over the bed. Shocked by her own reflection, she didn't even wonder at the strange placement of the mirror. Her face was black and blue, distorted with swelling, and she hardly recognized herself.

The door opened, and Rita entered carrying a tray. "Well, I see you're awake, honey." Then she frowned and shook her head. "But you look like hell. How do you feel?"

Liza grinned painfully at the woman's blunt, but honest remark. She was right, Liza admitted. She did look like hell. "Awful," she mumbled. Then, suddenly remembering, her hand flew to her abdomen.

Rita noted the movement. "Now, don't you fret. The baby's fine."

"How did you know about the baby?" Liza asked in surprise.

"The doctor who checked you over told me," Rita answered. "He said you didn't have any broken bones or serious injuries, and that the baby was fine, too. But just to play it safe, he thought you should stay in bed a few weeks."

Liza was alarmed. If it was the doctor from the fort, he would have recognized her from the dance. "What doctor?" she asked. "The doctor from the fort?"

Rita looked at the frightened woman and frowned. What was she so upset about? she wondered. "No, it was a doctor who . . . was sort of passing through. But he's a good doctor," Rita assured Liza.

Liza felt a wave of relief. At all costs, Alex mustn't find out where she was. She needed time to recover from her attack before she could continue her trip. She smiled, hoping that the older woman hadn't noticed her panic. "I'm sure he is."

Rita placed the tray on her lap. "Think you can manage some of this?"

Liza looked down at a bowl of oatmeal, two soft-cooked eggs and a cup of tea. "Tea?" she asked, looking up in delight.

"Sure it," Rita answered. "I thought you English liked tea?"

"We do," Liza answered. "But how did you know I'm English?"

Rita chuckled. "Honey, you've got an accent as broad as a donkey's rump. Even though you didn't say much yesterday, I could still hear it."

Liza laughed, and then wished that she hadn't. Any sudden movement of her lips was still painful. Slowly she ate, the older woman encouraging, almost bullying her. When Liza insisted that she couldn't eat another bite, Rita laughed. "That's your share, honey. Now you've got to feed the baby."

When Liza had finished eating, she said, "You've been so kind, and I don't even know your name."

"Rita. And yours?"

"Liza."

Rita waited for the last name, but when Liza just smiled at her, she nodded knowingly. The older woman studied Liza critically. "Who beat you like this, honey? Your husband?"

Liza was stunned by the question. Of course, she owed Rita an explanation, after all the woman had done for her. For a brief minute, she considered lying, and then, looking down at the bare finger on her left hand, decided against it. "No, I'm not married."

Rita's brow rose. Well, there's an honest one. Anyone else would have jumped at that chance to lie. "Then your lover?"

"If you mean the father of my baby, no!"

Rita smiled knowingly, for although the older woman had never had much formal education, the one thing she did understand very well was the relationship between a man and a woman. Whoever the father of her baby was, Liza certainly loved him. Gently, she persisted, "Then who?"

Liza wondered how much of the truth she could tell her without revealing anything about Alex or his ranch. Carefully, she chose her words. "I was traveling east from Salt Lake City. When we stopped at Fort Laramie for the night, I asked about a place to sleep, other than the stage depot. A big, blond-headed man told me he'd show me to a hotel, and I followed him. It was almost dark, so I couldn't hardly see where we were going. Before I knew what had happened, he had pulled me into an alley, gagged and tied me, and then dragged me to his horse. I tried to fight him, but he knocked me out." Liza glanced up to see the big woman's reaction to her story. Rita nodded silently for her to continue. "When I regained consciousness, we were out on the prairie. He dragged me off the horse and tried to . . . to rape me."

"But how did you get away?" Rita asked.

"I pretended to faint. You see, he was half-drunk. Then I hit him over the head with a rock."

"Good for you!"

"At first, I thought I had killed him, but then he moaned and moved his hand. I finally managed to get up on his horse and get away." Liza looked up at Rita. "I don't know if I killed him or not."

"I hope to hell you did!"

"But you don't understand," Liza said in a tormented voice. "If I killed him, I'm a murderer."

Rita looked down at the pale, frightened young woman. "Now, you listen to me," she said firmly. "You get that idea out of your head right now. If you killed him, it was self-defense. That ain't murder."

"But the law," Liza objected. "I'll be arrested. There'll be a trial."

"Arrested? Trial?" Rita repeated the words in disbelief. Shaking her head, she took Liza's hand in her big warm one. "Honey, now you stop worrying about that foolishness. Even if the marshal came looking for you—which I doubt will happen—all he'd have to do is hear our story about how we found you all beat up. A woman's got a right to protect herself, and believe me, the marshal ain't got time to go around arresting everyone who's killed in self-defense out here. If he did, he'd have half the population in jail. Besides, from what you told me, I doubt that you killed the man. You said he was moving his hand when you left him, didn't you?"

"Yes."

"See? You probably just knocked him out," Rita assured her. "Can't see a little bitty thing like you hitting a man hard enough to kill him, even if you did have a rock."

"But you said you hoped I had killed him."

"Yes. I said I *hoped* you had killed, not that I *thought* you did. A man like that deserves to die. Hell, honey, that's probably not the first time he's done something like that. The next time, he might kill the woman, if he already hasn't."

Liza remembered the way Lou had stalked her, his strange perversion of wanting her to scream and fight, and his threat to kill her. "He said he would slit my throat," she whispered.

"See, what did I tell you?" Rita looked down at the pale, trembling woman. "Now, look," she said, "let's not talk about it no more. It's upsetting you, and that can't be good for your baby. The only important thing is that you and your baby are both all right. Promise me you won't fret over it."

Liza smiled weakly and nodded. Rita looked at her doubtfully as she left the room.

The next time Liza awakened, Rita was placing her supper tray on the small table beside the bed. "I let you sleep through lunch since you ate such a big breakfast," Rita said. Her eyes searched Liza's face. "How do you feel?"

Liza smiled. "Much better."

Noticing the twinkle in her eyes, Rita laughed with relief. "Here, I want you to eat every bite," she said as she placed the tray on Liza's lap.

After she had finished eating, Liza glanced over at Rita. The big woman was standing by the window and looking out of it. Again, Liza noticed her dress. This time it was a hideous purple color and made the big woman look even larger. My God, Liza wondered, why did she wear such garish clothes? Then she rebuked herself. She should be ashamed of herself. Rita had taken her in and nursed her, and all she could do was criticize her.

Liza was startled from her thoughts by a man's deep laugh, followed by a soft, feminine one. The sound came from the hallway. When Rita turned from the window, Liza said, "You must thank your husband for me, for allowing me to stay here."

Rita frowned in puzzlement. "Honey, I ain't got no husband."

A voice, muted, but decidedly male, filtered through the walls.

Rita could tell by Liza's expression that she had heard the voice, too. Well, she thought, now was just as good a time as any to tell Liza the truth. Sighing deeply, she said, "I didn't tell you this earlier, because I didn't want to upset you any more than you already were. But sooner or later, you're gonna realize where you are." She hesitated and then blurted, "This is a whorehouse and I own it."

Liza's mind flashed back to Alex's words of long ago, *Rob started sneaking off to Rita's place. He'd come back still half-drunk and reeking of cheap perfume.* Suddenly all of the pieces of the puzzle fit together: the overly decorated, gaudy room, Rita's garish clothes, the mirror over the bed. Liza blushed profusely at the last. Of all of the places that that stupid horse could have dumped her, Liza thought, he had to choose a house of prostitution. She threw her head back and laughed.

Rita looked at Liza, alarmed. She had expected shock, indignation, or perhaps anger, but certainly not this reaction. "Are you upset?"

Liza finally controlled herself. "No, should I be?"

Rita was flustered. "Well, you being a lady and all," she answered nervously.

"*Lady?*" Liza laughed harshly. "I'm pregnant and I'm not married. I'm hardly in the position to cast stones. And I certainly don't deserve the title of lady."

Rita hadn't missed the bitterness in the younger woman's voice. Placing her hands on her broad hips, she glared down at Liza. "Now, you listen to me, honey. I ain't so smart, but if there's one thing I do know, it's how to tell a whore from a lady." She thumped her big bosom. "I'm a whore." Then nodding her head at Liza, she said, "You're a lady." Her eyes bored into Liza's. "You loved that man, didn't you?"

Liza was so surprised by Rita's tirade that she never even considered lying. "Why, yes."

"Humph, thought so!" the big woman grunted and then continued. "Giving yourself to the man you love doesn't make you any less a lady, and it sure don't make you any whore."

Rita sat down beside Liza. The bed lurched and groaned under her massive weight. "And let me tell you something else. Being married doesn't make the difference between a whore and a lady, either. Some women don't love the men they marry. They don't even care about them. They're using that man and selling themselves just as much as any whore. The only difference is, we deliver, and most of the time, they don't." Rita's eyes grew warm with concern. "What's the matter, honey? Wouldn't he marry you?" she asked gently.

Liza looked away from Rita. It would be so easy to lie, only she didn't want Rita to think badly of Alex, even if she never knew his identity. "I never told him about the baby," she admitted.

Rita frowned. "Why? Was he already married?"

Liza hesitated, thinking this would be the easiest explanation. "Yes," she muttered, already hating the lie.

"And I bet he didn't even tell you he was married," Rita remarked bitterly.

Liza couldn't lie anymore. "He was honest with me from the very beginning." That was true, Liza thought, and if Rita drew the wrong conclusions, it wasn't her fault.

Rita looked at Liza sadly. Yes, she thought, Liza loved him all right, still did, and probably always will. "Gee, that's tough, honey."

Liza turned her head away, fighting the tears that threatened in her eyes.

"Look," Rita said kindly, "I've already asked too many questions. I promise I won't ask any more." Her big hand touched Liza's shoulder gently. "But if you ever want to talk about it, I'm a good listener."

Liza could only nod, afraid any attempt to speak would only betray her more. Not until she heard the door close quietly, did she allow herself release. Then she sobbed into the pillow, "Oh, Alex, I need you."

Chapter 18

A week later, Liza finally convinced Rita to allow her to get out of bed. Her soreness and headaches were gone, and the bruises slowly fading.

"If I don't get up pretty soon," Liza argued, "I'll be too weak even to walk. Besides, I've shown absolutely no signs of miscarrying.'

"I don't know, honey," Rita replied. "The doctor said a few weeks." Seeing Liza's pleading eyes, she melted. "Well, just to the chair and back."

Liza was delighted with her small victory, but true to her words, she was almost too weak to make it to the chair. She sat gazing out of the window as Rita straightened the bed linens. Her eyes locked on the sight of a huge black man chopping wood below her. Liza had never seen such a massive man. He was almost six-and-a-half feet tall, with huge shoulders and powerful arms. She watched in awe as he swung the ax, shattering the wood beneath.

"You have a slave?" Liza asked, her voice strongly tinged with disapproval.

"A slave?" Rita asked, baffled, and then peering out of the window, she laughed. "No, that's Sam. He works for me. But he used to be a slave."

"He's a runaway?"

"No, he's a free man now," Rita answered. "His master freed him about twelve years ago. Seems the old man heard all that abolitionist talk and got to feeling guilty, so he freed all his slaves."

"You don't sound like you approve," Liza said resentfully.

"Now, don't get all het up, honey. I don't much cotton to slavery, either. But I don't think the old man did Sam any favor. Now, if he'd freed him and then hired him back, it might be different. But he just freed him, sold his plantation and moved on. Poor old Sam didn't know what to do with himself. He didn't know nothing except hoeing and picking cotton. That's all he'd ever done all his life."

"But couldn't he get a job hoeing and picking cotton someplace else?"

"In the South? A free black man?" Rita laughed harshly. "Not hardly. So he went north and got a job in one of those work houses. Found out he was in worse shape than he had been when he was a slave. At least then, he was given food, clothing and some kind of shelter. Then he drifted west, taking odd jobs here and there. I found him on my door step one winter morning, half-starved and half-frozen. I needed a man around the place for the heavy work, so I hired him."

Liza watched as the big man lifted the split logs in his arms. For the first time, she realized that he was grey haired. "How old is he?" she asked curiously.

"Don't know. Sam don't even know himself. But he's pretty old. You don't see too many of them cotton-tops. What's surprising is that he's still strong as an ox." Rita laughed, adding, "And gentle as a lamb. You've heard my piano, I'm sure."

"Yes, I have," Liza answered.

"Well, Sam is also my piano player."

Liza's expression was one of surprise and disbelief.

"Yep, it's true. You see, I picked that piano up off one of the wagon trains one year. I didn't know how to play it, but I figured it would give the place some class. Well, one morning I caught Sam picking a tune out on it. I don't know how he figured it out. Just came natural to him, I guess. Anyway, I made him my piano player. At first my customers seemed to resent Sam being in the same room with them, but after a while they got used to it. Now Sam's real good at it. Sometimes, a man will go over to him, hum him a tune, and Sam picks it out on the piano. Most times, the man gives him a little something, and that tickles Sam to death."

"But he's so huge, you'd think he'd break the keys," Liza said in amazement.

Rita chuckled. "Well, he did break that silly, little stool that came with the piano. Had to build him a big, sturdy stool to sit on."

Liza laughed.

Rita smiled, pleased to see Liza laughing. The young woman had looked so pitiful when she first came and then was so depressed and withdrawn for days. Mooning over that man, Rita knew. The older woman sensed that something in her story didn't quite ring true. A man would be a fool to let a beautiful young woman like her go. Hoping to distract Liza further, Rita continued. "Of course, Sam don't much like his job as bouncer."

Liza frowned. "Bouncer?"

Rita grinned. "That's one of them fancy ideas I picked up from Harry."

Liza grinned back. "And who's Harry?"

Rita chuckled and settled her big body into a rocking chair across from Liza. The chair groaned ominously, and for a minute, Liza feared it would collapse under Rita's weight.

"Harry was a gambling man who passed through here some seven or eight years ago," Rita explained. "Seems Harry wasn't always honest with his gambling. Some man caught him cheating and put a bullet in his shoulder. Leastways, that's how I found him on my doorstep."

"Your doorstep seems to have a way of attracting strange people," Liza remarked, laughing.

"Yep, it sure does," Rita agreed good-naturedly. "Anyway, Harry had to hang around for a few weeks until he was fit to travel. Seems he had been a gambler in one of them fancy whorehouses down in New Orleans, a bor . . . bor . . ." Rita frowned.

"Bordello?"

Rita's brown eyes sparkled. "Yeah, and they call the whores there cort . . . cort . . ."

"Courtesans?" Liza supplied.

Rita nodded and grinned. "Now, ain't them some fancy words?"

Liza laughed.

"Anyways," Rita continued, "Harry gave me a lot of suggestions on how to fix up my place so it'd be classier. Things like serving good whiskey instead of that rotgut, and little knick-knack foods with the drinks, and dressing my gals up fancer. He even helped me decorate this room," Rita said, looking about the room proudly.

Tactfully, Liza omitted commenting.

Rita didn't notice, being caught up in her own story. "Back in those days, I wasn't as big as I am now. Besides, Harry said he liked his women big." Rita shook her head, her voice fading as she remembered. "That Harry, he was sure something in bed. The things he taught me—" Rita came to an abrupt halt and glanced at Liza, who was blushing. "Oh, honey, I'm sorry," Rita apologized. "I plumb forgot who I was talking to."

Liza laughed nervously. "That's all right. After all, I'm not an innocent virgin. Did you love him?"

"Harry? My God, no! We were just friends," Rita answered. "Besides, he didn't stay long. He went to California to make his fortune."

"Digging gold?"

"Not Harry! He wouldn't get his hands dirty for nothing," Rita answered with a laugh. "No, he was gonna make it gambling."

"And did he?"

"Who knows? Never heard from him again," Rita answered, shrugging her shoulders. "Anyway, to get back to the bouncer story. That was one of Harry's ideas, too. I was having a lot of trouble with some ruffians at the time, and Harry told me down in New Orleans, in those fancy whorehouses, they used big men called bouncers to keep the men in line. He suggested Sam for the job."

Rita wiggled her big body further into the rocking chair. "I told Harry I didn't think it would work out here. All the men carried guns and knives, and I was afraid if Sam tried to throw out someone who was misbehaving, they'd kill him. Harry told me to make them leave their weapons at the door, like they did in New Orleans, and then said he'd handle it that night and show me it could be done."

Rita took a handkerchief and dabbed at the perspiration on her face and neck. Liza watched and then asked impatiently, "Well, what happened?"

Rita chuckled. "Well, I was scared to death that night. When the men rode up, Harry and Sam met them at the door, and Harry told them I had new house rules, that they'd have to leave their guns and knives at the door and that Sam was the new house bouncer. Well, the men didn't like that at all. Some of them just turned and walked away. But Harry sweet-talked the rest of them, telling them how they didn't need protection from the little ladies inside, that all we asked was no fighting and mistreating us, and in turn, we'd give them an enjoyable evening." Rita chuckled. "That Harry, he sure could talk fancy."

"And did Sam ever have to throw a man out?" Liza asked.

"Well, kinda. A few nights later, one of the ruffians showed up, and sure enough, when he got to drinking, he started pushing one of my gals around. Harry told Sam to go over there, give that ruffian the meanest look he could, and ask him to leave. Sam didn't like the idea at all; but he did what Harry told him, and sure enough, the ruffian went for his gun. I wish you could have seen the look on his face when he realized it wasn't there. He looked up at Sam's mean glare and his big shoulders and arms and turned plum green. He was so scared . . ." Rita started giggling.

"Well, what?" Liza asked in exasperation.

Rita gasped, struggling to control herself. "He pissed in his pants. Then he couldn't get out of the place fast enough. Plumb forgot his gun. Didn't come back for it, either."

Rita and Liza both laughed.

Rita sat rocking in the chair, muttering, "Yep, that Harry, he was something else. . . ." Her voice trailed off as she rocked back and forth in silence. The broad grin on Rita's face left no doubt in Liza's mind of what the older woman was remembering.

That night, when Liza went to bed and looked up to see the mirror, she laughed to herself. *I bet that was Harry's idea, too*, she thought.

A week later, Liza asked Rita where she had been sleeping.

"Down the hall in the spare room," Rita answered.

"Wouldn't it be better if I moved in there?" Liza asked.

"Why, don't you like this room?" Rita asked, a hint of hurt in her voice.

"Oh, yes, it's lovely," Liza lied graciously. "But don't you . . . don't you need it?" she asked, blushing.

Rita looked at Liza dumbly for a minute and then laughed. "Lordy, no! I retired from the business years ago." She laughed again. "Ain't no man crazy enough to crawl into bed with a mountain of fat like me. Besides, I was getting too old for that foolishness. The gals all give me a part of their earnings, and after expenses, I clear a nice profit. Of course, I still have a few personal customers, but I don't charge them. They come to talk."

"Talk?" Liza asked, incredulous.

Rita smiled. "You know, the men don't just come here for sex. A lot of them are just plain lonely. Some of them just want a woman to talk to. They can tell a woman things that they could never tell another man. So they talk, and I listen."

Liza was amazed at this revelation, but she had a problem of her own. "There's something that I've been wanting to talk to you about myself."

"Sure, honey. What is it?"

Liza hesitated. "Well, actually I wanted to ask a favor. But you've done so much for me already that I—"

"Don't be silly," Rita interjected, exasperated. "Now, what can I do for you?"

"I was wondering if you could loan me some money. Just enough to get me to St. Joe."

"What do you want to go there for?"

"Well, for heaven's sake, I can't stay here!" Liza retorted, exasperated.

"Why not? Look, honey, you're five months pregnant, and whether you realize it or not, you're beginning to show. Who's gonna hire a pregnant woman? Besides, the doctor said you should take it easy. That stagecoach ride would be awfully rough on a woman in your condition, all that jiggling. You don't want to lose this baby, do you?''

"No, of course not. But I can't stay here living off you until it's born.''

"You can work to earn your keep," Rita said calmly.

Liza was shocked; her legs buckled. Her voice was a mere whisper. "No, I can't do that. I won't!"

"Oh, hell! I don't mean that way," Rita said. "I told you a long time ago I knew you weren't no whore. Besides, I don't go looking for my gals. They come looking for me. I mean you can work in the kitchen, helping Sally."

Relief swept over Liza; then she was filled with guilt. "You're just making a job for me. You don't really need me."

"Nonsense. Sally can always use some help, and you'll be good for her. She gets pretty lonely down there all by herself sometimes. Besides, even pregnant, you couldn't each much.''

Liza laughed.

Rita's voice was soft and entreating. "Stay at least until the baby is born. Then, if you still want to leave, I'll loan you the money. But if you leave now, I'll worry about what happened to you the rest of my life.''

Liza was surprised at the depth of Rita's concern for her. A strange bond had been forming between them for the past few weeks, and Liza admitted to herself that she really didn't want to leave. She felt safe and cared for here.

"Unless you don't like the idea of working for a whore," Rita said, her voice a little hurt and defensive.

That cinched it. "I'll stay," Liza said, and both women laughed in relief.

"When do I start my new job?" Liza asked enthusiastically.

Rita frowned. "You're sure you're feeling all right?"

"I feel wonderful," Liza replied. And truthfully, she did, as if a great weight had been lifted from her shoulders.

"How about tomorrow?"

The next morning, Rita brought Liza some clothes. "Always got extra dresses around here," she explained. "Tried to pick something more modest-looking. Of course, you'll be busting the seams in no time anyways," she teased.

After Liza had dressed, Rita led her down to the kitchen. A horrendous pile of dirty dishes and glasses sat on the table. A tiny girl stood at the sink washing dishes.

"Sally, come here," Rita said. "I want you to meet someone."

The girl turned and walked toward them, smiling shyly. A few years younger than Liza, she was blond and blue-eyed, her face heart-shaped, with a tiny cleft in her chin.

"My, you're pretty," Liza said impulsively.

Sally stood staring at Liza in awe. "You're beautiful," she whispered.

"Well, if you two can stop admiring each other for a minute, I'll introduce you." Rita's words were amused and teasingly gruff. "Then maybe you can get some work done."

Liza laughed, but Sally quickly averted her eyes

and flushed. Liza frowned, thinking the girl was too shy, too sensitive.

"Sally, this is Liza. She's going to help you here in the kitchen from now on," Rita said.

Sally looked up, surprised. "You mean she's not one of *them?*"

"No, she's going to work here just like you do," Rita said kindly.

Sally looked at Liza and smiled, a radiant glow coming over her face. "I knew you were special the minute I saw you," she said quietly. Liza was strangely touched by the girl's words.

As Liza worked with Sally in the kitchen the following weeks, the girl warmed to her. Soon, she chatted gaily—unless one of the other women came into the kitchen. Then she became quiet and withdrawn. When she learned of Liza's pregnancy, she cried excitedly, "A baby? Oh, I love babies. Can I hold it?" From that day on, Sally pampered and petted Liza, until Liza thought she would scream.

Liza found herself wondering about the girl. On several occasions, she had almost asked Sally how she had come to be in a house of prostitution, but some premonition always warned her away from the inquiry.

One night, when Liza and Sally were finishing up for the day, one of the customers accidently blundered into the kitchen. Sam was right behind the man. "Sorry, sir, but you can't come in here."

"Oops, sorry, ladies," the man apologized, bowing politely as he left good-naturedly.

Liza smiled at the accidental intrusion, but when she turned, she saw Sally crouching in the corner of the room. Alarmed, she hurried to the girl. "Sally, what is it? What's wrong?"

Sally was pale and trembling, her blue eyes wide with fright. "Is he gone?" she asked in a whimpering voice.

"Yes, of course, he's gone," Liza said gently. "He just came in by mistake. He didn't mean to frighten you."

Frantically, Sally pushed Liza away and ran up the stairs to her room. Liza followed, but no amount of pleading could induce the girl to open her door. Something was wrong here, very wrong, Liza's instincts told her, so she went searching for Rita.

She found the madam in her office. Papers were scattered all over the floor. When Liza walked into the room, Rita looked at her with eyes just as wild as Sally's had been. "Oh, Liza. I'm glad to see you, honey. Would you mind pouring me a drink?" Rita pointed to a whiskey bottle on a table near Liza.

"What's wrong?" Liza asked, handing the glass to Rita and then watching in total shock as the older woman downed the entire glass of whiskey without even blinking an eye.

"Nothing. Everything. Oh, hell!" she swore. "My bookkeeper quit last week, third one this year. I know the little bastard was cheating me, but I don't mind that. It's when they quit and leave me with a mess like this that I get so mad!" Furious, she swiped at a pile of papers on the desk. They fluttered all over the room.

Rita looked up sheepishly, her anger apparently appeased by her attack on the papers. "I'm sorry, honey. Only, I can't add two and two, much less make heads or tails out of this mess. Things were sure a lot simpler in the old days when I just buried my money in the backyard. Then the only thing I had to worry about was some wild animal digging it up." She sighed. "I'd give my right arm for a good, steady man to keep my books."

"How about a good, steady woman?" Liza asked.

Rita stared at her dumbly.

"I've had some bookkeeping experience," Liza said, and then held her breath for fear Rita would ask where. Silently, Liza cursed her impulsiveness.

The madame looked at her with amazement and admiration. "No fooling? You think you could straighten this mess out?"

Liza expelled a silent sigh of relief. "I could sure try."

For a moment, Rita hesitated. "I don't know, honey. It's a lot of work."

Painful memories returned. Hadn't Alex said the same thing? Quickly, Liza said, "You don't really need me in your kitchen. I think I can earn my way better by doing this. Believe it or not, I enjoy working with numbers."

Rita stared at her in disbelief.

"Besides," Liza added, "if I stay in that kitchen much longer with Sally pampering me, I'll be as big as—" Unconsciously, Liza glanced at Rita's big body, and then realizing what she had almost said, blushed and looked away.

Rita laughed good-naturedly. "God forbid, let's hope you never get that big."

Rita leaned back in her chair, and as it groaned, Liza winced in anticipation of it collapsing beneath

401

the huge woman. Some day, some day, Liza thought.

"Well, honey, the job is yours," Rita said. "I'll pay you the same money I pay the men."

"Oh, you don't have to pay me," Liza objected. "I'm working for room-and-board, remember?"

"Hell yes, I'll pay you!" Rita retorted. "I gave them bastards room-and-board plus their salary. At least I know you won't cheat me. That way, after the baby's born, you'll have a nice, little nest-egg and won't need to borrow money."

"You've got yourself a bookkeeper," Liza said.

"Great!" Rita said, looking immensely relieved. "Now, hand me that bottle, honey. I feel like celebrating."

Liza handed the bottle of whiskey to Rita. "There's something else I wanted to talk to you about."

"Sure," the older woman replied, absently pulling a drawer open and reaching for a cigar. Seeing Liza's dumfounded stare, Rita asked, "You mind if I smoke, honey?"

"No . . . no, of course not," Liza muttered and then watched, fascinated, as the older woman lit the cigar and took a deep drag. The rich aroma of cigar smoke filled the air. A wave of longing for Alex swept over Liza, so powerful she had to clench her teeth to keep from crying.

Thankfully, Rita didn't notice. "What is it you wanted to talk to me about?"

Liza was glad for the distraction. "It's about Sally." Then she told Rita about the incident in the kitchen that night and Sally's reaction.

"Damn, I wish that hadn't happened. I try to keep the men away from her," Rita said.

"But it was an accident," Liza objected. "He didn't do anything. As a matter of fact, he was very polite."

"That don't make no difference to Sally. A man's a man, as far as she's concerned," Rita replied bitterly.

"I don't understand," Liza said.

"I don't reckon you do." Rita looked up at the young woman standing before her and studied her carefully before saying, "Well, I guess I can tell you. Don't nobody around here know about it, but Sam and myself. Don't reckon Sally would mind you knowing, though, being as she's so crazy about you. Sit down."

"I'm fine," Liza replied.

"No, you'd better sit. And you'd better have a drink first, too."

Liza sat and accepted the glass of whiskey. "Why should I sit down?"

"Because what I'm gonna tell you ain't pretty. But it's the only way you'll ever be able to understand Sally." Rita looked thoughtful for a moment, then said, "Let's see. Sally is about eighteen now, so it must have been about six or seven years ago. Well, one day this miner comes knocking on my door, telling me he wants to sell his daughter to me. I told him I don't buy people. Then he told me he thought she'd make a good whore."

Rita sighed deeply, as if she were steeling herself to continue her story. "Well, I was disgusted enough, but then he pulls out Sally. My God! I never seen nothing so pitiful in my life. She was a skinny, half-starved little thing, covered with cuts and bruises from where he'd been beating on her. I asked him if

403

he was sure that was his daughter, and he said yes. Then I asked him where her mother was, and he told me she was dead.

"I looked down at that little gal. She looked like some trapped, terrified little animal. I told him I'd give him three bottles of whiskey for her, but she wasn't gonna be no whore."

Rita stopped her story and took a long drink to fortify herself. "Then do you know what that bastard said? 'She'll make a good whore. I ought to know. I broke her in myself.'"

Liza gasped; bile rose in her throat. Quickly, she covered her mouth.

"Yeah, I know how you feel, honey," Rita said bitterly. "I was never so shocked and disgusted in my life. She was just a kid, his own daughter. Well, I got so mad, I slugged him. Wish I'd been as big as I am now, 'cause maybe I would have killed him. There's been many a time since then that I wish I had."

Rita wiped away a tear. "I figured she'd outgrow her fear. Maybe forget what happened. But she hasn't. She's terrified of men—all men. It don't matter to Sally if the man is young or old, polite or not. As long as she's known Sam, and as gentle as he's been with her, she's still scared of him."

Liza was crying quietly. "I've never heard anything so awful. That sweet, pretty little girl," she sobbed.

"Yeah," Rita agreed sadly. Then her face brightened. "But you know, she's kinda blossomed since you came. She always was shy and kinda quiet with the rest of us. I hate to see you leave the kitchen for that reason."

"I'll visit her every day," Liza promised. Then she had an idea. "Maybe we could room together. That way we could spend more time together in the evenings."

"Well, well, honey, if that's all right with you, I know Sally would love it. But are you sure you don't mind?"

"No. I want to help her if there is any way I can." Rita nodded in perfect understanding.

As Liza was leaving the room, she turned and smiled back at the older woman. "You know, Rita, you're wonderful. You take in stray people like some people do dogs and cats. Sam, Harry, Sally, myself, and no telling how many others I don't even know about. Now I know why you're so big. It's all heart."

Rita flushed in embarrassment; her eyes filled with tears. "Oh, hell, honey! Stop talking silly and get out of here!"

Chapter 19

Summer merged into fall and fall into winter. Liza adopted Sally as a sister and slowly drew the younger girl out of her shell. In a few months, Sally was chattering happily with the other girls and Sam, much to the old black man's delight. Wisely, Liza did not push, and she was careful to avoid any mention of men or sex.

The two of them took long walks in the afternoons, and at night, Liza tutored Sally. She had been shocked to learn the girl had never learned to read or write. Sally was a quick and enthusiastic student. As the time for the baby's birth drew nearer, Sally helped Liza with the layette, often badgering the other women for bits of lace and embroidery thread.

One day, Liza asked, "Don't you think those baby clothes have too much lace on them, Sally? What if it's a boy?"

A horrified look came over Sally's face. "But it can't be a boy. It's *got* to be a girl."

Liza smiled and said calmly, "We'll see."

One cold winter evening, Rita and Liza sat in the older woman's room talking. Liza had been unable to pry Sally away from the baby clothes. Now that the layette was finished, the younger girl was constantly rearranging the clothes, admiring them, fingering them with awe.

"I don't know who is more excited about this baby, you or Sally," Liza said with a laugh.

"Well, it's not every day I become a grandma," Rita replied.

"A grandma?"

"Sure. The kid's got to have a grandma. Every kid deserves at least one." Rita's eyes twinkled. "Of course, he may not want a whore for a grandma."

"Not unless it's you," Liza answered. She looked at the big woman fondly. "Why are you so sure it's a boy? You're just as determined for a boy as Sally is for a girl."

A strange look crossed the older woman's face. Quickly, she looked away. "I'm just sure, that's all."

Later, Rita looked at Liza with concern. "You're sure you won't let me get the doctor from the fort when the time comes?"

"No," Liza answered emphatically. "I don't want a doctor. I want you. You told me you've delivered babies before."

"That sure don't make me no midwife," Rita objected.

"I don't care. I don't want a doctor," Liza insisted.

"Okay, honey, okay," Rita said in a soothing voice. "You sure got a stubborn streak, though."

Liza just laughed. "I've been told that before."

Rita gazed at her curiously. She couldn't help but

wonder who the man was Liza loved. She had hoped that someday Liza would confide in her, but the young woman had held her secret close to her heart. She sensed that Liza's determination not to have the doctor from the fort had some bearing on the puzzle. She wondered if it could be someone from the fort.

Liza was curious about something herself. "Rita, how did you end up here?"

"I came west with a boy from a nearby farm. We were heading for Oregon."

"You were married?" Liza asked in surprise.

"Nope. Oh, Fred kept saying we'd get married when we reached Oregon, but I didn't much care if we did or not. I didn't love him in the first place. Only reason I ran away with him was to get away from my pa. You see, he fancied himself a self-made preacher. Always raving about hell and damnation and telling us kids how bad we was and beating on us. I finally had enough and took off with Fred."

"But why did you stay here, instead of going on to Oregon?"

"Fred got to gambling and drinking on the trip out. When the wagon train reached Fort William— that's what they used to call it before it became Fort Laramie—we stopped to rest up for a few days. Fred disappeared. The morning the train was gonna pull out, he was still gone, and so were the horses, the gun and all our money. I told the people on the train to go and we'd catch up with them."

"Did he come back?"

"No—the little bastard!" Rita spat. "Didn't come back all that day. And then, the next afternoon, three trappers showed up claiming they'd won the wagon

408

and horses from Fred gambling. Sure enough, they had his IOU. Then I knew for sure he wasn't coming back. Told the trappers I was sorry, but Fred had took off with the horses."

"And then?"

Rita laughed harshly. "One of the trappers eyed me up and down and asked me if I wanted to go along with them, since I was stranded and all. I thought it over. They didn't look like such a bad lot. But I knew I'd be cooking, washing and cleaning for them, as well as being used by them all. I turned him down."

The older woman sighed heavily and sat back down before she continued. "Then one of the trappers asked me if I'd give them a tumble. I looked around at the open prairie, and for the first time, I realized the fix I was in. Hell, I didn't even have a pot to pee in! Didn't have no horse, so I couldn't even ride after the train. And that was the last wagon train going through that year. So I asked the trapper what they'd give me for it. He said they'd give me the wagon, since they were trappers and didn't have no use for a wagon."

Rita rocked a few minutes in silence and then said, "I thought it over real good. Figured I could sell the wagon at the trading post. If nothing else it still had some food in it. So I agreed, and that's how I started my career as a whore." She laughed—an ugly, bitter sound.

Liza shivered. She looked at her friend compassionately. Liza was surprised by this new revelation. Rita had always been so frank and open about her profession that Liza had always assumed she had chosen it of her own free will. Now, she realized that her friend had been forced into it by circumstances beyond her control. Like so many of her sisters since the beginning of time, she had survived by selling the only thing she had to her name—her body. Gently, Liza said, "Go on."

"Well, when the trappers left me that evening, I stood on the back of my wagon and waved them off, telling them to come back and see me in the spring. Then I went back into the wagon and bawled all night.

"The night morning I got up and walked to Fort William. I told the man at the trading post I had a wagon I wanted to sell. He told me he didn't need a whole wagon, but he'd buy the parts off it. When he found out I was stranded, he offered to let me stay with him, but I knew it'd be just like with the trappers. I'd be working all day and putting up with him all night. I told him no, I was going into business for myself."

Rita laughed. "I wish you could have seen the look on his face. You would have thought I told him I was the Queen of England. Anyway, we went out to my wagon, and he took off all the wagon wheels, the axle, and some things I didn't even know the name of. When he left that night, I was left on the prairie with a wagon that wouldn't even roll no more. I bawled myself to sleep that night, too."

"But how did you ever survive?" Liza asked.

"I damn near didn't," Rita answered. "I almost froze to death that winter and would have starved to death if it hadn't been for Shining Water." Rita grinned. "Now don't laugh, but she was an Indian girl I found half-frozen outside my wagon one winter morning. She'd picked up some English here and there. Enough so I could piece together her story. Seems she'd been deserted, too, left behind by the fur trapper she'd run off with. I told her I was going into business for myself, and she said she'd join up with me. Like I said, if it hadn't been for her, we would have starved to death that winter. She snared rabbits for us, and that's how we survived." Rita shuddered. "To this day, I can't look a rabbit in the eye."

Liza squirmed in her chair, trying to get her awkward body more comfortable. "Then what happened?"

"Look, honey, it's late. Don't you want to go to bed?"

"No, I want to hear the rest."

"All right, but tell me when you get bored," Rita relented.

Rita was smiling now, apparently recovered from the bitterness of her earlier memories. "That spring, the three trappers came back, and they were plumb tickled to see us. Strange how word gets around out there. Before we knew it, we had all kinds of business: miners, trappers, men from the wagon trains. Then when the army came, our business really picked up. That's when we moved from that little house out back and into this big one."

"But what happened to Shining Water?" Liza asked curiously.

There was a long silence before Rita finally answered, "She got killed."

"Killed? How?"

There was a sadness in Rita's voice now. "One day, one of our customers came in saying there was an

411

Indian out front asking for Shining Water. She and I looked out the window, and sure enough, here's this buck standing out there. I asked her who the Indian was, and she told me it was her brother. Then Shining Water got the strangest look on her face and walked right out of the house and up to him." Rita shook her head, a haunted look in her eyes. "I should have known. I should have stopped her."

"Why, what happened?"

"He killed her. Stabbed her to death right there in front of us all."

"But why?"

"Because she had disgraced her family by becoming a whore. Indians are even more strict about that than white men. She told me once her tribe felt the only honorable thing for a woman to do who had disgraced herself, was to kill herself. I guess her brother figured if she couldn't do it, then he would."

"My God!" Liza gasped.

Rita stood and lumbered slowly across the room to the window. Recalling Shining Water's death had depressed her. Suddenly she felt the weight of her years. "If you don't mind, honey, I think I'll go to bed."

After Liza had left, Rita poured herself a large shot of whiskey. Her eyes were misty as she raised the glass in a toast, muttering, "Here's to you, Shining Water."

Liza's baby was born one January night, in the middle of a howling snowstorm. For the first few hours of labor, Rita allowed Sally to stay with them, but after Liza's water broke and the pains were

412

coming closer and harder, Rita pushed the pale, frightened younger girl from the room.

"But I want to help," Sally objected.

"Okay," Rita said calmly. "Here, you take these scissors and put them in a pot on the stove. When they've boiled for thirty minutes, you bring the pot and all back to me."

When Sally brought the pot with the scissors back, she asked, "Now what can I do?"

The big woman looked at her blankly. Flustered, she answered, "Just keep boiling water."

"What do you need so much boiling water for?" Sally asked.

Rita looked about the room wildly, as if searching the walls for an answer.

Liza answered for Rita, her voice weak, but calm. "Because when the baby is born, he'll need a bath. We'll need warm water for that."

"Oh," Sally said, smiling in understanding. "I'll keep the water heated. Let me know when you need it."

A haggard Rita turned to Liza and smiled. "I'm sure glad you have your head on, honey. I didn't know how we were gonna get rid of her."

All that evening, and into the small hours of the night, Liza labored. And if Liza suffered that night, Rita suffered three times more. The big woman soothed her, wiping the perspiration from her face. She rocked Liza like a baby in her big arms, crooning and offering her encouragement.

All the while Liza was in labor, Rita struggled with a growing terror, fighting visions of Liza, or the baby—or both—dying. What if she was too small? Rita thought. What if something went wrong? The three birthings that she had attended had all been with women who had borne children before, twice with her mother and once with a woman on the wagon train. As Liza whimpered in pain below her, Rita began to vent her fear and frustration on the baby's father. *Bastard! Son-of-a-bitch! Whoreson!* she cursed silently.

When the time came for Liza to push, Rita encouraged her, almost bullying her. "Push harder! Hell, honey, you can push harder than that. Push!" Liza gave one final, tremendous heave as the head crowned and the baby slithered out between her bent legs, howling its indignation to the world.

"It's a boy!" Rita cried excitedly. "Didn't I tell you, honey? It's a boy!"

Rita handed the slippery, crying baby to Liza, who was sobbing with happiness. As she buried her face into the warm body of the squirming body, Liza sobbed, "Oh, Alex!"

Rita frowned. She knew it had been the name of the man, but it had been too muffled for her to understand. Besides, the danger wasn't over yet, and she still had a lot to do.

After the cord was cut and tied, the baby wrapped in warm blankets, the placenta delivered, and most of the blood cleaned up, Rita lumbered heavily to the door. Opening it, she bellowed down the hall, "Sally, get that damned hot water up here!"

Later, after Liza and the baby had both been bathed and tucked in warmly, Rita pushed an excited Sally out of the door, saying gently, "Now Liza and the baby need some rest. You can see them in the morning."

Rita turned and gazed lovingly at Liza and her baby. "What are you gonna name him?" she asked.

"Daniel Robert," Liza answered sleepily.

Rita frowned. Neither name sounded anything like the muffled one she had heard. "That's a real nice name. Now, if you don't mind, I think I'll have a good stiff drink." As the big woman waddled wearily to the door, she mumbled, "Hell, I must have dropped twenty pounds tonight."

Liza lay in the dim, silent room, one hand gently stroking the silky, black hair on her sleeping son's head. She whispered into the night, "We have a beautiful son, Alex. Thank you, my love."

In the following weeks, Liza didn't get to spend much time with her new son. If Sally wasn't holding Danny, crooning to him, then Rita was rocking the baby, singing bawdy tavern tunes lustily. The lyrics of the songs were bad enough, but Rita's singing voice left much to be desired. Liza would sit by resentfully, wincing each time Rita hit a wrong note. It seemed to Liza that the only time she was allowed to hold her baby was when she was nursing him. Therefore, she deliberately drew the procedure out.

One day, when Liza was nursing Danny, Rita stood by waiting impatiently for her to finish so she could hold him again. "I still don't understand how you were so sure it was a boy," Liza remarked.

"Because you carried him the same way I carried mine," Rita blurted, then blanched at her own words.

Liza looked up in astonishment. "You've had a baby?"

The older woman turned away so that Liza

couldn't see her tears. "Yes, I had a baby once."

"What happened to him?"

"He died when he was three years old," Rita answered sadly.

Instinctively, Liza clutched her baby tightly in a fierce, protective embrace, and Danny howled in protest.

"Now look what you've done!" Rita cried harshly, rudely snatching the baby from Liza. "You've gone and upset the baby. Hush, honey lamb, hush," she crooned, rocking the baby in her big arms. Liza was too upset by Rita's revelation to resent the big woman's words or actions.

In a few minutes, Rita gently placed the baby back in Liza's arms, saying in an apologetic voice, "I'm sorry, honey. I shouldn't have done that. I guess I was upset. But I loved that little boy something awful, even more than I did his daddy."

"Then it wasn't an accident?" Liza asked in surprise.

Rita laughed, once more composed. "We whores have ways to prevent 'accidents' as you call them. No, honey, I wanted that baby. Not just any baby, but Kurt's baby."

Rita sat in the rocking chair, her big body rocking back and forth, her face pensive. Finally, she said, "You see, I did something no whore is supposed to ever do—fell in love with one of my customers. But I couldn't seem to help myself. Kurt was a big Swede, gentlest man I ever knew. I decided I wanted his baby, so I deliberately got pregnant."

"Did he love you, too?" Liza asked kindly.

"I don't really know. If he did, he never got the

chance to tell me. He left that fall to go fur trapping and told me he'd be back the next spring. Well, spring came, and I was as big as a house. His partner came instead and told me Kurt had been killed in an avalanche."

Liza gasped.

Rita continued, unaware of Liza's reaction. "He said all Kurt talked about that winter was how much he loved me and how he was gonna come back and ask me to marry him. I don't know if it was true, or just some story his partner made up to make me feel better." Rita's smile was wistful. "Anyway, I like to think it was true."

"But it had to be true," Liza insisted. "His partner wouldn't have come all that way just to tell you a story he'd made up. If Kurt had never said anything, he would have just gone on."

Rita's face brightened. "Well, you know, honey, I never thought of it that way." She sat smiling for a few minutes, savoring her new knowledge, and then said, "Anyway, I had his baby. Big, blond, blue-eyed, just like his daddy. I sure loved that little boy. He was my whole life."

Rita hesitated, wiping a tear from her eye. "The winter he was three years old, he got diptheria. Me and Shining Water worked like crazy to save him, but he died. I went stark raving mad. Would have killed myself if it hadn't been for Shining Water. She tied me to a bed and kept me there for a whole week, me ranting and carrying on the whole time. That's one reason I always felt so bad about not stopping her that day her brother killed her. Kinda figured she saved my life, and I owed her one."

Liza had been crying throughout the whole story. At the last sentence, she raised her head. "But you did save her life once. You said yourself she was half-frozen when you found her."

Rita looked up in surprise. "Well, you know, I plumb forgot about that."

Liza was half-laughing and half-sobbing. "You know, Rita, you have a way of plumb forgetting an awful lot of good things about yourself."

Rita blushed, looking uncomfortable. Liza gazed at the big woman fondly, thinking what a remarkable person she was. Rita had suffered so much loss and pain, and yet, she never showed any bitterness or hate. Instead, she was always doing something for others, kind and gentle, in her own gruff way.

Liza looked down at her son. Having finished nursing, he was sleeping at her breast. Gently moving his head, she closed her bodice. Then rising, she said to Rita, "Would you mind taking the baby while I take a nap? I seem to be a little tired today."

Rita's whole face lit up. "Why, sure, honey," she said, taking the baby and grinning down at him. "Come on, Danny boy, I'll sing you a little song."

Liza winced at the mention of a song, but then smiled as she left the room.

A week later, Liza and the baby moved into the little house out back that had been used as a storeroom. Rita had explained, "That way the baby won't be disturbed by all this racket around here at night." Then she laughingly added, "Besides, can't you just imagine the men's reaction if they heard a baby crying in a whorehouse?"

Liza had been delighted, and she certainly didn't

want any gossip going back to Fort Laramie about a baby at Rita's place.

Sally had wanted to move with Liza, but Rita had disagreed, telling Liza, "I don't think that would be a good idea, honey. You don't want her getting too attached to the baby, since you're gonna be leaving. That wouldn't be good for her, either."

One day, when Sally was visiting and playing with Danny, Liza asked, "You're not sorry he's a boy?"

"Oh, no, he's the sweetest, most wonderful baby in the whole world."

"You know, Sally," Liza said gently, "all men were once babies. Then they were little boys."

Sally's head shot up, her look suspicious.

"Would you like to have a baby like Danny?" Liza asked.

"Oh, yes," Sally sighed wistfully.

"Then you'll have to get married first. Married to a man," Liza said calmly.

"You're not married!" Sally spat.

Liza was surprised by Sally's vehemence, and then, remembering how painful the subject was to Sally, she bit back her own retort. "No," Liza answered quietly, "I'm not. But I think you know what I mean."

Sally's face was deathly pale. "I'm not ever gonna do that again. No man is ever gonna touch me again!"

"Not even if it meant you could have a baby like Danny?" Liza asked.

The girl looked at the baby with such intense longing it made Liza's heart wrench. "No," Sally whispered.

Liza sat down by the pale, trembling girl. "Sally, listen to me," she pleaded. "You know I wouldn't lie to you. It's not like it was with your father. It's not an ugly, hurting thing. If you love the man, and he loves you, it can be beautiful. I know."

Sally's jaw was set stubbornly, her eyes flashing.

Liza continued. "Sally, I used to feel like you do. I couldn't stand the thought of a man touching me, either. An older woman told me, someday, when the right man came along, the man I loved, I'd feel different. I didn't believe her, and then I met . . . met the man and found out that she was right."

"Danny's father?" Sally asked.

"Yes."

For a minute, the girl hesitated, looking from Liza to the baby. Then her face hardened. "If love was so wonderful, then why did you leave him?" she asked sarcastically.

Liza slumped and whispered, "Because I had to." Her eyes pleaded with the younger girl. "But not because I stopped loving him, and certainly not because making love with him wasn't a beautiful experience."

"No! You're lying!" Sally screamed. She jumped up and ran for the door, pausing at the doorway to look back at Liza, her eyes wild. "I don't believe you!"

Liza sat on the bed, feeling drained and sick to her stomach. "Oh, my God, what have I done?" she muttered. After a few moments, she picked up the baby and went looking for Rita.

The big woman listened patiently to Liza's story and then sighed deeply. "Don't blame yourself, honey. Someone had to try and get through to her. But I don't think Sally is ever gonna get over her fear of men."

"But it's such a shame," Liza said. "She'd make such a wonderful mother."

"I know, honey," Rita said sadly. "But I think that dirty old father of hers has scarred her for life."

When Danny was three months old, Liza's milk suddenly and unexplainably dried up. She was sitting in Rita's kitchen trying to spoon sugar water to the fretting baby. Rita was pacing the room frantically, while Sally sobbed uncontrollably in a corner of the room.

"We'll have to find a cow," Liza said, trying to sound calm.

"Honey, you can't feed cow's milk to a baby that small. It's too rich. He'll get sick for sure."

Liza's fear rose. Her mind searched for a solution—any solution. "Maybe we could find a wet nurse."

"*A wet nurse?*" Rita asked in disbelief. "We're sitting in the middle of a whorehouse and you want a wet nurse?" she cried, her voice shrill. Liza trembled; Sally cried harder.

"For God's sake, Sally," Rita bellowed, "will you stop that damned blubbering! I can't even think straight." Sally bawled all the louder.

"Wait a minute," Rita said, her face brightening. "I think I've got an idea. Sally, tell Sam I said to come here." While Sally was gone, Rita wrote a quick note.

When the black man entered, Rita handed him the note. "Sam, take this note to the fort and give it to that big Irish quartermaster. You know the one I mean?"

The old man nodded and trotted off with the note.

An hour later, Sam returned with the sergeant in tow. Rita met them in the parlor. Looking up at the big, beefy soldier, Rita asked anxiously, "Did you find any, Shawn?"

The Irishman grinned down at her, shaking his head. "I couldn't believe me eyes. Tinned milk? Now what would you be wanting tinned milk for?"

"None of your damned business!" Rita retorted. "Did you find any?"

Shawn stared at her incredulously and handed her a box. "'Tis all I could find."

Rita looked down at the four tins of milk and her heart sank. "Do you think Jake might have some?"

"No," the Irishman answered, his look still puzzled. "I stopped at the trading post and asked. 'Twas thinking the same thing, meself."

"Well, thanks anyway," Rita answered, her big shoulders slumping.

"Ah, lass, would ye be minding me having a wee drink?"

"No . . . no, help yourself," Rita answered absently, waving him toward the bar.

Rita carried the milk back to the kitchen, even more worried than before. When she entered the room, she said, "He could only find four tins. I don't know what we're gonna do when that's gone."

Quickly, Liza opened a tin, mixed the milk with the boiled sugar water, and started spooning it to the hungry baby. Now that the immediate pressure had been removed, she could think more clearly. She remembered Alex telling her they had used goat's milk for little Andy. "I know!" she cried. "We have to find a goat."

"A goat?" Rita asked incredulously.

"Yes," Liza answered, "I heard somewhere that goat's milk was good for babies."

"And where in the hell am I gonna find a goat in the middle of a prairie?" Rita thundered.

Liza hesitated. Even if she told her at Tanaźin's camp, would Rita know how to find it?

"I know!" Sally cried. "There used to be a herd of goats where my father was prospecting for gold."

"And where was that?" Rita asked, her spirits lifting.

"The South Pass District of the Wind River," the girl answered.

Rita waddled to the parlor and caught the quartermaster just as he was stepping out the door. "Wait a minute, Shawn," she said, panting from her exertions. "You gotta find me a goat."

"A goat!" the Irishman exclaimed, not believing his ears.

"Not just any goat. A nursing goat."

The big man exploded. "Jesus, Mary, and Joseph, woman! Are ye daft? First tinned milk. Now a goat? Now where in the hell would I be finding a goat?"

Rita looked up at the man glaring at her. Finally, she shrugged her shoulders. "Okay, Shawn, come on back to the kitchen. I'm gonna show you something. But if you ever say a word about what you saw here— I'll cut your balls off!"

Three days later, the Irishman returned with a stubborn goat in tow, her kid bleating frantically behind her. "Damned near got meself drowned because of that fool goat," he complained.

It was the quartermaster who suggested the bottle fashioned from a deer bladder. Apparently, he had noticed an Indian woman using one. Liza was vastly relieved that she had not had to suggest it herself.

Several weeks later, Rita noticed one of her customers after he had returned from a visit to the outhouse. The man looked unusually pale, his hands trembling as he wiped perspiration from his brow. When Rita offered him a drink, the man shook his head. "No, thanks, Rita. I think I'm going to lay off whiskey for a while. You know," he said in a shaky voice, "for a minute there out in the yard, I could have sworn I stumbled over a goat."

Danny thrived on the goat's milk, but Liza's trip back East was delayed until the baby was weaned. She could hardly take a goat on a stagecoach. Naturally, Rita and Sally were delighted.

"It's probably for the best anyway," Rita consoled her. "Traveling with a small baby would be awfully hard on you, and besides, this way, you'll have a bigger nest-egg to tide you over until you can find work." The big woman looked at her sadly. "Are you sure you won't stay?"

"No, I can't stay here," Liza answered. "As much as I'd like to."

Rita shook her head mournfully and looked down wistfully at Danny, sitting in his mother's lap. The dark-haired baby gazed up at her, his grey eyes wide, one little dark eyebrow arched. The big woman frowned and studied the baby. He reminded her of someone. Someone she knew but for the life of her, she couldn't remember who.

Chapter 20

Three months later, Rita was busy entertaining her customers when she looked across the room and saw Alex standing quietly in a corner. She was surprised, because she hadn't seen that good-looking rascal around there in a long time. Rita looked closer, shocked at what she saw. He looked terrible. What in the hell happened to him?

She lumbered heavily toward him, and as Rita approached, Alex smiled down at her. "Damn, Alex, you look like hell!" Rita blurted.

Alex chuckled and took another sip of his drink.

Rita studied him as he drank. My God, look at his eyes, she thought. She had never seen eyes that looked that empty and pained. She frowned. This man had been hurt, hurt real bad, and the only thing that could hurt a man that badly was a woman. "I got just the thing to fix you up," Rita said. "A new girl. Prettiest little thing you ever saw. And she's good, too, real good."

Alex grimaced, wondering why he had even come

to Rita's place. He didn't want a woman, hadn't since Liza had left him. She had taught him the true meaning of sex—an expression of love. After Liza, it would be meaningless and distasteful with any other woman. He shook his head. "No, but thanks anyway." He looked down at the big, kindly woman. "Would it surprise you, if I said I just wanted to talk?"

"Hell, no," Rita said, laughing. "But why don't you come back to my office? It's quieter there, and we can have more privacy."

Alex followed Rita through the crowded parlor and out into the hall. As they walked toward her office, the realization suddenly hit Rita like a thunderbolt. This was who Danny looked like, the spitting image. Alex was the man! Liza's lover and Danny's father. She turned to look at Alex.

But Alex was not looking at Rita. He had come to a dead halt, his eyes locked on the figure coming out of Rita's office. The madame glanced at her office door and saw Liza walking out. The young woman was smiling as she looked up, and then, seeing Alex, her eyes widened.

Alex and Liza stared at each other in shocked disbelief. Liza paled, her legs trembling, her heart pounding in her chest. She ran out the back door.

Rita watched as Alex's look of disbelief turned absolutely murderous. "I've changed my mind, I'll take her after all."

Rita knew what Alex was thinking. That Liza was her new girl. She blocked the hallway with her big body. "No, Alex. You've got it all wrong. Liza's not one of my—"

"Dammit to hell!" Alex roared. "Since when am I not good enough for one of your girls?"

Rita's heart was pounding hard, and she felt strangely dizzy. "Alex, you're making a mistake." From the corner of her eye, she saw Sam moving up behind Alex. She shook her head, motioning the huge black man away.

"Get out of my way, Rita," Alex snarled.

Rita looked up at the angry man. His eyes glittered, the same eyes that had looked so empty only minutes before. This was the man Liza loved, Danny's father, and somehow, Rita sensed Alex still loved Liza just as much. *God help me if I'm wrong,* she thought silently, moving aside.

"Where is she?" Alex asked.

"In the little house out back," Rita answered.

As Alex rushed down the hallway, Rita called after him, "But, Alex, you're fixing to make an ass of yourself!"

Alex barely heard Rita's words, for his heart was pounding, drumming in his ears. He raced across the yard and pushed at the door of the small house. It was locked. Rattling the door handle, he called angrily, "Dammit, Liza, open this door before I kick it in!"

A moment passed, and as Alex heard the lock snap, he hurled himself into the room. The momentum threw Liza halfway across the room, where she stood pale and trembling.

For a brief time, Alex stood staring at her, as if seeing her for the first time, utterly awed by her beauty. Then he remembered where he had found her, and his anger returned.

He kicked the door shut behind him with the heel

427

of his boot and smiled perversely when he saw Liza jump as it slammed shut loudly. His eyes were cold, appraisingly, deliberately insulting as he raked her body. "Well, I see you're even more beautiful than I remember you."

The tone of his voice was harsh and cruel. She had expected him to be angry, but couldn't understand why he was acting so outraged. Her voice trembled as she said, "Alex, I can—"

Alex ignored her, cutting into her words. "Or maybe you don't even remember me. Maybe there've been too many other men in the meantime."

Liza stared at him, dumfounded. She couldn't believe his hateful accusation. "No!" she whispered.

Again, Alex ignored her. "You can't imagine my surprise . . . and delight," he added sarcastically, "when I realized that you were Rita's new girl. She said you were pretty. Now that's an understatement if I've ever heard one. She also said you were good." He laughed harshly. "I always thought you'd make a good whore."

Liza felt his cruel words like a physical blow. She gasped, her knees buckled.

Alex caught her with one hand, his fingers biting cruelly into her arm. "You're looking at the biggest fool this side of the Mississippi," he snarled. His free hand fumbled in his shirt pocket, and then he held a ring before Liza's face. "I brought this back with me to put on your finger, but you were gone. I looked high and low, east and west. For a year I looked. And all the time you were sitting right here under my nose. Right here in a whorehouse!" Furious, he threw the ring across the room.

Liza had stared at the ring totally stunned. A ring?

Then he *had* planned to marry her when he returned from Fort Kearney. The realization of her mistake made her feel weak, sick at heart. "Alex, please, can't we talk?" she pleaded.

"*Talk?*" Alex laughed harshly, roughly throwing her away from him. She stumbled against the bed. "Hell, I didn't come here to talk."

Liza knew what Alex wanted, but the thought of him making love to her without love was more than she could bear. "No!"

"*No?*" A dark eyebrow arched. "You're telling *me* no?" he demanded. "Have you forgotten that I'm the man who taught you?" Roughly, he pulled her toward him, his fingers digging into her back, "How much? How much, Liza?" He tossed several bills on the table. "Twenty dollars?"

Liza shook her head, unable to believe what was happening.

Alex's silver eyes glittered with rage. "No? Not enough?" He scoffed, "I should have known you'd be one of those high-priced ones. All right, fifty!" He slammed the money down on the table. Roughly, he shook her, his eyes flashing. "But you'd better be good, Liza. You'd better be damned good."

He threw her on the bed, and Liza watched in horror as he undressed. "What are you waiting for?" he taunted. "Strip! I want to see what I bought." He sneered. "Believe me, I intend to get my money's worth."

Frantically, Liza rolled to the other side of the bed, but Alex caught her. She fought, kicking, biting, clawing as he laughed and ripped her clothes from her.

One powerful, muscular leg held her thrashing

ones, and one hand caught her wrists in a cruel grip as Alex's mouth came crashing down on hers in a long, hot, punishing kiss. His free hand explored her body, bruising her tender flesh. Then, slowly, his kiss softened, his hands gentled. Finally, his lips left hers as he buried his head in her throat, muttering thickly, "Damn you, Liza! Damn you!"

The curse sounded like a caress to Liza's ears. She heard the agony behind it, the longing. At that moment, she knew Alex still loved her despite everything. "Oh, Alex," she sobbed, her arms enfolding him, her hands stroking the powerful muscles on his shoulders and back.

Alex's anger dissipated completely. The feel of Liza in his arms again, her warm, pliant body pressed against his hard one, drove all thought from his mind. His hands caressed her breasts and stroked her hips and thighs. His mouth seared kisses up her throat and across her jawline. His lips nibbled and supped greedily at the corners of her mouth, and then capturing her lips, he kissed her hungrily, thoroughly, deeply.

He was a starved man. He couldn't get enough of her. His hands, mouth and tongue feverishly searched, caressed, and devoured every inch of her, rediscovering all her secrets, awed by her silkiness, intoxicated by the feel, the taste, the scent of her.

And when he drove deeply into her, savoring the feel of her pulsating heat surrounding him, he felt whole, complete for the first time in over a year. *This is where I belong*, he thought. *This is where she belongs. This is where we belong—together.*

He began his thrusts, bold, masterful, sensuous

strokes that lifted them higher and higher. They were in their own world then, the mystical, wondrous world of a man and woman joined in love, locked body and soul, striving together, climbing together, cresting together and soaring together. They touched the moon, the stars, the heavens, eternity itself—but always together.

For a long while, Liza and Alex lay in the sweet after glow, their bodies still joined, each awed and deeply touched by their experience. Slowly, reality returned.

Abruptly Alex rolled from Liza and off the bed. Pulling on his pants, his hands still trembling, he said in a husky voice, "Well, I'll have to admit, Liza, I certainly got my money's worth. You're still the best I've ever had."

Liza flinched at the cruel, biting words. They cut her to the depths of her soul. No, she thought, choking back a sob, not after what they just shared. She turned her head away to hide the tears that slid down her cheeks.

The ugly silence of the room was shattered by the cry of the baby. Liza rolled from the bed and wrapped her robe around her. Turning, she faced Alex across the bed. He stood stunned, a look of total disbelief on his face.

Lifting her head proudly, Liza walked regally from the room and into the small room next door. Picking up the baby, she rocked him in her arms, crooning, "Hush, sweet, hush," and then turned to face Alex. He stood in the doorway, his face pale, still shocked.

"His name is Daniel Robert, but we call him

Danny. He's seven months old," Liza said in a flat voice.

The door behind Alex opened as Rita entered the cabin. Using her big body, she rudely pushed him out of the way, hissing as she passed, "I told you, you were going to make an ass out of yourself." Waddling over to Liza, she explained, "I heard the baby crying. Here, let me take him."

Rita looked closely at Liza and then at Alex. They both looked pale and shaken. "I'll take the baby with me for the rest of the night," she said. "I think it's about time you two sat down and had a long talk."

After Rita had left, Liza and Alex stood staring at each other for a long while, each waiting for the other to speak. Finally, Alex asked in a voice full of pain, "Why did you leave me?"

Liza stood pondering the question. She knew now that he had planned to marry her, knew that he still loved her, but all she could think of was the agony she had gone through when she had made her decision to leave him. Her anger rose. "What did you expect me to do when you left me with no word, no message, no nothing?" she spat. "Was I supposed to wait until you came back and found me pregnant and then married me because of some stupid sense of honor? How was I supposed to know you were bringing a ring back?"

Alex glared at her. He had been to hell and back over the past year. Having Liza leave him was like having a part of himself wrenched from him. He'd spent months looking for her. He'd gone through blizzards, floods, grueling heat and sandstorms. He had suffered the agony of the damned. His own anger

432

rose. "What in the hell do you mean no message? What do you call my note?"

Liza blinked in confusion. "What note?"

"The note I left for you, dammit!" Alex roared. "I left it on the table by our bed."

Liza suddenly felt sick, her face paled, her legs trembled. "Alex," she whispered, "I didn't find any note."

Suddenly, Alex, too, knew something had gone wrong. "Oh, my God," he muttered, and in three quick strides, she was in his arms. For a long time, he just held her, soothing her with his trembling hands. When he did speak, his voice was ragged with emotion. "Rita was right. It's time we had a long talk."

He swept her up into his powerful arms and carried her into the next room. At first he headed for the bed, then swerved to a large overstuffed chair. Sitting down with her on his lap, he said, "Now you first. Tell me everything, even your thoughts. I don't want there to be any more misunderstandings between us."

"Where should I start?" Liza asked.

"The day before I left on the cattle drive," Alex answered.

Liza told him everything. When she came to the part of her abduction and Lou's attempted rape, she felt his muscles tense and saw the murderous look in his eyes, but he didn't interrupt. He listened patiently until she came to the story of Danny's birth and then he exploded. "You let a whore deliver our baby? What in the hell were you thinking of?"

"And why not?" Liza spat back.

"Because you could have died, that's why! What do whores know about delivering babies?"

"As much as any other woman," Liza retorted. "And don't you dare call Rita a whore!"

"Well, that's what she is," Alex snapped.

Liza jumped from his lap and glared down at him. "Not to me, she isn't! To me, she's the kindest, most generous, most wonderful woman in the world!"

Alex looked up at her intense face and grinned sheepishly. "You're right, sweetheart. I'll be forever in debt to her for keeping you and Danny safe for me. I'm sorry."

Liza hesitated and then smiled. "Now, can I finish my story?"

Alex nodded and pulled her back down on his lap. "You know," he said, "I have a feeling things are never going to be dull between us." He nibbled her ear.

"Alex!" Liza warned.

He chuckled. "Okay, sweetheart, finish your story."

Liza ended with, "And so, tonight, when I coudn't sleep, I thought I'd slip into Rita's office and bring the books back here to work on. When I looked up, there you were."

Alex nodded. "And just as Rita said, I made an ass out of myself. But, sweetheart, when I thought of another man touching you, I went crazy. I wanted to hurt you, just as I felt you had hurt me. Only the minute I kissed you—"

"I know," Liza interjected, smiling. "Now, tell me your story."

Alex grinned, his hand tenderly caressing her

434

breast. "Can't it wait until tomorrow?"

"No," Liza said firmly, pushing his hand away. "Now."

Alex pulled her tightly against him, as if he were afraid he would lose her again. "I was never angry with you, Liza. When I saw Lou pawing you, I was furious, yes. But it wasn't until he said something about you, that I went crazy. Hell, I would have killed him with my bare fists if Manuel hadn't pulled me off him. I rode off that afternoon because I was angry with myself for my own stupidity, for what I had done to you."

Alex looked deeply into Liza's eyes. "I should have never insisted on our waiting to get married. Being the selfish, arrogant bastard I am, I never realized how it might be hurting you, the price your pride was paying. And I was wrong about something else, too. I told you once love doesn't last forever. Well, maybe some loves don't. But, Liza, nothing could ever take away my love for you—not time, not death, not anything! It comes from deep down inside me. My soul, I guess. And as long as my soul lives, so will my love for you."

Liza smiled. Sighing, she laid her head back down on his shoulder. She felt warm, safe and secure.

Alex nuzzled her hair as he continued. "I came back that night, intending to tell you all this and tell you I would bring someone back with me to marry you, but you were asleep. You looked so exhausted, I decided to let you rest." He laughed harshly. "I thought I was being unselfish, for a change. Anyway, I wrote you a note and left it on the table by our bed."

Liza raised her head. "But I didn't—"

435

"Sssh," Alex said, "I know that now." Tenderly, he laid her head back down on his shoulder. "When I came back and found you were gone, I couldn't believe it. Hiram gave me your note, and it just didn't make sense. I went looking for you. First, I went east, following the trail of the stagecoach, but no one had seen you. Let's face it, sweet, a beautiful woman like you would have stuck out like a sore thumb. So I turned around and headed for Salt Lake City, figuring you'd gone west instead. But the same thing happened. No one had seen you. It was as if you had disappeared into thin air, and that scared the hell out of me. I was afraid you were dead."

"What did you do then?" Liza asked, hating herself for having put him through such anguish.

"I went back to Fort Laramie. Kathleen kept insisting you weren't dead."

"Kathleen? You went to Kathleen?"

"Yes, of course. Hell, I've got half of this territory out looking for you," he said, remembering his fear and frustration. "But, dammit, Liza, I never thought to look in a whorehouse!"

Liza laughed. "Then what did you do?"

Alex sighed deeply. "I started all over. I badgered everyone at Fort Laramie. Finally, I found a stable boy who had seen you talking to a big, blond-haired man. From the way the boy described him, I knew it was Lou. This was the first lead I'd gotten, so I started following his trail."

"His trail?" Liza gasped. "Then I didn't kill him?"

"You thought you had killed him?"

"I didn't know," Liza answered. "Rita told me she didn't think I had, but all this time I've worried. I

436

didn't want his death on my conscience."

"Well, he's dead, but you didn't kill him," Alex said in a hard voice.

Liza looked at him with alarm, a silent question in her eyes.

"No, I didn't kill him, either," Alex said. "Although I wish I had, now. I tracked him as far as Salt Lake City, but he'd been killed in a knife fight a couple of days before I arrived."

Liza sighed in relief. "I'm glad he's dead, and I'm glad it's not on our consciences."

"God, sweetheart," Alex said, "we've both paid a hell of a price for our mistakes." He nuzzled her neck and kissed her ear, whispering, *"Micante, tecihila."*

Liza pulled away and looked up at him, her heart pounding in anticipation.

Alex smiled, his look tender. "I know. I promised I'd tell you what it meant. I should have told you that night. It would have saved us a lot of heartache."

"But what does it mean?" Liza asked impatiently.

"My heart, I love you."

Liza frowned. "But you told me you loved me before."

Alex shook his head. "It's not the same. The Dakota words have a much more profound meaning. You see, an Indian only says this to the woman he loves, his soulmate. It's a commitment—for life."

He bent his head and kissed her tenderly, a long, lingering, searching kiss. Rising, he carried her toward the bed.

Liza pressed against him. "How is everyone? Andy and Hiram and—"

Alex laid Liza on the bed and placed one finger

437

over her mouth to silence her. His eyes were warm with love. "You know, sweetheart, you still talk too much." Then his mouth replaced his finger in a searing, consuming kiss.

The next morning, Liza and Alex lay in bed quietly talking. "Then you will marry me?" Alex asked, his heart racing in his chest.

A teasing glimmer came into Liza's eyes. "What would you say if I told you no?"

"Cut it out, Liza!" Alex said irritably. Rolling on his side so he could see her face, his look intense, he said, "I've never been so serious in my entire life."

Liza's hand stroked his cheek. "Yes, I'll marry you."

"When?" he demanded.

"My, you're anxious."

"Damned right, I'm anxious," Alex answered. "This time, I want everything tied up nice and tight. This time, it's going to be done right."

"Do you think you could find Father . . ." Liza's brow furrowed.

"Father William?" Alex asked.

Liza nodded.

"I'll start looking for him today," Alex promised. Then he chuckled. "But he's going to think I'm crazy. I brought him back with me last summer to marry us."

That must have been embarrassing for Alex, Liza thought. A blow to his male pride added to his anguish over her fate. Yes, they had both paid a high price for their mistakes.

"Do you want to be married here, or at the ranch?" Alex asked.

438

"At the ranch. And, Alex, could we have all our friends? Kathleen and Tom, Tanaźin and Waĥcawin, Jake and—"

"My God," Alex groaned.

"Can we?" she pleaded.

He bent and kissed her lips. "Sweetheart, I'd give you the moon if you wanted it."

Liza grinned impishly. "Well now, I hadn't thought of that."

Alex's eyes were warm as he lowered his head and nuzzled her neck, his tongue circling and playing in her ear. "I'll get it for you later," he muttered, his hands caressing her breasts.

The door opened, and Alex jerked away guiltily, quickly pulling the sheet up over his and Liza's naked bodies. He blushed furiously as Rita ambled heavily into the room.

The big woman stood holding the baby and grinning down at them. "I forgot to take napkins for Danny," she explained. Calmly, she walked over to Alex and dropped Danny on his naked stomach, the baby's sopping wet diaper making a plopping noise. "Here," she said. "It's about time you got to know your son."

Liza laughed. She had never seen Alex embarrassed before. That he was blushing in front of a madame, of all people, amused her even more. Calmly, she rose from the bed and pulled on a robe.

"You two get things straightened out?" Rita asked her.

"Yes, Alex is going to start looking for Father William today, and we're going to be married at the ranch."

"About time," Rita said, stealing a look at Alex. *Now, that's more like the man I remember,* she thought. She studied the powerful muscles on his shoulders and chest, the flat, tight abdomen. *Yep, all man,* she thought approvingly.

Alex was oblivious to the women's conversation. He was totally absorbed with his son. The baby scrutinized his father just as carefully. Finally, Danny cocked one little eyebrow, grinned, and reached for a dark curl on his father's chest.

Laughing, Liza reached down to pick up the baby.

"No, leave him!" Alex said, his voice firm.

"But he's sopping wet," Liza objected.

"I don't care," Alex said, fascinated with the baby, his eyes glued on him. He gently stroked Danny's head, saying softly, *"Micinksi."* Looking up to Liza, he explained, "My son."

Liza nodded, her heart in her throat, tears in her eyes.

"He's beautiful, Liza." Alex said in a voice barely above a whisper. Then, looking back up at her, his voice choked with emotion, he said, "Thank you, sweetheart."

The day after Alex had left to look for Father William, Liza asked Rita to be her maid of honor.

The big woman's look was one of disbelief. "You ain't serious, are you?"

"I certainly am," Liza replied.

"Well, that's plumb sweet of you, honey, but I think that would cause too much scandal if you had a madame for a maid of honor. Besides, look at me, I'm as big as a house, and you want a real pretty wedding. Why don't you ask Sally instead?''

Liza frowned. "I don't know. There are going to be a lot of people at the wedding, and you know how Sally is. Do you think she'd agree?"

"Don't rightly know. But it can't hurt to ask her."

"All right, I'll ask her. But only on one condition."

"What's that?"

"That you take the place of mother of the bride," Liza answered with a warm smile.

Rita blinked back tears. "Why, honey, I'd be plumb proud to."

Several days later, Alex arrived, announcing that the wedding would take place in two days.

"That's impossible, Alex!" Liza cried. "There's too much that has to be done first."

"Sweetheart, you said you'd marry me as soon as I found Father William," Alex pointed out calmly. "Besides, what all has to be done?"

"We have to move to the ranch, send the invitations, prepare all the food, and I haven't even got my wedding dress made yet. As a matter of fact, I've been so busy packing for the move that I haven't even started on it yet."

Alex chuckled, then said patiently, "We'll move to the ranch tomorrow. I stopped by there on my way back to tell them the news. Hiram and Bright Star are already preparing the house and the food. Manuel is riding to Tanaźin's camp to invite him and Waḣcawin, and I stopped in Fort Laramie and asked Kathleen and Tom and Jake and Little Songbird. And as for your wedding dress—" he pulled a big box from the back of the wagon and handed it to her—

"with Kathleen's compliments."

Liza was astonished to learn that Alex had been so busy and accomplished so much. Excitedly, she carried the box into the house and laid it on the bed. Pulling off the lid, she gasped in delight. A beautiful, ivory lace gown, its bodice edged with delicate seed pearls, lay in the box. "Oh, Alex," Liza cried, her eyes filled with tears, "it's exquisite. But where did Kathleen get it?"

"I stopped at the fort to tell them the good news before I went looking for Father William. You know, Kathleen has been absolutely frantic with worry about you. She must have sewed like mad while I was gone, day and night, because when I got back, she had the gown finished. She also told me a message to give you. She said to tell you that you were right, she had been trying too hard." Alex frowned in puzzlement. "Does that make sense to you?"

So, Kathleen was pregnant, Liza thought, smiling. "Yes, it makes sense."

"What did she mean?" Alex asked.

Kathleen and Tom hadn't told Alex their good news yet. Well, she certainly wasn't going to rob them of their pleasure. "Women's secrets," she answered.

Later, Liza asked, "Alex, how did you ever get Father William to come for the wedding so soon?"

Alex grinned. "I told him if he didn't hurry, we'd have another bastard in the family."

Liza gasped. "Alex, you didn't!"

Alex's grin faded. "No, I didn't. But even if I had, it wouldn't have shocked him. He's seen too much out here. I doubt that anything would shock him. Liza,

442

he's a remarkable man, a true man of God. But I shouldn't have made that crack about bastards. That wasn't funny."

He pulled her down to sit on the bed beside him. "I've been feeling rotten about this whole mess, particularly little Danny. Father William and I had a long talk. He said something that got me to thinking."

"What?" Liza asked.

"He told me God doesn't bother with marriage dates. His chief concern is what's in a man's heart. And he knows that long before the man does himself." Alex lifted her chin and looked deeply into her eyes. "I know this can't take back all the pain I've caused you, but, Liza, in my heart, you've been my wife since that first night in the Indian camp.

"And I intend to do right by Danny," Alex continued in a determined voice. "As soon as we're married, I'm going to give him my name, just as it always should have been."

That night, when they reached the door of the little house after a visit with Rita and Sally, Alex bent and kissed Liza lightly on the lips. Then he turned and walked away.

"Where are you going?" Liza asked.

Alex turned to face her. "To find myself a bed, I hope." A grin spread across his face. "You see, I promised Father William I'd behave myself until we're married."

"You what?" Liza gasped.

Alex chuckled. "Well, he didn't exactly tell me to stop sleeping with you. He was much more subtle than that. He suggested that if I really regretted everything that had happened, I might show God my sincerity by denying himself something that I really wanted. But I knew what he meant. He was telling me to behave myself. And it was Father William who set the date for the wedding in two days, not me." Alex laughed ruefully. "I don't know whether he was just being compassionate—or he didn't trust me."

Or he was afraid the bride would fly the coop again, Liza thought, laughing. "Good night, my darling."

The reunion at the ranch the next day was a joyous, emotional one for everyone. Much to Liza's surprise, it was Manuel who took Danny from her first, grinning at Alex and saying, "This one you could not deny, amigo."

As he walked away with the baby, Liza looked up at Alex. "Well, that was a surprise."

"Manuel? Sweetheart, he's crazy about kids. Didn't you know that?"

Rita and Sally had returned to the ranch with them since the wedding was to be the next day. That night, when they were all in the parlor, Liza looked up to see Manuel and Sally off in a corner of the room. The handsome Mexican was smiling down at Sally, who stood looking shyly down at her clasped hands.

Liza tugged on Alex's sleeve frantically. "Alex, you've got to stop Manuel. Sally isn't one of Rita's girls."

Alex glanced across the room at the couple and smiled. "He knows that, sweetheart. Besides, if you look closely, you'll see he isn't trying to get her into bed. He's courting her."

"But he can't!"

Alex glared down at her. "Why not? Because he's a half-breed and a bastard?" he asked angrily.

"No," Liza answered, her own eyes flashing. "You know better than that." Then she told him Sally's story.

"That son-of-a-bitch!" Alex swore. "I wish I could get my hands on him. Her own father!"

"But don't you see?" Liza asked. "It's impossible. Rita thinks Sally is scarred for life. You've got to talk to Manuel and stop him."

Alex glanced again at the couple across the room. "I'll talk to him, caution him to go slowly. But I think it's a little too late to stop him. Look."

Liza looked up to see the couple strolling out to the porch. Sally was smiling up at Manuel, her arm linked in his. Liza couldn't believe her eyes. Her shock was slowly replaced by hope. "Do you think it will work out for them?"

"Yes, I think it will, Liza. You know how kind and gentle Manuel is. Besides, they share a common bond."

"What bond?" Liza asked, puzzled by his words.

"They've both been the victims of their fathers' lust. I think if anyone can understand and appreciate Sally's problem, it's Manuel."

The next day, Hiram gave the bride away. The old man walked beside Liza, his stance proud and erect, his limp barely noticeable. Manuel was Alex's best man, and Sally was Liza's maid of honor.

When the ceremony was finished, Father William said to Alex, "You may kiss the bride now." Alex grinned at the priest and pulled Liza into a tight embrace, molding their bodies together. He kissed

445

her deeply, thoroughly, and much too passionately for a wedding kiss.

Father William blushed beet-red. Sally ducked her head in embarrassment. Manuel cleared his throat loudly. Tom coughed nervously, and Jake found sudden interest in the rafters on the ceiling. Hiram giggled, while Rita and Kathleen stood, mouths gaping. The only onlookers that seemed unaffected by the display were the Indian guests.

When the kiss finally ended, a sigh of relief was heard, and then silence. Finally, Tanaźin said something in the Dakota tongue. Father William laughed. "Tanaźin said that's one white man's custom he may adopt."

Everyone laughed, and Liza glared at Alex. He grinned sheepishly in return.

"Wowee!" Rita cried. "After that kiss, I gotta sit down." She plopped her heavy body into a chair. A groan, a cracking noise, and then the sound of splintering wood was heard.

"Oh, my God," Liza gasped. "I knew it would happen some day."

Rita crashed to the ground, and the room shook from the impact of her fall. The big woman lay sprawled on the floor, a look of surprise on her face. Then she laughed. "I knew I should have brought Sam's piano bench."

It took Alex, Tom, Manuel and Jake to get the big woman off the floor. Not because of her size, however, but because they were all laughing so hard, Rita the hardest of all.

Later that night, Liza and Alex were standing off to one side of the room. Liza looked fondly at all of their friends. It was hard to believe that only two years ago she had stepped off the boat in New York City and thought she had left her life behind her. What she hadn't known was that she was just coming to meet it. But Anne knew, and Liza offered her old friend a silent thanks.

Her eyes glanced over the people present, whose lives had entwined with her own, each contributing something to make her what she was today: Hiram, Bright Star, and Andy, Manuel and Sally, Tom and Kathleen, Tanaźin and Wańcawin, Jake and Little Songbird, and Rita. And first and always, she looked up to the man standing beside her, Alex.

He stood watching her, his smoky eyes warm with love. "I can't believe you're really my wife," he said gently.

Liza smiled. "Let's go out on the porch for some fresh air."

The night reminded her of a night long ago, the first night she and Alex had stood on the porch together. The landscape was bathed in moonlight, and a million stars glittered in the sky. *I could touch one if I wanted to*, she thought.

She leaned into Alex, who was standing behind her, and reveled in the feel of his powerful body against her. She pulled his arms around her possessively. "I've changed, Alex," she said. "I'm not the same person who stood on this porch with you two years ago."

Alex's arms tightened around her as he pulled her closer. He rubbed his jaw against the top of her head. "I know. You were a girl then. Now, you're a woman."

Liza turned in the circle of his arms and looked up at him. "Are you sorry? Won't you miss the girl? After all, she was the one you fell in love with."

Alex shook his head. "No, I find the woman intriguing and devastating. Besides, I don't think that's the last I've seen of that girl. I have a feeling I'll get a glimpse of her now and then."

He kissed her nose. "I've changed, too, Liza. I guess that's what life is all about, changing and growing." He smiled down at her, one finger tracing her lips. "But there's one thing that can't change, can't possibly grow any more—my love for you." He bent his head, and his lips met hers.

Liza stood in Alex's warm embrace, her head on his chest, listening to the strong, steady beat of his heart. She smiled as she remembered Anne's words, Anne's voice from the past, *You will love once, deeply—and then forever.*